THE LAST

THE LAST

THE WAR OF SOULS BOOK ONE

CHRIS A. JACKSON

Charlotte, NC

FALSTAFF
BOOKS

WWW.FALSTAFFBOOKS.COM

Copyright © 2022 by Chris A. Jackson

Cover Design by S. H. Roddey

Editorial by John G. Hartness

This is for all of you out there who do good not because you are told to do so by some institution or organization, but out of the goodness of your heart. Thank you. And of course, thank you to my fans. Don't worry "The Last" is not my last... Not even close.

ALONE

I walk alone through a sea of humanity, untouched by the pestilence of a dying world, the last of my kind. *Desperation, pain, loneliness, fear...* I feel it, smell it, taste the bitter tang of it on my tongue. I don't know if it's mine or from the poor wretched humans huddled in plastic and cardboard, dying by degrees around me. A wide street looms at the end of the alley, wet from rain that can never wash it clean. Putrid steam rises from the sewer gratings to invade my senses with rot and decay that can never touch me.

I've been away too long, hiding, isolated, afraid, hunted, but time has caught up with me. The years mean nothing, but humanity changes at such a frantic pace these days—a thousand years from bronze to steel and only a hundred from sail to space flight. *Fifteen years...too long.* Coming out of hiding is dangerous, but I can't ignore those I was put on this Earth to redeem. It's harder now, alone.

Am I destined to wander for eternity alone?

I hear my father's voice, as always. *Not to Heaven will you go without a hand to send you there.* It's an answer of sorts. The years don't touch me; centuries mean nothing, but I'm mortal. So, yes, I'll wander forever unless something kills me first.

I remember my lessons. *Awareness, vigilance, readiness is a constant state. Steady spirit...*

I step out onto the broad asphalt path, feeling someone in the shadows only steps away, watching me. I also know it is not one of *them*. Hate emanates from the Nephilim like heat from a furnace. Here I feel only cold, need, determination, and fear.

I can't read intentions or memories without physical contact, so I feign ignorance as I pass his hiding place. He's young and has a knife or a small sword; I feel the courage he takes from his grip on the blade. I'm past him, then I feel another presence, this one ahead of me, more fear, worry, anxiety. *Mine or his?* Maybe both. His unease mounts.

Please, don't do this.

When I'm two strides from the second one, he steps out of hiding in front of me. Rain plasters his hair to gaunt dusky features, young, with hunger and desperation in his eyes. His gun is small, ugly, and pointed only vaguely in my direction. It trembles in his hand, not entirely from fear. Thousands of years have honed my senses to recognize infirmity, weakness, and disease. My gift, my father's only gift, tells me he will die from it in less than a year, and pity rises in me. I've always felt sympathy for them; it's my nature. *Heal them, love them, give them hope. Love will conquer hate.*

Damn you, Father, for lying to me...

I stop.

"Yer money, bitch. All of it. Now!"

"No." I take my hands from the pockets of my duster, empty, unthreatening, and bridle my emotions, swallowing my fear. *Face all situations with calm: High spirit is weak, low spirit is weak. Do not let your enemy see your spirit. Steady spirit.* I feel his confusion, his uncertainty.

"I'll put a slug in yer gut, I swear it!"

"No, you will *not*." I put all I am into that, and the gun wavers.

The larger man moves up behind me, his sodden shoes squishing in the rain. The knife stroke is well-timed, but one does not live five millennia without learning survival. The world is a violent place, and I've learned from the very best of humanity—*Arigato, Musashi~san.*

I pirouette around the attack that would have put four inches of steel into my back, snatching the wrist of his blade hand. Touching him, his panic surges through me. Using his momentum, I bring his arm up over my head, pivot under, and twist until his hand is pinned behind his back. My thumbnail in the nerve plexus at the base of his wrist sends the knife clattering to the concrete.

The gun cracks, dull and deafening, shattering raindrops into mist, smashing flesh and bone into pulp. I feel the shock of impact through the man's body.

Please...no...

My move placed him between the shooter and me. Sudden weakness and pain, his not mine, and he exhales as he collapses. I had not intended to kill either of them, but now a groaning body lies at my feet, and the boy with the gun stands staring down in shock.

I move before he can recover and take the ugly little revolver from his limp grasp.

He stares at me in horror, rain dripping from his gaunt mulatto features. "Wha... What *are* you?"

"Old." My voice gives him all the grief of ages, all the blood on my hands, all the thousands, *millions* of souls I couldn't save. "I'm older than you can imagine, boy." I toss the gun into the refuse. "I'm sorry for your friend. You should pick your prey more carefully, lest you become prey yourself."

I step past him and walk on. *You can't save them all, Empa...* He splashes to his knees next to his companion, his horror hammering at my back. The man might live, but I tell myself it won't matter. *What are a few more years but strokes of a hummingbird's wings? What will any of it matter?* I'm alone, all my cousins silent, likely dead, and eventually, through malice or by accident, I'll be sent to Heaven... and humanity will perish.

I gird my sorrow—*Survive, Empa...just survive, keep moving. Keep searching. Maybe someone else has survived.* A street sign, and I know where I am. I've watched empires rise and fall and could find my way through the streets of Pompeii as easily as those of Denver, Paris, or Moscow. I've seen the rising sea overtake the monumental metropolises of Manhattan, Hong Kong, London, and Tokyo. Cincinnati isn't likely to bring me any surprises.

GIPPY KNELT in the rain and held his dying friend, watching the bitch walk off as if she'd just taken a piss on them and didn't care. Cold rage smoldered behind his rheumy eyes, rage at what she'd done, at what she'd made him do.

Lennie coughed blood and drew a wet breath. "Gip. What the fuck..."

"Shot ya." Gippy sniffed and pressed a hand to the bleeding mass of his friend's chest. "Sorry. She..." *She what, you stupid fuck? Made you shoot your friend? No, she didn't! You're just stupid and clumsy, that's what!*

"Can't...breathe..." Lennie coughed again, blood bubbling on his pale lips before the rain popped them.

"You be okay. I'll git ya to Dad. He'll fix ya up." Gippy tried to lift his friend but couldn't. *Weak, stupid, slow...* "Hang on. I gotta jack a ride."

"Gip!" Lennie grabbed his wrist with hysterical strength. "Don't...leave me..."

"Gotta! Can't carry ya. You gotta let me go, Len. I gotta jack a—"

Lennie trembled all over, his mouth gaping, eyes wide for a terrified moment, then went limp.

"Len..." Gippy shook him, but Lennie's eyes just stared up into the rain, unblinking, unseeing. "Len! Don't!" Gippy shook him again, to no avail. "Don't leave me alone!"

Tears mingled with the rain.

"Fuck." Gippy sniffed and laid his friend down, staggering to his feet, legs shaking. *Alone...* "Fucking *fuck!*"

He glared into the rain, up at the heavens, crying into a sky he couldn't see, raging at a God he didn't believe in. It wasn't supposed to be like this. He wasn't a killer, a murderer...

Until now.

Gippy lowered his eyes, his glare, his rage, redirected toward the bitch who had made him a killer. "Fine! If that's what I am, that's what I am."

He rummaged through the garbage and recovered his piece. Shaking the water from it, he jammed the revolver in his pocket and started after the woman who had shattered his wretched life, the one who had made him kill his best friend in this whole stinking world.

"You next, bitch."

2

COLD COMFORT

I cross the street at a walk and traverse the next block through another alley, weariness dragging at my steps. There's no traffic, even though it's barely 9 p.m. Global fuel shortages, famine, and scarcity of raw materials have made automobiles a waning luxury. Not even two hundred years they lasted. I wonder why I bothered learning to drive.

I came to Cincinnati looking for any sign of my cousins in one of our information drops. I found it empty, just like the previous five. The days of bus travel and walking are taking their toll. I may not age, but I do need a good night's sleep occasionally. I'll move on in the morning, Atlanta next, I think.

I turn right and enter a shallow alcove, a glowing stylized blue S shining above it like a neon beacon. I step up to a blank recess, tap it with a finger, and a numeric pad rotates out of the wall. I type in a ten-digit number and wait.

"Reservations?" a computer voice asks.

"No."

"Number of guests and length of stay?"

"One and one night. Something with a bathtub." Just because I can't be infected by the filth of ten billion humans doesn't mean I don't get dirty.

"One point four one kay North American Dollars," the computer voice announces. "Will that be credit, debit, or PFT?"

Damn inflation... Things change so *fast.* Computers...barely a hundred years and they control everything. Ninety-eight percent of my life, computations were done in sand, stone, wax, and finally pen and paper, abacus, and slide rule. Now it's all electrons, and machines think for humans. I feel ancient, tired, and alone. "Cash."

"This terminal is not equipped to accept currency of any denomination. Please enter and see the manager for assistance. Thank you, and have a pleasant day."

"Thank you, but I won't." The memory of the poor boys I left moments ago rides heavily on me. *So many...so fragile...so mortal.*

The magnetically sealed door pops open, swinging out on motorized hinges. The door is thick enough to stop an anti-tank round, a ridiculous measure of security since the brick wall surrounding it would barely stop an armor-piercing round from a high-powered rifle. Technology has changed warfare so much in the last three centuries it's hard to keep up.

I enter.

The light of the broad Securotel atrium washes over me in a wave of brilliance. I pull the hood of my sweatshirt back and squint until my eyes adjust, glancing around the white tile lobby as a matter of habit, checking for threats. *See everything. Readiness is a constant state.* Of course, there are none, unless you count the two heavily armed guards flanking the detector grid, but I know they're here for my protection.

My protection... The thought brings a cold smile to my lips.

I approach the grid. A slim brunette attendant behind a counter— *young, so young*—smiles and says, "Please place any weapons, ammunition, explosives, or personal electronic devices in one of the bins, ma'am."

Ma'am? I grit my teeth. I may be five thousand years old, but I don't look a day over thirty. "Of course."

This is the part I always hate, though it's a necessity. I desperately need a good night's sleep, and security here is tight enough to allow me that. But to sleep soundly, I have to respect their rules.

I pull the Glock 20C from the small of my back, thumb the magazine out, and jack the round from the chamber. I lay the pistol in the bin. Four magazines clatter after it, two painted red and two green, then the two small concussion grenades I keep for quick escapes.

Next, I pull the two long fighting knives from the sheaths sewn into the lining of my duster and the two throwing daggers from my boots, laying them carefully inside. A slim phone from an inner pocket joins the pile. Leaving that behind is dangerous, but again, I have no choice. The last thing I place in the tray is the long black-scabbarded blade given to me by Miyamoto Musashi. It is priceless and very dear to me, as he was. Placing it in the tray with my other weapons is physically painful.

I watch the girl at the scanner as her eyebrows rise. Swords aren't common anymore. Swords like this one are unique. I smile thinly. "The sword holds sentimental value for me. I'll take it *very* personally if it's damaged or goes missing."

"All your possessions will remain untouched by human hands, ma'am. They'll be returned to you when you check out."

I wonder about *inhuman* hands as I watch the girl fit a lid on the bin and lock it. She moves it to a row of lockers in the wall behind her, places the bin inside one, then locks that with a key fob that dangles around her neck.

"Good." I walk through the detector. It beeps.

"If you would please step over here, miss?" One of the guards retrieves a hand scanner from a table. The other turns slightly, his slung rifle pointing at the floor a foot from my toes.

"Certainly."

"Are you carrying any metallic items?"

"Yes."

"Would you please place them in the tray?"

"Of course." I withdraw the heavy belt from my waist and lay it in the tray. To the man's credit, he doesn't even ask what's in it. I also place a keychain holding several keys and an old-fashioned rabbit's foot on the tray. That does raise an eyebrow, but he doesn't say a word.

"Is that all?"

"Yes."

He passes the hand scanner over me once more and nods. "Would you please open the belt?"

"Certainly." I unzip the outer case, folding it out to reveal the rows of slim 100-gram platinum bars, all stamped with the Swiss National Bank seal and individual serial numbers. Money...one human invention that has endured.

"You can take the belt and your keys, miss. Thank you." He steps back, waving me onto the wide marble front desk and the smiling attendant behind it.

I thank him and remove one of the slim bars from the belt before fastening it back around my waist. I approach the counter, admiring the polished stone. It looks real. I doubt it is.

"Nice to have you back, miss." The attendant has never set eyes on me before, but the courtesy is appreciated. "Will there be any additional preferences other than the bath?"

"Just privacy for now, please. I'll call down for dinner later."

"Very good. Payment for the room must be in advance."

"Fine." I drop the bar of platinum on the counter. "Please put the balance on my account."

"Of course." He takes the bar and runs it through a scanner, smiles, and taps his collar mic. A bellboy appears as if by magic. "Jimmy here will show you to your room."

"Do you have bags outside, miss?" the young man asks.

He smiles at me, and I have to grit my teeth to keep my face from betraying my anguish. Physical pain and mental distress assail me like a hail of broken glass. He's being horribly abused by someone, and the shame in him is almost as overwhelming as the pain. The stoicism of his casual demeanor impresses me.

"No bags." I nod for him to show me the way, though I could find the room easily enough on my own if they just told me the number. *Well, appearances must be maintained, I suppose.*

"This way, please."

I follow him to the elevator and stand in uncomfortable silence while he fidgets up seven floors. The rooms don't have numbers, I discover, a change since the last time I stayed in a Securotel. *So long ago?*

Jimmy waves at the door and says, "Here we are, miss." He hands me a small plastic card with a hole in it for a keychain.

"Thank you, James." I wave the card over the lock, and the door beeps softly and clicks open.

"Will there be anything else?"

"Yes, actually." I produce a banknote from my pocket.

"That's not necessary, miss. Your account—"

"Please." I hand it to him, careful not to touch his fingers. "Bring me something to drink in about an hour. Something cold. Whatever you like."

"Wine, or..." his eyes widen as he sees the denomination of the note in his hand. "Champagne?"

"Do you like Champagne?"

"Uh, no, miss."

"What do you like?"

"To drink? Uh. I like Coke, but I don't think—"

"That'll do nicely, James. One hour. No sooner." I smile as the closing door obliterates his astonished features and the waves of his suffering.

I lean against the barrier, the fingers of my hand splayed against it. *Why do you do this, Empa?* I have no answer other than I am my father's daughter. I am what I am, and I must do as my soul guides me. *Love will conquer hate...* I pray it's so, but I doubt it.

"Lights, medium." I turn as the elegant suite is instantly illuminated in soft yellow light. "Draw a bath. Hot." The water starts running in the bathroom. I sigh and shrug out of my duster.

The coat weighs a ton, it seems, and my legs feel immediately springy with its weight divested. I hang it in the closet by the door, removing the slim carbon fiber blades secreted in the Kevlar liner. There are several other hidden items, but these I keep close at hand. Their molecule-fine edges are insanely sharp, and they don't set off metal detectors. I place them and my money belt on the wide table beside the window, peel out of my damp sweatshirt, then sit down and begin unbuckling my boots.

Five minutes later, I let the scalding water of the bath envelop me, the scents of expensive oils and salts overwhelming my senses, washing away the stench of the world.

Bliss...

Memories of a hundred thousand faces, friends, lovers, enemies, and strangers, sift through my mind as the water infuses heat through my sinews. Names I forget, but faces, never. I let them come and go, wondering why I remember them all.

Why am I? I wonder for perhaps the millionth time in my existence. If an all-knowing God put us here, She must have known what would befall us. I've met others of my kind, my cousins, sons and daughters of the Seraphim. We were many in my earlier centuries, but our number has dwindled. I've not heard from another Ageless in more than two decades. After the catastrophe of St. Louis—*The desperate fools...revolution, uprising, guns and anger against air power and suicide drones, my face on the net, screaming for justice...blood on my hands. What was I thinking?*—I went off-grid, hiding, barely connected to world events, savoring small victories in the tiny communities in the remote north. Now, judging it time to again move and try to make contact with my cousins, I've found our secret message drops empty. The covert channels of communication have fallen silent, no longer safe under the scrutiny of the Nephilim.

Technology is our enemy in that regard.

Our true enemies, the Nephilim, never diminish in number, even though more than a few have died at my hands. They always renew, always take a fresh human shell. Hell's other allies have proliferated as well, fed by the growing hate. Now, with enemies outnumbering friends and indistinguishable from the endless mass of humanity, I'm alone, the last of my kind.

Perhaps…

The door chime brings me surging up from the tepid water, reaching for the blades I placed on the tub's rim. Two steps, and I stand with my back pressed against the bathroom door, dripping and listening. Surely it hasn't been an hour. But the steaming water is now only warm, and my skin is pallid and wrinkled.

I edge through the door and check the clock beside the table. An hour and five minutes have passed.

"I must be getting old," I mutter beneath my breath.

I stash the blades out of sight and slip into the thick Securotel robe as I check the video pickup. Jimmy stands outside the door with an ice bucket in one hand, fidgeting from foot to foot. The poor boy probably thinks I'm going to seduce him. Well, he's in for a surprise.

I cinch the robe tightly and open the door.

"Your timing is very precise, James. Please, place the drinks on the table." I smile through the wave of pain and shame that passes through me as he walks by.

"Yes, miss." He puts the heavily iced bucket on the table. "Is that all, miss?"

"No, actually. I'd like to talk to you for a few minutes if you'd allow it." I move to the bar and put ice into two glasses, trying hard not to smile at his apprehension. His anguish beating against me like waves on a rocky shore makes it easier. "No obligation, of course. You may leave if you wish."

"Wha… What would you like to talk about, miss?"

"Please, call me Emma. I've been away for a few years, and I'd like the local news from someone who isn't trying to sell me something." What I really want he'll discover shortly, but news will be welcome. Things change so quickly. The news channels are now state-run. Propaganda and hate fill the net. "That, and I just like to talk to people." I nod toward one of the chairs. "*Just* talk."

"Oh, uh, sure." I feel his relief as he sits stiffly, fidgeting again as I open one of the sodas and pour two glasses full. "Not much to tell, really." He sips nervously as I sit, his eyes flicking to my legs, though the robe covers me to the ankles. "Things keep getting worse, now that NAFAS runs everything."

"Yes, NAFAS has become…a problem." The North American Freely Associated States—even the name is an ironic slap in the face. I sip and wonder how much of the political push to unify all of North and Central America into one massive empire was driven by the Nephilim. It certainly exhibits their modus operandi: unify under the promise of peace and security, then tighten the grip of tyranny. It's an old song I've heard too many times.

"It's hard to make a living, which is why I work here. My mom doesn't make much, and I've got two sisters."

"Do they pay you well?"

"Oh, not bad. I uh—Oh, God, I almost forgot your change! I'm sorry." He pulls a wad of bills from his pocket and thrusts it at me, but I'm already smiling and pushing it away.

"No, James. You keep it. Think of it as a—" My palm brushes his fingers, and I get his most horrific memories in one furious rush…

A girl's face, her lips on his, then his neck, then everywhere…a scream…an older woman, crying…the young girl laughing…words…tears…anger…shame. The shame… The lash he keeps hidden under his bed, wire twisted around a stick…

I was wrong; he isn't being abused. He's doing it to himself.

The girl is his stepsister; she'd been whoring for more than a year and laughed at him when he caught her at it. Then she showed him how she could earn more in one hour than he could in a week as a bellboy. Their mother blamed him, or so he thought. She didn't punish him; she only cried and cried. So, he punishes himself…every day.

I jerk my hand away, fighting to hide my horror. "Please, James. Keep the money. Your time is valuable to me."

He hesitates, puzzled by my reaction, then slowly stuffs the money away. "Um, thanks."

The question now is what to do about this poor boy. I can take his pain, absolve his guilt—it was what I was put on Earth to do, after all—but to do so, I'll need to delve into his soul. Without his consent, that would be a violation and might send him screaming from the room. I can't, however, just let him go. He's killing himself. *One more innocent soul…* I don't think about the futility of what I'm about to do. I just do it. I *have* to do it. *Damn you, Father…*

"James, I'd like to ask you a favor."

"Um…" He looks uncomfortable.

"Nothing that will put you or your job at risk, I promise." I sip the sweet cola and clear my throat. "I'm very good at reading people. I can tell when they're troubled. I can see you're in pain, and I can help you, but you have to allow me to."

He gapes at me. "You *what?*"

"I can *help* you, James, but you have to consent." I put my hand out flat on the table. "All you need to do is take my hand and look me in the eyes."

"N...nobody can help me." His denial is a plea.

"*I* can. I can take your pain. I promise." I breathe deep and feel the grace of Raphael coming into me, filling me like a cup overflowing. "Just take my hand."

Five millennia of persuasion and all the gifts of Heaven radiate from me, and his quaking hand inches closer. He places his hand in mine, and I grasp it. He gasps, for he feels the angelic power swelling in me, Raphael's grace pulling him in.

"*Look at me!*"

He can't resist. His eyes meet mine and lock. I delve down into the chasm of his soul, firmly but gently, soothing, calming... *There...* I find the center of it, a ball of self-loathing so putrid as to make me want to retch. *How can anyone live with that festering inside them?* I realize no one can, which is why James is slowly beating himself to death. The physical pain is his only release, his only way of dealing with what he thinks he's become.

I ease myself around the anguish, encompassing all the horrors that fill him, and back out, taking the entire loathsome mess with me, into me. I feel it inside me, trying to infect me, but like the viruses that kill these people I love so deeply, it can't. It is in me; I can feel it, but it will not master me. And slowly, ever so slowly, I'll kill it. I start to release his hand, then, almost as an afterthought, I take the wounds from his back as well.

I sigh and let him go as the physical pain lances through me.

"What the *hell?*" James bursts to his feet, panting in shock, backing away from me in fear. "How did you... What the hell did you *do?*"

I smile through the pain, his pain, and the shame that's even now waning. A deep drink of soda settles my stomach. His bewilderment is still plain on his face, but there's a lightness there, too. He knows what was growing in him and that I took it away. I watch his face as he tries to find it, to recall that pit of self-hatred, but it's gone. His guilt seems now ridiculous, trivial, pathetic. He's *free.*

"Feel better?"

"I—" He swallows hard, steps forward, and drains his glass. "I feel...*good*."

One soul at a time... This is my only weapon against the hate of the Nephilim. If I can keep hope alive in only one living human, the end of times will not come. A gift, or a curse... I've never known which it is, but I am what I am for a reason.

"Good." I stand wearily. "Now, be a dear and fetch me something from the kitchen, would you?"

"Anything!" A grin splits his sweet face. His lightness of heart fills me. "What do you want?"

"A steak would be good. *Real* steak. Medium rare." The wounds I've taken will be healed by morning, but the energy has to come from somewhere. "And I'll take you up on the wine. Have the steward pick out something that'll complement the meat."

"Sure. I'll bring it right up."

"Thank you."

"Are you kidding?" He laughs, the sweetest sound in the world. "I don't know what you did to me, lady, but I owe you big time. I'll be right back. Maybe fifteen minutes." He grins again as he lets himself out.

My smile fades as his joy leaves the room, as pleasant to me as his pain had been abhorrent five minutes before. I've taken a risk doing this, but the chances of him betraying what just happened are slim. Nobody would believe him, and he'd endanger his job. I judge the risk worth it.

I move to the bathroom slowly, stiffly. The pain's fading, but some cool water will help. I toss the robe aside, grateful that it isn't stained, and look at myself in the mirror, dusky skin, dark wavy hair, not a wrinkle or mark of age, and not a scar or blemish, save on my back. The cuts and welts, formerly James', aren't bleeding, and I'm already healing.

"Why do you do this, Empa?" I ask again as I step into the shower and let the cool water trickle down the tattered skin of my back. "It won't make a difference..."

But I know the answer: it's the only difference I can make. There is a bit less hate, loathing, and pain in the world. One less soul likely to be corrupted by the Nephilim. It may not matter in the end, but if only to hear the boy laugh, it had been worth it.

HUNKERED in a shadowed doorway half a block from the fancy hotel entrance, Gippy gripped the cold handle of his gun and watched. He shivered in the cold but just kept watching. Hunger gnawed at him like a rat, but that, too, was nothing new. If a street kid learned anything in twenty years, it was patience.

"She'll come out," he muttered, grinding his rotten teeth. "Don't you worry, Len, she'll come struttin' out in her fancy coat and thousand-nad boots, and I'll bust a cap in her head."

Her boots alone would buy him food for a month, and that jacket... He fingered his threadbare hoodie, long since permeable to the rain, and offering little against the coming winter. The jacket he might just keep.

"And a bitch like that's got to carry some scratch." Gippy mumbled on, keeping up a conversation with himself more to stay awake and alert than any underlying psychosis. He fantasized about finding a wad of thousand-nad notes in her pocket, maybe even a real credit card, or a fancy ring or something he could sell. "Don't you worry, Len, I'll come out on top of this one. You just—"

A vehicle hummed up the street, near-silent in the rain. Gippy hunkered back and pulled his hoodie low, for this was the type of ride rarely seen in this part of town. Sleek, black, and shiny, one of the new electric South African sedans, worth more than he could imagine. Even more interesting, it stopped in front of the fancy hotel, and a woman got out. The car drove on before she even entered the vestibule.

"Another fancy bitch..." Gippy watched her push buttons on the trick electronic gadget. The door popped open, a wedge of light scything across the street. She strode through, looking back over her shoulder.

For an instant, he caught a good look at her face, pale with shocking blond hair, but cold dark eyes.

Gippy shivered as the door swung closed, but not from the rain or cold. He gripped his gun closer and told himself he was imagining things, but he could have sworn the blonde woman looked familiar...and that she knew him...and hated him.

No, he decided, grinding his rotten teeth again. *Not just me... That bitch hate the whole fuckin' world.*

3

ENEMIES

Morning. I wake feeling better than I have in months, perhaps years. The combination of the restoration of James, a wonderful dinner, wine, and a perfect night's sleep was exactly what I needed. My hope is renewed.

Sometimes, it's good to be alive.

I stretch under the crisp sheets, remembering James's clumsy proposal that he share my bed. I gently refused him, of course. For an empath, lovemaking is a serious undertaking, for obvious reasons. James was sweet and didn't take it personally.

I've convinced myself this is the better way. I've been down that path too many times. Aside from the overwhelming intensity of lovemaking, experiencing not only my own rapture but that of my partner or partners as well, I've watched too many lovers grow old and die, or die young, bleeding in my arms, to seek that kind of companionship again. I've endured the torture of leaving them before those things happened, never to look back, and wondering what became of them. Only one, the Samurai and Zen Master, Miyamoto Musashi, did I well and truly fall head over heels for. His inner peace, his calm, his mental poise fulfilled me like no other man or woman I've ever known. In the end, it was he who sent me away, not wishing that I witness his final years. I miss his grace every day. Sometimes, alone is better.

"Drapes open." The heavy draperies whisk aside. The window isn't real, of course; not for what I paid. The image is the view from the top of the building projected on a flat screen, but it isn't a bad view. And the sunlight edging under the haze of smog feels real.

"Phone, audio only. Room service."

The phone twitters once before a female voice answers. "Yes, miss?"

"I'd like breakfast. An omelet, toast, orange juice, and coffee, please. *Real* coffee."

"Of course, miss. Ten minutes?"

"Make it fifteen."

"Very well."

The line clicks off.

I take a luxuriant five-minute shower, towel dry, get dressed, and even have time to dry my hair before the door chimes. The video shows a young blonde woman holding a huge tray. I key the door open and turn away.

"Put it beside the window, please."

"Yes, miss."

The woman walks through the door, and the wave of hatred warns me just in time to save myself from being riddled with bullets. The tray flies aside, and a short machine pistol with a thick silencer sweeps a spray of hollow-point slugs in an arc that would have cut me in half.

My twisting roll sends me crashing into the closet. Another spray of eerily quiet gunfire rips holes in the flimsy door but only ruffles my hair. A click and a thud tell me my assailant is reloading. I have about two seconds.

I dive out of the closet with my duster, right through the door into the hall. A hail of bullets tugs at my coat and slams the door behind me, but I'm not hit. I glance down the long corridor in both directions and realize I'm trapped. Whichever way I run, the woman will be out the door in time to shoot me down. On top of that, my carbon blades are still inside the room.

"Shit!" I don my coat and scramble back beside the door to crouch below the video pickup, my back to the wall. I hold my breath and wait. *Readiness...opportunity...steady spirit.*

When the door clicks open, I move.

As the gun sweeps toward me, I'm already inside its arc of fire. I trap the weapon under my arm and lash out with an elbow. The blow splatters the woman's nose across her face and drives us back through the door. A shattered nose would have at least stunned most women, but this is no woman. It is one of *them*, a Nephilim, and they're tougher than human beings. The blow will daze it momentarily but certainly won't stop it.

The gun chatters, chewing holes in the wall across the hall as I force us back into the room, but the real threat comes from the assassin's other hand. The woman-thing draws a curved knife and slashes at my throat. I block the dagger with my forearm, and the Kevlar keeps it from cutting to the bone. On her backstroke, I trap her wrist—my flesh touches hers, and I get a wave of unbridled rage—thousands of years, dozens of lives, Daughter of Af, Angel of Anger, cast out from Heaven—and lash out with a heel to trip her.

We land heavily, but I'm on top, her knife immobilized, one arm pinned across her neck, the gun still clamped under my arm. She tries to knee me in the groin, but I wrap my legs around hers and lock my ankles. We are, for a moment, immobilized face to face.

My beloved Miyamoto Musashi's lessons come to me: *Do not let your enemy see your spirit. Steady spirit. Thinking all aspects, a high vantage, even when pressed, is strategy.* Fighting these creatures for centuries has taught me one thing: humor really pisses them off.

"Can't say much for the room service."

"Join your siblings, bitch!" The thing tries a headbutt, but I turn to make it a glancing blow. She pulls the trigger of her firearm in frustration.

Just the response I'm hoping for.

The gun chatters, sending plaster and drywall clattering down from the ceiling until the weapon clicks empty.

I relax my grip on the gun and bring my free hand up to the knife. A twist and the wrist cracks, but the woman-thing's grip doesn't slacken. The butt of the gun cracks against my head, but there is little force in it. A short blow to my opponent's elbow bends the joint backward with a sound like a drumstick popping free from an overcooked chicken. This brings the blade right down into her chest.

I roll off and dash to recover my blades and money belt. When I turn, I realize I'd missed. "Well, shit!"

The woman is standing up, the knife protruding from just to the right of her sternum. Only a killing blow—head, spine, or heart—will stop a Nephilim in its tracks. The dagger had not been immediately lethal. The body will probably bleed to death in moments, but the Nephilim will try to kill me until it does.

The arm that held the knife hangs broken and useless. Her other still grips the empty machine pistol, which is almost as useless. While the

Nephilim fumbles to hold the gun between her knees and retrieve a fresh magazine, I whip one of the heavy chairs into her legs. She folds over, the gun clattering away. With only one weapon left, she wrenches the knife from her chest, but my boot comes down on her hand.

She hisses through bloody lips. "I'll kill you in my next life, cousin."

Cousins we are, but from parents estranged.

My carbon blades cross her throat in opposite directions. I evade the arterial spray as the woman-thing gurgles, convulses, and finally dies.

I retrieve the two remaining magazines for the machine pistol, reload it, clean and sheathe my blades, and glance around the room. The platter and plates lie scattered, the coffee up-ended on the rug.

"A perfectly good breakfast shot to hell." I pop a single round into the dead woman's forehead, partly to make sure and partly out of sheer petulance. "Now I have to eat at a damned Waffle House!" I squeeze another round home—this one's pure petulance—and stride from the room, tucking the pistol under my duster. What really makes me angry is that I've been tracked down, and I need to know how.

Morning, and Gippy stirred in his huddled rags: wet, cold, but still vigilant. No one else had come or gone from the hotel. A few cars had passed, but no more fancy jobs that drew his attention.

Soon... He gripped his gun and began working his stiff muscles, stretching slowly to unkink a night of immobility. He would have to move quickly when the bitch showed; survival on the streets had taught him to prepare. He'd only get one shot at her and would have to be close enough for a headshot. He didn't want to put a hole in his new coat.

Frail though he might be, lean muscle began to warm with the stretches. His joints ached horribly, but that, too, he was used to. The sky had cleared, save for the smog, of course; that never cleared. *Price of progress...* All the bullshit about climate change never changed the smog. Gippy had never seen the climate change, except the political one, but that was like a fly worrying about spiderwebs. Governments were a fact of life and likely to kill you someday. There wasn't a fucking thing someone like him could do about it.

Take what you need, help where you can, and fuck the rich fucks and their fucked-up world. The mantra had kept him alive so far, though others, like Len, hadn't been so lucky.

A loud rumbling made him hunker back into his nook, survival reflex momentarily overriding his curiosity. Shadow concealed him as a positively massive vehicle roared past, spewing black smoke from its exhaust. The black and gold paint job, a golden eagle gripping arrows and swords in its talons, ignited every nerve in Gippy's body. *NAFAS!* The urge to flee, find a nice dark hole somewhere and crawl in, rose in him like a tide, but he held his position.

"Fuckin' naffies..." Gippy knew one thing and one thing only about dealing with NAFAS goons: be invisible. *You run, you look guilty, you get shot...* He'd seen it happen too many times to make that mistake.

Then the armored vehicle stopped...right in front of the fancy hotel.

"What the fuck?" Curiosity vied with the urge to get up and walk away. Gippy had no idea why the NAFAS would have any interest in a hotel, but the hairs on the back of his neck began to stand as the vehicle slowly backed up, its front wheels turning until the dual back tires hopped the curb across from the big steel door. In the dim daylight, the armored vehicle's glaring headlights reflected off the shiny stainless steel door.

Gippy's mouth fell open as the powerful engines roared, smoke billowed from the stacks, and the massive tires howled and smoked on the pavement. He barely had time to cover his ears before the titanic impact shook the whole city beneath his feet.

4

CHECKING OUT

At the front desk, I ring the bell for attention. I consider just checking out, but leaving a dead woman in my room without an explanation will damage my reputation with Securotel. I need these havens, even if they've proven less "secure" than the name implies. I also want to find out how a Nephilim found me. In situations like this, the best defense is a strong offense.

The desk clerk greets me with a smile. "Checking out, miss?"

"One of your waitstaff just tried to kill me. I'd like a refund."

"Wa...wa... One of our waitstaff did *what?*" The man's eyes are so wide I think they might pop out, but at least his astonishment is honest.

"One of your waitstaff, a young blonde woman, brought me breakfast and then tried to shoot me," I pull the machine pistol from under my duster and place it on the counter, "with this. I'm afraid there was some damage to the walls and ceiling." He gapes at me, then at the gun, then back at me, but I hear the security guards moving to flank me. I pull my hands away from the gun. "Oh, and there's quite a mess on the carpet, too."

"Where is she?"

"Still in my room," I say, then add, "staining your carpet."

"Security detachment to room seven-oh-two," the clerk says into a microphone on his lapel.

"And my refund?"

"We'll have to confirm this, miss, and the authorities will have to be notified. I'm sorry, but you will have to answer some questions, at least."

"No, I *won't*," I say with a tight smile. "Your corporation *guarantees* anonymity to your patrons. My life has been threatened, my room shot up, and my breakfast *ruined*. I will *not* relinquish my anonymity as well."

"But the authorities—"

"Will *not* be brought into this." I take a half step back from the desk to put the nervous guards at ease. "I might add that the threat on my life was no random act of violence but directed *specifically* at me. *Someone* has penetrated your security. It would be a shame if your clients discovered Securotel to be *insecure*." I'd thought about this in the elevator on the way down. They must have hacked the company's computers or the serial number scanner on the currency reader, or facial recognition software hacked into the security cameras. There are too many possibilities.

"I don't believe—" His lapel beeps softly, and he presses a finger to his ear. "One moment, please." He listens, and his eyes widen again. He nods several times before saying, "Very well. Call a clean-up team. Move all the other guests off of seven." His eyes focus back on me.

"Authorities?" I ask, arching an eyebrow.

"No, miss. We'll keep your identity out of this."

Well, they didn't really have my identity, but they have *an* identity; one I'll never be able to use again.

"And my refund?"

"Shortly, miss. I'll have to get a manager."

"Soon would be good." I turn to one of the security guards. "Would you please have the technician pull my locker? I'll be leaving."

"Yes, miss." The man turns and speaks to the attendant.

"Thank you." I *really* want my weapons back.

I stand waiting while the clerk summons his boss, wondering why five thousand years has not taught me patience in situations like this. Then I realize it has. I feel rushed, as if I'm late for something, but I have no idea why. But I've also learned to trust my intuition. I need to move.

I step back up to the counter. "Can we hurry this along?"

"It'll be one moment, miss, while we draw the funds."

"Would it be quicker to simply credit my account?" Money means nothing to me. Three centuries of investments have left me with more than I can ever spend.

"Why yes," the manager says with a forced smile. "We can do that right away."

"Good. Do that. I'll be leaving now." I still have no idea why I feel like I should hurry, but the sensation is unmistakable.

"Thank you for—" The clerk's eyes suddenly widen again, but then, so do mine.

A truck driving through the front of a building is a legitimate cause for surprise.

The building's armored door and much of the wall surrounding it explode inward, steel and masonry ripping through the foyer and security station. The attendant has just placed my locked bin on her table. She barely has time to look up and scream before she is flung aside like a ragdoll, half-buried under bricks, concrete and twisted rebar. One of the two guards is knocked down by flying debris, but the other remains standing. His reflexes are good. He empties a full magazine into the front of the truck before it stops. Unfortunately, he may as well have been using a water pistol against the armored vehicle.

The truck is massive, a fully armored urban assault vehicle painted in the black and gold of the NAFAS Security Force. The fire from the security man's rifle inflicted less damage than the armored door and the reinforced concrete wall, and those only dented the grille and ripped off the side mirrors.

I'm over the counter with the assassin's machine pistol in my hand before the spray of debris hits. The manager and clerk duck reflexively, but the former stands back up too soon. He shouts something I don't bother hearing, then falls, riddled with bullets as automatic weapons open up. There is a thud and clatter as the security guard who fired at the vehicle goes down. More rifle chatter rattles from the direction of the security man who was knocked down by debris. As I risk a quick glance. Two NAFAS troopers have left the vehicle to gain better firing positions on the remaining guard, while two more remain standing behind the open armored doors.

I brace my weapon over the counter and spray thirty rounds at two of the men. Even at this short range, the machine pistol is about as accurate as throwing a rock, but the big silencer offers a good grip, and they don't even realize I'm firing until they're hit. Puffs of dust from their torsos without any blood tell me they wear body armor. I duck back as one attacker crumples from a leg wound. Crouching under the hail of fire that chews away the false marble facing of the armor-plated counter, I jack my last scavenged magazine into the weapon and skitter sideways to the end of the barrier. I risk another peek, but they're watching for me, and the three still standing fire immediately. A shower of shattered rock and plaster lances across my face, stinging like a whip. The cuts aren't deep, but my hand comes away bloody when I touch them.

A glance tells me two assailants have left cover to advance. Only three of the enemy, including the one I shot in the leg, are standing, and both of the security men's guns have gone silent. One enemy lies with a pool of blood encircling his helmet. One of the dead security guards has evened the odds a bit, but not enough.

"Not good." I look around for something, anything to increase my odds of survival. Behind the counter, there is only the dead manager, the terrified clerk, and the typical array of computer and communications gear used to run a hotel.

Communications!

I crab over to where the clerk hunkers. "Call for help, for Christ's sake!" *Poor, poor prophet of Nazareth; go not to Jerusalem...* I banish the flashback—five millennia of PTSD comes to roost occasionally—and grab his arm. "Call in your security team!"

Nodding frantically, he touches his collar and starts shouting for help, drawing the attackers right to us. But there's no way to reach us except over the counter.

A boot crunches broken plaster, and I fire a burst blindly. *Fire and move! Never stay put.* I take three crouching steps before the clerk screams behind me. I whirl to find one of the attackers rolling over the counter to land between us. He faces the clerk, his helmet and visor blocking me from view. I fire at the same time he does. My burst takes him at the base of the neck, just below the rim of his helmet. He pitches forward on top of the man he's just murdered. They obviously intend to kill everyone here.

Covering their tracks... It's an age-old Nephilim strategy—*Dead men don't write history*—and it makes my blood boil.

"Who's next?" I shout, dropping the empty machine pistol and pulling the dead man's sidearm. His rifle is pinned beneath him, and I don't have time to get it. I creep toward the far end of the counter, crouch there, and wait, knowing the last two will come over at the same time. Or they'll throw a grenade, which would be very bad.

A shout and an immediate hail of fire not directed at me catch me by surprise. The security team has arrived. I peek up and, seeing the last two troopers occupied, roll over the shattered counter. Bullets are flying in both directions, the security team pinned down in one of the elevators, the two NAFAS soldiers firing from cover.

There's daylight beyond the battered vehicle and the wreckage of the security station, but I can't leave yet. The bin with my possessions has been thrown with the poor girl—*Young...so young*—and is also buried under a good amount of concrete and steel. It's dented but in one piece. I dash to it and slide to a stop. The dead girl's eyes stare at me as I heave the wreckage off the bin and flip it upright. Guilt surges up from my gut, even though I know her death isn't my fault.

I put the muzzle of my stolen pistol against the lock, wait until there is a volley of gunfire from the automatic weapons, and pull the trigger.

The bin springs open, and I stifle a whoop of glee.

I grab the sword first, stow it in my duster, then retrieve and load the Glock with a green-painted clip. I don't have time to take my other knives. I do, however, snatch up my shattered phone—It's trashed, but I can't leave it for them to hack—and the concussion grenades. One goes into a pocket. The pin of the second falls back into the bin. The nearest assassin is crouched behind a piece of fallen table about twenty feet away, his concentration focused upon the one remaining security guard.

I roll the grenade carefully. It bumps gently against his knee. He has time to look down, but that's all.

The grenade is concussion only, made to disable a group in a confined space, but from so close, the results are devastating. Suffice it to say, I feel safe in not making sure this one is dead, which is good because I don't have the time to spare. I'm too busy finding cover from the last assassin's hail of bullets. When the onslaught stops, I'm up and running, firing as I go. The Glock's armor-piercing slugs peel chunks of concrete from the pillar the man hides behind, forcing him to keep his head down or lose it. The assassin is so concerned with my fire that he forgets the last security man. Moving around the pillar to evade my bullets places him in full view of his former adversary. A careful burst from the elevator sends him sprawling.

I don't wait to see if he's alive but sprint around the huge truck toward daylight. I allow myself to think I might make it.

The armored door of the truck flings open, and I feel a flash of hate an instant before the door hits me.

The impact sounds like Jackie Robinson's first Major League homer. I'm on my back, my mind swimming with the smell of hot dogs, popcorn, and stale beer, crowds cheering around the Polo Grounds. *Too bad the Giants won...* I don't remember for a moment how I got here or where I am. I know only that my head hurts, my ears ring, and the surface beneath me is lumpy and uncomfortable.

Boots crunch on debris through the ringing in my ears. Camouflage-clad pillars take positions on either side of my chest. My vision clears just enough to make out the pistol in the man's hand. *Not a man...* Its hate washes over me like a crashing wave.

I try to raise the Glock, but a boot comes down on my wrist, grinding my flesh into the fragments of concrete littering the floor. I grit my teeth —which makes my head pound—and reach for a dagger. The pistol barks and my elbow explodes into shattered bone.

It's playing with me.

I squint up at it, grimacing against the agony. *Not to Heaven will I go without a hand to send me there.*

"Your time is ended, cousin," it says, aiming the gun at my forehead. "Your purpose has failed."

Never give up! You think there's mercy in this world. Fuck no! You fight, or you fucking die! Sergeant Gattish, you were an asshole, but you've saved my life more times than I can count.

"Has it?" I heave my hips up to drive a kick into the small of its back. The gun goes off, the bullet ruffling my hair and sending concrete fragments scything into my scalp. He falls to his knees, straddling my chest, his fist grasping a handful of my bloody hair.

"Yes...it...has!" The Nephilim punctuates each word by slamming my head against the floor.

My vision swims, but I feel the warm barrel press against my forehead. I struggle to move the Glock, but my wrist isn't working.

The shot is deafening but different. I don't feel dead. Death would probably hurt less. Weight on my chest, my face, makes it hard to breathe. The crushing mass rolls off me, and I gasp for air. Then a hand grabs my broken arm, and I know for certain I'm still alive.

I bring the Glock up but hold my fire as my vision clears, and I behold the angular dusky face of the boy from the previous night. The one who tried to rob me.

"Ya need ta git up." He holds a smoking revolver and looks into my gun without apparent fear. "Others might still be kickin'."

"Who?" I hiss against the pain as he pulls me to a sitting position. My head pounds with my pulse, but at least I have a pulse. "Why did you..." I look down at the Nephilim who would have killed me. Its face is blown away. The boy must have shot it in the back of the head from point-blank.

"Come on. I got a hidey-hole nearby. You come on. I got a friend who'll getcha fixed gooder'n new."

"But *why*? Why did you *do* that?" I feel his confusion through the waves of pain. "Why did you save my life?"

"Dunno." He pulls me to my feet and out onto the street. Distant sirens sing in the air. "Sometimes ya just do shit, ya know. Come on."

"Yes, I *do* know." I tuck the Glock out of sight and put a bloody hand on his shoulder for support. My finger brushes his neck, and I feel exactly why he saved me. The pivotal moments of his life surge into me. *Guilt and loneliness, a mother who died with a needle in her arm, two sisters...gone. Lennie gone. Alone. Friends gunned down in cold blood by soldiers in black and gold. Hatred, but more for the naffies than even for me.* "And thank you. You're a good boy."

"No, I ain't. Just felt like doin' it, is all. Now come on, a'fore more naffies git here."

"All right. I'm coming." I follow, wondering where my savior will take me.

5

MY ENEMY'S ENEMY

The morning commute saves us. Sirens wail through the diffuse morning light, NAFAS patrol cars tearing down the streets, sending the deluge of bicycles and scooters scrambling for the sidewalks. A few electric and ore-emulsion vehicles pull to the side to avoid the screaming gold and black SUV's. Among the masses of rain-soaked humanity, two more bedraggled figures go unnoticed.

Pain sings up my broken arm with every step, but as my head clears, my steps firm. I remove my hand from my savior's shoulder, no longer needing his support. His tumultuous emotions continue to assail me, but it's nothing like the torrent I felt when I touched him. I recognize the street we're on and realize we've come several blocks. *Concussion. Memory gaps. Wonderful...* I touch the back of my head and feel a tangle of blood-matted hair. I thank God that my dark hair hides it. As if She designed Her granddaughter with this moment in mind. I reach back and pull up my hood.

The sirens fade behind us, and the morning commuters ignore the disheveled pair, intent on their own destinations, setting up their shops or tent stalls in the New Market District. A woman rolls up the door of her butcher shop, and the odor of blood floods out with the squeaks, barks, and yowls of her pre-deceased wares. As she puts out a chalkboard sign displaying prices for various species, both butchered and live, she glances at me and wrinkles her nose.

Drawing attention? Not good, Empa. I wonder why, reaching up to flip up the collar of my duster against the rain and curious eyes. Something cracks as I bend my left arm, sending a jolt of pain through me. I bite my lip to stifle a yelp. The shattered bones of my elbow are realigning, nothing I've not felt before, but pain is pain.

"Where are we going?" I ask.

I look down at my hand and flex bloody fingers. The rain has washed away much of the blood. A flattened forty-five caliber slug falls out of the sleeve of my duster to the wet sidewalk. The Kevlar slowed the bullet significantly, but a point-blank round will break bones, regardless. *Like a broken pikestaff hitting chainmail*—the memory comes to me in a rush, charging pikes—*what glorious fools we were, dear Robert.*

It'll be hours before I'm fully healed, but I'll live.

"Told ya," he says, not looking at me. "Got a hidey-hole. Come night, Dad'll fix ya up gooder'n new."

"Your father?" We turn down a side street, leaving the markets behind. "Is he a physician?"

He gives me an incredulous snort. "Dad's no doc, and he's not my paw, neither."

The contradictory statement makes me wonder if I heard him correctly or if the Nephilim damaged my skull more than I'd surmised. I fall silent for a block, glancing at my benefactor. He really is a mess, hair cut at odd angles like he'd done it himself with a dull pair of scissors, his face narrow, gaunt, mulatto skin reminding me of my youth in the Middle East. He wears a ragged old hoodie and threadbare jeans. His shoes are cut-out pieces of tire strapped to patched-together high-top basketball shoes, the logo long since gone. He keeps his hands in his pockets, his eyes alert but cast down, studiously ignoring me. I can still feel his confusion, a cloud of questions he dares not ask.

"What's your name?" I don't know why I always need to know.

He glances at me, then away. "Gippy."

"I'm Empa." I wonder why I tell him the truth. *I must be concussed.*

He doesn't respond.

"Your friend," I begin as we cross another busy thoroughfare, "the one who was shot."

"Dead," he says. "Weren't no friend, neither. Just a guy." I taste the lie. Regret and anguish for the death well up in him for a moment, then subside.

"I'm sorry."

"Why?" He glances at me again, a flash of scorn on his face before he turns away. We pass into an alley, narrow and reeking. "'Twern't yer fault. I's the one who shot him. He'd a put a shiv in yer back fer that fancy coat you got."

"And yet, he has passed, and I remain, and for that, I sorrow." *Carnage on a once green field, the misty fells of Scottish Highlands, tearing sobs of anguish shivering the air. Robert's voice as he stands cleaning his Claymore with a rag. Weep not for the dead, fair lass, for they're beyond suffering. Weep for the living.* "I sorrow for you, Gippy."

"Me?" He stops, his gaunt face hardening, eyes like drowned embers glaring at me. "Don't *need* your pity. Don't *want* it."

"I didn't mean to—"

"You talk too much." He walks past me, shoulders hunched.

A morass of feelings I can't sort out washes over me. I have to hurry to catch up and resolve to remain silent for the remainder of our walk.

Two blocks later, in another refuse-strewn alley, Gippy sifts through a heap of garbage to retrieve an iron bar. Under the pile is an old street elevator door, rusted and caked with filth. He inserts the bar into the handle and pries it up. The hinges complain, sounding like wailing children. *Auschwitz, Belzec, Krakow, Dachau... Handiwork of the Nephilim. Can't save them all... can't save them all...*

"In," Gippy orders, nodding at the hole.

I grimace but comply, finding the rusty rungs and climbing down, still favoring my mending arm. About a dozen feet down, my boots splash into a shallow puddle. I blink and pull an Everlite from a pocket. The door screeches closed above me as the light illuminates the dismal surroundings. The space is perhaps a dozen feet square, an old shipping pallet offering a relatively dry spot, a moldy mattress lying atop it. Syringes and used condoms litter the corners of the space along with empty alcohol containers. There's a door that once led to the basement of a building, but it's been welded shut. Surprisingly, the space is relatively free of vermin.

"You sit. We got all day, and you best not go out a'fore dark. There's cameras in that fancy hotel, and yer face is all over town by now."

Wiser words were never spoken. "Thank you." I sit gingerly, but my head still swims. "I'll be fine in a few hours."

"Yer tougher than ya look, then." Gippy frowns. "Thought you was shot, but yer movin' that arm good."

"I'll be fine." The last thing I want now is to freak out my only ally.

Besides, he still has a gun, and he could probably live for years on what I have in my pockets, not to mention my money belt. "Are you hungry?"

He snorts in derision. "*Stupid* question."

I realize he's right; I *am* being stupid. Gippy lives on the street. Hunger is his life. I pull a wad of paper money from a pocket and thrust it at him. "Go buy us some food. I'm hungry, and you're starving."

He blinks at the money, eyes disbelieving. "Jesus fucking *Christ*, lady."

Ah, Mariam, of all the men to love, why... "Don't blaspheme, Gippy."

Something in my tone gives him pause, and he looks like an altar boy caught in the sacramental wine.

"Take the money. Buy us some food. Don't get followed back here."

"Sh...sure." He takes the wad of cash and stuffs it in his front pants pocket. "Just more scratch than I've seen in one place ever is all."

"Don't worry. I've got more. Now go." I really need peace and quiet.

"Sure." He climbs two rungs and looks back at me. "Wha'd you say yer name was?"

"Empa." *Daughter of Raphael, Healer of Her Highest, Ageless granddaughter of God.*

"What kinda name's that?"

Now it's my turn to snort derisively. "An old one, Gippy. Now go."

He leaves me in the darkness, silence...no emotions invading mine. I wonder if he'll come back or take the money and run. *Time will tell...* I check my phone, but as I suspected, it's trashed. A kerchief over my Everlite softens the glow, and I lay back on the filthy mattress. My eyes close, and I let my mind rest. *Saved by an unredeemed soul. How ironic is that?* I would laugh, but my head hurts so I sleep instead.

GIPPY WALKED the streets of New Market, hoodie up, face down, the practiced posture of the willfully anonymous. He wouldn't have been more ignored if he had a big sign painted on his back that read, "Do Not Fuck With Me!"

Buy us some food... don't worry, there's more... Jesus... If I had any sense, I'd just keep walkin'.

He had more money in his pocket now than he'd ever had in his life, enough to eat for a month if he stretched it, and this crazy bitch had handed it to him like it was garbage. He stopped at a line before a hole-in-the-wall vendor, teasing out a fifty from the wad without showing it. He shuffled forward, head down, waiting for his turn, mouth watering with the smell of food so close.

"One, the works, no hot sauce." He handed over the bill, received a tencoin back, and seconds later was handed a foil-wrapped packet, warm to the touch.

Gippy found a disused doorway, tucked in, and ate. Fresh flatbread, a quarter pound of fried mystery meat—probably rat—peppers and onions, went into his stomach in ravenous bites, barely chewed. *You get food, you eat fast*, an old codger had told him when he first hit the streets. *What's in yer gut nobody can take from you.* Good advice.

His stomach stretched painfully, but pleasantly, Gippy ditched the wrapper and started off into the markets. *Me first...* He found a gun shop and stepped in. The stocky woman behind the Armorglass looked up from her phone disinterestedly. It was early still, and she looked half-awake.

"What you need?"

"Two thirty-eights. Brass."

"Twenty."

"Twenty?" He wrinkled his nose. "Na. Ten."

"Go somewhere else then." She went back to her phone.

"Ten, and I got the spent brass."

She looked back up. "Show 'em."

Gippy pulled his piece, thumbed out the chamber, and picked the two spent shells out of the cylinder. One of them had killed Len. *So why you hangin' with the bitch who made you kill him?* He still didn't know why he'd saved the woman's life; other than anyone the naffies were so determined to take down had to be someone worth saving. Gippy had very few friends left, many enemies, and acquaintances of varying degrees of mistrust. He put his piece away and held out his hand flat on the counter, the spent shells on his palm.

The woman squinted at the brass, shrugged, and nodded. "Ten with the brass."

"Deal." He pulled the tencoin from his pocket and put it and the spent shells in the slide tray.

She inspected the shells, nodded with a grunt, and picked two out of a box under the counter. The bullets clanked into the tray, and she slid it over, already back on her phone.

Gippy inspected the rounds, but at this point, the deal was done, and he couldn't squawk even if there was something wrong with them. He wasn't worried about getting cheated. A vendor pushing crap would get a bad rep on the street and would be out of business in a week. Of course, they were reloads, which made them cheaper by half than new and a tenth the price of caseless. He topped up the cylinder of his piece, put it away, and went back out onto the street.

Considering the money in his pocket, he started looking for a shop to buy food he could carry back. She'd given him too much. He felt like people were staring at him, knowing he was flush, planning to rob him. He kept a hand on his piece in his pocket and his head down. The food in his stomach gave him a warm, sleepy feeling. He'd been up all night and longed to get back and bed down, but he had to buy food for her first.

Empa... What the hell kind of name is that?

She'd told him twice that she was old, but he wouldn't peg her for over thirty. She talked strangely and acted even stranger. Beautiful, but he wasn't interested in that. Memories of Lennie rose up unbidden, safe, warm, familiar... Not that Gippy didn't like girls, too, but this one...no way. She was of a different world than his, untouchable. He would never even consider asking her.

He spotted a used clothing shop across the street and mentally counted his money. He had plenty for a new hoodie, even a jacket to keep the damp off, but they had a sign—red circle with a diagonal line over the outline of a gun—and that meant a scanner and guards. He walked on, thinking about food. What should he get her?

Fancy bitch probably eat nothin' but cow meat and chocolate cake!

"Need somethin', brah?"

Gippy glanced at the dealer leaning in the doorway and considered the money in his pocket. His mouth watered again.

He stopped. *Shouldn't...she said buy food.* "Yeah. Couple of Vickies." They helped him sleep and took away the dreams he knew he'd have. He peeled a cee off his wad, exchanged it for two oblong white pills in a tiny plastic bag, and walked on. He tucked the baggie in his other pocket, resisting the urge to take them now.

Food...gotta buy food. He ducked into a market and grabbed a basket. She wanted food? Well, he would buy her a fucking feast!

COMBAT BOOTS CRUNCHED through the rubble of the Securotel foyer. Her team fanned out ahead of her, and she paused to inspect the corpse of her cousin.

"Fool, get of Baraqiel. All balls and no brains." She fingered the hole in the back of his skull. "Or were you ambushed?"

The Nephilim, daughter of Ariquiel, Fallen Angel of Judgment, brought the bloody finger to her nose and sniffed the charred flesh and gray matter. The wound was ringed by burned hair and skin. Powder burns. A point-blank shot in the back of the head, execution-style. How many hundreds of times she'd inflicted that very judgment... Poland, Croatia, Serbia, Arkansas... It seemed almost ironic to see one of her own felled by that method.

"Perhaps your next life, you'll learn to duck." She stood and approached the bullet-riddled counter and the stiff Securotel executive standing before it with two armed security goons at his shoulders. The man looked shaken but stoic, Asian, expensive haircut, a corporate executive with all the courage that lawyers, a pension, and a ten thousand nad suit could give him.

"I'm Unit Commander Westerhouse, NAFAS Federal Security Force." She removed her hat and tucked it under her arm. She didn't offer to shake his hand. "Unless you are cooperative, we'll be pressing federal charges of harboring terrorists and assaulting NAFAS security troops against Securotel. Your name?"

"My name is Hiamatsu, Commander. I'm regional chief of operations for Securotel." He executed a short bow from the waist, his Asian features unyielding. "And you will *not* be filing any charges against Securotel, nor will we be offering any assistance in your investigation. Your vehicle smashed through *our* building, killing innocent people, and your men opened fire without provocation or announcing themselves as federal authorities. Our people returned fire to protect themselves and our clients only. Our security recordings show this clearly."

Westerhouse gritted her teeth and suppressed the urge to pull her sidearm and put a bullet through the man's skull. "I can have a federal judge here in five minutes with an injunction, Mister Hiamatsu. We require your security recordings and guest records for the last forty-eight hours. If you don't comply, I *will* arrest you."

"Your injunction will do no good, Commander. All recordings and guest records of this facility have been expunged." He smiled at her and bowed again. "Save for those showing your unprovoked attack and murder of innocent civilians. Arrest me if you will. I'll be out in time for lunch."

"I doubt that." Westerhouse pulled her sidearm and put a bullet through the astonished executive's gaping mouth. His cheeks puffed out with the muzzle blast, and the back of his skull sprayed the fake marble wall behind the counter. Her next two rounds exterminated the security guards standing behind him.

The echo of her pistol rattled around the once lavish foyer. Her team didn't flinch at her use of deadly force; they knew her and knew what would happen if they did.

"Justice..." She holstered her pistol and looked around the room. "Sergeant, I want someone to crawl through this facility's computers with a fine-toothed comb, and I want everything in my hand in an hour. I also want the dash recordings from our assault vehicle and full reports of ballistics and forensics."

"Yes, ma'am," the sergeant barked, waving his people into motion.

The daughter of the fallen angel of judgment turned and started for the exit, pausing only briefly at the corpse of her cousin. "We'll find her. We'll find her this time, and Hell will have its due."

6

HIDING FROM GOD

I wake feeling better. Not good, but fed, rested, and mostly healed. My head doesn't spin when I sit up, and my arm bends without much pain. I finger the hole in the elbow of my duster. The round must have been steel-jacketed to pierce the Kevlar. My hair is still a matted mess, but the wound and my concussion are healed.

Gippy snorts in his sleep, and I consider him, feel the cluttered confusion of his dreams, and remember his intoxication after we ate, a giddy sleepiness that spoke of narcotics. I don't know what drug he took. I should have known better than to give him so much money. *Should I leave without waking him?* It would probably be best for both of us, but I'm curious about Gippy. He saved my life, and I need to know why.

And I'm alone...

I touch his arm and shake him awake. "Gippy. It's evening. We should go."

"Huh?" He starts awake, blinking at me in the subdued light. "Who the... Oh, yeah." He shakes his head, runs his fingers through his stringy disheveled hair, and lurches up to his feet. "Food?"

"Please, and something to drink." I stand without difficulty and stretch out the kinks while he retrieves a wrapped bar and a can from the plastic bag he's hung from the ladder. I accept both, peeling back the wrapper with my teeth and popping the top of the canned imitation cappuccino. We all have our drugs, our demons to feed. I've been addicted to caffeine for five centuries, and the world shortage of coffee is slowly driving me insane. Who am I to judge another's addiction?

We eat in silence, and Gippy packs up our trash. I retrieve my light, and we leave the hidey-hole exactly as we found it.

Light rain is falling, and even though it's early, the streets aren't heavily traveled. Coming winter has put a bite in the damp air. Gippy guides us north along less-traveled streets. I count the blocks and keep track of where we are in my head. The area becomes less urban but not quite suburban. An hour or so and three miles later, we turn onto a narrow street dominated by an old stone Catholic church, Saint Luther's.

Dear Martin, you really should have known better... One of the few who truly deserved sainthood and he started a war that wasn't reconciled for five centuries.

To my surprise, Gippy turns up the walk that skirts the church grounds and descends a stairway to a basement door. I follow reluctantly. As odd as it may seem, I don't generally get along well with organized religions. Too much money and power, not enough faith.

Gippy pushes a button beside the door, and we wait.

A small viewing slot clicks open. I get a flashback of a speakeasy I frequented in Newark during prohibition. The tiny door snaps closed, and a lock clicks. The door opens to reveal a middle-aged woman in a black dress and sweater. Her hair is tied back, and her eyes are sharp. She wears a crucifix and a simple silver ring on the third finger of her left hand. A nun.

"Gippy." The woman's eyes dart to take me in. "Friend of yours?"

"Hey, Sis. I'll vouch." The door opens wider, and Gippy motions me to follow him in. "Dad around? She's hurt."

I open my mouth to object since my injuries are mostly healed, but the things he's said click into my mind: *Church... Sis... Nun... Dad... a priest.* This can make things difficult, but with the NAFAS and probably others looking for me, and who knows how many Nephilim among them, I'm loath to turn down a refuge.

"He's busy," the nun says, letting us in. It is warm and dry inside, tidy, orderly, and smells like church. I wonder about that smell sometimes. "Follow me."

She guides us down a hall, doors set to both sides, and another at its end. The walls are painted a pale green that reminds me of a mental institution. *Time ill-spent.* I remember the screams, the smell of urine, the hopelessness. One malady I've never been able to help in humans is psychological disorders that aren't resultant from trauma. I can feel them, but I can't find the boundaries to surround them and take them away. Believe me, I've tried. I follow her into a small room. Furnishings include a cushioned table, several chairs, and counters of black material like laboratory benches. The walls are lined with cabinets.

"How bad?" The nun takes down a tray wrapped in blue paper from a cabinet. I recognize the autoclave tape sealing the package and raise a hand.

I beat Gippy to the punch this time. "Not so bad that I'll require surgery, Sister." I resist the urge to call her sister-in-law. They never understand the joke, and it draws attention I don't need.

"She's shot," Gippy insists, pointing to the hole in the arm of my jacket.

"Take off your coat." The woman puts down the tray and reaches to help me.

"You needn't tend me, Sister." I evade her grasp.

This is where my nature always becomes problematic. Gippy saw me shot, but I know what my arm will look like if I remove my jacket: a ragged hole in my shirt caked with dried blood, powder residue, but no gaping wound. The bone is still knitting, and I likely have a hell of a bruise, but the bullet hole will be closed. Explaining how I heal so quickly often brings out the worst in people, even nuns, and *especially* priests. I've gotten good at explaining things away, however.

"My coat's lined with Kevlar. The bullet didn't penetrate." I raise my hand, most of the blood washed off by rain. "I was only bruised. This blood isn't mine, but that of my assailant, from whom Gippy here saved me."

"Naw I—"

"*Without* his timely intervention, I'd have been killed." That, at least, is the truth.

"What about your head?" the sister asks, peering sidelong at my blood-matted hair. "Or is your *skull* armored, too?"

"A few cuts that'll heal well enough." I try a smile but get nothing in return. *Why is she so suspicious?* "Head wounds, as I'm sure you know, often bleed more than their severity warrants."

"They also become infected if they're not tended properly, but I can't *make* you sit still if you don't want to." The woman's reticence surrounds her like a field of nettles.

"I appreciate your concern *and* the shelter, truly, Sister, but a shower and a clean shirt are all I truly want. That and food, if it's not too much trouble." I withdraw another roll of NAFAS bills from a pocket. "I'm able to pay."

"Christ on a *cracker*, lady!" Gippy stares wide-eyed at the money. "You flash around cash like that, some ganger gonna—"

"None of your blasphemy, young man!" The nun's comment makes me smile. Poor Gippy can't get a break. "Now, go find Father Farrell. I'll show our guest to the common room." She gives me a glare and points to a sink. "You can at *least* wash your hands and face."

Gippy mutters something under his breath and leaves the room.

"Thank you." I put the money away and begin a quick but thorough scrubbing. A lot of blood washes down the drain. No wonder the butcher lady stared at me.

"We don't take payment from the *needy*," the sister begins, as I towel dry, "but I won't tell you that a donation to the church wouldn't be welcome." I feel a twinge of avarice from her.

"Take it, then." I dig the roll of bills out of my pocket and press it into the woman's hand. Our fingers touch, and I get her peak memories in a flash: *fatigue, resentment, the life she wanted, the baby she lost...* "If, as I suspect, you're serving the *truly* needy, then the money will be well spent."

"Thank you." The money vanishes into a pocket of her dress, and the prickly aura surrounding her eases somewhat. "It's still early, but supper will be ready soon. Father Farrell will have to approve the use of the rectory for a shower, and he *is* busy."

"The shower can wait."

I follow her down the hall to the larger door at the end and through. Beyond, I find myself in a large room crowded with folding tables and chairs and smelling of food. A serving counter to her left is open, and a group of bedraggled men, women, and a few children are beginning to line up. They stare, and I find myself staring back, their attire, their hair, their jewelry, gaudy and garish; styles have changed in fifteen years. Wildly colored hair, tattered or oddly cut clothes, and a myriad of tattoos and facial piercings catch me off guard. Toronto and Detroit, Chicago and Indianapolis...recent images of the people of this new nation flash through my mind. I've been seeing, but not seeing, too focused on my search for any sign of my cousins. Styles change, clothes, hair, tattoos, jewelry, come and go so fast, every *decade* now, something new. I haven't been paying close enough attention.

Empa, you need to get out more.

There are a couple of lounge chairs and a tattered sofa along the walls, a bookcase, and a windowed cabinet of stuffed animals and toys. One figure lies snoring on the couch. The first few in line are served and sit at the tables, quietly eating whatever's being doled out. The smell of coffee is like a breath of fresh air.

"There's stew, bread, and coffee or tea," the nun says, pointing to the line. "But before you accept our generosity, I must tell you that we have a few rules."

"Of course." More eyes are drawn to me, some merely curious, others gauging me. I can feel their suspicion, their hunger, their need. The press of their directed emotions bleeds into me, scouring me like steel wool, leaving me raw. I don't like being the center of attention. I can't block feelings directed at me, be they benign, positive, or hateful, so I let them fill me. I take them in and let them become me. I don't let them change me, however. I alter *them*, reflect them back transformed. *Love, hope, solace.* I can't change what people think, but they can usually pick up what I feel. I see the mood shift; a few look away as if embarrassed, others keep watching, as if hungry to feel something good.

I understand all too well.

"We do not tolerate violence, theft, drug use, or carnal relations among our residents." The woman glances pointedly at my long coat. "We don't ask that weapons be relinquished, knowing that nobody would willingly comply, but if one of our staff sees one, it'll be confiscated."

"I understand." I wonder how she plans to disarm someone if they flash a gun.

"We don't ask for names or, as you know, payment, but we accept volunteer work or donations. Those who stay longer than seven days will be asked for one of the two."

"I won't be staying that long. Thank you." I give the woman another smile. "My name's Emily." I hold out my hand.

The woman purses her lips and ignores the gesture, filled again with suspicion. "Thank me by following the rules." She turns away, exiting through a door beside the food window.

I join the end of the line, keeping my eyes from meeting others' and my hands in my pockets until I'm handed a bowl of stew, a biscuit, and a cup of coffee. The older man serving flashes me a brief smile and a nod, which I return. I find a seat at an empty table and start eating. The stew is surprisingly good, savory, with some kind of meat. I don't speculate *what* kind. I've eaten far worse. The coffee is hot but tasteless, likely synthetic. Despite NAFAS promises that the unification of North America would bring prosperity for all, international trade has been devastated by the slow-motion cataclysm of climate change and rising sea levels. The coffee plantations of South America have been drowned by decades of unrelenting monsoons, and Central America by so many sequential hurricanes that they have stopped naming them.

One hundred fifty feet of rising sea has put most of Florida and the coastal cities of the gulf states underwater, not to mention many of the greatest cities of the eastern seaboard. Millions perished, either in cataclysmic storms or from the ensuing pestilence that ravaged the refugee camps. Despite the diminishing population, the mass exodus of these cities has put undue pressure on those not flooded. NAFAS promised stability, security, and prosperity, all the things usurpers have promised through the ages. They've delivered a police state, security through brutality and fear, obliteration of human rights, and protection for only those who support their regime. Elections were last held in 2050, two decades ago. NAFAS declared a state of emergency in 2054, rescinding the democratic process. Then, the St. Louis Revolt, and I went into hiding.

It seems that humans sometimes have no memories, ignore their own history, or are perhaps too short-lived to recall the tyrannies of the past. I remember them all, and I weep to see another in this once free land. I suspect the Nephilim at work, for they feed on strife like a leech feeds on blood.

A snort from the couch draws my attention, and the man sleeping there lurches to his feet, tall and broad-shouldered. He looks around, and his eyes fall on me for a moment, then pass on. He walks to the serving window with a gait that speaks of some chemical intoxication or the lack of it. With a bowl and cup from the window, he walks right over to my table.

"Nice coat." He sits down. He's unshaven and smells of sweat and a lack of proper dental hygiene. He slurps his coffee and takes a bite of stew.

"It is." I give him an even smile, tolerating his mix of feelings. Mostly there is avarice, the need to feed his habit.

Desperation breeds addiction like rats breed plague—*Thousands are dumped into the mass graves, covered with lye, then soil... I help as I can, but there are thousands more to follow... One third of Europe dies*—and again, I feel the Nephilim at work. There never seems to be a shortage of chemicals to numb the senses.

He eats and smiles back, but there is no warmth on his face. "Coat like that in a place like this…you either got a lotta guts or no brains."

"I was brought here by a friend." I finish the last bite of stew and the final swallow of my coffee. "And I'll be leaving soon." I get up and return my bowl to the counter.

"More coffee?" the man behind the counter asks after taking my bowl.

"Please."

"Don't mind him." He pours the coffee-like liquid into my cup. "Just you aren't the usual type we see here."

"I understand." I sip and give him a tentative smile, feel a spark of surprise that simple gesture evokes, and the quirky sense of humor the man wears like a thin suit of armor.

"Not many understand street folk, but a lot *think* they do." He gives me a gap-toothed grin, his gray stubble creasing into deep lines.

"I've been poor, homeless, and hungry before," I tell him, keeping my voice quiet. "*I* understand."

"Heh. Yer not old enough to understand."

"I'm older than I look." *Older than you, this building, this city, this nation…* I take my coffee back to my table and sit down exactly where I was.

The man who passively threatened me fires a short glare, bluster to hide his surprise that I show no fear, and returns to his food. I feel a twinge of curiosity pierce the wall of his greed.

The door beside the serving window opens, and Gippy enters accompanied by the nun and a diminutive man in a checked flannel shirt and jeans. He looks perhaps fifty, though it's hard to tell, has a slight paunch, and, surprisingly, a closely trimmed moustache and beard of gray whiskers. If he is, as I suspect, Father Farrell, the facial hair's unusual, discouraged as a sign of vanity by his church. His eyes are a startling blue and dart about the room, never settling on one thing for more than a second. His hair is sandy, with a touch of salt and pepper at his temples. His hands brush at his pockets, fingers fiddling with the belt loops, twiddling, fidgeting. His eyes find me, settle for a second, flick away, then back.

He is different; I can't feel his emotions, or at least anything cohesive. A confusion, a million details in a whirlwind of information, sounds, scents, faces, numbers, music only he can hear, a concerto from years ago. The mannerisms and peculiar emotions strike a chord in my memory.

Autism; high on the spectrum, but clearly there. I've felt the minds of autistics before, and it always amazes me how those high on the spectrum can function with so much data flooding their minds constantly. A million inputs, memories, sensory overload, and still they manage to think through it. I can't even carry on a conversation during a concert. I try to remember if I've ever met an autistic priest and fail. *Interesting.*

Gippy goes to the counter for food, but the priest and his stern escort approach me. I stand and prepare myself. There will be questions.

"Welcome to Saint Luther's. I'm Father Emil Farrell." His eyes flick over me from head to foot, his hands folded at his belt. "Our guests generally call me Father Farrell, or Father."

"Emily Johnston." The name is one of my many identities, not the one I used at the Securotel the previous night. I'll need to change my identity, my looks, my clothes... *Such a pain in the ass.* I watch for him to extend a hand—priests usually do—but he doesn't. I would just as soon not touch him. I don't relish experiencing his chaotic thoughts. I also feel a slight uneasiness that I can't place, like a flicker of light on a cloudy night. I can't decide if the priest is uneasy with me, the nun, or maybe the man at the table.

"Gippy tells me you were involved in some...difficulties this morning, and Sister Janice said you wanted to get cleaned up."

"If it's not too much trouble and doesn't break your rules, yes, I'd like that very much." I glance around the room; Gippy has taken a seat and is eating. A pale skinny girl in goth clothes, spiky black hair, garish makeup, and too much jewelry sits beside him, speaking in whispers, shooting me furtive glances. "If we could speak in a less public place, I'll explain."

Father Farrell's eyes narrow for a moment, flick away, and he smiles disarmingly. "You needn't. I'll let you use the rectory washroom to get cleaned up. I'd like to talk to you afterward, but rest assured, I'm not going to ask you for details that would make things difficult. We have no secrets there, but we respect our guests' privacy."

Sister Janice stepped in. "Father Farrell, I don't—"

The priest waves a hand to forestall her argument. "Don't worry, Sister. I'll take care of it."

"Very well, Father." The woman gives a slight nod and leaves us, flushing with resentment.

"Come." Farrell waves toward the door he came in through. "The rectory's this way."

"Thank you, Father." Still, the uneasiness lingers. I get no pure thoughts from the priest through the chaos of his autism, but there's something peculiar there, too.

"You're welcome."

He leads me upstairs, through a labyrinth of halls at a brisk pace. I hear a baby crying from one of the doors we pass and wonder if that was what he had been busy with. It seems he offers more services than a simple bed and breakfast for the needy, but I'm not about to ask any questions.

He works a key in a door and opens it into a hall with thin red carpet and the usual décor of a place of worship. I smile at the likeness of Christ on a crucifix, so anglicized, so different from my memory of the man. I remember his laugh, his touch, his strong carpenter's hands, the openness of him, the simplicity of his thoughts... *Go not to Jerusalem...* The sound of the hammer driving spikes through his flesh.

"This way." Farrell takes me down a long hall to another door and opens it with a key.

A brass plaque overhead reads Rectory. Inside is homey, warm, and comfortable, without a hint of ostentation. He guides me through an open door, white and black tile Wainscoting, a green bathmat and shower curtain that don't match, sink, and toilet.

"Sister said you wanted a clean shirt. We've got some castoffs." His eyes flick over me again, and I feel that strange unease, almost anger, like a scent of something burning on a distant stove. "Size six or eight? Something warm, yes? Lose or fitted?"

I blink at him, surprised. The clothes I wear are cut to fit—online shopping is the best use of computer technology yet—but I still wear my coat. He has a sharp eye. "Eight, please. Fitted."

"I'll see what I can find. There are towels in the closet. Take your time." He flashes a smile and closes the door. The uneasiness vanishes.

It is him. But what? His autism? Some hidden personality disorder?

There is no lock, but even if there were, it would be pointless. He would have a key. I sigh in resignation and take off my coat, hanging it on the back of the door. My sweatshirt is just as bad as I thought it would be, bloody from the elbow down with a ragged hole and powder burns. There are splinters of bone—*my* bone—stuck in the fabric. I pull it over my head and run cold water into the sink, soaking it thoroughly while I look at my arm. Bruised from bicep to forearm, but whole; it's healing well. I always heal well. By tomorrow, I won't even have a bruise.

I peel out of my stretch top and then my sports bra, mankind's best invention, in my opinion. They landed on the *moon* before they got around to making one. Tell me again this isn't a male-dominated world, even now. I run the water in the shower while I divest myself of boots, socks, pants—rolling them up around my holstered Glock to keep the weapon out of sight—and scanties. That, of course, is when a knock sounds at the door.

"One moment, please." I grab a towel from the closet, wrap myself, and crack the door. I feel it again, faint, like the heat from a radiator, uneasy, unhappy, angry. Father Farrell holds out a folded shirt, his eyes pointedly directed elsewhere. "Thank you, Father."

"Take your time. I'll be in the den just down the hall when you finish." Still, his eyes focus down the hall, darting around like mice looking for a place to hide. "I'd like to speak with you after."

Questions...always questions.

"Of course." I close the door and look at the shirt. A woman's flannel plaid cut to fit, something a suburban wife would wear to weed her flower beds. I put the towel aside and step into the scalding shower. *Glorious...* Okay, maybe the sports bra is the *second*-best invention.

I luxuriate, washing my hair twice to get all the blood out, and soak the back of my neck to ease the stiffness. When I close my eyes, I see the hate-filled face of the Nephilim as he presses a gun to my forehead. I'm lucky to have survived, and I have Gippy to thank, which I really haven't done yet.

One question, however, plagues me: *How did they find me?* The morning's events, the room-service assassin, then the brute-force attack, stack up in my mind like a dam threatening to burst. Two Nephilim in one place means they knew who I was and wanted me very badly. Some kind of computer hack seems the most likely Judas. They have someone high up in NAFAS, that seems certain, but they've controlled heads of state before and I've never experienced a focused attack like this.

And I've only been out of hiding for two weeks...

I've survived dozens of human wars, more than once as a soldier, but I won't survive this one. They're gunning for me, me specifically, and eventually they'll get me. The odds have been stacked against me far too long. Technology has made their job easier and mine harder. The problem is the same as it has always been: too many enemies, not enough friends.

Five thousand years of war between the Ageless and the Nephilim— God's grandchildren locked in a deadly family squabble that will decide the fate of mankind. I lean into the hot spray and pray. I know She hears me. I know She loves me, for She loves everyone. But I also know She won't help me. She abandoned this war more than twenty centuries ago, vowing to take no more hand in the conflict. I guess watching one's only mortal son crucified can do that even to God.

One day, I'll die, and Her love will take me to her side. When a Nephilim dies, the hate of the Serpent sends that soul into another new life. How ironic that love can lose a war while hate can win it.

GIPPY SAT down with his stew and soykaf, his head down, ignoring and hoping to be ignored. He was also trying to forget the last twenty-four hours. As usual, he was failing miserably.

Saw her shot... saw the blood... Kevlar coat or no, she took a bullet. The memory was just too clear, the hole in Empa's coat, ragged meat showing through, blood dripping steadily from her sleeve, leaving a trail down the rainy street. Then, when he returned with the food, she was moving the arm, and the bleeding had stopped. When she woke him, she seemed right as rain, and insisted she was fine when they arrived at the church. *Saw her shot...*

While he was still trying to reconcile what he'd seen with the physical world he knew, Jeri sat down with her usual lopsided smile.

"Hey, Gip. Worried about you last night. You okay?"

"Fine," he lied, shoveling a bite of stew into his mouth. Jeri was always nice when she wasn't teasing, which was pretty much always, but he didn't feel like talking.

"So, who's *she*?" Her ebony-lined eyes flicked toward Empa, her piercings clicking against her teeth.

"Nobody." He didn't know what to call her. She'd given him one name and Father Farrell another. "Just someone need a place."

"You meet her last night?" Jeri nudged him under the table. "Get lucky, maybe?"

There she went with the teasing again. Why did it always have to be about sex? "Ain't like that, Jer."

"What's it like then?" Her eyes followed Empa as Dad took her away. "She's wearin' a—"

Drake sat down abruptly at the table, his mere presence cutting Jeri off. Gippy tried to think of someone he would like less to talk to and couldn't.

"Where's your boyfriend, Gipster?" Drake grinned his bully grin.

Another flash of memory: *the woman in the long coat moving like a blur*

45

in the rain, his finger squeezing the trigger of his gun, the shot shattering the raindrops into mist, then Lennie staring at him in shock, one hand on the bloody hole in his chest.

Gippy dropped his spoon and swallowed forcefully, his eyes rising slowly to meet Drake's. "Len's *dead!*" It came out too loud, drawing stares from all around the room.

Jeri drew in a sharp breath, and for once, Drake faltered, gaping at him.

"H...how?" Jeri asked, her black-nailed fingers raising to her mouth.

"Shot." Gippy pushed back his chair and grabbed his bowl, his appetite gone. "Don't wanna talk about it." *Because you shot him, you stupid fuck! You killed your best friend!*

He got up and took his bowl back to the serving counter. Hank, at least, saw the look on his face and didn't say anything, but when he turned around, Jeri was there. He bowed his head and tried to walk past her, but she put a hand on his arm.

"Gip, I'm sorry. I know you and he was tight. If you need...anything..."

He looked at her and knew that anything included someone to hold, cry with, feel human with, and feel safe with. Gippy needed that but knew where it would go, and he couldn't do that to Jeri. *You're a dirty needle, Gip.* He couldn't kill another friend.

"No, Jer. I need ta be alone."

"Be safe, huh?"

He snorted a laugh, not knowing where it came from. "Right." He took her hand—*warm, human, safe*—and pulled it from his arm. "I'll see ya, Jer."

Gippy left the church and just started walking. He had quite a bit of Empa's money still. Maybe he could score some Vickies or even some fent, make the world go away for a while. He rested his hands in the pocket of his hoodie out of habit, curling his fingers around the butt of his pistol.

Maybe make the world go away forever.

Behind him, Drake sidled up to Jeri. "Holy shit, Lennie dead, and he walks in here with some rich bitch? What the fuck? Gipster finally grow a dick or somethin'?"

Jeri glared at him. "Fuck off, Drake." She walked away, seriously worried about Gippy. If he and this woman were involved in some trouble, as she guessed from the conversation with Father, and Lennie ended up dead because of it... She considered going after him but knew he'd brush her off. Still, maybe she should tell someone.

7

REVELATIONS

Clean and feeling somewhat better, I pull my last pair of fresh scanties from an inner pocket of my jacket—*I really need to pick up my stash and find a laundry*—and get dressed. My mangled sweatshirt, rinsed in cold water until the blood is gone, I hang over the shower nozzle to drip dry. I then arm myself, drape my jacket over my arm to keep Musashi's sword hidden, and step into the hall. The fitted flannel shirt I leave untucked to hide the Glock. This may be a safe place, and it may not be. The centuries have taught me caution.

Father Farrell's den opens out from the hallway, a warm, cozy space with a couch, three chairs, a few lamps, and an old-fashioned fireplace that's been refitted with natural gas. It almost looks real and puts off enough heat to make the room comfortable. The priest sits in an armchair reading a book—a real paper one, and my fingers itch to touch it, recounting decades as a librarian, time well-spent—but his eyes rise to meet mine as I stand in the entry.

"Come in, Emily, Please." He folds the book and sets it aside, rising to his feet. I glimpse the cover, *Realizing Awakened Consciousness. Buddhism?* Not what I expect from a priest. "Coffee?"

"Please." From across the room, I get no feelings from him at all, no confusion, and no unease. What is it about this man that unnerves me? I look around, but there's no coat rack. "Is there somewhere I can hang this?"

"Oh, just drape it over a chair. Please, make yourself at home." He pushes through a swinging door into a small kitchen.

I place my duster over the back of a chair so the sword hangs straight. Cups clatter, a kettle clanking on a stove.

"I'm afraid all I've got is instant, but it's real coffee."

"That'll be fine, thank you." I take in the room; much more memorabilia than I would expect, pictures of people, places, cities, and countryside. I don't know why I expect priests to be austere monks. Most are just regular folks, after all. Images of Father Farrell as a younger man, a wide-eyed, enthusiastic look on his face, and what looks like the ivy-covered walls of a university. Maybe a seminary. He looks very...happy.

The door creaks, and he leans out, an amiable look on his open face. "Something to make the coffee a bit more palatable and drive off the chill?"

"You mean alcohol?"

"Jesus drank wine, after all, and I'm Irish." He blinks, and his eyes dance around the room, a wave of too much information touching my senses but no unease from this distance. "A dram of whiskey, or not?"

"Please." I find myself smiling for no apparent reason. There is something different about this priest that I haven't yet figured out. I think I might like him but for that strange feeling when he's close. *A multiple personality disorder, maybe?* The healer's curiosity in me is insatiable.

I continue my inspection of the room as I hear a cupboard open and the clank of a bottle touching the rim of a cup. Above the faux-fireplace several framed pictures are poised on the mantle. My heart skips a beat: two of the pictures include a blonde woman I recognize.

"Terpsichore..." I lift the frame from the mantle and stare into the face of my Ageless cousin, daughter of Israfal, Angel of Music. "Oh, Cora..." My hands shake.

"Put that *down*, please."

I whirl to find Father Farrell standing in the doorway with two cups in hand, both of them trembling. I feel a wash of emotion from him for the first time—worry, love, heartbreak—that pierces the confusion of information.

"I'm sorry." I turn and put the picture back on the mantle, trying to reconcile what I'm feeling from him. *He loved her?* "I just—"

"No, it's fine." He moves to a table between two chairs and puts down the cups. His emotions are again clouded in a deluge of information I can't parse. "Please, have a seat. Never mind the picture. Just something I hold dear...an old friend, you understand."

"Of course, I understand, Father." *More than you know.* A million faces of friends long lost race through my memory in a torrent. "I have quite a few myself, old friends, that is."

"Do you?" He sits and gestures to the other chair with a twitchy hand. "You don't look old enough to have *too* many old friends."

"I'm older than I look, and I've traveled quite a lot." Reluctance to get close to him wells up, but I can't show it. I sit, quelling my reaction —*unease, deep anger, an urge to break things*—and pick up my cup, sniffing the aroma of instant coffee and Irish whiskey. I wonder how old the liquor is; Ireland hasn't had a crop to distill in two decades. I sip—not bad, all things considered. The urge to ask him about Cora burns in me, but these things must be eased into. I need to find out some things about the good Father Farrell first. "You wanted to ask me some questions?"

"Not as such. As I said, we respect people's privacy here, but I'm concerned about... the effect your presence will have on our other guests."

"I'm not your usual street person, is what you're saying."

He smiles, his eyes still flicking around. "You must admit that you're not. Your clothes alone say so."

"And that will cause disruption." I see where this is going. "Gippy hinted at that, and another of your guests mentioned that coming here and wearing a coat like mine was foolish."

He shrugs and sips his coffee. "Not foolish, perhaps, but careless."

"I didn't have a choice."

"I understand that, but it could provoke...things we're not prepared to deal with."

"You needn't worry about me, Father. I can take care of myself."

"Oh, I don't doubt it!" He gestures vaguely at me. "Gippy said you were shot, but Janice told me your coat's lined with Kevlar, and I can see for myself that you carry weapons. It seems everyone does these days. But it's not *you* I'm worried about; it's my...flock if you will. One doesn't wave money in front of someone so poor without provoking a response."

"Don't blame the victim for the crime, Father."

His face hardens, and I feel his annoyance sifting through the deluge of information. "You may be a lot of things, Miss Johnston, but I don't believe you're a victim."

"No?" I take a healthy draught of my heady draft and stand. It's time for some truth. I can't trust this man fully, of course, but I judge he won't call the authorities, and it's nothing he won't learn from the news feeds anyway. "May I show you something, Father?"

He stiffens in his chair but doesn't look scared or particularly daunted. "Yes."

I unbutton my sleeve and roll it up to my bicep, the dark bruise livid. "This is the result of being the *victim* of an assault, Father. I was shot, and my coat saved me." His eyes widen at the sight of the injury. "I was *also* assaulted in my room at the Securotel on Washburn Street this morning. If you check the news feeds, you'll see that a NAFAS assault vehicle drove through the front of the building. They'll undoubtedly call this an action to apprehend a suspected terrorist, since that is the current language."

"This is the incident you told Sister Janice of?"

"Yes." I roll down my sleeve. "You're a man of God, Father. You know the scriptures." *The scriptures that made it into print, anyway... So much lost, so much deemed unsavory or unworthy, redacted by politicians...* "You know they used similar language to describe the Son of God before they cruci-fied him." *Oh, my dear uncle...go not to Jerusalem.* "The Romans called your prophet, Jesus, a terrorist, a blasphemer, and a seditionist, an enemy of the state. Your church labeled thousands as heretics in their hunt for those who wouldn't back their agenda. They tortured, and crucified, and burned at the *stake* those who fought their reign!"

Sweet Joana, don't do this...they will not submit to the truth! They will burn you! I close my eyes against the tears of my memories.

"Emily, please, sit down. I'm not accusing you of terrorism."

My teeth are on edge, and I don't know why. I know this man isn't my enemy, but there's something dark there, something that wants to lash out. I sit and swallow my temper. "Father, I *am* the victim here. I'm being hunted by people of power, people who have control over the law and those who enforce it. Gippy saved me this morning from the bullet that would have ended me...fired by a NAFAS *captain*."

"Sweet Jesus, Mary, and Joseph." The priest sits back and picks up his whiskey-laced coffee, downing it at a draught. "I prayed it wasn't so."

"I'm afraid your prayers haven't been answered, Father Farrell, for an enemy of the state and one of God's own finds herself on your doorstep. Remember the dictates of your own faith? When a *nokri* lives with you in your land, do not mistreat him."

He blinks at me. "Nokri? Hebrew?"

Watch your tongue, Empa... "Yes. I said I'd traveled, and the word has more meaning in the original."

His eyes flick around again. "And you know scripture. Leviticus."

I cannot but smile, but I gird my thoughts. "As I said, I'm one of God's own. Does that surprise you, Father?"

"Frankly, yes." He stands, seeming to solidify, settle himself. "But we digress. Our *problem* is now redoubled. You're a fugitive from the law. We cannot harbor you here."

"I understand, Father, but ask yourself which you serve. The law of man, or God."

His face hardens again before my eyes, his thoughts bristling with contingencies, problems, consequences, and that underlying, mysterious anger. "Miss *Johnston*, I serve only *one*, but I also have to think of those under my care." He shrugs helplessly, and I feel it. "Tell me what would happen if the authorities stormed this place looking for you?"

I see it in my mind even as he asks the rhetorical question...blood and death, more on my hands. I can't countenance it.

"Then I'll go, Father." I nod respectfully and stand. This wasn't how I had planned this conversation, but I'm not leaving until I find out more about my cousin. "And I'll thank you for your aid, but first," I have only one card left to play, "I'll ask you how you know this woman." I snatch the picture of Cora and a much younger Emil Farrell from the mantle and thrust it at him.

"What?" A surge of worry, love, heartbreak. "Why?"

"Because she's my cousin, and I love her and don't know what's become of her." I watch for his reaction. Even prepared, it catches me off guard.

"*Cousin?*" He staggers a step back, his thoughts an incomprehensible torrent. "You! You're *one* of them!"

Good God, he knows! I need to find out how much, and there is only one way.

"Emil, please!" I reach for him, but he jerks away, stumbling back, eyes wide.

"No! Don't touch me!" He's trembling so hard I suspect some kind of seizure. "You *can't* be! She...she said..."

"Emil, *please.*" I put down the picture and hold out my hands, open and empty, pleading for calm. "If you truly know what Cora was, believe me when I say I *am* her cousin."

"Cora?" His eyes twitch. "Her name is *Teri.*"

"Teri, then. She's gone by more than one name, as have I." I clutch my hands together. Cora knew this man, trusted him with her secret, and now he knows mine. He's hard to read through the storm of information that fills his mind, but I feel no malice in him. I *have* to trust this man, if for no other reason than to find Cora, if she still lives. "You have nothing to fear from me. I loved her, as I know you did."

"Do." His lip trembles. "Still do... Always will." He staggers to another chair and sits. "Dear God, *why?*"

"Why?" The question catches me off guard. Feeling for his emotions is like listening for whispers in a rainstorm. "Why what?"

He looks up at me, his eyes pleading. "Why did He send you to me?"

I know he means God, and I wonder if it could be true. But if God has sent me here, this is far bigger than just my search for other Ageless. Only once in five thousand years have I been guided like this; when I was sent to her son. That event changed the entire world. I dare not hope that this one could.

COMMANDER WESTERHOUSE STARED out into the rainy night, watching the lights of sparse interstate traffic, her hands clenched hard at her sides. *Where are you, cousin?*

The office wasn't hers, but the regional director's. He wasn't happy with her—the summary executions had caused a kerfuffle in the halls of corporate-influenced government. The daughter of Ariquiel didn't care. Securotel could scream and posture all it wanted. The whole city could burn down for all she cared. All she wanted was Empa.

Maybe that's the answer. She looked up at the low deck of clouds, burgeoning, angry, and imagined raining fire from the sky down on this whole rotten city. *Rather like burning down a house to kill one rat, but if I could be sure...not like St. Louis.* She had the NORAD number on speed dial and could have a tactical nuke deployed in minutes. *And the media would blame a terrorist.*

"Commander, we have images of her. The system's primed with the search parameters. Ninety-four percent of cameras are active."

She turned to face the technical officer. "About time." She glanced at the clock. "Twelve hours. Not very good performance, Lieutenant."

"The memory was damaged, ma'am. We only got a few images."

"Show me." She gestured to the director's desk.

"Yes, ma'am." He tapped his phone, and a flat screen rose out of the desk's shiny surface, rotating to face them. Images sprang up, slightly grainy, a beautiful woman's face, mid-length black hair, dark eyes, a frightened look on her face, different angles, different expressions.

There you are, Empa. The Nephilim hadn't met this particular Ageless but had seen her image before. The strike force had been deployed on suspicion only, and with their operative and the captain of the team both dead, these images were the only concrete confirmation that this woman was indeed the one they sought.

"Tighten the noose, Lieutenant. This terrorist *must* be neutralized. Priority one." She dragged her eyes away from her nemesis to the tech officer's. "Do you understand me?"

"Yes, ma'am. We're on it."

"Good." Commander Westerhouse turned back to face the window. "If she slips away, I'll find out who is accountable."

"Yes, ma'am." He hurried out.

The daughter of Ariquiel folded her hands and squeezed hard, imagining her fingers around the throat of the very last Ageless on Earth. *Soon father. Soon I will be free of this place. Soon, I will come home.*

GIPPY WALKED WITHOUT A DESTINATION. South toward downtown, toward people, toward something...anything to take his mind away.

Saw her shot... Killed your best friend... Shot that naffie right in the head... Murderer... Saved the bitch who made you a murderer... Saw her shot... saw the blood... day later she's right as rain... Fuckin' miracle...

Flashing blue and yellow lights strobed through the rain, tires howling on wet pavement. The NAFAS cruiser blasted past Gippy at a hundred KPH, its big coal emulsion diesel belching black smoke. He wondered idly where it was going, who they were going to gun down this time.

Your tax nads at work... The thought almost made him laugh. Gippy had never paid taxes in his life, had never had a real identity. He was truly an off-gridder, an OG, which was why he wasn't too worried about the naffies looking for him. Even if one of their cameras caught his face in that fancy hotel lobby, it wouldn't register in their system. He'd never been arrested, never been added to their database.

No one... nothing... murderer.

His steps took him to New Market, perhaps by coincidence, perhaps by subconscious intent. Finding a dealer this time of night was about as hard as taking a piss. Gippy scored a bag of Trix. It cost him most of his remaining money, but he didn't care. He'd never been able to afford the new designer shit, a speedball blend that came in multi-colored one-cc syringes, pre-mixed and pre-loaded for your convenience, guaranteed clean, and ready for use. The pharm corporations had to make up for their losses in the healthcare crash somewhere, after all.

He kept walking, hands in his hoodie pockets, one clutching the bag of syringes, the other the butt of his piece. *Death in both hands.* The thought almost brought a grim smile to his gaunt face...almost.

Out of the markets, he looked for a place. *Someplace out of the fucking rain.* It was late, and his hidey-hole was probably taken by now. Most of the good spots were already taken, so he kept walking. He'd find someplace.

Again, by chance or subconscious intent, he found himself passing a building swathed in blue tarps and police tape. *The fancy hotel.* Grim security troops, not NAFAS, but sporting the stylized "S" emblem of the hotel itself, stood in a line behind the tape, their blue uniforms almost camouflage against the plastic tarp. It surprised Gippy that the naffies would let the hotel take over the site of their so-called terrorist attack, but corporations had real power in NAFAS, sometimes as much as the government.

Cameras were undoubtedly watching every passerby, so Gippy kept his head down and continued walking. *Stupid, coming back here! But that's your MO, right? Stupid, clumsy, weak... murderer.*

He turned a few more corners and recognized the street where he'd shot Lennie. There was no police tape here, no chalk outline, no security troops or cameras... no sign of any investigation at all. He stopped at the spot where Len died, looking for a trace, but the rain had washed away the blood, the stiff wagon had taken away the corpse, and the scavengers had picked the rest clean.

Nothing left...no sign, no headstone...no Lennie. *The only person left in this fuckin' world you cared about, and you fuckin' murdered him.*

Gippy wiped his face—rain or tears—and walked on. He knew he was lying to himself; there were other people he cared about. Jeri was nice to him, which is why he pushed her away, and Father Farrell was always kind. Maybe that was *why* he lied to himself. The people he cared for, the ones who cared for him back, like Lennie, his mother, his sisters, Macie and Jami, invariably ended up dead, gone, strung out, or slaves.

Alone's better. Safer... for them.

He found a spot, an alley with a deep doorway, the back door to some fancy shop that was never open at night. Hunkering out of the rain and tucked into a ball, he let his shivering warm him. That was the problem with syringes: he needed a steady hand or a friend with one, and Gippy had no friends left. But he'd eaten well today and had calories to burn. Eventually, the shivering subsided.

Fishing out his fix kit, an old shoelace with a loop tied in one end, and a lighter, he pulled up his sleeve. The baggie held three syringes of meth-ball laced with PCP. One was enough to get seriously fucked up. He laid them out in his lap, looped the shoelace around his arm, cinched it tight, and took the end in his teeth. He struck the lighter, and in the flickering light, flicked the first needle open. It took two tries to get a vein.

The first syringe went in, and he eased the tourniquet, felt the rush, and reached for the second. The vein bulged, the needle slid in, and he pushed.

Fuck yeah...

He slipped the tourniquet and reached for the third syringe, but he couldn't get a vein. The shoelace kept slipping through his teeth, his hands shaking, his mind reeling with the buzz. His heart thundered in his ears, racing like a runaway train.

Come on...come on...

The lighter fell from his hand.

Darkness.

He let the shoelace go, images, light, memories, fantasies all popping up around him like firecrackers in his mind. He felt...good, powerful, sad, happy, unstoppable, vulnerable...everything and nothing all at once. Lennie was there with him, holding him, strong and warm. Gippy was crying. *I'm sorry...I'm sorry...*

Fuck it.

He jammed the last needle into his thigh and pushed.

8

I SHALL NOT WANT

Father?"

I whirl toward the hallway, my hand moving reflexively to the small of my back. Sister Janice stands there with a wide-eyed girl, the one I saw with Gippy. The nun's eyes harden on me, and I leave the Glock in the holster, stifling my survival reflexes. *Stance, combat readiness is a constant state.* Some lessons never fade.

"Miss Johnston, please." Father Farrell seems to recover his composure before I do.

"I'm sorry. Old habits die hard."

He frowns at me then turns to the doorway. "Yes, Sister. Is there something wrong?"

"Yes, Father." Janice ushers the girl into the den. "Jeri insisted that she speak with you. She's worried about Gippy."

"Gippy?" Emil glances at me, then gestures the girl in. "What's wrong?"

A cold ball forms in my stomach.

"Well, Father, I'm just worried he might do something...you know... drastic. You see, well, you know his friend Lennie, right?"

"Yes."

I think of the young man who was shot, and the knot in my gut tightens.

"Well, you know they were...well...close." Jeri's dark eyes flick to me,

56

then back. I feel her concern like a chill blanket around her. "Turns out Lennie was killed last night. Gippy's...taking it hard."

"Dear lord..." Emil turns to me. "Do you know anything about this?"

"Yes, Father, I'm afraid I do." I fold my hands to keep from reaching for my duster, pulling it on, and walking out of here. They're all looking at me, and I know there's no escape from the truth, that Gippy's life may depend on it. *My savior.* "I didn't know the other boy's name. They tried to rob me, and he was shot."

"Did you..."

"No, Father." Sorrow rises up in me... *Don't need your pity... don't want it.* "I disarmed the larger boy, and Gippy fired his pistol. The bullet struck his friend in the chest."

"Oh, God!" Jeri's hand covers her mouth, her wide eyes suddenly filled with tears. Her horror floods the room, a tide of blood and grief. "Oh, *God*, no."

"Where is Gippy, Jeri?" Emil asks.

"He...left. I wanted to help him, but he said he needed to be alone." Her hand drops away from her mouth, and the tears spill. "Please, Father, if he shot Len, even by accident..."

"But..." Emil turns to me. "You told Sister Janice that Gippy saved your life."

"And he did, Father. I don't know why, but he surely did." I turn to Jeri. "Do you know where he might go?"

She shakes her head. "There's a million places. He'll probably try to score if he's got any money, but—"

"He does. I gave him some...for food."

"Gippy's an *addict*, Miss Johnston." Sister Janice's voice is hard, admonishing. "Food to an addict means drugs."

"I realize that, Sister. I didn't know he was an addict when I gave him the money, and he *did* buy food for us." I face Emil again. "Please, help me find him. I can help him."

Farrell's gaze flies around the room like a hummingbird, the unfiltered deluge of data, possibilities, options, consequences, and fears jumbling, and that roiling anger beneath. "I..." He swallows hard. "Very well. We can use my car. Jeri, please come along. You know more about where we might find him than either of us."

She nods. "Sure."

I grab my duster and follow them out, enduring a glare from Sister Janice as I pass. I can't please everyone, but I owe Gippy my life. I should have helped him before, but once again, I'm blinded by my own survival instincts.

Emil's car turns out to be quite a piece of work. A rusty old diesel Mercedes converted to burn cooking oil. These conversions have become more popular in recent years, but they're maintenance nightmares and don't handle frigid weather well. This one, at least, is not infested with cockroaches drawn to the putrefying oil.

"Downtown," Jeri says from the back seat. "If Gip wants to score, he'll go downtown."

"Of course." It takes a few minutes for Emil to get the beast started, but it runs remarkably smoothly.

Unfortunately, downtown is a big place, and it's crawling with NAFAS cruisers, most of them probably looking for me. I flip up my duster's collar and try to keep my head down while also watching for Gippy.

Father Farrell drives a precise search pattern, his mind a morass of data. Jeri asks me questions that I can't answer. Her curiosity burns like a bonfire, concern for Gippy, sorrow for Lennie, fear and awe of me, love of Emil, desperation, loneliness, longing. She's one of the most complex and conflicted people I've ever felt, all wrapped up in a seventeen-year-old girl.

Humans...they never cease to astound me.

Finally, I have to put her off. "I'm sorry, Jeri, but I can't tell you about myself. It'll only put you in danger, just as it has Gippy."

"A little late for that, ain't it?"

"What do you mean?" I look over the seat at her.

She shows me her phone, a blurry image of my face on a news feed with a bright headline, 'Wanted Fugitive, Suspected Terrorist.'

"We're kinda harboring a fugitive already."

She's got a point. I consider telling Emil to pull over and simply leaving them, but Gippy...and Cora...I can't. Not yet. I scan the street. We turn down another block on Emil's search grid, and I see what's left of the Securotel where I stayed the night before. I hunker as we pass but note the hotel security without NAFAS presence. Someone in the corporation is pissed but not pissed enough to keep my picture off the nets. I'll need to look into that later, but now, Gippy.

Instinct grabs me; I've learned to trust it. "Turn left."

Emil, God bless him, turns without argument.

"Why?" Jeri's curiosity is undiminished.

"Because this is where Lennie died." I point ahead at the mouth of the alley. "Gippy feels guilty. He might have come back here."

Jeri nods and rubs her nose. "He would."

We pass the very spot; nothing of the night before remains. "Slow down."

Emil complies.

It's getting late. Few cars and fewer pedestrians roam the streets. Fear, despair, hunger, and desperation mingle like blood in rain.

Another surge of instinct, like a slap in the face. "Stop."

The Mercedes stops on screechy brakes. "Do you see something?"

"No, Father, but he's near." I get out, rain plastering my hair flat. *Maybe you should buy a damned hat, Empa.*

"Here." Emil hands me a stocking cap. "You're too distinctive."

I pull it on, glad he's thinking along the same lines as I am. But that inner core of anger, unease, worries me still. There's definitely something different about him, and I wonder if that was what attracted Cora to him. *Later, Empa. You can get your answers later.*

I walk the street, feeling, taking it in, all the pain and desolation. Instinct, empathy, or God guides my steps, and I turn down an alley. A doorway, a huddled figure. I fish my Everlite out of a pocket and press it on. Gippy, gaunt, slack, one arm bare, a strap loose around it, and a syringe sticking out of his leg. Two more syringes lie empty beside him.

"God no…" On my knees, I jerk the syringe out and feel for a pulse. Nothing at the wrist, and he's deathly cold. At his throat, I find one, fast and thready. His mind is a cloud of racing thoughts, hallucinations, memories, dreams, and nightmares. Guilt, a shining light at the core.

"Is he alive?" Jeri's horror washes up my spine like cold water.

"Yes, but he's in grave danger."

"Do you know what these are, Jeri?" Farrell says beside me, holding up a syringe.

"Trix. Don't know exactly, but it's speedballing."

Speedballing…heroin and cocaine, usually, but this is stronger, different, more. I've felt the effects of a thousand different drugs, but never this.

"I have Narcan in the car." Farrell gets up, but I forestall him.

"No. It'll only block the opioid, not the stimulant. He could go into cardiac arrest."

"Then we take him to a hospital!" Jeri's panicked.

"Wait." I press a hand to Gippy's brow and *delve*.

A tortured soul but good at its core. So much guilt… I probe delicately, for there's as much danger here for me as there is for him. Three drugs, yes... only three. If I take only one or two, the others can kill him and me as well. If I take it all, I may die before my body neutralizes it. Like drinking wine or coffee, I feel the effects, but they don't last long. Sometimes I wish they did.

Compromising, I take most of it, as I took James's wounds. I also take the illness that will kill him, the infections here and there, and lastly, the core of guilt.

The drugs hit me like cavalry charge—*A voice in Gaelic: Ye gotta learn ta duck, lassie*—and I feel myself falling. Jeri gasps. Strong hands, warm thoughts, confused...too much data...and a core of something that makes me shiver.

I wake in the back of the Mercedes, Jeri holding my head. I blink and clear my throat, tasting vomit. *So much for dinner.*

"Gippy?"

"In the front seat." Jeri looks into my eyes; awe, fear, longing. "You gonna puke again?"

"No." I try to sit up, and my head swims. Jeri helps me. Drugs still fight for supremacy inside me, but they're losing. "How is he?"

"Still unconscious but alive," Emil says from behind the wheel. "His heart's beating strong, and his breathing's regular."

I don't recognize the street we're on. "How long was I out?"

"Only a few minutes. You were sick. We were afraid you'd aspirated, but Father did a Heimlich on you." Jeri smiles wanly. "*That* was pretty gross."

"No doubt." I wipe my lips. My head is still spinning. "Where are we going?"

"Christ Hospital. It's close, and they know me."

Of course, they do. I lean forward and place a hand on Gippy's shaggy hair, feel his vitals, weak but getting stronger. I take a bit more of the drugs from his system, just some, not enough to put me out again, and the car moves and pulses around me like a living thing. *Sleep now, poor Gifford...sleep and dream of your lost friend, but with a heart free of guilt.*

I lean back in the seat, fighting down the euphoria. "Please, Father, take us back to your church. Gippy will be fine, and so will I." And regardless of how well the ER staff knows him, they'll have my picture.

He glances back at me, and I hear Cora's name in his mind, curiosity, fear, then the deluge of data drowns it all out. I wonder how he can think at all with no filters in his mind. I wish I could help him. *You can't save everyone.*

"Very well, Miss Johnston, but we need to *talk*." He takes the next left and heads north.

"Yes, we do." I close my eyes but open them again when I feel Jeri's hand on my brow. Curiosity, wonder, and an insatiable eroticism well up in me at her touch. *Jeraldine, you naughty girl...* I stifle a smile. They're all Her creatures, in so many varied ways.

"What did you do back there?"

I shrug, shake my head, and pull away. *How do I explain?* "I...helped him. It's a gift I have."

"Gift?" One dark eyebrow arches, the silver stud there glinting in the passing streetlights. "Like poetry or *music*? Ha. Looked more like freakin' *magic* to me, lady."

How can I say it without frightening her? "Not magic, Jeraldine. It's simply how I was made."

Her brow furrows. Suspicion. "Who told you my name?"

Oops. The drugs are still there, and my judgment's not very good. "I can't remember. Gippy, maybe." I shrug and close my eyes, willing the drugs to go away. Life was so much simpler before humans discovered chemistry.

GIPPY WOKE in a small room that smelled of fabric softener and air freshener. Clean sheets against his skin startled him fully awake.

Where the fuck?

The room was dark, but a dim nightlight burned in one corner outlet. There was a small desk and a chair, and in the chair, Jeri slumped with a blanket pulled up to her chin.

What the fuck? He sat up and realized he was naked under the sheets. "Shit!" He looked around for his clothes, trying to remember what had happened, how he got here.

Jeri stirred, blinked at him, and smiled. "Hey. It's alive!"

He pulled up the sheet. "Where are we? What happened?" He felt strange, clear-headed as he'd not felt in...forever. He felt...*good.*

"Chill, Gip. Yer safe. We're in the rectory at Saint Luther's." She grinned and nodded to the bed. "Father put you to bed. I offered to help take off your dirty clothes and clean you up, but he wouldn't let me. Such a buzzkill."

"What...what *happened*, Jer?" He shook his head. "I remember..." Rain, sorrow, wanting to die, scoring some Trix, needles in his arm...

"You OD'd." Jeri sat up and twisted her neck. "How do you feel?"

"I'm...fine." He was better than fine. He felt amazing, as if somebody had wrung all the filth out of him and scoured his soul. "How'd you find me?"

"Oh, that chick, Emily, found you. She's...somethin'." Jeri stood and sat down on the foot of the bed. "She saved your life, Gip."

He just stared at her, trying to catch up. *Saved my life?*

"I'm really sorry about Lennie, Gip. Emily told us what happened. It wasn't your fault."

Sorrow welled up, but it didn't drown him this time. He remembered still, the trigger, his fear, she moved so fast...and his world exploded. The guilt, however, wasn't there any longer. Sorrow yes, longing, regret, but Jeri was right; it hadn't been his fault.

"Wait, she *saved* me?" You don't save someone from an OD, not without a hospital. "How?"

"I never seen anything like it. She just touched you, and..." She shrugged. "She passed out and puked, like she'd...taken the shit right out of your veins or something."

"Jesus H..."

"Yeah. *That.*" Jeri smiled again.

"I'm...havin' a little trouble gettin' my head around all this, Jer. Sorry."

"Don't be. So am I." She twisted her neck again. "Look, it's not even morning yet, and that fuckin' chair's killin' me. You mind if I lay down with you?"

"Jeri, I'm not..."

"Chill, Romeo." She smiled and fetched her blanket. "Strictly platonic. I'm too tired to fuck anyway."

Gippy found that hard to believe—she'd told him herself that she'd fuck just about anyone, anytime, anywhere; male, female, gay, straight, or other—but he'd seen a lot of things in the last two days that were even harder to swallow. "Sure, then." He scooched over.

"Thanks." She lay down on top of the bedspread and pulled the blanket over her. The bed was too narrow for two, so she threw an arm over him and pulled him close.

He felt like he should protest, but she just sighed and lay there against him, warm, soothing, comforting. She felt good, like a warm blanket on a cool night, something he hadn't felt in far too long. Gippy lay there for a time, trying to reconcile everything that had happened. Lennie, Empa, Jeri…the needles…and fully intending on not waking up from his final trip.

But he *had* woken up.

He was alive.

And he felt *good*.

9

HOPE OF SALVATION

I snap awake at some sound and find myself in an armchair in Father Farrell's den. The scents of coffee and food and a clatter from the kitchen tell me my host is awake. I'm stiff—an armchair is better than a floor for sleeping, but I don't recommend it—and stand slowly. The blanket that covers me falls to the floor. I remember being groggy when we arrived back at the church, helping put Gippy to bed, the argument from Sister Janice about allowing Jeri to stay with him, and the girl's snide comment.

Jeri has a mouth on her, all right.

Emil had settled it with a single word: "Enough!"

Sister Janice stalked off in a sulk.

I remember brushing my teeth and sitting down, but that's all. I look for my coat and can't find it. I took it off and draped it over the chair as before, but it's not there. *Musashi's sword...* My pistol, at least, is still there; it's left a serious kink in my back. Before I can get upset, the door opens, and my host emerges from the kitchen with two cups in his hands.

"You're awake. Good." He hasn't changed, still outwardly calm and cheerful with an impenetrable confusion of nonsensical data clouding his emotions. The unease rises as he nears me. "Coffee?"

"Please, but I need to use the bathroom first. My coat?"

"I hung it in the closet there." He points to another door. "It weighs a ton."

"Yes, well, I keep a lot of essentials in the pockets." I start for the closet.

"Like a katana?"

"Yes." I can't read him, but his features remain calm, mildly inquisitive. If he knew Cora, truly *knew* her, then he knows what I am. "Among other things." I open the door to find numerous coats, vestments, and my duster hanging side by side. I fish my toothbrush out of the inner pocket and check Musashi's sword. It's still there. I decide to leave it there for now and close the door. "Be right back."

"I'll be here." He sits and lifts his cup.

Five minutes in the bathroom, and I feel human again. Aches and pains never last long, and the dregs of last night's ordeal are gone. I thank God that Her grandchildren don't get hangovers and return to the den.

Emil gestures to the other chair, and I sit. "So, I'm sure you have many questions about Teri, or Cora if you prefer, and I have just as many for you."

I sip the coffee, strong and hot, forcing down my unease with him. I feel no malice, no hate, no scorn, but that underlying urge to lash out will not leave me. "I do, and I'll answer your questions as best I can."

"Let me start." He gestures to the picture on the mantle. "I met Teri in graduate school at Brown. She was taking non-degree graduate courses in music, and I was working on my PhD."

That surprises me. "In Western Religions?"

"No. Psychology." A wistful smile flicks across his face. "I always wanted to help people."

"And you *are*, Father."

"I try." A sigh, and I feel his regret through the cacophony of his mind for an instant. "Teri took an interest in me, though I had no idea why. She was so…" Words fail him, but I can guess what he's thinking.

The get of angels are a comely folk, and thousands of years have taught us poise, grace, and a way with people. We can't help but be attractive. Seduction comes easily when we wish to, and sometimes unintentionally.

"We met at a play, *Julius Cesar*, and I couldn't figure out why she thought it was amusing."

I can't help but smile. "But you do now."

"Yes." He meets my smile with a frown. "When she told me what she was, I thought she was joking. When she persisted, I considered she might be delusional. Then…she showed me."

My smile fades. "How?" I also wonder also *why*, for we don't generally reveal our true natures to humans. It causes problems. *Confess, witch! Confess, and the pain will end...*

Emil puts his cup down with a sigh. "She...cut herself. I just about called the authorities to have her committed, but then she showed me the injury had already closed. In ten minutes, it was gone."

Oh, you poor man. I can imagine his confusion, his disbelief. All of the Ageless heal quickly, but only I can take the injuries of others. Cora's gift was bringing joy to humans through her music, as mine is healing, but she was still a survivor. "Did she tell you *why* she revealed her nature to you?"

He nods, his lips pressed tightly together. "She said...I had an interesting soul."

"*Soul?* Not mind?"

"No, and I had the same thought." He makes a jittery gesture. "I'm high on the autism spectrum, so my...mind is...different than most people's."

"I know."

His eyes flick up then away. "After that...things got complicated."

"How so?"

"We made love. I didn't...I couldn't understand why she wanted to, but..."

Neither could I. "And you fell in love with her."

"Yes." A humorless, nervous laugh. "How could I not?"

Indeed. What had my cousin seen in him? I had to know. "Emil." He looks at me, and I hold out my hand. "Will you take my hand? It'll help me understand."

"No." He recoils. "No, I know what that means to...your kind, and I'm not ready to share everything with you." He stands and walks to the mantle. His shoulders shake, and he sniffs. "Forgive me."

"There's nothing to forgive." I can offer little solace, but... "I loved her, too." There's one thing I must know. "Emil, what did she tell you about herself. What do you *know* of us?"

"She said her father was an angel sent from Heaven." He shook his head, and I hear music in his thoughts, Cora's music. "Israfal, Angel of Music."

The truth. But why?

He turns to me. "When...did you last see her?"

"Long ago, in Mannheim." *His soul is filled with music, Empa...and love. Love is his genius!* She was always a sucker for a composer, but Emil doesn't fit that profile as far as I know. "I thought she'd died. I haven't heard from her in half a century, but I've been out of touch for more than a decade. Hiding, really. I've been checking the places where my cousins might leave a message, and found nothing. I thought I was alone, but now...Emil, this is important, more so than you know. Do you know where she is?"

"No. She...left me." I feel his heartbreak like a knife. "Not long after we took that picture."

"Damn." I can see the pain in him, but I must delve deeper. "When was that taken?"

"Summer of fifty-two, at Brown University." He touches the frame. "We'd been together about a year. Then she told me—left a note, really—that she had to leave."

I feel his heart breaking anew. I can't pry further. That Cora was alive eighteen years ago doesn't mean she's alive now. The world has changed so much. Brown University is on an island now, very nearly underwater. I'm still alone, still the last. There's nothing more for me here, and I'm putting everyone in danger with my presence.

I stand and head for the closet. "I should go."

"Wait, please." I turn to find him looking at me imploringly. "She...left some things."

"What?" That also takes me off guard. Leaving anything personal with a former lover, a *human* lover, would be dangerous.

"She left me a rather detailed note and a lot of junk. She wanted me to keep it for her." He sighed, pain edging through. "I nearly threw it all out, but she said someone might come someday to collect it. I suppose she meant one of...you, now. If you'd like to see it."

Hope sparks like steel on flint in the dark, his or mine, I don't know. *Maybe I am here for a reason.*

"Please."

GIPPY WOKE with an erection and a dire need to urinate. Jeri still curled up against his back, warm and breathing deeply. Light through the drapes illuminated the tiny room, but he couldn't see his clothes anywhere. Maybe he could sneak out before she woke. He tried to ease out of her embrace, and she stirred.

Damn. He turned to watch her blink awake and smile. "Hey, Jer. I gotta get up."

"'Kay." She drew her arm back and stretched. "Go ahead."

He sat up. Tiptoeing to the bathroom buck naked in his current state was out of the question. "Jer, I need clothes. I gotta pee."

She blinked at him and nodded. "Morning wood, huh? Father put a robe in the closet." She rolled out of bed and pulled a thick terry robe from the closet, handing it over and turning her back. "Your clothes were ripe. Sister took 'em to be cleaned. Go ahead, but hurry. I gotta go, too."

"Sure." He donned the robe, tied it tight, and held one hand to his crotch to hide his erection as he hurried past her and down the hall to the bathroom.

A long piss and a quick wash eased his condition, but his face in the mirror startled him. He hardly recognized his angular features. He felt ridiculously healthy, the grayish, jaundiced coloration gone, the rheumy bloodshot eyes clear and sharp, the ache in his joints nothing but a memory. Even his teeth didn't hurt. He knew he wasn't as healthy as he seemed; there was no cure for H2V, and he had the virus. The HIV variant was burning through the population like wildfire. *You're a dirty needle...*

Still, he felt amazing, and not only physically, but in his head, too. The anguish was still there but manageable. He wondered if his near-death experience had somehow changed him in ways he couldn't fathom. All because he saved the life of a woman he'd intended to murder.

Weird life you got, Gip...

Gippy stepped out of the bathroom and heard voices down the hall, Father Emil and the woman, Empa, or Emily. The memory of seeing her injured, then later well, still unsettled him, but her use of different names made sense now. The naffies were after her, that much he knew. *Drove a fucking truck into a building tryin' to get her.* False identities would protect her *and* Father Emil. *Smart woman... Gotta thank her and Father fer savin' my worthless life.*

He opened the door to the tiny guest bedroom. "Bathroom's open. I gotta talk to Father."

"Thanks." Jeri stood and joined him in the hall. "Want me to back you up?"

"No thanks. Just need ta thank 'em fer last night is all."

"And get some clothes, maybe." She grinned evilly and tweaked the tie of his robe. "Though this *is* pretty hot."

"Back to yer teasin', huh?" He'd never confronted her like that before.

She stopped at the bathroom door and gave him a curious look. "What makes you think I'm *teasing*?"

"Jer, you know Len and I was…" What were they? Lovers? Fuck buddies? Friends with bennies? He couldn't say it.

"I know, Gip, but Len told me you like girls, too." She shrugged. "So do I. What the fuck does it matter what's downstairs, anyway? It's what's *upstairs* that counts." Jeri tapped the side of her head. "I know you and Len were doin' it, and I know you probably don't want anyone in your bed right now. I just want to let you know you're not alone, okay? I'm *here* for you. *Really!*"

Gippy opened his mouth to put her off, as he always had, but again, he couldn't say it. Instead, he said, "Thanks, Jer. Really. I mean it."

She smiled, winked, and vanished into the bathroom.

Gippy ventured down the hall to Father's den. Leaning in, he started to say something but stopped, befuddled at the sight of Empa and Father seated on the floor, a big cardboard box between them, and junk strewn all around. Notebooks, an ancient computer, pictures, clothes, knick-knacks littered the carpet. And they were both in tears.

10

IN FOR A PENNY

mil pulls a large and dusty cardboard box down from the top of his closet and places it in the middle of the floor. The tape sealing it is yellowed, and the corners are worn. I can barely restrain my eagerness—what clues might lie undiscovered within? Might Cora still be alive?—but I can see that delving into these memories will be painful for him. I gird my impulsiveness. These are *his* treasures; the least I can do is let him open the box.

"I haven't looked at these in years." He wipes the top with a kerchief and unfolds a pen knife from his pocket. I suppress a sneeze. "Teri left in a hurry, you see. She didn't even warn me. No goodbye, nothing but a note and that picture. She wrote…something on the back, asking me to keep the picture where I'd see it every day, and know that she loves me. I was… bitter for a long time." His fingers brush the top of the box.

She wanted one of us to find this! I can see the tracks of her thinking now. Any Ageless who met Emil would feel what I've felt in him, this uneasiness inside. It's nothing I've ever sensed before short of a multiple personality disorder. Any one of us would be curious, and if we saw Cora's picture, we'd know she was with him. *She left this on purpose!*

I also know why she left without saying more. More always brings pain. A flash of memory, slipping out from between crisp linen sheets, dressing in the dark, scrawling, *I am sorry, sweet Pedanius. But I must go,* on a scrap of vellum and slipping out through the servants' entrance. "Is that why you became a priest?"

His eyes lift to meet mine for an instant before looking away. "After a fashion, I suppose." He sighs and cuts the tape. "I was in trouble after she left… Six months from a Ph.D. in psychology, and I couldn't even diagnose my own depression. I stopped taking my meds and lost contact with reality for a while. I did some things I'm not proud of in those years."

"We've *all* done things we're not proud of." *You can't save them all…* I've lost count of the number of souls I've sent to Heaven and Hell. "But then you got help?"

Again, a flash of eye contact, a weak smile. "Help got me." He looks back down at the box beneath his fingers. "After being with Teri, it's not like I could deny the existence of God, despite all the evidence to the contrary."

"Evidence to the contrary?" This, from a priest, catches me off guard.

"I'm a *scientist* as well as a priest, Emily. I look at everything according to facts, data, evidence." He opens the box. "There's not much factual corroboration to the Bible."

"Because the Bible wasn't written by God, but by *men*, Father. It's been edited, rewritten, poorly transcribed, entire chapters deleted, and altered to fit political goals. Surely you know this."

"I do now." He lifts a folded sweater of deep crimson from the box, holding it reverently. "I didn't then." He presses his face to the tight weave and inhales. His shoulders shake, a tremor of rekindled grief, and he puts the sweater aside. "It took me a long time to realize that scientific evidence doesn't disprove the existence of God."

"I wish more than anything that others could do so." The age-old battle between the church and science, from Galileo to Sir Isaac Newton to Charles Darwin. Memories of those men, their brilliance repudiated by the fear of *men* of *faith*, sickens me. I wonder how much of that opposition was the work of the Nephilim. How much still is, with the resistance to science so prevalent? Even with fifty meters of sea covering coastal cities, people still decry climate change. False prophets claim God's will, punishment of the wicked, a worldwide Sodom and Gomorrah. "Science was *designed* to ask questions. Somewhere, someone decided that to have faith in God, one *couldn't* question. It's the greatest lie of mankind."

"You won't hear an argument from me." Emil lifts a folder from the box, a blue plastic cover protecting an inch-thick stack of loose-leaf papers in clear plastic sheaths. He holds it out to me without making eye contact. "Her music."

"She left her *music*?" I kneel beside him and take the folder, surprised that Cora would leave this behind of all things.

"Yes. I don't know why she would, why she would leave *anything* behind, but she did."

I open the cover of the folder and hear her voice in the notes, feel her soul in the melodies, her love in every stanza. *Oh, dear cousin...* As I turn page after page, her songs playing in my mind, I hear Emil taking other things out of the box, laying them aside in orderly piles, but the music fills me. Tears sting my eyes. I let them fall. There is so much love in her music. That was her gift, to give her love to all mankind in song, as it is mine to feel human pain, take it into myself, and heal. I question, once again, how love and healing can fail to hate and brutality.

The answer is simple: lies, fear, the Nephilim.

"And there's this." Emil's voice cracks as he lifts out one more item, a rectangle of plastic the size of a notebook.

"She left a *computer*?" I put down the treasure of Cora's music, stunned. "That *really* doesn't seem like something she would have left behind, Emil."

"I know." He shrugs and puts the now empty box aside, precise piles of clothes, books, knickknacks, jewelry surrounding him. There's clearly a bit of order compulsion in him. "It still works. The battery's shot, and it's got a hopelessly outdated OS, not even ultranet compatible. You can look through it if you like, but she wasn't very organized."

"Teri *reveled* in chaos." I stare at the device, suspicion tingling my nerves. *Why?*

There can't be anything important in it; she never would have left it if there had been. *Unless...* I look around at the items, clothes, books, little trinkets, a charm bracelet. My cousins and I have used information drops to communicate for centuries. Safe stashes, safety deposit boxes, online data dumps, even geo-cache troves, encryptions, secret codes. Most had gone empty and silent before I went into hiding when the NAFAS cracked down. Now, there was nothing left. The information age was our death knell; our secrets were hacked, our identities doxxed. We were named terrorists, hunted, incarcerated, tortured, murdered... Could this be Cora's final cache, her last desperate attempt to preserve something for one of her surviving cousins to find? If so, I received no message to look here. Would she risk her records falling into the wrong hands by leaving them with this man? I couldn't imagine it.

Nevertheless, I have to find out for sure.

But there was a problem.

"Emil, I need to look through her files, her music, her books. It's *critical*. She may have left something important, some clue."

He looks at me, his eyes brimming with tears. "A clue to what?"

"To where she went, why she left." I resist the urge to tell him more. Humans don't handle the news that their entire civilization is nothing but a battlefield for the offspring of squabbling angels very well. They accept that Heaven is losing the war even less well.

"I've been through it all a hundred times, but you're welcome to look." He waved a hand dismissively. "Mostly a lot of music theory, compositions, history; not much personal."

He's not getting the ramifications. "Emil, to study this, I'll have to *stay* here, at least for a while, but you're right that my presence is putting you and your flock in danger."

"Oh. Yes." He blinks hard, and his tears spill unchecked into his beard. "I...forgot." He looks down at the precious relics of his lost love, anguish tearing a rent through the deluge of information that constantly assails his mind. Even the inner unease, the impulse to lash out, is drowned to silence for a moment. "I guess I could...let you..." A sob wracks his shoulders.

"Emil..." I long to touch him, to comfort, to take his sorrow, his pain, but I have to respect his desire for privacy. "I can't ask you to give me these things, but I don't want to put everything you've built here in jeopardy. It should only take a few days."

"Yes, well..." He sniffs and his shoulders steady. "There's no easy answer, is there?"

"Father!"

The voice from behind me, male, urgent, catches me off guard. I react as the millennia have taught me. *Lunge, twist, roll, draw, acquire the target, point, finger from safe to trigger, aim center mass...and...*I stop half an instant before putting two rounds in Gippy's chest.

"Jesus!" Gippy pales, staring wide-eyed at me.

"Sorry." I lower the Glock and holster it. "Don't do that, Gippy. I'd hate to kill you after going to all the trouble of saving your life."

"Miss Johnston, *please!*" Emil gets up. "I'll ask you to keep your weapons—"

"No, Father, it's okay." Gippy steps into the room, his hands clutching the tie of his thick robe. "My fault. Shouldn't've barged in like that."

"It's *not* okay, Gippy." Emil gives me a glare.

"Is *so*, Father." Gippy sounds different, and I realize that was why I didn't recognize his voice. He faces Father Farrell and, even in a robe, there's a solidity to his posture I've not seen before. "She's got the whole... um... The naffies are after her. She gotta be careful. I shouldn't've barged in, but...you *can't* let her just *go*, Father." His eyes focus on me. "She's...special."

I wonder how long he's been listening. I open my mouth to protest, but Emil beats me to it.

"I *know* she's special, Gippy, but eavesdropping is *not* polite."

"I weren't droppin' nothin', Father. You gotta know she's..." He gropes for a word. "Jeri told me what she done. I was *gone*, Father. Good as dead, and she brung me back. I feel..." Again confusion, denial, then finally resolve, and his eyes turn to mine. "She *saved* me, Father, and I don't just mean my life. She...*fixed* me." He clutches a hand to his chest, his bony knuckles cracking. "I feel...*new* inside."

Emil looks at me. "I thought you just cured the overdose."

I shrug helplessly. I am my father's daughter. "In for a penny..."

Gippy faces me fully now, his eyes clear, intense, spears of pleading. "What *did* you do to me?"

"I..." Revealing my true nature is anathema to my survival instinct. I look to Emil but find no refuge there.

"He deserves to know the *truth*, Emily."

"The truth..." Love has lost the war, and hate has won. What is the truth now? What does it matter, except to a confused, frightened boy on the verge of believing he is a good man, that he can have a life, love, mean something to himself and others? I nod once to God's shepherd. "So be it." I face Gippy and try to think of how to explain in terms he can accept.

"I am the daughter of a great healer, Gippy. He gave me gifts to take pain, harmful things, from people." I see his confusion and try again. "I took the drugs from your blood, the anguish from your soul, and the sickness from your body. I took it into myself and destroyed it. It's gone. You're free to start anew, healthy and clear of conscience. What you *do* with that freedom is *your* choice, as is the choice of all of your kind."

There's still confusion in him, but fear now, too, and a core of wonder, hope, and curiosity. "How'd you do that?"

I almost laugh. *There are no easy answers.* "As you said, I'm...special."

"You said before..." Gippy cocks his head, and a razor of sorrow crosses his soul, scoring a line of pain. "After I...shot Lennie, I asked what you was. You said you was *old*. Older than I could imagine. *How* old?"

"I don't know, exactly." I smile ruefully. *In for a penny...* "There were no calendars when my mother gave birth to me. Five thousand years or so, give or take a century, is my best guess."

"The *fuck?*"

"Gippy!" Emil glares at the poor boy, then looks at me curiously. "So long? Teri never said exactly."

The cat's out of the bag now, lassie. There's no puttin' it back until it's had its due. You were a proper bastard, John Rackham, but I learned as much from you about the hearts of men as I did from any monarch. Again, there is no easy answer, but I need to stay here, study, learn what Cora left behind. Perhaps there's a clue, and I must convince him to let me find it.

"I'll explain, Father." I sigh and gesture to Gippy. "It's a *very* long story, and I'll tell it if you wish, but mightn't we *eat* something and get poor Gifford some *clothes* first?"

"Yes, I—"

A stifled snort from the hallway catches us all off guard. I reach for the Glock again, but Emil waves me back. Gippy looks stricken and leans back out into the hallway.

"Jer! How long you been—"

"Sorry!" Jeri steps into the doorway with a rueful smile. "Couldn't help it. She called you Gifford, and I lost it."

I grit my teeth to stifle a curse. "How much did you overhear?"

"Enough." Jeri cocked an eyebrow at Gippy, then looked back at me. "So, no bullshit. What *are* you?"

I look to Father Farrell, but he just shrugs. I've already shown Jeri more than I should have, and there is no way to assuage her curiosity other than to tell her the truth. There's nothing else to do. I gauge them carefully. Emil I have less concern for, but young minds, wary minds, street smart and feral, often lash out when confronted with such truths. They'll either believe me or not. If they don't, if they risk my safety, I'll have to leave, and I'm not going without Cora's things. Even if I must do it at the point of a gun.

In for a penny...

"I'm the daughter of the Seraphim Raphael, Angel of Healing. My cousins and I were begotten to balance the forces of Hell, the Nephilim, spawned by the Grigori, Angels cast out of Heaven, whose goal it is to corrupt every human soul on Earth."

Suffice to say, jaws drop all around the room. Gippy and Jeri look at each other wide-eyed, and both of their faces split into hapless smiles.

Emil stares at me in shock. "The *Nephilim*? They're *real*?"

Evidently, Cora didn't mention that part.

"Very much so, but as far as I know, I'm the last of my kind." I sigh with the pain of the admission. Gippy's and Jeri's smiles fade as they stare at me. "I'm afraid the war between Heaven and Hell is all but lost."

"Lost?" Gippy shook his head in denial. "Can't be."

"I'm sorry, Gippy, but it's true. I haven't heard from any of my cousins for a long time. I've been searching for them the last few weeks and found nothing." Empa gestured to Father Farrell. "Emil knew one of them some twenty years ago." She waved to the pile of junk at their feet. "All this is hers, but she left, and we have no way to know if she's alive."

Pieces started to fit together in Gippy's mind. This was big, way bigger than a local naffie gunning for a fugitive. "So…them naffies who was after you. Was them these Nefa-whatever?"

"Two of them were, yes. A woman who attacked me in my room, and the captain of the strike team whom you shot. The others were simple soldiers, deceived into believing they're fighting for the right side. Yours was a noble action, and I thank you for my life, Gippy." She smiled at him, and his heart skipped a beat, but it wasn't just because she was beautiful. It was more. *Her daddy was an angel.* "Unfortunately, the Nephilim you killed will only respawn."

Jeri's brow furrowed. "Respawn? Like Doctor Who?"

Empa smiled at her, and Jeri's cheeks flushed. "Not *exactly*, Jeraldine. Unlike my kind, the Ageless, Nephilim age and, eventually, their bodies die, or they're killed. Unfortunately, their souls don't go to Hell, where they belong. They're cast back to Earth by the Serpent, and they occupy a newborn child, supplanting its soul with their own. The process is random, but the Nephilim is born knowing all that its former lives have experienced."

Jeri snorted a laugh. "Man, and I thought *my* childhood was screwed up."

"They're very good at hiding their true natures."

"And you can't do that?" Gippy asked. This was all just about too much to wrap his head around.

"No." Empa looked down at the litter of junk on the floor. "God's love takes the children of the Seraphim to Heaven, as it does all good souls."

Father Farrell sat down hard, staring at the junk on the floor. "I can't… believe this. A *war*? Five thousand years, and it's *lost*?" He looked up at Empa. "What of the fate of mankind?"

Empa shook her head, and Gippy felt something, a wrenching stab of loss. "Once I'm gone, the Nephilim will work to corrupt or kill every last human on earth. They've caused wars and spread plagues aplenty in the past. When they succeed, the Serpent will win. The Apocalypse will come. Earth will be swept clean by the four horsemen."

"No. *Can't* be." A stab of anguish, unfairness, anger lanced through Gippy's heart. It wasn't *fair*; he felt good for the first time in his life, and now he was being told it all meant nothing. Humanity was a lost cause. "They can't murder *all* the good people!"

"I'm sorry, Gippy, but they *can*, and if nothing opposes them, they *will*."

"*Fuck* that!" Jeri had tears in her eyes now.

"Jeri, please." Father looked up at her imploringly, then blinked at Gippy. "I'm sorry, Gippy. You need clothes, and we could all use some food." He got up.

"Food?" Gippy stared at him. "How can you *eat* when she just told us we're doomed."

"No, Gippy, not you." Empa stepped over the pile of junk to him, her hands out, empty, welcoming. She grasped his shaking hands, and he felt a warm thrill, a calm presence. "You're a *good* man. You'll stand at God's side for eternity. Your soul's not corrupted."

"But I…tried to…" He swallowed hard. It was difficult to think with her touching him. But if she really was what she said, if angels and devils were real, if *God* was real… "Don't the Church say suicide's a mortal sin? Ain't I damned for what I did? For killin' Lennie, for tryin' to die?"

"No, Gifford." Empa smiled at him, squeezed his hands, and his heart felt like it would explode with joy. "The Church doesn't know the mind of God. She loves you. She loves *all* of mankind. Only those truly corrupt, those who reject Her love, will be claimed by the Serpent."

"Her?" Jeri smiled at them both. "God's a woman? Effing *knew* it."

"God is neither male nor female, Jeri." Father Farrell waved a hand in dismissal. "What Emily is saying, I'm *sure*, is that God is in all of us. I, therefore, identify with God as male, whereas she identifies with God as female."

"That's the gist of it, yes." Empa smiled and let go of Gippy's hands. The room seemed suddenly darker, colder. "Now, why don't you get some clothes on, and we'll have breakfast together. We may be on the cusp of Armageddon, but coffee makes everything seem brighter."

Gippy snorted a laugh. "Yeah, fightin' the armies of Hell in a robe ain't quite kosherized, I suppose."

He didn't know why, but both Empa and Father Farrell burst out laughing.

11

THE MOUTHS OF BABES

hen I'm right, I'm right. Food, coffee, and being busy always makes things seem brighter. The four of us are cramped sitting at Emil's tiny kitchen table, but nobody complains. Eggs, ham, toast, and coffee soothe frazzled nerves. They have questions. There are always questions.

"So, how many of these nefa-whatevers are there?" Gippy is grim, his jaw clenched as if ready for a fight.

"Nephilim. There are two hundred." That, at least, the Bible got right. "There were two hundred Ageless in the beginning as well, put here to balance the forces of Hell. Now, only me, that I know of. That's why I need to find out if Cora's still alive."

"You said you went into hiding. Couldn't she have done the same?" The hope in Emil shines through. I hate to crush it.

"It's possible. I pray it's so."

"Where'd you go?" Jeri asks. She seems to be handling these revelations best of the three, or she simply doesn't believe me.

"The far north. There are still a lot of isolated Inuit villages that are off-grid." I'm not going to tell them why I went there. *Blood... screams... all for me.* I remember the years of cold, hopelessness, the drugs, and violence I found there, the hope I left behind. "I did some good there, I think."

"So, what *are* these Nephilim?" Gippy asks. "Like, demons?"

"No, Gippy. They're like me, the offspring of angels. Their sires, the

Grigori, were cast out of Heaven. The Serpent commanded them to beget children to corrupt mankind."

Gippy looked to Emil. "The Church know about 'em?"

"The *official* word of the Church is that they don't exist."

"Which also might be due to the efforts of the Nephilim and their allies."

"Allies?" Gippy's eyes widen. "Who's crazy enough to help somethin' like *that*?"

"People seduced by power, money, or forced into servitude by Hell's minions." I give him a grim smile. "There *are* true demons in the world, Gippy. Evil souls transformed by Hell into succubi, incubi, or others. They possess humans, corrupt their minds, poison their souls. They strive to corrupt every last human on Earth."

Silence settles on the table for a moment, the mood darkening.

"So, I gotta ask." Jeri nudges my elbow with a sideways smile. She's been touching me covertly at every opportunity, her insatiable hypersexuality an intoxicating warmth. "You've probably had about a *million* lovers. How come you don't have a bazillion kids?"

"Jeri, that's not—"

"It's all right." I smile at her and shrug. I'd thank her for shifting the subject, but it's a sore topic. *Children... You can't miss that which you've never had.* How to explain. "Relationships are...not as easy for us as they are for humans. Especially for me. I...*feel* too much, so I generally avoid them. But children...no. Neither the Ageless nor the Nephilim can bear children. We're barren."

"Well, *that* sucks." Jeri frowns and stuffs another bite of ham into her mouth. "Why?"

I shrug. "Even I don't know the mind of God."

"I can't buy that you're gonna just give up." Gippy feels he's been cheated of a future, and he's not wrong, but it wasn't I who cheated him.

"I'm not giving up, Gippy. I can't. It's not in my nature. As long as I live, I'll continue to save as many as I can. As long as there's one good soul among you, the end won't come." I have to tell him the truth. "But I can't beat the Nephilim. Knowing you're losing is different than giving up."

"So, what's your plan, then?" Jeri counters. "If you're not givin' up, what's your strategy to win?"

"*Win?*" I'm always stunned by the naivete of humans. "I *can't* win, Jeraldine. Not alone. The Nephilim can't be destroyed."

The two youngsters look at one another, then back at me. "Ain't alone. You got us."

"He does have a point." Emil gets up to make more coffee. "Why haven't you amassed your own army? You're certainly charismatic enough to gain followers. Why not try to fight the Nephilim?"

War... I close my eyes in anguish, the memories of a thousand battle-fields, the stench of a million corpses, the cries of a billion maimed, burnt, blinded, starved, gassed, tortured... Another St. Louis looms up in my mind. *I can't. Not again.*

"My cousins and I have *tried*, Emil. More times than you can imagine. In the end, it only draws attention to us." I open my eyes to find them all staring at me. How do I explain? One example shines through. "*Hitler* was a Nephilim, the son of Sathariel, Angel of Lies. You may think he lost, but in the long game of Hell, he won. He bred hate, bigotry, intolerance, used misinformation to corrupt a generation, and in the end, he laughed and blew his brains out to respawn and do it again in Africa, then again in the Middle East. I can*not* ask more millions to die fighting something that can't be destroyed."

"She right." Gippy holds out his cup for Emil to refill. "Can't fight NAFAS. Them Nephilim run the show, or most of it. But that don't mean you give up."

"As I said, Gippy, I'm not—"

"Bullshit!" Jeri gets up and takes her plate to the sink.

"Jeri, please, your language."

"Cursin' helps me think, Father, and *thinkin's* what's gonna win this war, not guns or soldiers." She scours her dishes as she talks, her motions abrupt, angry. "You ain't *listenin'* to us! Just because you can't fight these fuckers on the battlefield don't mean you can't fight 'em."

I struggle to keep my despair at bay, knowing it will infect them if I let it get out of control. *I can't save them all... Just survive... Steady spirit.* "With all due respect, Jeri, I've been fighting them every way I can think to for a *very* long time. It's all I can do to stay alive, now."

"And that don't mean there ain't *new* ways!" She rounds on me and glares. "Just 'cause you're old, don't mean you know *everything*!"

She's right, but I can't get distracted from Cora. *If she's alive...* "No, it doesn't, and I'll welcome any ideas you have, but first, *today*, I'd like to look through my cousin's things." I shrug and stand. "I may find some clue to why she left or where she's gone."

"I'll help you get started," Emil offers, taking our plates. "I know her password."

"Thank you." I doubt he knows *all* her passwords, but I'll accept whatever help he can provide. If this is truly Cora's computer, and it has anything worthwhile to me in it, there will be layers of encryption.

Gippy still sits there staring into his coffee cup. I put a hand on his shoulder, offering the only comfort I can. "Don't despair, Gifford. You've got your whole life ahead of you."

"Just thinkin'." He stands and nods to me. "What can we do ta help ya?"

I open my mouth to put him off, then reconsider. There is something he can do for me. "Actually, you can help me recover some things, a bag in a locker at the bus station. My face is all over the net, so going out in public isn't a good idea right now. I'll have to change my looks before I leave."

"Sure." Gippy brightens. "Just gimmie the key, and I'm on it."

"And I can help you with your look." Jeri smiles and brushes my cheek with the backs of her fingers, erotic visions flashing through me at her touch.

She really is over the top, but I don't get many flashes of peak memory, pivotal points in her life that might have precipitated her clear hypersexuality. The healer in me can't help but diagnose. She's low on the spectrum of sex addiction, no violent, obsessive, or debilitating impulses, simply insatiable thoughts and desires. I dare not delve her looking for the cause if there is one, and frankly, it's not my business. She seems healthy, reasonably able to control her impulses, and good at heart. I pull away just enough to break physical contact.

Her smile twitches and fades. "Just tell me what you want, and I'll make a run to the store."

"The problem is cameras." I sigh in frustration. *Damn computers to Hell...* "Technology, facial recognition software. I've got to look different enough to fool it, so hair, maybe a wig, makeup to change skin tone, and some jewelry. Something to change the shape of my face, my features, and maybe blend into the current fashion."

"Got it!" Jeri's grin returns. "When I'm through with you, baby, your own *mother* won't recognize you."

I don't bother to say that my mother's been dead for fifty centuries. I sometimes wonder if she *will* recognize me when we finally meet. "Thank you. Both of you." I turn to Emil. "May I stay for a few days?"

"Of course." He chuckles and shakes his head. "God would never forgive me if I turned you, of *all* people, away from my home."

"Yes, She would." I reach out to touch him, forgetting, but he draws back. A pulse of anxiety, the urge to lash out, hits me like a blow. I drop my hand. "I'm sorry."

"Never mind." He starts in on the dishes. "We've got work to do."

A CITY of homeless lived beneath the interstate, and Gippy knew it like his tongue knew the chips in his teeth. Wearing his old clothes, though clean and mended, he strode through the familiar squalor as he had a thousand times, head down, ignoring and ignored, one of the invisible.

No fancy coat, no flash boots, ugly, skinny, hungry... That Empa may be hot shit, but she way too proud to ever be invisible.

Gippy crossed an underpass and stepped out from under the freeway, grateful that the rain had let up. He glanced up to cross Gilbert Street and continued on toward the bus station, past the massive parking structure of the old casino, squat and ugly. A few tricks were lined up there, strutting their stuff for the people with money who went there to lose it. Gambling never seemed to make sense to Gippy. Money was to be spent before someone could take it from you. Survival was gambling enough.

The security guards at the bus station ignored him. Nobody gave a shit about some scumbag kid. As long as you weren't openly breaking the law, nobody cared. There were plenty of others like him there, begging, scrounging, whoring, some even waiting for a bus, having scraped enough together to head south before winter. *Not far enough south, unless they got tickets to Mex-City.* He shivered at the thought of snow. *Winter's too cold, summer's too hot, and rain like a muthah in between...* It was all he'd ever known. He shook it off and headed for the lockers, glancing up sidelong. There were cameras here, of course—there were cameras everywhere— but his face wasn't yet on the news feeds, so he figured he was safe.

Eyes trained by a lifetime on the streets spotted first one, then another NAFAS goon. They weren't standing together, but they were dressed too similarly and were far too clean-cut to be anything but naffies. They stood with their hands in their long trenchcoat pockets, eyes scanning the sparse crowd. Their gazes passed him by without even pausing. *Dumb clones ain't got nothin'.* They were watching for Empa, no doubt, not for a street kid.

Still, he had to be on his game; Empa's warning rang in his mind.

"Be careful, Gifford. These people are ruthless. They may be looking for anyone recovering a bag from the lockers. If they suspect you, they'll apprehend you, and you'll tell them everything you know."

Like they'd fucking believe me if I told them the truth, he thought, but she had a point. If they showed him Empa's picture and started pulling fingernails, he'd break. Gippy was no stranger to pain, but nobody could take that and keep his mouth shut.

He matched the number on the key she'd given him to the locker—he couldn't read, but numbers were easy—and jammed it in the keyhole. The locker was one of the bigger ones, and when he opened it, he stared at the single bag inside with sudden dismay.

"What the fuck was she thinkin'?" The duffel was huge, new, and spotless, not something a scumbag kid would carry. Not unless he'd stolen it.

But he had no choice. He'd come here to get this bag and get it he would. Maybe the naffies wouldn't notice the difference between his threadbare clothes and the flash new bag. He pulled it out—*Damn thing must weigh as much as me!*—looped the strap over his shoulder and tried to walk normally. He didn't head for the exit. The goons might notice someone coming straight in, getting a bag, and heading straight out. Instead, he walked into the nearby men's room. Bored people had short memories. If he stalled in there for a while, they might forget they saw him pick up the bag.

The place stank worse than any of his hidey holes. Someone had taken a shit in one of the sinks, probably because he didn't have a tencoin to open one of the stalls. Gippy would never have used a toilet here for that very reason, but he also wouldn't have dumped in a sink. Some people were just disgusting.

Now, however, Gippy had zero interest in his bowels and good reason to spend a tencoin. He slotted the tin disc and stepped into the stall—not quite as bad as the sink, but still pretty ugly. He hung the heavy bag on a peg, wiped the worst off the toilet seat with a scrap of paper, dropped his pants, and sat down to wait.

He thought to give it ten minutes, then leave. Bored and curious, he looked at the lock on the bag's zipper. It was one of those three drum travel locks, pretty pointless against anyone who had time and patience. Gippy had both. He started going through the numbers: click-pull, click-pull, click-pull, and struck gold in less than five minutes. Pulling the zipper open, he peered inside. Neat, clear zip bags packed mostly with clothes, energy bars, some medical supplies. Deeper, he found a couple of long knives and more zippered pouches of heavy dark plastic. Inside those, boxes of ammunition, magazines, a holstered automatic pistol, and a black plastic box that looked like a big egg crate and weighed a lot more than it should. He popped open the lid and stared at the six dark metal spheres, each with a pin and a handle, painted with different colored dots.

No wonder they think she's a fucking terrorist. Gippy started to close it up, then stopped when the bathroom door opened. Footsteps crossed the hard tile floor slowly. A muttered curse.

Gippy eased a hand into his hoodie pocket and pulled his piece.

The footsteps passed over to the wall of urinals, and he heard pissing. A pause, more footsteps, and water ran at one of the sinks. The water stopped, and the footsteps started past again, then stopped right in front of him.

Mother fuck. Gippy pointed his gun at the door. Pulling the hammer back would make a distinctive sound and probably get him killed, but for all he knew, the goon was pointing a piece at the other side of the door. He waited. His hands shook, the gun slick in his sweaty palm.

"Any paper in there, man?"

Gippy swallowed. "Yeah."

"No towels out here. Could you hand some out?"

"Sure." He pocketed the pistol, pulled off a handful of paper, and held it out under the door.

A hand took it. "Thanks, man."

"Sure."

More footsteps, and the door opened and closed again. Gippy waited, listening. He had no idea if that was one of the goons or just some guy who had to piss. Hearing nothing, he closed up Empa's bag, wiped his ass, shouldered the bag, and left the stall. He started for the door, then stopped to stare at the paper towel dispenser...the *full* paper towel dispenser.

"The fuck?" The cold hand of fear gripped the back of his neck.

Why would a guy ask for paper when there was plenty right there? It didn't make sense. He looked down at his hand. He hadn't touched the guy's fingers, and even if they could get his DNA from the paper, he was a non-person, an OG. His genome wasn't on anyone's database. Then he realized there was one more thing the guy could have gotten. *My voice!* He'd heard rumors that there was voice-recognition software that could pin you to a crime, just like face-recognition software, and there was no doubt they had his pictures from the lobby cameras. If they'd gotten a recording of his voice or his image when he shot the NAFAS captain, they might be able to match one or both.

Shit.

There was nothing he could do about it. If they could, they could. He doubted they could do it in the next minute or so. The best thing he could do was to get the hell out of there. But before he left , he opened Empa's bag and picked out one of the grenades from the case, one painted with a red stripe. He stuffed it into the other pocket of his hoodie, put everything else back inside, shouldered the heavy bag, and headed out.

The goons were still there, and one of them might be watching him. He couldn't make sure without looking suspicious. The question was whether to just leave the station or hop a bus. If they were looking for someone connected to Empa, they'd probably be watching for a bag to be picked up and taken right out of the station, not someone taking a bus. He shuffled up to the line and bought a ticket for Louisville. The ticket got him past the gate to the loading platform. Now the problem was the bus.

A guy was stowing bags in the undercarriage bins, affixing tags, and handing out stubs. He couldn't board the bus, then have them stop later and get the bag, and he didn't want to ride all the way to Louisville. Dodging the bus would look suspicious, however.

Well, shit. He risked a glance back through the door and spotted one goon but not the other.

Before the driver could tag his bag, Gippy stepped out of the line and left the boarding platform by the turnstile through the chain link. That put him back on Gilbert Street. He headed toward the underpass, half a block, the back of his neck itching. *Don't look back, just walk casual; you're nobody, just a scumbag kid carrying a shiny new duffle full of grenades.* When there was a lull in the traffic, he stopped and looked up to cross. Goon two was walking toward him, eyes fixed on him.

Shit, shit, shit! He put his hands in his pockets and gripped the grenade in one, the pin in the other.

Gippy crossed the street and picked up his pace toward the underpass. He dared not look back now, and running from a naffie was asking for a bullet in the back. At the underpass, he crossed without waiting for traffic, earning a horn, screeched tires, and a shouted curse. Then he was in the city of homeless, one of hundreds, invisible, at least to anyone who didn't belong. He shot a glance back but couldn't see the goon through the jumble. *If I can't see him, he can't see me.* He picked up his pace.

A shout rang out from behind, a curse. Eyes came up, some looking back and some at him.

A big man stepped in front of him. "What's in the bag, bro?"

"Yo' fuckin' head, if ya don't move, *bro*." Gippy jerked the pin from the grenade and pulled it out to show the thug. "Now fuck off or die."

The guy's eyes widened, his face a mask of surprise and fear. He took a step back, tripped, and stumbled over a sleeping form. Gippy was past them before the shouting started, his hand back in his pocket, his palm sweating on the steel handle of the grenade. He wove through the maze to the next set of support pillars, took a right, and emerged on the next street. Father Farrell's ancient Mercedes was right there across the street, the engine still idling, Father behind the wheel.

Thank God.

Gippy crossed the street at a jog and opened the back door with his free hand. "Got a tail, Father. Best move before he spots me." He dumped the bag inside and followed it, slamming the door and lying low.

"What does your tail look like?" Father asked, shifting the Mercedes in gear and pulling away from the curb.

"Tall, thick, short hair, wearin' a black trench." Gippy fumbled the pin out of his pocket and tried to fit it back in, but his hands were shaking. *Come on, come on!* The steel sphere was slick in his grip.

"I see him. He just came out from under the freeway." They merged into traffic.

Gippy tried again to fit the pin back in the tiny hole. *Damn shaking...* What he wouldn't give for a Vickie to calm his nerves. Maybe the pin wouldn't go back. Maybe once it was pulled, you had to use the grenade. Maybe his sweat-slicked grip would fail, and they'd die in a fiery explosion.

"He's not looking at us." The Mercedes accelerated. "We're safe."

We're safe if I don't blow us to Hell! Gippy held his breath and tried one more time to fit the pin back into the grenade. It stuck halfway in, and he had to wiggle it to get it the rest of the way. When it finally poked out the other side, he let his sweaty grip slowly relax. The handle stayed firmly in place. *Safe.*

Behind them, the NAFAS surveillance officer scanned the traffic for the street punk with the big new duffle bag and bit back a curse. He keyed his collar mic and said, "Suspect lost. He made me. Sending the voice print." He tapped his phone.

"Affirmative. Received. Send the video asap." His section commander didn't sound pleased. "Continue surveillance."

"Will do." He started back for the bus station.

In the mountains of data being compiled in the search for Empa, a voiceprint and matching video ran through the analysis software. It found no match, but Gippy's picture and the recording of the three words he'd spoken were placed in a file for future reference.

1 2

TEMPTATIONS OF THE FLESH

I sit on the floor of Emil's den with my cousin's life spread out around me, a jumble of memories, loves, fears, comforts, and an ancient and dilapidated computer full of nonsense. The machine's battery won't hold a charge at all, so I have to keep it plugged in. Two function keys are missing, the screen has permanent lines across it, and the caps lock sticks. The only saving grace is that the operating system is so outdated the machine could never be hacked.

Cora organized her files like a freeway pileup at rush hour. The desktop is a litter of icons, folders, games, pictures, and music. The documents folder is empty. Her music library is massive—the two terabyte SSD is nearly full—but the old machine's speakers are shot. I've scrounged a pair of earbuds from Emil's desk and listen to her favorites on shuffle. Never was there a more eclectic mix, from Mozart to Hans Zimmer to Adam Duritz to Hugh Masekela.

There are few real traces of my cousin here; I recognize camouflage when I see it. As I told Emil, Cora reveled in chaos—*Manheim in 1777, stacks of loose-leaf music so thick she was using them as furniture*. Her favorite way to hide something was in the midst of a massive pile of nonsense.

Deep within layers of folders, temp files, game saves, and cat gifs, there is a trove of hidden encrypted files. I'm confident most of these are decoys, junk, more camouflage, and traps. There are two I deem important, their file names seemingly random alphanumeric strings that pluck chords in my memory. Cora loved music more than life itself and had long ago devised a complex cipher to convert melodies into strings of characters. With good old-fashioned pencil and paper, I decode them. The file names are excerpts from two of her favorites, Mozart's Symphony 41 "Jupiter" in C-minor, and a riff from Bohemian Rhapsody.

There is something here, but I'll have to discover the keys to the encryption.

The solution, of course, must be music, but the wrong answer will likely destroy the files and my chances of finding out if Cora still lives. I've got to be sure.

I start the endless process of searching through her music files, but after a time I realize the futility. If Cora left these things for one of us to find, which her letter to Emil and her request to display her picture prominently suggest, then it can't be an insurmountable task.

But the computer wasn't all she left behind.

Putting the ancient laptop aside—*How ironic that something only thirty years old can be considered ancient*—I look through her books, trinkets, and clothes for clues. The plastic binder of Cora's music gives me a glimmer of hope. Maybe she's left me the keys to the kingdom right here.

I listen to the Jupiter Symphony while I flip through the plastic-sheathed pages. Cora was a genius with music and could compose beautiful works as easily as I can delve into human feelings. The works here are definitely original and her own—I can see her distinctive style in them—but they are not, by far, her best. Only someone who knew her would realize this and see the key for what it is. I search for phrasing that matches elements of the Jupiter symphony in the pages, find twelve that are clear, and jot them down. *But are they in order?* If Emil changed the order of the pages, even by accident, it would give the wrong key. I hate to wait until he returns, but I must.

Now, for the other. The riff from Bohemian Rhapsody is simple to decode, and I play it on repeat as I search through her music. Nothing. *Come on, Cora...it has to be the music!*

I search again and come up blank. Granted, it's a lengthy tune, but I find no elements in these pages at all. *Damn!*

The music in my ears continues, Freddy Mercury's dulcet tones teasing me, mocking me... *If not music...the lyrics?* There are so many obscure references in the lyrics, she could have picked any one of a dozen. *Galileo... Figaro... Beelzebub... a devil put aside for me... Scaramouche, Scaramouche, can you do the Fandango?* That catches a chord in my mind; no pun intended. *Fandango...* I flip through the pages of Cora's music again, looking for the unusual triple meter of that dance. There, a slip into triple meter in the midst of a composition. It doesn't really work, which tells me Cora put it there on purpose; she'd never make a blunder like that. I excise the phrase and apply Cora's alphanumeric cipher, jotting the result down on a scrap of paper.

I have it. I'm sure of it. And in this case, since there's only one entry, I don't need to wait for Emil.

I do a quick double-check of my translation and deem it correct. If I'm wrong, I have little doubt the encrypted file will be obliterated, maybe even the computer's entire memory. I consider copying the files to a jump drive first, but that, too, might trigger a catastrophe. No, it's now or never.

I double-click the file, type in the alphanumeric, check it twice, hold my breath, and click enter.

The file opens in a text window. It's a simple letter in ancient Hurrian, Cora's birth language.

Dearest Cousin,

I pray that someone survives to find this, though none of my queries have been answered to date. I cannot stay with Emil any longer. He is truly the devil that Beelzebub has put aside for me. I know not how or why, but the Nephilim soul in him cannot gain purchase on his mind to destroy the good in him.

Nephilim soul in him? A cold hand grips my stomach. *How...? I trusted him! He knows what I am, and there's a Nephilim...* Fear, panic, the urge to flee, hide, get away surge up in an inexorable tide.

Musashi's lessons revisit me: *Face all situations with calm: High spirit is weak, low spirit is weak. Steady spirit.* I breathe, center myself, and calm returns. I can think once again.

Emil hasn't shown any signs of being one of them...except for the core of unease I feel when he's near. It's not the wall of radiating hatred I get from most Nephilim, but it's something. But how could a Nephilim be there without destroying his soul at birth and taking complete control? *You need more information, Empa,* the diagnostician in me says. *Calm the hell down and get more information.* To that end, I breathe deeply and continue reading.

I'm no physician, but I suspect it's due to his autism. The mood-stabilizing medications he takes may also play a part, but those wouldn't have been there in his earliest years, so can't have kept the Nephilim from supplanting his soul. Without them, Emil is much less stable, and even dangerous, but not evil.

My theory is that the constant flood of unfiltered data makes his mind slippery, which keeps the evil at bay. What I do not know is if the Nephilim is aware. If it is listening to his every thought, if it knows me. If so, Emil learning of my research could be dangerous. Do not show him these files.

So much for getting his help with her music.

Emil's soul, however, is also full of love. He longs for nothing more than to help people. I love him, but I cannot stay with him, for if he finds out I carry his child, he will not let me go.

Carry his child? An inarticulate cry escapes my throat, all of Musashi's training forgotten. *Impossible! No, it can't be! She must have been mistaken.* My heart, my very soul, seizes in pain. To carry a life inside myself, bear a child, and bring a new soul into the world...a dream unfulfilled in five thousand years. *But what if...* A thousand recriminations, guilt, sorrow, seize me in a vise. "My love, Musashi..."

Please...go, my Emiko. Seek your bodhisattva without me. You have my love...always.

I wipe away tears and clamp my mouth closed on what might have been. I read.

I know not how this miracle has occurred, but there is no doubt. I am pregnant, and there can be only one father. Perhaps it's due to the Nephilim within him. I don't know.

Another exalted soul? Is that how it happened? But no, I've coupled with other Ageless, and I know my cousins have as well. Not one resulted in pregnancy. *But a Nephilim soul?* My mind stumbles over one question: *Why?*

This has, as you can guess, changed everything for me. There can be only one priority in my life now. It pains me to leave my research, the very impetus for which was Emil's unique condition, but I must go.

If you've delved my research file, you know there is hope, for Emil and for mankind. I must bear this child and see what God's plan for me is; then, perhaps, I will continue my search. If I fail, I am dead. Please continue my work. It's the only prayer humanity has left.

All my love to whoever reads this.

Terpsichore, Daughter of Israfal.

Hope for mankind... My heart hammers in my chest. *How in the name of God?* Could it be the Nephilim soul inside Emil that brought this about? If so, what will this child be? Is this some hidden plan? After five thousand years, the irony feels like a knife twisting in my gut. *Pregnant...*

"Any luck?"

I jerk up to find Jeri standing in the doorway with two bulging plastic bags in her hands, her amiable countenance intact. I close the file and shrug, trying to hide my raging emotions. *A child! Pregnant? How? With a Nephilim?* I can't answer these questions now. *Steady spirit...*

"Some, but it's a mess." I shut the computer down and stand. My butt is numb from sitting on the hard floor, so I twist to work out the kinks. "You?"

She grins and hefts the bags. "With *your* money, honey, nothing but the best. Wanna do your hair first?"

"Sure." I sense mischievousness in her but no malice. If anyone can come up with a new look for me, it's Jeri. Cutting my own hair never works out well for me, but she's assured me she's got experience there. Looking at her hair, spiky asymmetrical chaos in blue and black, I don't doubt it. I'm not familiar with current styles, so I'm relying on her. I follow her to the tiny bathroom. It's barely big enough for the two of us.

"Color first. I picked something light. I figured if you want change, go completely opposite, right?" She takes a box out of one bag and puts the rest down. "Best lose the shirt. This stuff'll ruin it." She opens the closet and pulls out a plain white towel. "Here."

"Thanks." I take off the shirt, wrap my holstered Glock in it, drape the towel over my shoulders, and sit on the lid of the toilet facing the corner.

Jeri mixes the bottles of hair dye, flips the switch for the ceiling fan, and reaches past me to open the window. "Stuff reeks, and it'll probably sting like shit."

"I'll be fine."

I sit still while she applies the mixture. She's right; it stings. Her hands are sure, quick, and surprisingly gentle. The vinyl gloves at least insulate me from her thoughts. I close my eyes and let myself enjoy the sensation of someone's fingers in my hair. She's done in five minutes.

"Give that ten minutes and rinse it off. You'll have to touch up your roots regular." She peels off the gloves.

I give her a wry smile. "I *have* dyed my hair before, Jeri." I could have done it this time, but she wants to help, and it's easier this way.

"Right. Sorry." She sits on the edge of the tub and looks at my face closely, like van Gogh looking at a blank canvas. "You don't pierce at all?"

"I have, but they always heal up if I don't keep earrings in."

"Oh, well, I had more in mind than your *ears*, but we can start there." She touches my chin and turns my head. *Curiosity, imagination, desire* enter me through her touch. "Just the right, I think. Your hair will cover the left. That and makeup will help change the shape of your face and hide your ear." She reaches for the bag and pulls out a piercing kit, alcohol, a box of tissues, and another bag that rattles like metal on plastic. "Turn your head."

I comply, and Jeri opens several tiny plastic boxes on the edge of the sink. An eclectic array of studs, loops, wire filigree, and dangly jewelry. It seems a lot. "All that?"

"You wanna look different, don'cha?" She applies a cotton swab damp with alcohol to my ear, completely unnecessary since I don't get infections, but I'm not going to argue. She's right, too; recognition software queues on ears, eyes, and facial architecture. "Hold tight and try not to jump."

I hold still as she punches holes in my ear and applies the jewelry, six in all. Her touch is more distracting than the jolts of pain. I resist the urge to delve too deeply. Her flashes of memories and fantasies are bad enough. Jeri's thoughts could make a succubus blush.

She fits the last in and then turns my head "Now, close your eyes."

"Why?"

"'Cause we're doin' your eyebrow, nose, and lip next, and I don't wanna get distracted by your freaky hot eyes on me." She holds up the piercer. "Okay?"

I open my mouth to protest but then reconsider. *Well, I'll certainly look different.* I close my eyes and hold still, though it's hard when she fits the piercer over my lower lip. Her thoughts of what she *really* wants to do with my lips make me grit my teeth.

After four jolts of pain, she says, "We could do your tongue, too, if you—"

"No." I have to draw the line somewhere. "It sends the wrong message."

"Or the *right* one." She sticks out her tongue at me, and I notice two piercings, one near the tip and the other farther back.

If she's trying to shock me, I've got news for her. "No, *thank* you, Jeri. It's a disguise, not a lifestyle."

"Suit yourself." She stands abruptly and goes to the door. I feel a surge of prickly dejection, petulance, pain. "Best rinse yer hair, then we'll do a cut and pluck yer eyebrows. I brought some makeup, too."

"Jeri." I stand and stop her. I have to be clear and honest with her. Alienating someone who knows my nature when one word to the authorities will bring a storm of Nephilim down on me isn't an option. "You have to understand something about me."

"What?" She turns but avoids my eyes.

I take her hand and squeeze. "I'm *not* what you think I am. I'm *old*, and intimacy with *anyone* is…complicated for me."

Her eyes flick up, then down. "Why does fucking have to be *complicated*?"

No easy answers… "Because it *is*, for me at least."

Anger flares up in her. "That's a *bullshit* answer, and you know it!"

"It's *not*!" I grit my teeth against all the feelings thrilling through me, her feelings, wanting, longing for closeness, fulfillment, because it's the only joy she knows. And mine… I won't lie to myself and say I'm not lonely, but I can't give her what she wants. I can, however, show her why. "*Look* at me, Jeri!"

She does, and I *delve*, open myself to her, show her every dark corner, all the love, all the empathy, all the pain of longing, all the anguish of leaving loved ones behind. Then I share with her the reciprocal rapture I feel in the throes of intimacy, her ecstasy flowing into me, mine back into her, into me, into her…

Jeri gasps, and tears pool in her eyes, her slim frame shuddering with tremors. A moan escapes her trembling lips. Her knees fold, and her eyes roll up. I catch her and break the connection. *Too much… I gave her too much. Damn you, Father.*

"Jeri? I'm *sorry*." I feel her shudder again, convulsive aftershocks. Her legs steady, a deep, wracking breath, and her eyes blink open. "Are you okay?"

"Holy *shit*, woman." She puts a palm against my chest and pushes me away, leaning back against the door and drawing another deep breath.

"*Now*, do you understand?"

She barks a breathy laugh and wipes away tears. "I understand I've gotta go change my *panties*." She shudders again and looks up at me. There is fear and awe in her eyes, along with the lingering desire. "How does anyone *survive* being with you like that? You didn't even fucking *kiss* me and I... *Jesus!*"

"I'm sorry, Jeri, but now you know why we can't be together."

"Yeah. I know." Jeri wipes the tears from her eyes and shakes her head. "Be a hell of a way to go, though." She turns for the door. "You better wash that shit outa your hair, or you won't have any left to wash. I don't think *bald* would be a good look for you."

She slips out, and I bend over the sink, washing away the dye and the color of my hair with it. I pray that I haven't just done something I'll regret. When I towel dry and look in the mirror, I see someone I barely recognize, platinum blonde, dark eyebrows, over the top piercings.

Jeri's right; with a haircut and some makeup to change the shape of my face, even a computer won't recognize me.

HAULING the heavy duffel from the garage up to Empa's room left Gippy gasping for breath. Funny how the bag seemed even heavier now. She wasn't in her room, but as Father Farrell locked the door behind them, he heard voices from the den.

Father gripped his shoulder and smiled warmly. "Let's see if the ladies had as much fun as we did."

"Fun?" Gippy gave the priest a sidelong look. "Don't call that *fun*, Father."

He chuckled as they strode for the door to the den. "Just a figure of—"

Father Farrell stopped cold as they stepped into the room. Jeri sat cross-legged on the floor with another woman, a striking blonde with dark brows, a bunch of stuff scattered around them. She was applying some kind of makeup to the other woman's face. *But who...*

"Jesus, Mary, and Joseph!"

Gippy blinked and realized who the blonde woman must be. "Woah! Nice *job*, Jer!"

Jeri looked at them and grinned. "Like it?"

Empa smiled weakly, brushed the bare stubble above her right ear, and got up. "It's going to take some getting used to, but I think it'll fool the facial recognition software."

"It'd fool the devil himself!" Father Farrell said.

"Mission accomplished." Jeri started putting away the makeup.

Gippy had to agree, and since the devil was pretty much who they were trying to fool, the drastic disguise seemed warranted.

Empa's hair was bleached white, about a third of it buzzed short above her right ear, which was now multi-pierced with a bunch of weird studs, spiderwebs of wire, and dangly shit. The rest of her hair was scooped over to the left and draped over one eye, jelled to stay in place. And she sported even more piercings: a silver stud pierced her right brow, a gold one her right nostril, and two gleaming black iron rings in her lower lip, which was painted with dark red lipstick. Her upper lip was painted black, which changed the shape of her mouth. Her eyes were made up black and dark red, and her skin seemed a shade lighter than he remembered. She looked younger, a punk, certainly not the dark beauty he'd first seen on the street.

"Got some contacts for her eyes, too. Just light enough to throw off the software."

"I thought you were going for *less* noticeable, not more," Father commented.

"More *is* less, Father." Jeri stood up and brushed her hands. "Everyone puts on this kind of...stuff to be noticed, right? There's so many kids out there way more punked-up than this, she'll be another grain of sand on a beach."

"She's right. I didn't really notice it at first, but there are a lot of outrageous styles popular now. My only worry is that it's a little high maintenance." Empa stepped over the piles of junk with her usual fluid grace. She picked up the old computer and sat down with it on her lap. "Did you recover my bag?"

"Yeah. In yer room." Gippy felt his heart lighten with her smile. "You don't pack light, that's sure 'nuf."

"No, I don't. Thank you, Gippy. Did you have any problems?"

"They was two naffie goons watchin', but we slipped 'em."

"Gippy slipped them. I did little but drive the car." Father Farrell gestured toward the neatly arranged junk that littered the floor. "Did you find anything important?"

"Some, yes." Empa typed something. "A letter that alluded to some research she was doing. The files are encrypted. I'm working on the key." She picked up a plastic folder and opened it.

Gippy didn't really care what secrets she'd found in the ancient computer, but something strange was going on here that he couldn't quite peg. A lifetime on the street had taught him to read people, especially when they were uptight, because uptight people were often dangerous people. Empa's eyes seemed to be avoiding Father's. Jeri was uncharacteristically quiet, too, like she was pissed off or something. Gippy looked back and forth between the two women. They weren't looking at each other much, either, which was odd for Jeri. She couldn't keep her eyes off Empa before. Something had happened, and knowing Jeri, it involved sex.

"In her music?" Father frowned and went to her side, but still, she didn't look up at him. "You think her music is some kind of key?"

"Yes, but I'm still working them out. This could take hours."

Jeri got up and caught Gippy's eye, flicking a pointed glance at the door. Her meaning was clear; this wasn't for them. Still, he couldn't shake the feeling something was wrong, either between Jeri and Empa, or between Empa and Father. Maybe both. Gippy followed her out and down the hall.

When the rectory door closed behind them, he asked, "So what's up?"

"Nothin'." She shrugged and continued on toward the shelter, her shoulders stiff. "Just tired of bein' cooped up."

Cooped up on a rainy, cold fall day? That didn't ring true. "Serious? It sucks outside."

"Better than in there." She shot a surly glance back toward the rectory.

He followed her downstairs, through the common room, and toward the shelter entrance. They only had to endure one glare from Sister. "What happened, Jer? You try to fuck her and get stuffed?"

"Kinda like that, but..." She shook her head and lowered her voice to a harsh whisper. "She's fucking *scary*, Gip. I didn't really believe what she said earlier, all that shit about angels, but then..." Jeri looked shaken, which wasn't like her.

"What happened?"

She paused at the outside door and leaned close. "So, I was helpin' her with her hair, right, and I came onto her a little. I mean, she's fuckin' *hot*, right, and I figured, why not."

Knew it. He tried not to smile as he said, "And she turned you down."

"Yeah, and I was a little pissed, but then she gets all apologetic, and I got mad. I wouldn't let up, so...she...showed me why she couldn't."

Gippy's jaw dropped. *"What?* How?"

"Fuck me if I know! I just looked in her eyes, and it was like we were in each others' *heads*." Jeri looked at him, and there was something strange in her face; fear maybe. "It was like she fuckin' turned me inside out. I came in my pants, I swear to God, and she didn't even *touch* me."

"You...*what?*"

"I shit you not, Gip. I...I fuckin' came like a *bomb* went off in my crotch. I nearly passed out!"

"Holy shit." He didn't know what else to say.

"Yeah, that's what *I* said." She snorted a laugh, pulled up the hood of her jacket, and shouldered the door open. "Come on, I'll buy you lunch."

"So, now you believe her, huh?" He pulled up his hoodie and followed. "About the angels and shit, I mean."

"Yeah, I think I do. After what she did for you, then this shit, I think so."

Gippy had believed Empa from the beginning, but he'd seen her shot and healed a day later. He didn't really think Jeri had doubted her either, but this... This was just freaky. "Well, wait 'till I tell ya what was in her bag."

13

A HIDDEN WEAPON

I glance up to make sure Emil is still occupied with his sermon—
convincing him to let me work without hovering over my shoulder
was as challenging as figuring out the encryption key. I've got to
hand it to Cora; she's clever. Finding the coded music fragments had been
something only one of her cousins could have done, but the order of the
pages is still suspect. Eight pieces of music, sixty-two pages in all, each
hand written, complete with tiny scratches and notations in the margins.

First, I excise the pieces that match Mozart's Symphony 41 and apply
the cipher. I have twelve short segments of the key, but I have no idea
what order. I examine the pages for clues. There are no hidden pages, and
the beginning and end of each page is different with no easily discernable
pattern. Each of the pieces is about the same length, which in and of itself
is suspect. *Where's your love of chaos, cousin?* I flip through the compositions. Six are eight pages long, the first and last seven. Way too regular for
Cora.

Eight and eight... Scales? I check the first note of each separate composition. Yes, they each have a different first note. I'm onto something. Next, I
check the first notes of each page of the first piece, which are also different. *That must be it!* Rising scales or falling, or both. There must be a clue,
maybe in her chicken scratched margins.

On the last page of the last piece, I find it. A pencil scratch, "Sound of
Music... Doh!"

Doe, a deer, a female deer... Cora you sly genius!

I arrange the pages so that the first notes of each piece and each page within those pieces follows rising scales from the start point. A double-check to make sure I've got it right, and I check the new order of the Symphony 41 segments, numbering them on my notes. I transcribe the code in sequence.

I have it!

The encryption key is over a hundred characters, and the damn caps lock is driving me crazy. I check all of my work half a dozen times before I trust that I've got it right. When I finally hit the Enter key, and the folder opens a text document, I allow myself to breathe.

"I love you, cousin." I start scanning the document.

It's titled Slippery Mind Theory, and it's in journal form with internal links to references and supporting documents. It's also a mess—Cora was an artist, not a scientist—but I get the gist quickly enough.

Emil's unique condition gave her the idea that if a Nephilim couldn't supplant the soul of an autistic infant, the reason had to be the structure of his autistic mind. Slippery is the term she coined, the inability for the Nephilim to get a grip, to latch onto Emil's mind well enough to destroy it. The theory seems reasonable, but how this could be the hope of mankind, I don't get until I find a note amongst the rambling narrative.

...and if his mind is too slippery to grasp, mightn't it also be too slippery to hold onto? No Nephilim has been successfully exorcised to my knowledge, but with Emil, it might work. I can't just strap him down and try, however. Also, the practical application of this theory to other Nephilim is the real goal. The question is, how can the state of "Slippery Mind" be induced in the non-autistic?

An admirable goal indeed, and something we've been trying to do for millennia to no avail. If Nephilim souls could be exorcised—banished *permanently* to Hell, as succubi, incubi, and other demons can be—they could never respawn again on Earth, and the balance of power would shift in Heaven's favor for the first time. Taking this method to war would mean tracking down and capturing every single Nephilim on Earth, two hundred of them all told, each one a warrior as capable as I am. A seemingly insurmountable task, but one that has at least a minuscule chance of success. That's more than I have now.

Cora's research method, however, is utter madness.

She simply began a random internet search—no ultranet in 2052—using various search criteria: exorcism, brain injury, coma, autism, anesthesia, narcotics, zero-EEG, and a dozen more in different combinations. Each likely finding, she linked as an internal reference. There are hundreds. I begin flipping through them one at a time, a silent prayer running through my mind.

If she found a way to exorcise Nephilim, this would be even bigger than her being pregnant.

Most of the references are mercifully short. Brain injury patients with speech abnormalities deemed to be speaking in tongues but no change with exorcism. Cases of partial acephaly treated with medications and exorcism to no effect. Drug overdose that resulted in hypoxic brain injury where the family called in a priest to exorcise the demons from their loved ones, again to no effect. Even brain cancer patients with altered mental states, also exorcised to no effect. All the failures are noted with a red-highlighted "NO" at the top of the reference, which saves me time. Some are indicated with a yellow-highlighted "Maybe," which I look into. Changes in EEG patterns post exorcism seem promising, but any with brain activity at all afterward are certainly not cases of Nephilim being successfully banished. Demons, perhaps, for the world is a battleground, and Nephilim are not Hell's only soldiers. Incubi, succubae, dybbuk, and others possess humans, but they don't supplant the human soul. If they're exorcised, the human mind remains, though sometimes damaged. If anything remains after exorcism, they aren't cases of Nephilim possession, for there would be nothing left of the human soul to generate brain activity.

Except, perhaps, if the Nephilim within Emil could be exorcised.

Then I find one entry marked with a green-highlighted, "Promising!"

Case - Laurence K. Caldwell. 2048. Young politician from Albuquerque injured in a car accident. C-spine injury, quadriplegic.

No family, became agitated then suicidal, injured a nurse in the ICU. Psychoanalysis yielded nothing. Caldwell wouldn't even speak to a psychiatrist. After several unsuccessful attempts to take his own life, he was sedated and sent to a care facility staffed by brothers of a monastic order, Our Lady of Healing, just outside Flagstaff. Several medications were tried to stabilize his psyche but he started raving, begging people to kill him, screaming things in languages nobody could understand, later determined to be Aramaic, spitting and trying to bite. He bit his own tongue so badly he had to be restrained with a bite block.

A priest-physician requested permission to perform an exorcism. Church authorities gave the okay, citing "speaking in tongues and self-mutilation" as adequate evidence this wasn't a case of mental illness. The priest performed the ritual with Caldwell under light sedation to facilitate communication with the patient.

The patient went into a deep coma, and subsequent EEG's showed flat-line.

See references:

Caldwell's profile *could* be that of a Nephilim. If he was, the exorcism may have worked.

The question is, why? The injury? The drugs?

Need to follow up on this one, but med records, attending physician, and everything else important are HIPPA restricted, and I don't have the credentials to get past that.

I look through the references, news articles, political segments, school records, and see that Caldwell certainly had the profile of a young up-and-coming Nephilim. Brilliant in school, not many friends, some questionable incidents in his youth. He left home at sixteen with a GED and worked while attending community college. A loner. Politically active. Lived alone as an adult. Money, but no apparent source from parents or relatives. Both parents died in a car accident when he was twenty-four. One accusation of inappropriate congress with a minor, but no charges were filed because the accuser and her entire family perished in a house fire. That sounds like the minions of Hell in action. He was elected to city council and ran for mayor before his accident. Quite a following from the hard right-wing.

A fifteen-year-old work-study student died in the accident that para-lyzed Caldwell. If he indeed *was* a Nephilim, I shudder to think what Caldwell was doing with the girl. *Memories of other victims tear through my mind like a hail of broken glass—seduction, corruption, bondage, slavery, torment, sacrifice...* Sometimes I wish I could forget.

The flatline EEG is certainly interesting. I've encountered very few cases in all my years, mostly post-operative or trauma-induced hypoxic brain death, but none post exorcism.

Cora theorized that Caldwell's attempts at suicide and apparent delu-sions were merely his attempts to evacuate his broken host body and respawn. If she was right, and the exorcism worked, I now only have one-hundred ninety-nine Nephilim trying to kill me. This could be the weapon we've sought from the beginning.

But how could it work?

Cora intended to investigate this, but I have no way to know if she ever did. She left Emil eighteen years ago. If she discovered the means to exorcise a Nephilim, she would have returned and performed the ritual on him; she loved him, after all. Of course, she never did, which gives three possibilities: Cora is dead, she investigated the Caldwell case and found nothing, or she never investigated at all. If she actually bore a child, that might be a reason she never explored this opportunity.

Motherhood... I banish the longing that rises up in me. *Steady sprit.*

I consider what to do. I have two options: find Cora or follow up on the Caldwell case. I long to learn of her, what her pregnancy meant, if she gave birth, who and what this child is. *The offspring of an Ageless and a Nephilim? What is God's plan in this?* But if this truly is the weapon we've sought for five thousand years, I can't let the opportunity to discover it pass. Without it, the war is lost. With it, there is a slim but real chance of victory.

Victory... I never even prayed for it. Now I might have it, my unuttered prayers answered. It's like a knife in my soul, but I have no choice. I *must* find out if this weapon is real.

"Coffee?"

I look up to find Emil rising from his chair. "Please." With that core of unease still palpable within him, I consider another option. Cora didn't want to try an exorcism on Emil, but I might.

"Any luck with Teri's research?"

"Yes, actually." I close the file, shut the computer down—I can't have him digging into Cora's research—and follow him into the kitchen. "She may have found a case of successful Nephilim exorcism; if she's right, it's the first."

"*Religious* exorcism?" He looks at me from the stove, his face skeptical but his mind a blur. "Does that really work?"

"Not against Nephilim. At least not in my experience." I stretch my neck and lean against the kitchen table. "Unlike the demons and spirits that the Serpent sends to possess and seduce humans, Nephilim destroy the host soul when they respawn. They have an inexorable grip on their host body."

"There are truly demons possessing humans in the world..." He still looks skeptical. "I always thought that was just myth."

"Oh, it's real enough." I shrug. "Mostly lesser ones sent to corrupt humans; I've encountered a few."

"And..."

I give him a tight smile. "They don't like me and usually try to kill me before I can exorcise them."

Emil dumps heaping spoonfuls of instant coffee into two cups, looking sad. "I suppose you've had to defend yourself hundreds of times over the centuries."

"Yes, but if Cora, or *Teri*, is right, and Nephilim *can* be expunged, truly banished to Hell *permanently* so that they can't respawn... Well, that's a game-changer." I dare to hope.

"But you didn't find anything that says where she went or why she left?"

I hate myself for the lie I must tell. "No, Emil. Only that she wanted to continue her research, look into this particular case."

"And where was this case?" The water starts to boil, and he fills the cups. His hand is shaking.

"I...can't tell you, Emil."

He spills boiling water on the counter. "What? Why not?"

"Because I intend to go there, and if the Nephilim somehow track me here and interrogate you, you'll tell them where I went." Actually, if they discovered the Nephilim soul inside Emil, they'd kill him instantly to allow their cousin to respawn, but they'd torture my location out of him first.

"I...understand." He finishes with the coffee and adds sugar and creamer to his. He slides the other across the counter to me, black. "Might you also...look for Teri?"

"Of course, Emil, but you *must* understand that finding out if this actually *was* a case of successful Nephilim exorcism is far more important."

"Is it?" His eyes dart around again. "I can't... I mean, consider that if you find that this is true, that a Nephilim *was* truly banished, you're *one* person. If you die, the secret dies with you. Wouldn't it be better if you found her first and both of you—"

"No, it wouldn't."

He freezes in place, his eyes snapping to mine, almost accusative. "Why not?"

"Because, Emil, if my cousins and I have learned one thing over the millennia, it's that consolidating our forces is just what the Nephilim want us to do. That's why we meet so infrequently, travel alone, keep multiple identities, always moving. That way, if they find one of us, as they found *me* recently, only one of us is at risk."

"I see." His hands clench. "But still, you shouldn't go alone. This is too important."

He has a point, but traipsing around the countryside with Emil is not an option. He's too unpredictable, and I'm not sure about his motives. If it came down to helping me or finding Cora, I have little doubt which he would choose.

"Emil, I—"

"Not me. I can't leave Saint Luther's without drawing suspicion. Besides, I have too many responsibilities."

"I can certainly send word. I have a phone in my bag that's untraceable and I can keep in touch. Whatever I find out, I'll tell you."

He shakes his head. "Not good enough. Too much could go wrong. Taking someone with you doubles your chances of keeping both you and whatever you discover alive."

I can't argue with his logic.

"Then..." The only other two possibilities are not good ideas. Jeri is far too attracted to me, and her insatiable desires would draw attention and cause problems, not the least of which would be distracting me. Emil knows this. There's only one other. "Gippy's a good boy, but also an addict and emotionally fragile. I haven't known him long and don't know if I can trust him."

"Gippy is stronger than you think, Emily."

"Do you believe I can trust him?"

"He's already saved your life once, hasn't he?"

"Yes, but that was impulsive. Also, his addiction is problematic."

"Can't you..." He waves a hand. "...fix that?"

"No, unfortunately. I can deal with physiological and traumatic psychological problems, but not underlying genetic disorders or problems that manifest from them." I smile disarmingly. "The propensity for addiction is genetic, and his need isn't a disorder. I can't cure that. I wish I could."

"I still think he'd be an asset. You could teach him so much, and he's street smart. You really should have seen him today."

Again, I can't argue with that. His street savvy saved me when we were fleeing the hotel. But traveling with someone again after so long alone...

"He would be good for you, Emily."

"How do you figure?" It comes out harsher than I intend, argumentative, defensive.

"Because being alone isn't good for *anyone*, least of all for someone like you."

"You don't *know* me, Emil."

"Don't I?" He cocks his head at me quizzically. "What good is empathy if you're alone, Daughter of Raphael?"

Damn him for being right. "I'll ask him, then. I won't command him to help me."

"Of course, you won't, but he *will* help you. I know he will."

I consider for a moment that Father Farrell might just read people even better than I do. That's unusual for someone on the spectrum, but as a psychologist and priest, he's mastered the art to an astonishing degree.

GIPPY AND JERI hunkered out of the rain under the eaves of a Seven-Eleven, eating chewy hot dogs with the works and sharing a Monster Gulp. It felt strange having money, eating more than once a day. Well, *he* didn't have money, but Empa had given Jeri a bar of some precious metal to change into cash for her shopping trip. She'd given most of the change back, but Empa had insisted she keep some. Jeri even scored a Vickie for him to kill the shakes.

It was nice hanging out talking with her, even if she wouldn't stop talking about Empa.

"I'm fuckin' *scared*, Gip." She took another huge bite of her dog and wiped mustard from her mouth as she chewed. "All this shit just seems too big."

"Yeah, tell me 'bout it." He wolfed his last bite and wiped his hands on his hoodie. "I fuckin' shot a naffie in the back of the head."

"So, *think* about that." She tapped him in the chest with a rigid finger. "If she's tellin' the truth about this...*war*, you maybe saved the whole fuckin' *world* by pullin' that trigger."

He hadn't thought of it that way. It made him feel like puking. "Thanks a lot." He grabbed the cup and choked down a swallow.

"That's what I *mean*, Gip. This is too big for us." She nudged him, always touching, not coming on to him, but just her way. "Hey, I got enough to get us to Atlanta. Maybe we should cut out."

He looked at her sidelong, trying to figure out if she was serious. She wanted to go to Atlanta with *him*? "For real?"

"For real." She finished her dog and shrugged. "It wouldn't be bad, you and me. We'd make do. No angels and devils, no war, no bullshit, just get by and fuck each other's brains out every night." She grinned that mischievous grin.

It sounded a lot better than not bad; it sounded awesome. But things weren't that simple.

"Dunno if this is somethin' I can run from, Jer."

She made a sour face. "Sure as fuck ain't somethin' you can *fight*."

"No, not me, but I might help." He squinted at her. "You said so before, like *you* wanted to help."

"Yeah, well, I'm stupid." She looked away.

"'Cause she wouldn't fuck you, you wanna cut and run."

"No." She flicked a glare at him and chucked her dog wrapper into the gutter.

"What then?"

"Dunno. Just…scared, I guess." She stuffed her hands in her pockets and hunched her shoulders, withdrawing.

"Scared to get caught up in a *war*?" He snorted a laugh. "Join the fuckin' club, bitch."

"Not scared of that so much as I'm scared of *her*, Gip." She shivered and shrugged. "She freaks me out. It's like I can't get her out of my head, but I know she's fuckin' dangerous. Like heroin. Like I could OD on her and die smilin'."

Gippy knew that feeling all too well. "Yeah, I get that, but you know what else?"

Her eyes came up. "What?"

"She needs help."

"Her?" Jeri made that face again. "No way. Not her. She's a badass"

"True that, but she sticks out like a thousand-nad-bill in the gutter. Her clothes, her coat, that fuckin' bag she had me pick up, all squeaky clean and shiny new. Just the way she fuckin' *walks* tells everyone she ain't normal." He reached out and put a hand on her arm. That brought her up short, and she looked down at his hand and back up. She'd touched him a thousand times, usually teasing, but this was the first time he'd reached out to her. "She needs someone to teach her to be invisible, like us."

Jeri bit her lip, her teeth clicking her piercings. "She'll get you killed, Gip."

"Maybe, but people like me die all the time. and it don't mean shit. If the world gonna go up in flames, we gonna die anyway. I want dyin' to *mean* somethin'."

"What's it gonna mean if—" Her eyes slipped past him and widened minutely. "Naffie cruiser."

Gippy knew better than to turn and look but saw the black and gold reflection in the store window. "Just keep talkin' like it ain't nothin'."

"Pullin' up on yer left." She was watching them too closely.

"Chill. Just here fer donuts." He gave her a nudge. "Look at me and keep talkin'."

"No way! She didn't!" She nudged him back.

"Right there in front of her fuckin' mom, I shit you not."

"Her cousin?"

"Bitch got no shame, I tell ya."

They kept up the banter as the two naffies got out, their bulky reflections clear in the glass over Jeri's shoulder, one taller, the other shorter, maybe a woman, though he couldn't tell with the helmets, face shields, and body armor. They ambled past without even looking at the two punks talking shit. When the door swung closed, he nudged her again.

"Come on. Slow. Like it ain't nothin'."

She pulled up her hood against the drizzle, and they walked off the curb and across the lot without looking back.

"Slick as shit on a park bench," she said, elbowing him in the side.

"*That's* what I'm talkin' 'bout!" He gave her a bump back. "*She* couldn't have pulled that off. *That's* what she needs to learn." Empa was amazing but she was too old, too upscale, too poised, and way too knock-down beautiful to blend in on the street.

"Yeah, no shit." She frowned and peered at him from under her hood. "So, you gonna teach her?"

"Who better?"

"One thing. She could never pass for street trash." Jeri shook her head. "She's too much...all that."

"True. That hair and shit might fool cameras, but it don't make her look plain."

"Didn't think of that." Jeri grimaced. "Too much?"

"Not the disguise, Jer, *her*." He thought for a minute. "But she might pass for a trick."

Jeri barked a laugh. "Oh, she could *totally* pass, and naffies wouldn't give her a second glance. They don't see tricks. No laws being broke, not their business. But *would* she do it?"

"Yeah, maybe too proud fer that." He'd have to convince her that survival was more important than pride, even if it meant dressing up like a whore.

"Just be careful with her, Gip. She's fuck-all weird, I tell ya."

"Not weird, Jer. Bitch just *old*."

Jeri snorted in disgust. "May be old, but she's fuckin' hot. You be careful with her."

"Don't worry, I already *got* an addiction. She ain't my junk." Gippy wasn't just blowing smoke; Empa was beautiful, no doubt, but he found women more alien than attractive.

Jeri looked down. "Good for you, man. Bad for me."

"No worries, Jer. She be gone soon, and you can forget her." *And I'll be gone with her...*

"Dunno, Gip." Jeri sniffed and rubbed her eyes. "Don't think I'll *ever* forget her. She just... It's like she's got my soul by the nuts, and she's squeezin'."

Gippy knew that feeling. For the first time in her life, maybe, Jeri was in love, and it scared her. He was scared, too, but for a different reason. He didn't know where this might take him or if it might even kill him, but he felt something he hadn't ever felt before, too. He felt needed.

1 4

APPRENTICE

I spend the afternoon planning, sequestered in my room with Cora's computer and my phone. I've searched her files for any more clues and transferred her research files onto an encrypted folder on an encrypted Bluetooth drive. I make a list of some things I'll need. Emil has offered his car, which is both a boon and a problem; I won't have to stop at fuel stations where there are always cameras, and used fry oil is cheap, but that means stopping at greasy spoons to refuel. Just the smell of deep fried food makes me nauseous.

My face is still all over the news: terrorist, murderer, armed and dangerous, reward for information. The last worries me most, for others in the shelter saw me, and some would doubtless hand me over for money. If someone tries, Saint Luther's will be a crater before we hear the incoming missile. Emil seems to think they won't; street people trust the authorities less than anyone. I haven't shown my face outside the rectory since I arrived, except for our brief foray to rescue Gippy, so if nobody's betrayed me yet, they probably won't. With any luck, I'll be gone soon.

A knock at the door brings my Glock out from under the pillow. I asked Emil to send Gippy to me when they returned, so this isn't a surprise, but incaution is deadly.

"Yes?"

"Gippy. Need ta talk."

That sounds ominous but hardly dangerous. I put the computers down, holster my weapon, and open the door. Gippy's there, but Jeri's also with him. They're wet from the rain and look serious as death. Jeri avoids my eyes as she has since the unfortunate incident in the bathroom. Her fear of me hangs like a cloak around her. Gippy, however, is intense. Eager.

"Come in."

"So, we been talkin', and we got a plan." Gippy seems steadier, but his pupils are blown, probably drugs.

"Plan?" I gesture to the chair. "Please, have a seat and tell me."

Jeri sits, and Gippy leans on the arm. I sit on the bed, facing them.

"Look, you got it all, money, weapons, mad skills, all that angel-daddy shit, but there's one thing you *ain't* got."

I can't help but smile at the euphemism; it may be the first time I've ever heard it. "I can think of *many* things I haven't got, but you have one thing in particular in mind. Please, tell me."

The two exchange a glance. Jeri shrugs and nudges his elbow. Gippy takes a deep breath. "You ain't got nobody to watch yer back. Someone street. Someone who knows how to be a nobody."

I wonder if Emil told him what I was going to ask. I hadn't intended to do it with Jeri here. I pray that both of them don't want to accompany me. "I *have* been alone a very long time, Gippy, but I've been on the street for many, many years. I know what it is to be anonymous."

Jeri snorts a laugh and nudges Gippy's elbow again.

"Yeah, right?" he says to her, then looks back at me. "Look, you may *think* you all that, but you ain't. You been on the street, but not *my* street. Said so yourself, you been out of touch. You stick out. You flash and clean and all shiny. Why you think I pick *you* to jack the other night."

"Because I looked like I had money." He has a point, one I've realized. Things have changed a great deal in the last fifteen years. I don't know today's streets. Gippy might be just the person to help me with that. It worries me that Jeri's so quiet, however. "You're suggesting you could help me look less affluent?"

"Look, talk, walk, act..." He flicks a hand at me, then looks at Jeri. "You wanna tell her?"

"Your disguise'll fool *cameras*, but you're still too damn hot not to draw attention. Dressing you down would be even worse; a woman as beautiful as you don't dress in rags." She bites her lip, her teeth clicking on the rings there. "You're gonna stick out, unless..."

I've considered that, but I've been more concerned with Cora's journal and the disturbing trend of the news nets. They're hunting me. "Unless what?"

"Unless you trick," Gippy says.

"What?" The term isn't familiar. I really am out of touch with the common vernacular.

Jeri counts off on her fingers. "You wear that duster and boots, you look like a rich bitch slummin'. You wear rags, it don't fit. You draw *attention*. You need to dress like a woman who *wants* to draw attention. A woman who wants to draw attention is doin' it for a *reason*. Usually money."

Trick... It makes sense now. "A prostitute?"

"Yeah, a *trick*. You'll need new clothes and *definitely* ditch the jacket."

My duster. I've grown attached to it, so convenient to have everything in pockets. It's also nice that it'll stop a bullet. "But won't that draw even *more* attention?" I don't relish taking on the role of a prostitute...again.

Gippy shakes his head. "Not from them you *wanna* be invisible to. Naffies don't even *see* tricks, just like street trash. No laws bein' broke. You get someone to watch yer back, look like yer personal badass, yer pimp, and nobody gonna fuck with you but them who want what you're sellin'."

I must admit, Gippy's plan has merit. I get up and go to the closet to pull out my duster, fully restocked from my bag, clean, and mended as best I can. I turn it around, inside toward Gippy. "Try it on."

Gippy looks at the coat like it might bite him. "Me?"

"Who else?" I give him an encouraging smile. "You wouldn't have suggested it if you weren't ready to take on the role. And you're right, I'm out of touch with the street. You can teach me while we travel."

"Travel where?" He stands and shrugs into the coat. "Jesus H, it weighs a fuckin' ton!"

"Ten pounds of Kevlar, a pistol, four magazines, two grenades, four knives, and a sword." I settle the collar and turn him around. It fits well enough, but he doesn't look the part yet. "Oh, and my toothbrush and spare underwear. You'll get used to the weight." I look to Jeri. "He'll need better clothes, shoes, and a haircut. Maybe some jewelry. Can you help with that?"

"Sure." She nods and smiles to Gippy. "You *already* look like a badass, dude."

"And I'll need some clothes." I pull my money belt from the bedside dresser and withdraw a hundred-gram bar of Swiss Bank platinum. "Don't change it at the same place you did the last one."

"I ain't *stupid*." Jeri gets up and takes the bar from my hand. She doesn't touch my fingers.

"Size eight. Shoes are nine and a half. Don't get me anything I can't move in, and nothing too slutty."

Jeri looks skeptical. "You really gonna *do* this? Play the whore?"

"It *is* the oldest profession, Jeri. And since I'm very likely the oldest living thing *on* this planet, it seems only appropriate." I sigh in resignation and open the door for her. "And it won't be the first time." She gives me a startled look, but I cut her off before she can say anything. "I'd like to leave tomorrow evening. Be careful."

"Right." She tucks the platinum bar in her pants and leaves, casting another glance at Gippy. "*Careful*, dude."

"Fuckin' right," he replies with a nod.

The door closes, and I turn to Gippy. "First, let me tell you what you're getting into."

He squares his shoulders in my jacket. "Shoot."

"You've lived on the street, so you're no stranger to violence, but war is a different kind of thing, and the one we're fighting is...difficult."

"Didn't think it'd be easy."

"Not the way you think, Gippy. It's difficult because my enemies, the Nephilim and Hell's other minions, have seduced a *huge* percentage of the population into believing *they're* the good guys and *I'm* the bad guy. Sometimes, we'll be forced to fight for our lives. I need to know you're willing to take a human life to help me."

"Did it once before, didn't I?"

"Yes, you did." I breathe deep, trying to make the next as clear as I can. "The hard part, the thing that is difficult to deal with, is realizing that most of these people aren't evil; they're just on the wrong side."

"I get that."

I wonder if he does. I hope so. "The other thing you have to realize is that I'll try everything I can to *preserve* every human life I can, even if they're in league with the Nephilim. That means running, lying, bribing, drugging, or whatever, to win free and let them live. I cherish human life, *any* human life. Even those seduced by Hell. You understand?"

He nods, and I feel a little reluctance now.

"If you find yourself in over your head, you can leave me at any time.

This isn't *slavery*, Gippy. I need to know you're helping me because you *want* to."

"I *want* to, alright! First time in my *life,* I had a fight that *meant* somethin', ya know?"

"I know." I reach into the coat and pull my backup weapon, another ten-millimeter Glock. *Online shopping... buy one, get the second half price, and free shipping. What a deal.* "Now, let me show you a few things."

"Na, you talk too stiff. Say, 'Lemme show you some shit.'"

Language...so fluid, like the changing course of a river. I speak more languages than I can easily name, but changes in dialect catch me off guard. "Lemme show you some shit." I smile at him. "Have you ever fired a semi-automatic pistol?"

"Where would I?" He looks down at the weapon dubiously. "Flash piece like that *way* outta my price range."

"Then lemme show you some shit." I pop out the magazine and clear the round in the chamber.

AFTER THREE HOURS WITH EMPA, Gippy felt like his head would explode. He never dreamed that shooting a gun, using a knife, and throwing a grenade could be so complicated. The Glock felt big and clumsy in his hand compared to his little revolver, even though the custom grip was fitted for Empa's smaller hands. Her strength, speed, and grace left him gaping, and she insisted he continue to wear the heavy coat.

"And *eat*, Gippy. You're way too thin." She poked him in the ribs. "If you're going to be my muscle, you have to *have* some muscles."

"And if you gonna play a trick, you gotta talk like a bitch." He tried to poke her back, but she blocked it easily. "Say it *street.*"

She scowled. "You too skinny. Gotta eat. If you gonna be my muscle, you gotta *have* some."

"Not bad. You learn quick."

"I've had a lot of practice." She loaded the Glock, jacking a round into the chamber, then popped the magazine out to top it up before slapping it in and handing it back to him. "Holster and secure."

"Sure." He did as she'd showed him, securing the pistol with the Velcro strap of the belt holster. "What about that?" He pointed to the scabbarded sword lying on the bed. "Do I get ta learn how ta swing that?"

"No." She picked up the sword and ran a hand down the black scabbard. "Sorry, Gippy, but this is…very special to me. It belonged to a dear friend centuries ago. He gave it to me before he went into seclusion before his death."

"And he was a soldier, way back, I mean?"

"A samurai."

"Sam-a-what?"

"Like a knight, but in Japan." She drew the blade slowly from the scabbard, a silvery length of steel, faintly curved, with a wavy pattern along the edge. It was the most beautiful thing Gippy had ever seen. "Miyamoto Musashi was the greatest swordsman in the world at the time." She slipped the sword back into the scabbard so fluidly he feared she'd cut herself. "We were very close. This is my most treasured possession."

She loved him. Gippy swallowed the lump in his throat, taken aback by the realization. "He teach you?"

"Yes. Many things, not all of which had to do with killing." She smiled and lay the sword back down. "And I taught *him* many things."

He didn't know why she was telling him this, but she'd piqued his curiosity. "Like…what?"

"Like how to love, even if you are a warrior." She sat on the bed and looked at him curiously. "It's important that you realize there are more paths than violence, Gippy. I've just been given a clue that may be a chance to fight the Nephilim, but the weapons we'll use to win the war are as much teaching people to *love* instead of hate as they are killing those who oppose us."

Teaching people to love…

"So, why *didn't* you?" Gippy cleared his throat. He couldn't talk about this, not with *her.*

She knitted her brows. "Why didn't I what?"

He had to say something. "Jeri told me."

She stood up and turned away from him. "That was…a mistake, Gippy."

Making her feel good, a mistake? What bullshit!

"Yours or hers?" He didn't know where the question came from.

"Both." She turned to face him, and he saw something different. For the first time, she wasn't all hard lines and age-old poise. There was hurt there. "Jeri wanted sex. She didn't understand that sex for me means something more than just recreation. When I refused, she got angry, which was *her* mistake. Then I showed her…why. That was *my* mistake."

"You don't *know* her."

She hardened, her armor back in place. "I know her better than you think, Gippy."

"Not like I do. If you did, you'd've showed her that fuckin' *can* be more. She never had that. She needs to *learn* it before she gets in *real* deep shit. She's fallin' for you hard." *Like I did with Lennie.* Gippy took off the coat and flung it down on the bed, pointing at the scabbarded sword. "You say you showed this dude, Musashi, how to love. Jeri never learned that. You say you love everybody. You leave her hangin' with her heart cut out, she's gonna crash."

"I don't…know if that's a good idea, Gippy."

"Bullshit." He started for the door. "I'm late fer supper."

"Gippy, please, tell her—"

"Nope! Ain't yer messenger boy." He opened the door and looked back at her. "You wanna tell her somethin', *you* tell her."

Gippy closed the door and headed down to the shelter, unsure if he'd done the right thing or not.

15

SWEET SORROW

We finish packing the car about sunset. It's been a very long day, but we must get out of the city before we sleep. My searches on the nets tell me the noose is tightening. There's suspicion that I have an accomplice, someone sheltering me. I must leave to protect Emil and everything here, if nothing else.

And there's Jeri to consider.

We've come to an understanding. It took a lot of talking, and some *very* careful showing, but she's not afraid of me any longer. Gippy was right, she's fallen for me, and I can't deny she fills a void in me that's been empty for a very long time. I pray to God she can let me go, and that I don't do something stupid at the last minute like ask her to come along. She would, I think, but I can't. I *know* I can't. Jeri and I are like drugs to each other. The more of me I give her, the more she'll want, and I fear the converse is true, too. She's a drug I dare not get addicted to. I can't afford distractions right now.

"Well, that's it." Emil slams the trunk and sighs. He's worked diligently to get us on our way. "Just don't push it too hard, and don't forget to add oil about every five hundred miles. The rings are shot. Don't forget to empty the water reservoir in the centrifuge. If it gets cold, you'll have to run the preheater longer. The battery's new, but the alternator's a rebuild."

"I'll remember." He's gone through the car's idiosyncrasies thoroughly several times. I think tinkering with the machine feeds his obsessive disorder, and I'm taking that away, but I've given him enough money to buy a new piece of junk to fix up. "Please be careful about changing the bullion. They watch for big expenditures and might be tracking serial numbers."

"I will." He looks at me again and shakes his head. "You're *sure* about this…disguise of yours?"

"No, but they are." I nod to Gippy and Jeri. They're embracing, and I'm taking them apart. *Such sweet sorrow.* "I trust their judgment in *this*, at least."

"But you look…so…" He waves a hand at me, and I laugh.

"Lascivious?" I can't argue with that.

Jeri picked my disguise carefully, and I can move easily enough. The high-heeled boots are comfortable, and the stretch pants fit like a second skin. My bare midriff feels vulnerable, and the rhinestone in my navel will take some getting used to, but the skimpy crop top holds everything in place without being restrictive. It feels a lot like a sports bra but shows enough cleavage to get the point across, the equivalent in my first three thousand years of showing one's hair. *Times change…*

"As did Mariam of Magdala in her time, Father." *Loving him is not a demon within you, Mari. It is simply love…* I'm glad she also picked up a long vinyl coat. It's not Kevlar, but it covers me up, hides my pistol, and, with a little stitching, will conceal the katana.

Emil blinks at me curiously. "Well, yes. I'm just concerned it'll draw too much attention."

"It should fool the recognition software, and NAFAS security pays no attention to prostitutes." I'm lucky they legalized prostitution. *Just another trick trying to make a living…* "As far as drawing attention, people looking for someone will look for someone being unobtrusive. I don't look like who they're looking for, and I'm too eye-catching to be hiding from anyone. That's all that matters."

"I hope so."

"Gotta go, E." Gippy has started calling me that rather than Empa or one of my assumed names. He looks very different, too, hair cut short on the sides, clean and sharply dressed, a shiny watch, and a gold chain neck-lace. A proper pimp indeed. "You drivin'."

"Only 'cause you can't." Jeri shoves him playfully.

"He'll learn soon enough." I embrace Jeri unabashedly. Emil knows what's transpired between us and even told me he was happy I could bring some joy to her. As far as priests go, he's one of the finest I've ever met. I wonder if Cora was right about him, how such a good man could harbor such evil. And as far as young, impetuous sex addicts go, Jeri's exemplary. "You be good."

"And you be *bad*." She kisses me goodbye, her hands questing under my long raincoat, fingertips running along the smooth material of my stretch pants. She's relentless, and I have to pull back from feeling what she's feeling for me. *Too much... No distractions...* We part—*such sweet sorrow* —and she grins. "And don't you corrupt my boyfriend."

"Jeri..." Gippy scowls at her teasing.

"God be with you, Daughter of Raphael." Emil holds out a hand.

I look down at it, hesitate only a moment, and then grasp his hand firmly. The deluge of data floods me, a sea of information, feelings, thoughts, anguish, and a deep-seated longing to help people, an empathy that humbles me. But beneath it all, struggling, incapable of gaining purchase through the storm of information, a writhing core of hate and malevolence... I feel a name, Son of Azkeel, Angel of Ruin and Destruction. We're acquainted; I put a spear through his eye in Constantinople during the fourth crusade. Another war lost to the machinations of Hell's children.

"And you, Father." I grit my teeth against the storm, a hurricane of malevolence within him.

"Are you alright?" Emil looks concerned and releases my hand.

"Yes, your mind is...very complicated."

"Tell me about it." He smiles and holds out the car key. "Keep in touch."

"We'll be back when we can." I can't make any promises, and they know it, but now, knowing Cora was right, that a Nephilim resides within this good man and that I might find a way to banish it for good, I have a real motivation to return. *And there's Jeri.*

I get in the Mercedes, hit the preheat for a count of ten, and start it up. It coughs to life and idles smoothly. Emil opens the garage door into the rain-soaked night. I turn on the headlamps and ease us out into the storm, watching them waving in the rearview. The door closes, cutting off the warm glow of the light and their love. I pull onto the street and head south toward I-71, leaving Saint Luther's behind.

"Think we will?" Gippy asks, and I feel the wash of his anguish. "Come back, I mean?"

"Fuck yeah, bitch. Ain't doin' this for fun, ya know." I punch him in the shoulder.

"Funny." He rubs his shoulder, not fooled by my bravado. "You think?"

"Yes, I do." The truth? Maybe, or I'm as good at lying to myself as I am to others. If I can learn how to expunge the Nephilim from Emil, I'll certainly do everything in my power to do so. *And there's Jeri...*

"Where we goin'?"

I haven't told Emil or Jeri; what they don't know they can't divulge if the Nephilim find them. "Flagstaff, Arizona."

"No shit? Ain't that like a desert?"

"High forest, actually, but it's beautiful country, or was when I was last there." I forget the year, but I remember the blood, a peaceful people forced into a war they couldn't win. *Talk about irony.* "It'll be cold. Get some sleep. I'll wake you when we need to refuel."

"Sure." He slouches down and pulls up the collar of my duster.

I drive carefully through the rainy night, keeping under the speed limit. The last thing we want is to be pulled over. I find an onramp, and we make the freeway. I keep it under sixty, watching the antiquated temperature gauge and logging the mileage on my phone. The fuel gauge doesn't work, of course, gummed up by gunky cooking oil. Three hundred miles, and we'll have to refill the tank from the reservoir of five-gallon jugs in the trunk.

I relish the silence, the solitude, and the tiny kernel of hope in my heart. We *do* have a chance, albeit a slim one. And I'm not really alone. For the first time in more than a century, I've trusted a human to accompany me, and he's a fragile drug addict.

You gotta be fuckin' crazy, bitch. Not really, but practicing the vernacular in my head keeps me awake and will make it more natural when we have to stop.

THE DAUGHTER of Ariquiel glared out at the dawning sun, her hands clenched behind her back so hard that pain thrilled up her arms. "Tell me, Director, *exactly* what you mean by 'vanished.'"

"We haven't gotten a single hit on any of our cameras in over forty-eight hours. She's either gone to ground somewhere or left the city before the net came down." The regional director shifted, obviously uncomfortable with reporting his failure. "She may have had accomplices. The bus station video suggests—"

"She arrived on the 1430 bus from Cleveland. We have exactly two frames of her in the bus station." *Thanks to the crappy one frame per ten seconds cameras in the station.* "Our stakeouts in the station gave us *nothing*. People store bags in bus station lockers all the god-damned *time*, Director!" She'd seen the data; a few people coming in to recover bags from lockers meant nothing.

"One, in particular, is of interest, Commander Westerhouse. A young Afro-American man recovered a bag then purposefully evaded our surveillance team. He bought a ticket to Louisville, then skipped out of the boarding gate."

"And did you find anything on this young Afro-American man?" She knew the answer; she'd reviewed the files.

"No, ma'am. He's a non-person. Completely off our radar. This might suggest—"

"It suggests that he's a worthless punk, Director!" She rounded on him, sick of his weak attempt to explain his failure. "Criminals run from the law, in case you didn't realize that! He obviously spotted your surveillance team and ran. Our fugitive wouldn't be so foolish as to employ the aid of some homeless punk."

"Yes, ma'am." His tone stated clearly that he disagreed but was too cowardly to say so.

She longed to murder him on the spot but couldn't. Unfortunately, she needed him. "Widen the search. State-wide, and if that doesn't give results by noon today, region-wide." *Should have nuked this city when I had the chance.*

"Commander, the demand on computer resources is—"

"Not your concern, Director. I'll get the necessary appropriations for computer time." NAFAS had a dozen supercomputers running full-time analyzing facial and voice recognition data, tracking criminals, dissidents, and troublemakers. This, however, was a priority.

"Very well, Commander." The director gave her a respectful nod and left his office.

Commander Westerfield turned back to glare out at the city, considering her options. They were few. If the Ageless had learned one thing in five-thousand years, it was how to disappear.

GIPPY SNAPPED up from a light doze at the chime of Empa's phone. Sunlight lit the crack between the thick curtains. He hadn't meant to fall asleep, but boredom and comfort were a somnolent mixture. He poked the phone, ten AM local time, and she'd barely had three hours sleep, but she'd said to wake her when it chimed.

Empa lay dead asleep on the seedy motel room's bed. They'd made good time, ten hours and two fuel stops, but she finally pulled off for a rest. Some town called Joplin, or on the outskirts. The motel manager had been pissed to be woken so early, but he shut up when Gippy waved a T-note under his nose. A bed, a bathroom, a chair, and a TV that didn't work. She'd dumped her coat and was asleep in two minutes. He'd slept most of the way, so he sat in the chair to watch.

He got up and stretched, his back cracking like clicking dice. "E! Wake up."

She stirred, blinked, and looked at him. "Time?"

"Ten."

She rolled up and rubbed her hair. "Hungry?"

"Stupid question."

"Right." She stretched.

Gippy tried not to watch her. *Damn Jeri for dressin' her like that.* He hadn't lied to Jeri when he told her Empa wasn't his junk, but still. He looked away as she walked to the bathroom.

"Ten minutes. Find us a diner."

"Diner?" Some of the words she used baffled him.

"Restaurant. Greasy spoon. Food. Someplace that'll have used fry oil." She closed the door.

Gippy tapped her access code, then the little round thing that let him talk to her phone. "Find a restaurant near me. Fried food."

The screen blinked, and a map came up. He couldn't read the words, but there were several red dots labeled nearby. He poked one close to the flashing blue dot that was them, and a picture came up. *Looks greasy. Perfect.*

She was out of the bathroom, looking fantastic, armed, and in her jacket in nine minutes. By the time he peed, combed his hair, and drank some water, she had the car running and their bag in the back seat. He stepped out the door, squinting into the glaring sunshine. The rare break in the weather, an honest to God blue sky, seemed strange. He got in the passenger side.

"You in a hurry today." Gippy handed her the phone.

"No, just in road-trip mode." She grimaced at the picture on the screen. "Great choice."

"So, you pick."

She put the Mercedes in gear, and they drove six blocks in silence. He'd been watching her drive, and it didn't look that hard. *Gas, brake, steer...simple.* He'd driven a little bit, jacked a few cars, but never on a freeway or in traffic.

When they pulled into the near-empty parking lot of the restaurant, he asked, "Gonna let me drive today."

"Once we're out of town." She tapped his arm and popped a piece of gum in her mouth. "Time to put on our show, baby."

"Right." Gippy got out and put on his grim face. Jeri had helped him practice.

He'd seen so many pimps with their merchandise, it almost came naturally. He was still getting used to the fancy clothes, slick shirt with buttons and a belt to hold up pants that felt like they'd fall off. The coat still weighed a ton, even though she'd let him stash the sword under the back seat of the car. *Strut, important like, don't look at her, make her walk behind, don't hold the door...* He stepped into the restaurant and looked around, six customers, none of them naffies. A few eyes settled on them; some lingered on her, interested. *So far, so good.*

They took a booth in the corner, and a tired-looking waitress ambled over with two sheets of plastic. She dropped them on the table, eying Empa. "Drinks?"

"Two coffees." Gippy had never eaten in a real restaurant in his life, but he'd seen enough TV to know how to order. "And none of that fake shit."

"Nothin' but the real thing, darlin'."

The waitress left, and he picked up the sheet of plastic. There were no pictures, and the jumble of words and numbers meant nothing to him. *Fuck.* He dropped the menu and flicked a hand dismissively. "Order whatever. I don't give a shit."

"Sure, baby." Empa popped her gum and smiled.

Gippy hadn't watched her walk in, but she seemed okay with her role. She definitely drew more attention than he did, which was fine. The waitress came back with two chipped mugs of something black that was supposed to be coffee. Gippy reached for the sugar.

"Couple'a burgers with fries." Empa popped her gum and grinned at the waitress. "*Love* your hair, sweetie."

The woman looked a little startled, touched the dangly red curls that framed her face. "Thanks."

"And none of that fake shit. *Real* meat," Gippy said.

"Sure, sure." She walked off without looking at him.

Gippy stirred and sipped his coffee; it was bitter and strong. Empa drank hers quickly and even went up to the counter for a refill before the food came. Gippy watched her walk. She *definitely* knew her role. Eyes followed her.

The food came, two greasy burgers that *might* be real meat and slimy fries. Before the waitress could leave, Gippy peeled a C-note off the roll in his pocket and held it out to her.

"Yer boss got a barrel for the fry oil? We need some for our ride."

She took the note. "Sure! Out back." She smiled at him. "You want more coffee, darlin'?"

"Sure."

She brought more coffee, and they ate in silence. People came and went. A beefy man walked up to their table and asked if Empa was working, but Gippy put him off. Empa smiled at the man and said, "Sorry, sugar," and the guy left without a word. Gippy's burger was chewy but delicious. He ate every bite on his plate and half of Empa's fries. Food was one thing he'd never learned to waste.

The trouble didn't start until they were pulled up behind the restaurant with the trunk of the Mercedes open, filling the five-gallon jugs from the barrels of waste fry oil. They were both busy, trying not to get the smelly oil all over their clothes, and didn't see the cruiser until it pulled up behind them.

Tires crunching on the gritty pavement snapped Gippy's attention up to the late model police car painted in the black and gold of NAFAS.

Fuck! He tried not to look terrified. "Trouble, E."

"Just one in the car." She turned back to working the hand pump as if unconcerned. "No trouble yet, just rousting us. Offer money."

"Right." Gippy lifted two of the heavy jugs and shuffled back to the Mercedes as the cruiser's door opened. A big man stood up behind the door. He wore no helmet but had the usual flak jacket and gear belt. His face was unshaven. Not the typical naffie. Gippy hefted one of the jugs into the trunk. "Problem, officer?"

"Not yet there ain't, boy." He rested a hand on the pistol on his belt. "You pay for that oil?"

"Yep. Ask inside." He lifted the second jug into the trunk.

"You ain't from 'round here, are ya?"

"Nope. Just passin' through." Gippy walked back to Empa. The pump was slow, and there were still four empty jugs. He picked up two more full ones and shuffled back to the car. "Headin' south fer winter."

"Figured." The naffie stepped out from behind the car door and ambled up, hand still on his gun. "This is a God-fearin' community, boy. We don't take no truck with fancy city pricks sellin' loose women."

"Ain't sellin' nothin'. Just passin' through."

"You tellin' me she ain't yer hoor?" He said it more as an insult than a question.

"No, sir, I ain't tellin' you nothin'." He hefted a jug into the trunk. "Don't want no trouble." He lifted the other jug and turned back to find the big man in his face. Gippy tried very hard to keep his hands out of his pockets and empty, though they itched for his gun. He forced his eyes to meet the man's. "How much to make this go away?"

"You offerin' me a *bribe*, boy?" The naffie's breath reeked of alcohol. "I can *arrest* you for that!"

Gippy raised his hands defensively. "Don't want no—"

"Officer, *please*." The naffie jerked around to face Empa, obviously surprised that she had gotten so close without him noticing. She'd surprised Gippy, too. "My man and I just wanna travel on. I'm sure *somethin'* can be done ta help that along."

The trooper looked her up and down. Her coat was open, showing him the goods, and she gave him a sultry smile. His hand left his pistol. Gippy slipped his hand under the duster. With the man's attention stuck on Empa, he could draw and put a bullet in the naffie's head easy. Empa's gaze slipped off the big man to him.

"You don't mind if I talk to the nice officer, do ya, baby?" She shook her head minutely, looked back at the naffie, and smiled, her tongue running over her upper lip.

"You fuckin' *hoor*," the naffie spat.

Gippy *really* wanted to kill him, but Empa sidled up, moving like a snake through tall grass. *What the hell she doin'?* But it was obvious what she was doing; she was going to fuck him to avoid killing him. He couldn't believe it.

"Yes... I... am," she breathed through pearly teeth, close enough to brush her breasts against his chest. "I'm a fucking...sucking...banging, *whore*, and I can do you better than you've ever been done in your *life*."

The man's mouth dropped open. "You..."

Gippy's mouth dropped open, too, though her performance made him a little ill. *Goddamn, she the shit.* He didn't know if she was pulling some angel-mojo on the guy or not, but the naffie's pallid face had flushed scarlet, his loose jowls quivering. She had him by the nuts.

"Why don't you take me to your car and *interrogate* me while my man here finishes up." She turned to give Gippy a broad wink. "You don't mind, do ya, baby?"

Gippy would much rather have killed the man right there, but killing a naffie was all kinds of trouble they couldn't afford. He forced the words out. "Go ahead, E."

"Take my coat, baby." She slipped out of the long vinyl jacket and handed it over. It was heavy. She'd put her gun into one of the inside pockets. She held out her wrists to the naffie. "You can handcuff me if you want."

"I..." The naffie cleared his throat and pulled a long zip tie from his belt. "I might just have to do that." He grabbed her wrist and dragged her off toward his car.

Empa giggled and squealed, playing it up. Gippy felt like he might puke.

"Don't damage the merch." He put her coat in the back seat and got to work, trying to ignore the sounds coming from the back seat of the cruiser.

They were back on the road in twenty minutes, Gippy behind the wheel. Empa moved stiffly and looked a little pale through the makeup. There were red marks on her wrists from cable ties. Gippy gritted his teeth until they hurt and gripped the wheel hard, but she waved to the naffie as they drove past. The big man sat behind the wheel of his cruiser, looking stunned.

Gippy headed toward the interstate, concentrating on driving. He didn't, *couldn't* say anything to her.

They were only four blocks away when Empa said, "Pull over," in a tone that brooked no argument.

Before they even came to a complete stop, she opened her door, leaned out, and retched.

Gippy stifled a curse and fished a water bottle from the back seat and a few paper towels. *Wouldn't've happened in a city, but small-town dickhead naffie had to butt in.* This wasn't the time to bring that up, but he would have to soon, or they'd run into more trouble. He handed her the bottle first, then the towels. She swished and spat, then drank some water and wiped her face, smearing her lipstick.

She slammed the door. "Drive."

He glanced over his shoulder and pulled the Mercedes into traffic. "You okay?"

"No, but I will be." She drank more water and dragged a breath into her lungs. "Dear *God*...so much hate."

Gippy remembered how he felt after she helped him, all his guilt gone, like all the nasty shit had been wrung out of him. "You took it from him, didn't you?"

"Yes." She shuddered. "All of it."

He stared at her as he turned onto the onramp. *"Why?"*

"Because I *could*, Gifford." She gave him a weak smile and held out a hand. "Please, take my hand. I...need...to feel someone good."

"Sure." He took her hand and drove, wondering again what he'd gotten himself into. "Wish you'd of just let me kill the fucker."

"No, Gifford." She flipped down the visor and wiped the smeared lipstick off. "Remember, we'll fight if we have to, but if there's *any* other way, we'll take it. Love is sometimes the better weapon. Who knows what fruit this will bear?"

Far behind them, Officer Hennessy sat behind the wheel of his cruiser, staring at his big scarred hands, tears rolling down his unshaven cheeks.

16

LESSONS

By the time we take Highway 60 off the interstate to avoid Tulsa and Oklahoma City, the disgusting mass of hate in me is gone. I don't seem to be having much luck with meals lately. The bruises on my wrists will take longer to heal, as will the bruising elsewhere, but that's just pain. The encounter with Officer Hennessy brought back far too many memories that I've tried for centuries to expunge. Killing him would have been far too dangerous. I chose the only viable option but delving him to remove the core of hate choking his soul during the act had been...challenging.

Holding Gippy's hand for half an hour helped. He is genuinely a good soul, though he still doesn't consider himself so. I've learned much more about him than I intended, confusion and misplaced guilt about his bisexuality, loneliness, and a deep dread of intimacy due to the pain of his losses. We're kindred in the last, at least. Though I've lost thousands more loved ones than he, the pain is the same.

Gippy wants to stick to interstates and cities, which isn't surprising. He's a city boy. But his driving is less likely to draw attention in the country and I want to make a stop in the Osage reservation. By the time we pass the reservation border, the welts on my wrists are fading. The rest will take longer, but I've endured far worse for lesser causes. At least this time, it was my choice.

My reasons for this route are simple: seclusion and evading the authorities. While I'm reasonably sure Officer Hennessy won't put a bulletin out on us, I can't be certain. Native American reservations are still nominally under the governance of the tribes, and NAFAS rarely bothers to go there anymore. After all, the Osage oil is gone, and they have nothing else of interest. They make more money now on grass-fed beef and bison than anything else. They've always been astute at business.

I tell Gippy to pull onto a dirt side road. When we stop, I take two water bottles and a box of ammunition from the back seat. While Gippy tops up the fuel tank from the jugs in the trunk, I place the two bottles about fifty feet out onto the grassy flat.

"Wha'cha doin?"

"Time for a live-fire exercise." I draw my Glock and clear it.

"You mean shoot at targets?" He finishes with the last jug and closes the trunk. "Ain't that expensive?"

"Not as expensive as missing what you're aiming at when it really matters."

"Like when love won't work, and you gotta shoot some naffie fucker in the head?" He's still upset with my decision back in Joplin, but I know I was right.

"Yes, Gippy, but you can't always get so close to your target." The day is unseasonably warm, so I doff my coat. "We'll use standard rounds for practice. The hollow points and armor-piercing rounds are for combat only." I put my magazine and the chambered round on the top of the car and load a magazine of standard rounds.

"Why use that caseless shit? Big bucks for nothin'."

"Casings can be traced. Trade." I hand him my weapon and take his for my holster. "The armor-piercing rounds are Teflon coated, so the slugs don't retain markings from the barrel of the weapon. The hollow points are generally too deformed to allow good ballistics." I feel his confusion as I hand over the loaded pistol. "They can't be easily traced to the gun that fired them."

"Okay." I'm proud to see his grip on the Glock, just like I showed him. "Show me some shit."

I put him through a basic drill, concentrating on accuracy rather than speed. His hands learn quickly, and the motions become more fluid. After sixty rounds, fatigue begins to degrade his prowess. He's still not very strong, and the recoil has him shaking. The two bottles are still standing.

"I suck at this." He holsters the Glock and flexes his hands.

"No, you don't. You just need practice." I take his hands in mine and relieve him of his aching joints and ringing ears. "The first rule of the warrior is that *everything* is difficult at first. I was no better the first time I handled a firearm. That's why we practice."

He looks uneasy as he takes his hands back, his discomfort gone. "Yeah, but I ain't got a hundred years to learn."

"*Six* hundred, but a matchlock is nothing like a Glock."

"A match what?"

"Early firearms. It's not important. The point is, you don't *need* a hundred years. You just need to practice." I point to my bag in the back seat. "Get the cleaning kit. I'll drive while you learn how to break your weapon down and clean it."

"You *clean* guns?"

"Yes, or they betray you when you need them most."

"Well, *fuuuck* me."

I laugh at his coarse humor; I know he's not being literal. I've felt his confusion about me; physical attraction but no desire to do anything. He's still a little afraid of me, too, and I can't blame him. As he reaches for the bag, I spot a pall of dust on the road from the highway.

"Company." I retrieve the magazine and single round from the car's roof and hand them to Gippy. "Lock and load. They probably just heard us shooting and are curious. If they're Osage, we'll have no problem."

"And if they ain't?" He loads his weapon quicker than before, his hands sure, and holsters it behind his back. Good boy.

"We'll see." It's a pickup, three people in the cab. Two more stand up in the bed as it slows and finally stops about two hundred feet away. *Cautious...* Through the glass in the back of the cab, I see a rifle. That could be trouble. They're too far for a sure kill with a pistol. They look like Osage, but it's hard to be certain. I step out from behind the car and wave. "Hello, friends!"

One of the men in the bed raises a hand and shouts, "Heard shooting. Trouble?"

"No, only practice." I point to the two bottles.

The two in the back jump down, one holding the rifle. The three in the cab get out. Two are women. I don't see any more weapons. Musashi's lessons come to me: *Readiness is a constant state. High spirit is weak, low spirit is weak, steady spirit. See everything.*

The man who spoke before, the one without the rifle, points to Gippy. "He teachin' you?"

They walk forward slowly, casually. The rifleman holds his weapon easily in the crook of his arm. It's a hunting rifle, bolt action. I watch for nervousness among them and see none. A hundred fifty feet.

I smile. "No. I'm teachin' him."

"You?" They exchange glances and smiles, still walking forward. One hundred feet; well within my deadly range. "No offense, lady, but you look like a trick, not a fighter."

I shrug. "That's *why* I look like a trick."

"Yeah?" They stop at about seventy feet, still all smiling, obviously amused and skeptical. I can't blame them with the way I'm dressed.

"Yeah." I grin big and hold my hands out to my sides, empty. I don't think we'll have any trouble with them. They're still too far for me to get any feelings, but they're Osage, just curious and cautious. "You want a lesson?"

The man grins wider. "Sure!"

I nod, check to make sure Gippy's clear, then draw as I turn. I double tap both bottles and turn back, holstering the Glock.

They all break into laughter and smiles, one woman nudging her companion.

"Holy *shit*, E." Gippy gapes at me.

"Jesus tits, woman! You *bad*!" The man who spoke before strides forward with a hand out, grinning openly. They all follow. "I'm Honga."

His grip is strong and warm, his hand huge around mine. "Ellen." I feel no malice in him, just amusement, love, curiosity, and concern for his friends. I hook a thumb at Gippy. "My friend, Gif."

Honga shakes Gippy's hand and introduces his friends, his sister, her husband, and two cousins. "You road trippin'?"

"Yes, south for winter. Maybe Mex City." Necessary lies are the easiest.

"In that?" He points to the Mercedes. "It'll never make it."

"The car's like her." Gippy nods at me with a lopsided grin. "Bitch tougher than she look."

They laugh again. *Nicely done, Gifford.*

"Headin' west, I guess. If you stop in Ponca City, try the Tripple T. My cousin Monsa does the best steak in Oklahoma."

"We *will*. I could use a good steak." After losing my breakfast, too true.

"You serious, you can follow us." He jerks a thumb at his truck. "We're bringin' Monsa his monthly."

My mouth waters and I decide to trust first impressions. I really could use a good meal, and Gippy's a bottomless pit. I give him a formal curtsy from ages past. "Lead on, my good man."

They laugh and clamber aboard their truck.

"You sure about this, E?" Gippy asks as he gets in and clears his Glock.

"No, but I *am* hungry, and they seem friendly enough." I pull out and follow the pickup. "Ponca City's a half-hour. You can strip and clean your weapon before we get there. First, double-check to make sure it's clear like I showed you, then pull the trigger. It'll stay pulled. Now, take a firing grip, then wrap your gun hand fingers over the slide and pull back..."

GIPPY COULDN'T REMEMBER EVER BEING SO full, but he ate every last bite of the monstrous steak. It was the best thing he'd ever tasted. Honga and his friends were nice, too, and offered to put them up for the night. Of course, most of the men and some of the women looked at Empa with longing—they'd have to be dead not to—but Empa declined with casual grace. By early afternoon, they were back on the road, Gippy behind the wheel. Empa picked out a route to avoid Oklahoma City and Amarillo, told him to wake her when they were in Texas, and went to sleep.

Gippy didn't know what she had against cities but didn't argue. She was the boss.

Once in Texas, they stopped in a town called Stratford, where Empa insisted Gippy load up on practice ammunition. "Texans love guns like the French love wine," she said, which meant nothing to Gippy, but seemed to amuse her. She gave him one of the thin metal bars from her stash and told him what to buy. He almost balked at the cost but did as he was told.

The guy behind the counter looked at him with disdain—*Small town dickhead lookin' down his nose at the slick city prick*—but his little machine must have told him Empa's money was good because he didn't make a fuss. Gippy was also getting the shakes, which might have been the reason for the gun dealer's unease. He took a Vickie and got in the passenger side.

"Dude in the store didn't like me much."

"Old prejudices die hard." She pulled out onto the highway and gave him a glance. "You're lucky you were born in this century, my friend."

"You talkin' 'bout slavery?" He shrugged. "That shit ended like two hundred years ago, didn't it?"

"*Legal* slavery did, yes, but bigotry didn't, and human trafficking is alive and well."

"Yeah, I know." He frowned. *Jame...* "Lost a sister that way. Fuckin' pimp sold her like a piece of meat."

"I've been a slave more than once, Gippy. Time changes many things, but humans will always try to dominate one another."

"Don't I fuckin' know it." He looked at her, trying to imagine her in chains. He couldn't. "How'd you survive it?"

She glanced at him, and he saw the anguish in her eyes. "Any way I could. You do what you have to do to survive, Gippy. You know that."

"I *do* that." He thought about all the things he'd done, and a cloud of regret loomed up in him. "Fuck that depressin' shit. What *else* you been? I don't know nothin' 'bout you, E. Tell me some shit."

"Lord, where to start." She sighed. "I've always been a healer, which helped me avoid the worst of life's pain. It gave me value. My family—my *human* family—were farmers. They died before I really even knew what I was."

"You didn't *know*? Like, you didn't know yer daddy was an angel?"

"Not at first, only that I heard his voice." She smiled at him. "It's not like I got an instruction manual. When I was very young, I thought everyone heard voices, felt people's emotions, saw their memories when they touched." She shook her head. "I learned to hide my nature very early."

"So, what else?"

"I was born in the Middle East, near a small city-state called Lagash, but I've lived in almost every country on Earth at one time or another. I've met other Ageless from other cultures, the sons and daughters of angels nobody wrote down in the Bible, born in Asia, Africa, and Central America. Moving around's harder these days, with the weather and technology, the Nephilim hunting me online." She glanced at him. "I've been many things. So many I can't remember them all."

"Like?"

She sighed. "An apothecary, a merchant, a medical doctor, soldier, librarian, pirate, concubine... You name it, I've done it."

"Pirate?" He grinned at her, again trying to imagine and failing. "No shit?"

"No shit." She smiled at him. "Look up Anne Bonny some time. Not all pirates were murdering bastards, and not all were *men*."

He stared at her. "Well, fuuuck me."

"Get some sleep, Gip. We'll refuel in Albuquerque and drive through the night to Flagstaff."

"Sure." Gippy leaned his seat back and threw an arm over his eyes, trying to imagine Empa on an old-time pirate ship, sword and pistol in hand. The image came to him more easily than he thought it would. Fatigue and the Vickie dragged him down into darkness, and the image became a dream.

He was sleeping soundly when Empa touched his arm and jostled him awake.

"You should see this."

He blinked and sat up. It was dark. "See what?" Light flashed in the distance, illuminating mountains. "Storm?"

"No, just heat lightning. We'll be cresting the Sandia Ridge in just a minute, and you'll see Albuquerque."

She woke him for that? "Seen one city..."

Her teeth gleamed in the headlights of the oncoming traffic. "Wait for it."

They crested the ridge, and the glow he'd seen on the horizon blossomed into a sea of lights stretching as far as he could see. He caught his breath at the enormity of it.

"Mutha *fuck*." How could there be this many people in the whole world?

"The city's sprawled a lot in the last fifty years or so. Phoenix and Denver are bigger, but they've all more than doubled."

"Where they all *come* from?" He marveled at the sight, so many lights. His mind couldn't grasp it.

"Houston, south Texas, New Orleans, some from California, though not as many." She glanced at him. "You know about the sea rising, right?"

"The sea?" He'd heard some bullshit about the sea swallowing up cities before he was born but always thought it was just talk. How could water swallow a whole city? "That shit true?"

"Oh, yes. Climate change shifted ocean currents and melted the polar ice caps. I've never seen anything like it. The sea rose a hundred and fifty feet in thirty years. Whole *countries* were inundated."

"Countries?" He glanced at her skeptically. "You mean like Flor-day?"

"*Florida* wasn't a country, just a state. Almost thirty million people were forced to flee from there. That's why Atlanta's such a mega-city now. Bangladesh was a country in Southeast Asia that's now completely underwater. A quarter-*billion* fled. Most of them perished because other countries wouldn't let them in. There was nowhere for them to go. Wars broke out. Genocide." She sounded like she'd witnessed these things personally. Then he remembered how old she was.

Gippy didn't know what to say. He couldn't imagine numbers like that, let alone that they represented people. He watched the sea of lights grow nearer, trying to encompass what he saw.

"How many here?"

"About three and a half million, I think. Query the phone if you want real numbers."

He didn't. Gippy didn't know numbers well, but he knew a billion was a lot more than a million. He didn't want to show his ignorance but tried to imagine a hundred times the population of this massive city dying in a war. He failed, unable to visualize it. *A fuckin' mountain of corpses...*

"Find us a place to eat. Someplace near the freeway."

He punched up her phone and asked it to find a restaurant. It came up with dozens of options. The map was confusing beyond belief. The little blue dot kept moving, and he couldn't tell where the freeway was. He got frustrated quickly.

He put the phone down. "Can't find nothin'."

"Why not?" She glanced at him. "You okay?"

"Fine, just can't..." He looked out the window at the lights to hide his embarrassment. *Fuck it. She's gonna find out anyway.* "Can't *read*, okay?"

"Oh." She squinted at signs as they entered the city proper. "Well, we can fix *that*."

Was she *teasing* him? "How you gonna do *that*?"

They took an exit, and she turned onto a city street wreathed in neon.

"I'll teach you to read, of course."

There was no teasing in her tone, but he knew better. "Too old for that shit."

"Nonsense." She pulled into a parking lot. A restaurant, he guessed, from the neon sign of a pig in a funny white hat holding two massive plates of ribs and sausages. "I'll help you, and if technology's good for *anything*, it's learning." She snatched up the phone and grinned at him. "Come on, baby. Supper time."

"You keep feedin' me like this, I'm gonna get fat."

She laughed and slammed the door. "You on to my evil plan, baby!" She strutted for the door, her vinyl coat flapping in the cold breeze.

The place was busy for so late, which was good. Busy meant they'd be ignored. They got a booth, ordered Cokes and pulled pork sandwiches, and Empa started punching up things on her phone. Gippy ignored her, the other customers and the smell of food occupying his attention. There were a lot of younger people in the restaurant, and their clothes, hair, jewelry, and makeup made Empa's seem tame. Nobody gave them a second look. Empa had avoided big cities because there were always more naffies and cameras, but Gippy could tell their disguises were working here, while they made them stand out in small towns. Empa seemed not to have gotten that yet.

He sipped his Coke and watched her. *Hot shit, for sure, but she don't know everything.* He'd been reluctant to disagree with her on anything up to now but thinking back to the incident in Joplin changed his mind.

Finally, she looked up from the phone to find him staring at her. "What?"

How to say it... He shrugged and nodded to the phone. "You teach me plenty, but I got somethin' for you, too."

"You mean other than how to talk street?" She put the phone down. "Okay, what?"

"Look 'round."

"Where?" She did but didn't see what he saw. "I don't..."

"We invisible."

"What?" She blinked at him, uncomprehending.

"This place packed, and nobody give a shit about some skinny pimp and his ho sittin' down to eat." He nodded to her. "Big cities're like that. We don't stick out here, but that little shithole we got rousted in, we different."

"But there are risks. Cameras, surveillance, NAFAS."

"But we ain't on their radar. I'm an OG, and you don't look *nothin'* like you." He flicked a hand at the full tables, the diverse crowd, the bustling staff, not an eye lingering on them for more than passing interest. "Nobody *sees* us. Naffies could walk right in here, and *they* wouldn't see us. Little town dickhead naffie seen us, and we got fucked."

"Good point." Empa nodded, then frowned. "But *you* weren't the one who got fucked."

He leaned back in his seat, suddenly angry. "'Cause *you* didn't want me to bust a cap in the fucker's head. Don't blame me fer that."

"I don't *blame* you, Gippy. Killing him was *not* the best course of action."

"Wouldn't have had to mess with him at all if you didn't take us through Podunk Nowhere, is all I'm sayin'."

"There's a lot of nowhere between cities."

"No, *really?*" He made a face. "Don't mean we gotta stop in the middle of it to *eat.*"

"Point taken." She glanced at the phone. "So, I'll teach you to read, shoot, and drive, and you teach me to be invisible."

"I teach you *where* to be invisible." He grinned at her. "You got that ho shit down."

She smiled weakly. "Just like firearms. Lots of practice."

He couldn't believe that. "No way."

"*Way,* Gippy." She shrugged. "It's been a man's world most of my life. Girl's gotta make a living."

"But you got mo' money than God!"

She chuckled. "Only after banks were invented and women were *allowed* to have money. But there are other advantages to playing the whore."

He couldn't imagine one. "Like?"

She sighed and fixed him with a solemn look. "Like when cities are overrun by armies, soldiers and civilians are often lined up and murdered, while whores are generally *not.*"

He didn't have to ask why not. He couldn't imagine her going through that, submitting to it. But she was old and still alive, and he was young and stupid. "I guess we both got a lot ta learn."

"Yes, we do."

The waiter came with their meals, and Gippy asked about their waste oil.

"You kiddin', me? We can't get rid of that crap."

Evidently, cars running on vegetable oil weren't common here. That was a break. "Mind if we take some off yer hands?"

"No problem. I'll tell the manager. Just pull around back when you're done."

"Thanks!" Things were *definitely* cooler in cities. He dug into his meal and decided that meat was probably the best reason in the world for money. That and Vickies.

17

DREAMS, RIDDLES, AND MERCY

I have to force my eyes to stay open by the time I see the lights of Winslow. I'm tempted to ask Gippy to talk to me to keep me awake, but I can't. He's slouched in the passenger seat, earbuds in, muttering with the literacy program I downloaded, actually laughing occasionally—music to my ears.

Music... "I was standin' on a corner in Winslow, Arizona..." I sing softly as I pull off the first exit, my vision so blurry I can barely read street signs. I'm punchy with fatigue. Driving on to Flagstaff tonight is out of the question; I need to be on my game tomorrow. Sleep is now priority one. I pull into the parking lot of the first motel I see.

The manager doesn't ask questions, and we're in the room in minutes. It's cold here, but the room is warm. I dump my jacket, put my Glock on the nightstand, and head for the bathroom.

"I need a shower. Go ahead and crash."

"Don't gotta tell me twice." He dumps our bag on the floor, chains the door, doffs my coat, and collapses on the bed before the bathroom door even closes.

I strip out of my prostitute costume, put the pants and stretch top in the sink with some hand soap and hot water to soak, and step into the shower. *Hot showers...best invention ever.* My toiletries are in the bag, but I don't care. I use the motel shampoo and soap with abandon, scrubbing off the last vestiges of makeup, sweat, and the remnants of my encounter with Officer Hennessy. Though the physical damage of that encounter is long gone, the memory lingers, especially at times like this, exhausted and alone with nothing to occupy my mind. It dredges up a thousand others like it, some far worse. *My choice... At least it was my choice this time.* It's not the first time I've been faced with that choice: kill or save, damn to Hell or try to redeem. This time, I feel in my heart that my decision was the right one. I smile to myself as the hot spray pounds against the back of my neck. Officer Hennessy's wife is in for a surprise when he comes home a changed man, all his hate expunged.

As I speculate what might happen there, the hot water starts to cool. "All good things..."

I turn off the spray, scour myself dry with the rough motel towel, step out of the tub, clean and relaxed, and stop cold. My clothes are soaking, and my bag is in the room outside. "*Shit!*" And motel towels are roughly the size of postage stamps. "Shit, *shit!*"

While I try to think of what to do, I rinse and wring out my clothes. The thought of putting the clammy wet things back on to get my other clothes makes me cringe. Gippy's probably asleep by now anyway. I need a good four or five hours of sleep desperately. I wrap the tiny towel around myself as best I can, grasping the two corners together, turn off the bathroom light, and peer out into the room.

Gippy lays on the far side of the bed with his back to the bathroom. The bag is on the floor on his side, and the bedside lamp on my side is on. He's fully clothed on top of the spread, his skinny chest rising and falling rhythmically. Easy solution: I sleep on my side under the covers and send him to the bathroom first in the morning.

I slip out, pad to the side of the bed, and switch off the bedside light. The towel hits the floor, and I slide between the sheets. They're roughly the texture of cardboard and smell of bleach. *At least they're sterile.* I fan my damp hair out on the pillow and close my eyes.

"Ain't gotta worry 'bout me, E," Gippy says in the dark. "You know that, don'cha?"

I open my eyes. He's faintly silhouetted against the glow of the parking lot through the curtains. He hasn't moved. I can't pick out what he's thinking without touching him, and I don't want to give him the wrong idea. *Trust...* After so many betrayals, it comes hard, but holding his hand while I destroyed the hate of Officer Hennessy told me enough. "I know, Gippy. Thank you."

"Fer what?"

"For being you." I close my eyes and drift off without a worry.

A dream not mine, erotic turning violent, a gunshot in the rain, blood. I snap awake, and Gippy's face is inches away, his hand lying atop mine, his breathing shallow and fast. He's having a nightmare, and I'm in it. His friend, Lennie, dies in his arms again as I walk away naked in the rain. It starts over.

"Gippy." I jostle his hand, and his eyes flutter open. "It's morning. You're in the bathroom first."

He clears his throat, still waking up, and nods. "On it." He rolls up and staggers. I wonder if he remembers the nightmare and hope it fades fast.

When the bathroom door closes, I'm up and in my bag in a flash, picking out clothes. I check my phone for the weather. It's cold out but supposed to warm up to above freezing by mid-morning. I think of today's task and decide to shift my identity, trading the crop top for a sports bra, thermal fleece, the flannel shirt Emil gave me. Not exactly the look I'm going for, but a quick stop at a department store will fix that.

A knock sounds at the bathroom door, and it cracks open. "You dressed?"

"Yes."

Gippy comes out looking bleary-eyed. "New look today?"

"Yes. I have to talk to some people who probably won't appreciate being questioned by a prostitute." I grab my toiletries and makeup and slip past him into the bathroom. "It's cold outside. Layer up. We're going shopping when we hit Flagstaff."

"I'll get Mercy started."

"Mercy?" I look back at him, perplexed.

"The Mercedes." He grins at me and dons his hoodie over his shirt. "Girl's been good to us. She needed a name."

"Mercy..." I nod. "Perfect."

By the time I've finished morning necessities, gelled my hair into a proper coif, applied some more sedate makeup, and applied my dark green contact lenses, Gippy has the car running and warmed up. We pack up, and I get behind the wheel.

"Hungry?" He digs a granola bar out of our bag and hands it to me.

"Stupid question." I rip the wrapper off with my teeth. "Can you find a coffee shop?"

"Sure." He taps on my phone. "Find coffee near me."

We hit the drive-through at DD and are on the freeway before the coffee's cool enough to drink. There's crusty snow alongside the road, but the sky looks unthreatening. The car heater has barely overcome the chill when we pull into a Super T Mall in Flagstaff. I trade my flannel for a thigh-length sweater and my vinyl jacket for a dark blue blazer. My Glock rides under the sweater, making a quick draw impossible, but there's no other option. Gippy gets a tie—I have to tie it for him—and a sports jacket that makes him look like a young professional, though he doesn't believe me when I tell him so. We're back in the car and on the road by ten with Gippy driving.

"Where to, Doctor Winston?" He's practicing my new identity.

"South on I-17 and take the 89-A exit. The place is called Our Lady of Healing. It's kind of in the sticks."

"And it's run by a bunch of monks?"

"And priests, yes." I punch the location up on the phone and put it on nav-mode. "I just hope they keep good records."

Mercy struggles with the thin air as we wind up a side road off 89-A. We take it slow to keep the temperature gauge below critical. There's a simple sign at the driveway, gravel dusted with snow, and a wrought iron fence with a speaker box and camera. I'm glad Gippy's driving; there's no way to know if the optical feed's been hacked by Nephilim or linked into the NAFAS-wide network. The fewer cameras that record my face, the better. I coach him on what to say, and we pull up.

"Can we help you?"

"Doctor Ellen Winston, Johns Hopkins, Towson, to see Father Blake." Perfect. I'm proud of him.

"Is she expected?"

"Hope so. We come a long way. She sent an email." Not so perfect, but not bad.

"Let me check." A long pause. "We've no record of her email, but Father Blake can see her. Please drive forward and park. Someone will meet you at the door."

"Thanks!" The gate opens, and Gippy drives forward.

The place looks more like an old-fashioned ski lodge than a monastery. We park, and I touch Gippy's arm as he reaches for the key.

"Let it idle. It's *really* cold out, and I don't want her to freeze up." I don't mention that a quick departure might be necessary. If Caldwell was indeed a Nephilim, and his soul was banished to Hell from this spot, my enemies might have staked it out.

"Not worried about somebody jackin' it?"

"Not here." We get out. It's bitter cold, and a breeze whipping down from the mountains cuts through my sweater like a knife. *Memories of Arctic winters, famine, hungry faces...* By the time we get to the door, my teeth are chattering.

A youngish man in a brown robe opens the door for us with a smile. "Welcome, Doctor Winston. Sorry we seem to have misplaced your email."

"No problem."

He swipes a key card to unlock another pair of doors and ushers us into a warm lobby with a tiny reception desk. The computer sitting on it is older than Cora's.

"If I could just see your credentials..."

"Of course." I hand him my identity card. It's forged, of course, but only the date. I really *was* Dr. Ellen Winston from Johns Hopkins Towson...fifty years ago. That was a dangerous time of my life, but invaluable. Occasionally, even I need to catch up on medical advancements. Here, I'm hoping for only a cursory inspection. "The picture was taken before I went wild with my hair." I smile at him. "Mid-life crisis."

He chuckles and hands it back. "I understand. And the purpose of your visit?"

"It's just a data-mining study. Old records. We don't need access to any of your patients."

"I see." His eyes flick over my face, hair, jewelry—I ditched the two lip rings for the visit and toned down the makeup. I sense disapproval, but it doesn't reach his face. "Well, Father Blake's willing to talk to you. It's his decision."

"I understand completely."

We follow him down a side hallway to an office door labeled Father Vincent Blake, MD, PhD. Science, medicine, and faith together, as they should be; small things like this give me hope. Our escort knocks and opens it, ushering us in. An elderly man in a priest's casual attire and collar stands from behind a small desk, his face open and friendly. The room is sparse, the furniture functional, a crucifix and two diplomas the only ornamentation. I sense a stiff pride, ego, and a hint of suspicion. This is his domain.

"Doctor Winston. Pleased to meet you." He holds out a hand, and I shake it. Ego, certainly, but also curiosity, confusion, and definitely suspicion, but no malice. Without delving, I can't get much more, but I try to give him a feeling that I'm trustworthy, honest, curious. "Sorry about the mix-up. How can we help you today?"

"I'm doing a study on treatments of post-traumatic suicidal psychosis. The history of your facility states you've had many such cases, some of them successfully rehabilitated."

"Most not so successful, I'm afraid. The prognosis is dreadful." He sighs and sits, gesturing us to chairs. "Most of our patients are soldiers, you know."

"I know." I frown and sigh. "They see *so* much horror." Visions of battlefields threaten, but I banish them. *Steady spirit...* I have to focus. Blake could deny us access at a whim.

"They do indeed." He frowns. "My only concern is HIPPA regulations. Our patients' privacy is guaranteed in our charter."

"Oh, we're not going to take any personal identifiers." I wave a hand dismissively. "Just diagnostic data, treatment regimens, results, and the names of attending clinicians for follow-up interviews, you know."

"No names to be published, I hope."

"Of *course* not." I give him a smile. "In fact, most of the records we're interested in are decades old. Modern treatment regimens are well-established, but sometimes older techniques can shed new light. Some of your predecessors have used some unorthodox methods with varying degrees of success."

"Yes, that's true." He frowns and shrugs. "I don't see any harm, but I'll need you to sign a release."

"Oh, *absolutely*! I wouldn't have it any other way!" I sign his forms, and he gestures us toward the door.

I flash Gippy a covert smile. We're in.

Doctor Blake escorts us to the records room and asks if we want anything: coffee, tea, soda. I thank him and decline with a smile.

"Well, take your time. Just ask one of the brothers if there's anything you need."

"Thank you, Father. This shouldn't take long." *I hope...*

He leaves us alone.

Luckily, the records are computerized, though the system is antiquated. I do a search for Laurence Caldwell's record.

Nothing.

I pull out my notebook and try again, checking the spelling from my notes and get the same result. "Shit!"

"What's wrong?"

"I don't know. I'm not finding the record I need." I try a few different iterations of spelling, reverse the name, include the middle initial, and still get nothing. I even try a keyword search and sort through the results, but no Caldwell. "It's not here."

"Erased, you think?" Gippy's thinking clearly, at least. If the Nephilim learned what happened here, they very well might have expunged the data.

"Possibly. If so, we're screwed."

"Don't that mean this Caldwell really *was* a Nephilim, and the exorcism *worked*?" I look to Gippy, the hope in him infecting me. "Why else would they delete it?"

"Maybe, but we need to know exactly what was done, especially the drugs they gave him, and there's nothing here."

"And the guy's whole medical record is gone?"

"Yes."

"So, we drove all this way for nothin'?" His frustration rises like a breaking wave.

"We're not beat yet. I have the date of Caldwell's accident and the date of his obituary." I pull up all the records in that time frame and start sifting through them. "If I can find a list of attending physicians during that time, maybe we can find out who treated him."

I start jotting down notes, and Gippy looks at my pen and notebook as if I'm about to take up necromancy. Ah, the mystique of pen and paper in the digital age. Only four attending physicians had clinical privileges here during Caldwell's admission. One of them, Father Martin Pederson, a Doctor of Public Health, catches my eye. There are no clinical records for him after the date of Caldwell's death. I wonder what happened to him.

"Gippy, I need you to search a name. Pull up the Find-Me app."

He pulls out my phone. "What's it look like?"

"An eye with a smile beneath it." I give him the spelling as I continue to scan records.

"There's a shitload of 'em."

"Add 'Father' before his name and M.D. DPH after it."

He taps it in slowly. "Only one hit, but it's old. I can't read all this shit." He hands me the phone.

At a glance, I suspect this is the physician who treated Caldwell. Shortly after Caldwell's death, Father Pederson left the monastery, moved to Phoenix, was arrested for dealing narcotics a year later, and incarcerated for a year. The records grow sparse after that, but a deep delve into the net will yield more. I suspect he left after the attempt to treat Caldwell put his patient into a coma.

But I must be sure.

"I need to talk to someone who knew him." I go back to the database and check for names of current attending physicians. One name matches my notes, Doctor Vincent Blake. "Blake! He knew Pederson! I need to talk to him."

"Dangerous, E. If he makes a call to that Hopkins place and finds out you ain't there..." Gippy's nervous, and for good reason.

If Blake gets curious and investigates my credentials, we could have trouble, but I hope to be long gone before that happens. I check the time; we've been here only forty minutes. "We should be okay. Bureaucracies react slowly to questions like that, *especially* universities and medical institutions. If Blake gets a straight answer in less than a day, I'd take vows and don a habit...again." What a mistake *that* had been.

"Donna who?" Gippy looks at me like I started speaking Greek.

"Sorry. I mean, become a nun, like Sister Janice." I shut down the computer, and we go to Blake's office.

My knock receives a pleasant, "Come!" We step in, and Blake looks up from his desk in surprise. "A problem, Doctor Winston?"

"Not at all! We're finished. I just copied what I needed to a flash drive, so we won't need to bother you all for so long. I do have one question, though."

He stands. "Of course. What can I help you with?"

"A physician who worked here some years ago seems to have completely fallen off the register. A Doctor Martin Pederson? I believe you worked here with him."

"Ah, yes, poor Martin." His face goes grave. "He left Our Lady after a tragic case with a young quadriplegic. He was convinced he killed the poor man."

"Killed him?" I can't resist digging deeper. "You mean the Caldwell case? I thought he just went into a coma."

Blake shook his head. "Complete brain death. Zero EEG. He lasted only a couple of weeks after the...procedure."

"Procedure? You mean the exorcism?" I watch for a reaction, but if there is one, it's subtle, and I feel only sorrow from him. "Was there some problem with the anesthesia?"

"No. Or at least we didn't think so at the time." He sighed and spread his hands. "I greave more for poor Martin than I ever did for Mister Caldwell. Such a brilliant clinician and so thoughtful. I'm afraid it destroyed him."

"And you have no idea where we might find him? I'd like to talk to him about some of his cases."

"No, Doctor, I'm afraid I don't. I'm sorry."

"Well, shoot." I sigh despondently, but at least I know that Pederson's the man we need to speak to...if he's still alive. "Thank you for everything, Father. We won't take any more of your time."

"It's been a pleasure, Doctor Winston, but do you mind if I ask *you* a question?"

I fight the urge to tense. "Not at all, Father." *Steady mind, center your thoughts, see everything.*

"If all you needed was electronic data, why not file a request by email and save yourself the trip?"

"Well, I..." I don't really have an answer and kick myself for not having one prepared. *You need to start thinking ahead, Empa.* "I wanted to..."

"You busted now, Doc!" Gippy laughs harshly and gives me a nudge. "Best fess up!"

"Fess up?" Blake gives him a look.

"She's got family out here, Winslow, Denver, Phoenix, and wanted to see 'em. Boss said it was okay as long as she drove her own car and didn't ask him to pay fer our food." He shrugs and grins. "So, we get to take a road trip and see the country, and I get to sleep on her cousin's couch." He laughs again, and Blake joins him.

Bless you, Gifford.

"Well, I can't blame you for that. I've family I haven't seen in...far too long." Blake extends a hand. "Where to next?"

"Phoenix, then Denver." I shake his hand and smile sheepishly. "An aunt and another cousin." I feel no more suspicion in him; he bought Gippy's story completely.

"Well, drive carefully. Winter's upon us, I'm afraid."

We're out of the building in ten minutes.

Gippy gets in the driver's seat because I'm already on my phone looking for anything I can find on Pederson. "Where to?"

"Back to Albuquerque. Someplace we can hole up and be invisible. We need to do some digging." One thing good about the Information Age: nothing is ever really deleted. If it happened, or someone *thought* it happened, it's on the net somewhere. "And well done on the story! Quick thinking."

"Thanks. Albuquerque, here we come!" He puts Mercy in gear and takes us out of the parking lot. "Think you can find this priest doctor dude?"

I'm already on my phone looking up his personal information. "Martin Pederson was only forty-one when he left Our Lady of Healing. He'd be sixty-three now. If he's still alive, I'll find him."

GIPPY NEVER THOUGHT he'd admit it, but he was *really* tired of greasy takeout food and being stuck in a motel room with an incredibly hot woman he had no desire to touch. At least they were back in Albuquerque and invisible. One more pimp and his meal ticket shackin' up in a crappy motel. But three days of it left him bored and frustrated.

Empa had bought him a phone, at least. She was glued to hers all day and night. He studied the literacy course as much as he could. Learning to read was fun, and the net had everything he wanted to know, if you could weed through the bullshit, but staring at the little screen for hours left him fidgety, eyesore, and even more frustrated. He needed to *do* something, and one thing, in particular, came to mind.

"Been thinkin'." Gippy got up and stretched.

"About?" She didn't even look up from her phone.

"Mercy needs new tags. If that Blake dude asked about you, or your naffie boyfriend in Joplin called 'em in, we could get pulled over."

She looked up from her phone. Even exhausted, her hair a mess, no makeup, sitting on the bed in that ugly flannel shirt and stretch pants, she was hotter than any woman had a right to be. That was another reason he needed to get out of the motel for a while. Unlike Jeri, he had no interest in Empa that way. Quite frankly, she freaked him out. But being locked in a room with her was wearing on him. He needed a break.

"You want to steal replacements?"

"Na. Just find a chop shop an' buy 'em." He grabbed the trench coat and shrugged into it.

"Won't that come up as stolen in the NAFAS system?"

"Maybe, but Father's name and our pics won't pop up." Gippy clipped the holstered Glock to his belt and started for the door.

"I should go with you." She got up.

"Na. I got this, E." The last thing he needed was her coming along. "You do your shit; I do mine. 'Kay?"

She pursed her lips. "I don't know, Gippy."

"Look, I gotta get outa here. Stuck here with you's drivin' me nuts."

She blinked, startled by his admission. "Okay, go, but be careful. No drugs, and no trouble."

"Trouble's the *last* thing I want, E." He hadn't taken a Vickie in two days and hadn't gotten the shakes. His cravings were next to nil. *Maybe that angel-daddy shit rubbing' off on me.* "I'll be fine. Back in an hour."

He started Mercy up and headed south. After three days on the net and making runs for food and supplies, he knew Albuquerque pretty well. Finding a chop shop was about as hard as finding his dick. He pulled into one that looked to specialize in foreign cars, if the chain-link junkyard full of scrapped hulks was any clue, and got out. They did a legit business here, too, of course. All the good shops did. He pulled the registration slip from the glove box, strolled up to the first bay, and waited to be noticed.

"'Sup?" A stocky dark-haired man stepped from behind a car he was working on, wiping his hands on a rag.

"Got any tags?"

"Some." The guy's eyes flicked to Mercy and back. "Fer that?"

"Yep."

"Maybe." He grinned and waved to a door. "Step inna my office, homey."

Two other mechanics watched him follow the man into a cluttered little office. One entire wall of the place was nothing but bins and file cabinets. A curvy Latina sat behind a desk mounded with paper. She inspected him from shoes to hair and smiled, her teeth insanely white against flaming red lipstick. For some reason, her smile made him uncomfortable.

She just see the money. Gippy shifted his shoulders in the jacket. He hadn't considered that he might get jacked for the fancy coat and the money in his pockets just like he tried to jack Empa. He did now. If they tried, he had a surprise for them. With nothing else to do, he'd been practicing drawing the Glock quickly.

"Fifty-two, right?" the man asked cocking an eyebrow.

"Yep."

The guy turned to the Latina. "Tag for a fitty-two four-door Mercedes DLA. White."

"No problema." She tapped away on a pad, smiling at Gippy again. "Texas okay?"

"Sure." Gippy didn't care where it came from.

"Score." She got up and stepped out from behind the desk.

She wore a thin old T-shirt, cut short and torn in a vee at the neck deep enough to show the swell of tan breasts. Her jeans were so tight and threadbare that little slips of tan skin pressed out between the white threads, the T of red underwear an inch above the hem, something in Spanish tattooed there. An image of Empa looking so fine and sharp in her getup flicked into his mind, and he thought, *Trashy.*

She pulled a drawer open and rooted through the hundreds of license plates inside, finally coming out with one. "Need a sticker?" She slapped the plate against her hip.

"Yeah." Gippy ignored her—or tried to—and turned to the guy. "How much?"

He frowned and shrugged. "Trade yours?"

"Sure."

"It hot?"

"Nope. Owned by a priest in Cincinnati. I even got a reg slip." Gippy pulled it from his pocket to show the guy.

"Legit?" The guy's eyes widened, suspicious. "No bullshit?"

"No bullshit."

The guy squinted at him. "Why you wanna new tag, homey?"

"Naffies might be lookin' for me." Gippy shrugged; it was a common enough problem these days.

"Lemme run a check on yours. If you straight up, I cut you a deal. Even throw in a bogus reg sheet with your ride's VIN on it."

"Deal." Gippy handed the reg slip to the woman.

His fingers brushed hers as the slip of paper passed, and he pulled back, feeling suddenly uncomfortable, like he'd touched something slimy. She just smiled at him. Gippy smiled back and waited while the guy went outside to pull the tag off Mercy's bumper, trying to ignore the woman's interest as she ran the search and affixed a new registration tag on the stolen plate.

"Well?" the guy asked as he came back in with Mercy's tag in hand.

"Squeaky clean." She smiled at Gippy again. "Reg'd to a priest in Cincinnati, just like he said. Course the naffies could be lookin' for it under our radar."

"Not my problem." The guy dropped the plate on the desk and turned to Gippy. "Two C, and we even."

"And you print me a new reg?" That was a good deal, almost too good.

"Sure, homey."

"Deal." Gippy peeled two C-notes off his roll and handed them over, but the guy just pointed to the woman behind the desk.

"Chaki handle the cash, homey, I just do the greasy shit." He grinned and took the new plate outside.

"So, you in town for a while?" The woman eyed him again as she took the cash and dropped it in a drawer.

"Nope. Passin' through." He didn't want anything to do with her.

"Too bad." She tapped on her pad, eyes still on him. A printer he couldn't see hummed behind the desk. "I could use a new boyfriend." She bent down and pulled the printed sheet, her shirt sagging open to expose her tits. Sitting back up, she tore out the perforated margin and held out the bogus registration. "Wanna party tonight before you gotta go?"

He took the slip, and again their fingers brushed. The thought of her made his skin crawl, but he bit back the visceral response. "Na. Got a girl-friend." He shrugged and tucked the new registration in his pocket.

She ran her tongue over her upper lip, long red nails teasing a taut nipple under her shirt. "We could all three of us play."

Persistent bitch. He snorted a laugh at the thought of bringing Chaki back to the motel. "Don't think so. She the jealous type. Chew you up and spit you out."

She frowned at him, suddenly cold.

Gippy didn't care. He left the office without another thought of her. Outside, the guy was just finishing up with the new tag. Gippy waited to shake his hand, feeling uncomfortable, antsy, like he should get on the road. "Thanks, man."

"My pleasure, homey. I'm Ernesto." The man's grip felt like warm iron. "You need anything else, let me know."

"Won't be in town long enough, but thanks." Gippy got in and drove off, mission accomplished, money saved, and Mercy now as invisible as he was.

He checked the time; he still had half an hour. *No drugs and no trouble...* The thought of going back to sit in that room with Empa for more endless frustrating hours had zero appeal. The memory of Chaki and a sudden surge of petulance tightened his grip on the wheel. *Goddamn women. Why they always gotta be like that?* Jeri, Empa, Chaki. They all seemed hypersexual all the time, stuffing it in his face so he couldn't ignore it. Guys were different, familiar, less alien. Memories of Lennie dredged up a longing in him that no woman could understand or fulfill.

No drugs, no trouble... Really shouldn't, but...

Gippy cruised Barelas until he found what he was looking for. It didn't take long. He pulled slowly up to the curb in front of a slim Latino in tight jeans and a crop top tee, and rolled down the passenger window.

"Whassup, homey?" The trick leaned in the window, flashing white teeth.

"Not much. Just shoppin'." Gippy shifted in his seat. *Really shouldn't but... She didn't say no sex.* "How much for a little lip service."

"You, sweetie? I'd do you for free, but my chulo a bitch." He licked his lips. They were nice lips. "Where you wanna go?"

"Just drive 'round."

"C-note?"

Gippy grinned. "Step inna my office, homey." He was starting to like Albuquerque and having money didn't suck. The trick got in, and he pulled away from the curb.

18

LAWYERS, GUNS, AND MONEY

Gippy's quiet when he gets back, troubled in some way, but I really don't have time right now to find out why. The search for Pederson has led me on a merry chase through the seediest dens of the ultranet. I'm glad my phone's IP is encrypted.

Martin Pederson didn't just fall from grace; he took an express elevator. His plummet was so precipitous, in fact, I wonder if there mightn't have been a Nephilim or some other minion of Hell behind it. I didn't find anything solid on that score, but I'm still suspicious.

A year after leaving Our Lady of Healing, he picked up alcohol and drug abuse. His physician's license allowed him access to prescription drugs, which led to him dealing, which earned him his first arrest. His brief stay in prison didn't yield much in the way of information, but he must have made some interesting acquaintances. After his release, he took up his old ways, but focused on making money, not simply destroying himself. Another arrest and a longer stay in prison, but this time it changed him in a different way.

He came out deeply depressed and began associating with a doomsday cult that had arisen with the slow-motion global ecological disaster. The United States, Canada, Mexico, and the countries of Central America were merging into NAFAS at that time. Although federal law enforcement was following this cult, there were only minor interventions. Again, I wonder if the Nephilim encouraged its spread, for their message reeks of Hell's involvement. The last I found of Pederson was five years ago in New Jersey. He had a minor brush with law enforcement but was let go when a cult lawyer accused the officers of religious persecution. The cult has a major stronghold in the half-drowned remains of Manhattan. The net has given me everything it can. If I'm going to pick up his trail, I'll need to start a physical search.

"How did it go?" I log off and get up, working the kinks out of my back.

"No problem. Mercy's got a new Texas tag and reg." He starts to shrug out of his jacket, his eyes evading mine, his mood prickly. "Cost three C's, but she's invisible now."

I'm too preoccupied to worry about his evasion. I check the time. "Don't get too comfortable; we're leaving as soon as I get cleaned up."

"Find somethin'?"

"I won't know until we get there. It means a lot of driving. Pederson got involved with a doomsday cult called The Church of the Coming Dark." I start going through the bag, pulling out what I need. "He's fallen completely off-grid, but one of their primary enclaves is in Manhattan. He was there five years ago."

"Man-what? Where's that?"

I look at him, baffled by his ignorance. "Are you joking?"

He looks blankly at me, his lips tight with annoyance.

"New York City?"

"Heard of New York. Thought it was a state." He frowns and again looks away from me.

Annoyance? Guilt? Shame? It's hidden, but there, and it catches me off guard. Gippy's been uneasy with the inactivity, but this is new. *Not now, Empa. You can sort it out later.* "It *is* a state, but it was also a city, the biggest on the east coast. Most of it's underwater now, but some people still live there. This cult thrives in places like this; ruins, drowned cities, devastated areas, Houston, Jacksonville, Vancouver. They've carved out quite a little empire in what's left of Manhattan. If we go there, we might find Pederson."

"So, more drivin', huh?"

"Unfortunately, a lot more." I bundle my clothes and grab my phone. "And I'm afraid of what we'll find when we get there. Pederson was on a downward spiral. I pray he's still alive."

"You pray, I'll get our shit together." He reaches for our bag.

I feel more annoyance from him, but ignore it. "We'll have one stop before we leave town, and that'll mean jacket and tie for you. We need a few things if we're going to deal with people like this."

Now he looks worried. "Like what?"

"Lawyers, guns, and money, my friend." I head for the bathroom.

"Lawyers?" He obviously doesn't get the reference.

I glance back as I close the door and give him a smile. "Don't worry, G. I got this. You do your shit, I do mine, right?"

He snorts in disgust at having his own line thrown back at him. "Right."

I crank on the hot water and make the call. My phone's encryption key gets me into my lawyer's secure line, and a single flat tone sounds. "Voiceprint: Epsilon minus three whiskey alpha tango plus twelve."

"Processing." The voice is synthetic. Digital lawyers are the best kind; they don't argue and never skim more than their requisite ten percent. I peel out of my clothes and test and adjust the water while I wait. "Accepted. Submit query."

"One hundred thousand North American dollars in certified Swiss bullion to nearest branch, Albuquerque, New Mexico. Pickup today."

"Processing." A shorter wait. "Confirmed. Sending encrypted receipt voucher."

The call ends. I glance at the phone's screen. The voucher arrives along with the location of the bank where the money will be waiting. I smile, drop the phone on my clothes, and get into the shower. I murmur the old Warren Zevon song as I let the hot spray wash away three days in a motel room.

Gippy's behind the wheel waiting when I step out of the room, wearing his jacket and tie, our bag in the back seat. I smile to myself; he really does look like a young professional, even if his tie is still tied wrong. I get in, and the scent of cheap cologne hits me. Either Gippy has added an olfactory element to his disguise, or someone else has been in the car. Someone who wears way too much Polo. This piques my curiosity.

"Where to?"

"A bank." I turn on the nav app and tap the address in.

"A *bank*?" He blinks at me. "Gonna *rob* it?"

For a moment, I can't decide if he's joking or serious. "No, just make a withdrawal." I explain how I have money transferred.

As we drive, I start picking out our route to Manhattan, cringe, and change to a more southerly alternative. St. Louis is out of the question.

Fire... blood... screams... The southern route, Oklahoma City, Little Rock, Memphis, and Nashville, raises no alarms in my memory. About thirty hours on the road, two fuel stops at least, but the trip worries me less than our arrival. Getting anything from the Church of the Coming Dark will be dangerous, if not impossible. *Daniel in the lion's den.*

"So, what's the money for?"

"For finding Martin Pederson." I drop my phone on the seat. "There are two tactics for dealing with religious fanatics, Gippy: bribery or intimidation, sometimes both at once. That means money and weapons, though I doubt we'll be able to fight the entire Church of the Coming Dark." I fix him with a meaningful stare. "This will be dangerous."

"We already got guns."

"Not enough."

"Okay, bank for the money. Where we gonna get more guns?"

"Texas. Amarillo's our first stop. I know a place there that'll have what we need."

"Anythin' you *don't* know?"

"Quite a lot." I need to figure out why he's in such a mood. The cologne reek in the car is starting to give me a headache, so I crack a window. Then it hits me: *uncomfortable, short-tempered, embarrassed, reeking of cologne...* "For instance, I don't know how to find stolen license plates, or chop shops, or Latinos who wear too much cologne."

Gippy stares at me open-mouthed. "How—"

"You're *driving*, Gippy!"

He snaps back to the road, jerking the wheel to correct our drifting course. Fortunately, traffic is light. I should have known better than to broach the subject while he's driving.

"I'm sorry. I didn't mean to startle you."

"How the fuck you know?"

"Deduction. You're uncomfortable and the car reeks of cheap men's cologne." I shrug casually, trying to put him at ease. "You're young, Gippy. Seeking sexual gratification is normal. There's nothing wrong with it, as long as you're careful and nobody gets hurt."

"I...I couldn't do it."

"What?" Now it's my turn to gape at him. I've been sensing his sexual frustration like a background itch for a while. I thought he might scratch that itch eventually. "Why not?"

"Wanted to, but..." He frowns, gripping the wheel hard, embarrassment and guilt flowing from him in waves. The phone squawks instructions, and he follows them mechanically. "Shit complicated."

Anguish, loss, guilt, anger... I understand; too near his loss. "*Life* is complicated."

"Ain't for you!" He glances at me, an accusative glare and a flash of anger.

What's gotten into him? "What in God's name gives you that idea?"

"Kiddin' me?" Another accusative glance. "You got it all. Money, looks, mad skills, women, men, whatever you fuckin' want."

"Gippy, I'm not going to explain my life to you, but you're wrong. You see what I do, what I have, and you think it came easily. It didn't. It came with blood, heartbreak, and more years of loneliness, more loss, more pain than you will *ever* know in your lifetime."

"Oh, *fuck* you, E! You think I don't know pain?" He's shaking with rage now, and I'm afraid he's going to get in an accident.

God, please... I don't' have time for this. But then I realize I *do* have time, and this is important. Martin Pederson has been off the grid for years, and the Nephilim will be hunting me until I die. Gippy is troubled, confused, and angry with me right now, and I can't afford to alienate him.

"Pull over, please, Gippy. We need to straighten this out."

"Ain't nothin' to straighten out!"

"There *is*! You offered to *help* me, Gifford, and I *need* your help! You've made that obvious. Now *please* pull over so I can explain."

"Explain what?" Still, he doesn't pull over. His fear tingles along my nerves. Fear of me, fear of the truth, fear of me learning what I already know about him.

"It's not about you, Gippy; it's about *me*. I need to show you where I'm coming from here. Please."

Finally, he complies, pulling over to the curb. He jams the car into park and folds his arms defensively, refusing to look at me. "So, explain."

"Your loss is still acute, the pain sharp, I understand that. You're lonely and frustrated and sought solace in—"

"Stop usin' fancy shit words I don't know! What the fuck is so-lace?"

I grit my teeth. *Separated by a common language.* "What happened with Lennie is hurting you. You miss him and feel...like it's your fault he's dead. You can't feel better by having sex with strangers, and that makes you feel worse."

"Thought you said this was about you, not me."

"It *is* about me." A deep breath. It would be so much easier if I could just dump my memories into him, but I don't think he'll trust me to do that, and it might push him over the edge. "I don't know how to tell you this, but that pain will never go away. I've felt that pain and worse. You shot Lennie and think it was your fault, and even though it was an accident, it *was* your fault as well as his *and* mine." He finally looks at me, shaking with a hundred pent-up emotions. "I've *also* killed people I loved, Gippy. Not by accident. With my own hands."

His face slackens. "What?"

"I've killed...murdered...to save people I love from far worse; torture, rape, torment. It's happened more than once. Men, women...*children* even." I close my eyes... *Masada, Krakow, St. Louis... faces, tears, wailing, pleading.* "I carry the pain of those deaths in me still. So, *believe* me when I say I know what you're feeling."

"How..." He sniffs, his lip trembling. "How you live with that?"

"*Love*, Gippy." He blinks at me, uncomprehending. "I love people, *all* people. Every once in a while, I'm lucky enough to be loved back. What I did for Jeri helped me more than it helped her. She's a good soul. I never thanked you for that, but if you hadn't told me to go to her, I wouldn't have. But what I did for that hate-filled man in Joplin was *also* good for me because I could *help* him. I took the poison from his soul and gave him hope. And with *his* hope, *I* feel hope."

"Can you...do that with me? Take it all away?"

"I can't take your memories, and I don't think you'd want me to, but I can show you what it is to love and be loved." He looks startled, starts to draw back, and I realize his misconception. "Not sex, Gippy. That's different and something we probably shouldn't share. I mean love like a mother for a child, like *God's* love."

His eyes are wide with fear. "How?"

I hold out a hand. "Just take my hand, look into my eyes, and trust me."

Gippy sat in the idling Mercedes, waiting for Empa to finish inside the bank, feeling once again like his soul had been wrung out. The memories were still there, that horrible night, the gun firing, the look of shock on Lennie's face, and earlier, his sisters both gone, his mother screaming obscenities, finding her with the needle still in her arm. But there was something else there, too. Something he couldn't understand because he'd forgotten what love was.

Lennie... Jeri... and yes, Empa and Father Emil. People he cared about and who cared for him. Distant memories of his mother and sisters, the few good times when they were fed and happy, playing silly games together, watching TV, laughing. He'd felt like this when he woke up in the rectory after the OD, but something had happened, and he'd forgotten. Now that feeling had been unlocked inside him, and *she* had opened it. He'd never really doubted what Empa was, but feeling her wring out his soul like that had changed the way he thought about her, about life, death, and what would come after. It had changed the way he thought of himself.

Empa had been quiet afterward, like she'd done something taxing, and Gippy had been too stunned to talk. She'd told him to stay in the car and went into the bank alone like he was the getaway driver or something. He checked the time, suddenly worried, but it had only been ten minutes.

She came out of the bank looking like she always looked, but he saw her differently now. She wasn't just a poised, beautiful, badass woman; she wasn't a woman at all. She wasn't human. She was *more*. And *he* was more because of her.

She got in and looked at him. "You okay?"

"Yeah." He nodded. "Just feel...weird. You?"

"I'm fine, but there's something you need to know, Gippy." She sounded worried.

"What now?" Her tone sent alarm bells up his spine. "Got the money, didn't you?"

"Yes. That's not it." She pulled her pistol from under the seat—banks didn't allow weapons inside—and tucked it into her jacket. "Go ahead and drive, but I want to ask you some questions about the people you met while you were out."

"Sure." He pulled out of the parking lot and onto the street, heading toward the interstate.

"Tell me about this man you picked up. What happened exactly."

"Well, after I got Mercy's tag, I felt like maybe I deserved a little fun, ya know." He told her about the prostitute and the failed attempt. "Dunno what happened. I wanted to, and he was... Well, you know."

"Sexually attractive."

"Hot, yeah, but when he...I just couldn't." He gripped the wheel hard. "I kept thinkin' 'bout Lennie. Made me mad."

"And after, what happened?"

"Oh, he was all like sorry and kinda pissed, but not really. I paid him and dropped him off."

"Good." She took a deep breath. "Did you feel angry, too? Like you wanted to…blame him? Hurt him?"

Gippy thought back and frowned. "More pissed at myself, but…yeah. Some. Why?"

"Because that wasn't you, Gippy. That was something else."

The cold chill down his spine intensified. "What you mean?"

"I'll explain, but tell me about the people you met at the chop shop."

He told her about Emanuel and Chaki, how she came on to him, wanted to party. How she seemed trashy to him, slimy, made his skin crawl.

"And did she touch you?"

He looked at his hand. "Yeah. Twice. It felt…"

"Wrong, dirty, tainted."

"Yeah." He glanced at her. "What?"

"She was a succubus, Gippy."

"Suck my *what*?"

Empa barked a laugh. "You're lucky she didn't! A succubus is a demon, Gippy. You remember I spoke about how they're different than Nephilim?"

"Yeah, but I thought…like, horns and a fuckin' *tail*, or somethin'."

"No, unfortunately. A succubus is a human woman possessed by a minion of Hell, either willingly or forced. If she'd *really* gotten a grip on you, I'm afraid what might have happened."

"Mutha *fuck*!" He felt cold, as if an icy hand had just grabbed his testicles and squeezed hard.

"Just their touch is dangerous. That's how they begin to corrupt humans, and that's probably why you had the impulse to seek out sex, but you resisted the urge to pervert the sensual act, as is their impulsion."

He snorted and shook his head. "E, why can't you just say shit in simple words?"

"Sorry. Her touching you made you horny and angry, even violent, but you didn't hurt the trick like she wanted you to. You resisted." She smiled at him. "You're *good*, Gippy. Her corruption couldn't take hold of you."

"'Cause you…fixed it, right? You took it away." They reached the freeway, and he took the onramp.

"Yes, but the corruption was already dying." She sighed and leaned back in the seat. "Eventually, you would have destroyed it on your own."

"So, if you was there, would you of known about her?"

160

"Maybe. If I touched her, certainly, but she'd probably have spotted me, too, so it was better that I wasn't with you."

"Huh." He frowned, thinking back. "Thought it was the money."

"Thought *what* was the money?"

"Why she was comin' on to me. You know."

"I'm afraid it was your *soul*, not your money that she wanted, Gippy."

He barked a laugh. "Bitch *starve* to death eatin' *my* soul!"

"Don't sell yourself short." She smiled at him again. "You have a *beautiful* soul."

He didn't know what to say except, "Yeah...well, thanks."

"You're welcome." She leaned back and closed her eyes. "And don't sell yourself short in the looks department, either. You clean up nice and have a kind of a broody Will Smith thing going on."

"Who?"

"An actor who was popular a while ago. You can look him up when you're not driving." She reclined her seat. "Wake me when we're in Texas."

"Will do." Her eyes were closed, so he pulled his phone and looked up the name. A picture popped up, and he glanced at it. *My ears really look like that?*

———

As MERCY STRUGGLED up the Sandia ridge, behind the desk in Emanuel's chop shop, the beast behind Chaki's eyes glared down at her fingertips, wondering what exactly it had felt. Never in a thousand years and all the humans it had possessed had Duvara felt anything quite like the boy's touch. It smoldered in her like an unspent orgasm. Slowly, she brought her fingers to her lips, tasting the minuscule traces of him there.

Angel touched... A cruel smile graced her lips. *That's why he could resist me.*

She reached for her phone and tapped in a number she never thought she'd call. A female voice answered.

"Yes?"

"Daughter of Ariquiel. I have something for you."

19

THE HOUNDS OF HELL

I step out of the Waffle House bathroom and know instantly we're in trouble. Blue and yellow lights strobe in the parking lot, and Gippy sits in the far corner booth trying not to look terrified.

Steady... They might not be after us. I walk the length of the restaurant toward our table, taking in the scene in the parking lot. A NAFAS cruiser sits outside the windows near the door, two troopers standing by the Mercedes. A second NAFAS cruiser pulls into the lot and lights up, parking behind our car.

They're after us.

What the hell went wrong? Our trip so far has gone smoothly, the purchases in Amarillo and a stop for sleep in Oklahoma City uneventful. I started teaching Gippy the rudiments of Musashi's lessons, the philosophy of the Five Rings. He takes in new ideas like a sponge absorbs water. We spent the day at a gun range and made the seven hours to Memphis without incident. The city's big enough to make us invisible. Gippy catches my eye and glances to the service door behind me. *Run?* There is too much in the car that we need. I shake my head minutely and take a seat at the end of the counter instead of joining him.

Pick your position; fields of fire, cover, elevation, observation, escape routes. Never box yourself in. I thank Sergeant Gattish once again, and his insistence that even medics in his unit are trained in tactics. *Sand and blood, torture and beheadings, all in the name of God.* I snap back to task, swallowing my memories of the war. *Steady spirit...*

It's too late to avoid getting cornered, and the floor-to-ceiling windows offer zero cover, but from my seat, I can see well, and the counter shields me from the door. Missing my Kevlar coat, I slip a hand behind my back, release the Velcro strap on my holster, and loosen the Glock.

Two more troopers get out of the new arrival and clip short automatic carbines to their vests. The first two turn to speak to them, and I see they're similarly armed. They tap on wrist pads and talk into communications gear, looking down at the back of the Mercedes. They try the doors, but they're locked.

Not good. Something's gone horribly wrong, maybe the plate, but I can't worry about that now. I have to deal with the consequences. We're trapped here, but we need our car. The officers might or might not have our descriptions. They'll come in and find us, arrest us, or maybe even gun us down. *No way out, Empa.* Even if we could get to Mercy, we could never outrun the NAFAS cruisers. That leaves only one option. *More blood on my hands...*

I order coffee.

"Thought you was sittin' with yer boyfrien'," the waitress says as she fills my cup.

"Ain't my boyfriend, and I'm pissed at him."

"Too bad. He's cute." She doesn't seem upset by the NAFAS. Maybe they roust out-of-state plates all the time.

I doubt we're that lucky.

A few of the other customers gawk at the lights. I sip my coffee as the troopers converse. I wonder if any are Nephilim, but they're too far for me to feel anything, and the glass door blocks me anyway. The two new arrivals turn and approach the restaurant. I read a menu as they pause at the door and scan the tables and stools through the windows. Besides Gippy and me, there are only five other customers, one waitress, and a cook. It's late.

They come in, hands on their weapons, and look around again.

"Evenin' officers," the waitress says. "What can I get you?"

The troopers ignore her. I feel nothing but festering belligerence from them. They might not be Nephilim, but they are most certainly sent by my enemies. *The hordes of Persia, Roman centurions, the Third Reich, all unwitting pawns to darker forces, the Hounds of Hell, sent forth into slaughter.*

My choices are few, the equation simple; kill or be killed. I didn't live five thousand years by being a pacifist.

"Who owns the Mercedes?" one of the troopers asks loudly.

Everyone looks up, so I do, too, trying to look bewildered and concerned. We all look at them, then at each other. Shrugs from some, and two men who came in together mutter something low. Not many people are eager to cooperate with NAFAS; their record on public relations isn't good.

One of the troopers turns to the two men. "What's that?"

"Nothin'." The man facing them frowns and looks down. "Didn't see who parked it."

The trooper who spoke steps over to their table while the other watches the rest of the place. "Which car's yours?"

"The Tez Lightning. Plugged in right there." The guy points, and the trooper turns away to glare at the other customers.

"Everybody, put your keys on the table in front of you." He points his weapon at the table between the two men. "You first."

The man pulls a ring of keys from his pocket and drops it noisily on the table. The other trooper's eyes linger on me, and I smile sweetly. He looks away. I'm invisible. *Thank you, Gippy.*

The first trooper picks up the keys, inspects them, and drops them on the table. He steps up to the next table, a woman and her young son. "Keys."

"Leave us alone!" the boy snaps.

The carbine comes up to point at the boy. I tense—*not the child, please God, not the child*—but I don't have a clear shot, not with his body armor, and the other trooper would kill me.

"Don't be brave, you little puke." He faces the woman, but the gun remains aimed at the boy. "Keys! Now! Unless you want to see this little shit's brains!"

She digs in a handbag and hands over her keys. After a glance, he drops them on her table.

He turns to the waitress, the muzzle of his weapon raising to clear the counter. "You, too."

"My stuff's in the back, and I ride the bus anyways." Her eyes are fixed on the gun, wide, terrified. "I got no car."

"You?" The weapon twitches toward the cook, a massive African American man.

He raises his big hands. "I got no ride, officer."

The trooper looks at the other single man at the counter, and the customer dangles his keys. "Ford coal-burner, right there." He points to a big pickup truck.

I'm next. When he walks down the counter to me, I slide off my stool and smile at him. "I'm hoofin' it. Workin' the strip." I slip my coat off my shoulders to my elbows as if displaying my wares and wink at him. "Wanna *search* me, officer?"

"Shut up and get out of my way, whore." He turns to Gippy.

Invisible... Last mistake you'll ever make. The other trooper's attention has shifted to Gippy, too. I shrug into my coat and pull my Glock, keeping it below the counter.

"You, punk. Keys!"

"Sure." Gippy pulls our big ring of keys with the rabbit's foot from the trench coat pocket and drops them on the table. I can see the Mercedes key on the ring from here.

"You little *fucker*!" The trooper reaches for the keys, but his fingers never touch them.

Bullets rip up through the table as Gippy unloads, and the trooper staggers back.

I can't take the time to see how badly the trooper is hit. I'm too busy taking aim on the other before he can bring his weapon to bear. While screams and chaos erupt, I put four careful rounds into the trooper, two center mass, one head shot, and one at the joint of his helmet and body armor. Blood sprays the window behind him. I'm over the counter before he hits the floor. As I roll, I notice Gippy's on the floor beside the first trooper, but I can't tell if he's shot. I don't remember hearing any fire other than ours but I might have missed it.

As my feet hit the floor behind the counter, all hell breaks loose. Busts of fire from the parking lot send glass spraying. More screams, curses, the child's high-pitched wail. *Please, God, not the child...* I scramble past the waitress and the cook, both of whom have the good sense to lie flat. Bullets tear through the counter behind me.

"You alive, E?" Gippy shouts.

God, it's good to hear his voice. "For now!" We need cover, and there's only one thing nearby that will stop a rifle bullet. "Behind the cruiser, Gippy! When I fire. Ready?"

"*Fuck* yeah!"

"Go!" I rise to level my weapon across the counter and find myself staring into the dead eyes of the man who sat there. *Blood on my hands...*

Collateral damage... Fire bombs ripping through residential streets to destroy Germany's ability to manufacture weapons. Not your fault, Empa! You didn't kill him! The troopers are shooting at anything that moves.

As I lay down suppressive fire, the body jerks with more incoming rounds. Shattered Formica sprays up, and bullets clang against the metal grill behind me. Muzzle flashes traverse from my left to right as Gippy runs at a crouch. He's firing one of the troopers' carbines, spraying glass, lead, and harsh language. Good boy.

Movement to my right as I duck back, the door to the bathroom opening. I risk a glance. The woman with the young boy backs through the door, sheltering him, a small pistol in her hand and her eyes wide with panic. The other two men from the table are on the floor, but I can't tell if they're wounded, dead, or just hunkering. The cook is crawling toward the service door. The waitress is lying flat with her hands over her head. *Please no more killed because of me...*

I reload and scramble for a new spot, stepping carefully past the waitress. "Gippy?"

"I'm good!" He sounds remarkably calm.

Thank God. I gauge my position to be in line behind the parked cruiser by the lack of bullet holes in the counter. I'll have a good position if I don't get shot going over it.

If.

"Give me some cover fire, Gippy."

"Ready!"

"Now!" I wait for his first round and lunge up to roll over the counter.

Gippy blind fires one-handed around the side of the NAFAS cruiser, and both troopers return fire from behind their own. What little glass isn't already shattered disintegrates, and more rounds ping into the metal behind me. I plant a shoulder against the grille of the cruiser as Gippy dumps his spent magazine and reloads. The trooper's carbine lays at his feet, presumably empty. I have one more magazine, and Gippy should have two.

"Are the other two dead?"

"Didn't ask 'em."

"If they answer, shoot them again."

He stares at me. "How can you *joke?*"

"Gallows humor. You laugh, or you lose your shit and die!" He looks at me with disbelief in his eyes, and I see the blood. "You're hit."

"Huh?"

I touch the side of his face and show him my bloody fingertips. "Let me see."

"Fuck it. I ain't dyin'." He peeks over the hood, and a burst of fire pings against the back of the car. "We're *fucked*, E. They're shootin' from behind their car, and we shootin' from behind this one. Got nowhere to go."

He's got a point, and I have little doubt more hounds are on the way. *Gotta move, E!* I lean my head against the grille and try to think. The big cruiser's engine throbs against my temple. It's running. I glance up and check the angles to the other cruiser. *Maybe...*

"I've got to get in this car, Gippy, but they'll shoot me if I show myself. I need you to make them duck."

"Runnin' low on ammo."

"Grenade."

He looks at me like he did when I told him about the succubus. "No shit?"

"No shit. The flash-bang. Just don't roll it too far. We need Mercy in one piece."

"Okay." He fishes into a pocket and comes out with the grenade. "Wha'chu gonna do."

"I'm going to bring the fight to them." I tap the grille of the cruiser and holster my weapon. "Follow me. Use the car for cover. When they break cover, take them down."

He looks doubtful. "Sure 'bout this, E?"

"*Fuck* no." I say a short prayer in my head. *No high spirit, no low spirit, steady spirit.* "Do it."

"Okay." Gippy puts his pistol down, pulls the pin from the grenade, and picks the Glock back up. A glance over the hood elicits a burst of fire that cracks against the Armorglass of the back window. He lobs the grenade over the cruiser, and I hear it rattle against the pavement. I close my eyes, open my mouth, and cover my ears, but even so, the concussion rattles my teeth. I hope it did more than that to our opponents, but I can't check to make sure.

I'm up and to the driver's door in a second, my ears ringing. I stagger against the door as it opens—the explosion must have affected my equilibrium—and flop into the seat. Bullets ping against the inside of the door as I close it. The troopers aren't as rattled as I'd hoped. The rearview shows me muzzle flashes over the hood and trunk of the other cruiser. I slam the car into reverse and smoke the tires, aiming right at the flashes.

The impact slams me back against the seat, and I'm out the door and drawing my weapon.

Strange details register: my knees are weak, my grip on the Glock slippery, my ears ringing. The passenger door of the other cruiser is smashed in, the car flung sideways about six feet. Its lights are still flashing, the colors intense, pretty. I round the front of the smashed cruiser, firing at the dark form of the trooper flung back by the impact. Gunfire from my left. Gippy. I find my weapon empty and reach for my last magazine. It's slippery. I'm on my knees without knowing how I got there.

My hands, pistol, and magazine are slick with blood.

My blood.

Shit.

My weapon clatters to the pavement, and I catch myself before I do a face plant. I cough an astonishing amount of blood, frothy and bright red in the streetlights. *Lung, pulmonary artery, bleeding out...* I try to breathe and cough again. The pavement hits me hard, shoulder, temple, hip. I'm staring at the destroyed face of the trooper I just killed, flesh torn to pieces by hollow-point rounds. He's young, and his one remaining eye is blue. *Blood on my hands...* I wonder if he was a good boy, if his mother is proud of him, if he even knew he was one of Hell's minions. Will God tell him, or will the Serpent?

"E!"

Something touches me, a hand on my shoulder. Gippy.

"Oh, fuck, *fuck!*" He rolls me onto my back, and I try to scream as the pain finally arrives. Nothing comes out of my mouth but blood. Gippy looks terrified, his face contorted, bloody, but he's alive. "E, don't! Don't die. I don't know...what to do!"

"C...ar. Drive." I cough again. My lung is filling with blood. I don't have long. *Not to Heaven will I go without a hand to send me there.* "Go."

"*Fuck* that!" He looks angry, and I feel his hands moving me.

I black out as he lifts and wake up in the Mercedes, sitting in the passenger's seat. We're moving. Street lights passing. Trees and houses. A residential area. I'm breathing, sort of. Wet, gurgling sounds. I cough again, weakly, and blood dribbles from my chin.

"E? You alive?" A hand on my shoulder.

"Stu-pid question." I cough again. Pain and horrible weakness. *Don't talk; just breathe.* I'm not dead, but I've got a bullet in my chest, a collapsed lung, and the left pleural space is probably full of blood. I haven't bled out, so I probably won't, but if blood fills my other lung, I'll suffocate.

"I've gotta jack a car, E. Mercy's on their radar now. That bitch Chaki must have ratted us out."

He's thinking, not panicking. *Good boy.* I breathe carefully, trying not to cough. *Don't want to knock a blood clot loose.* Decades of medical training...sucking chest wound, pneumothorax, lacerated pulmonary artery. I need an Asherman dressing, then a chest tube, but I'm not likely to get either one.

We pull over behind an ancient and rusty SUV. "We get outta town, I'll find someplace to hole up."

I try to tell him something, but he's out of the car now. I must have blacked out for a moment, can't remember what I wanted to ask. He's into the SUV in a flash—*mad skills with a slim jim*—then he's back and shifting our gear into the other vehicle. I hear the groan of the trunk opening, the clatter of metal, curses, then my door opens.

"Can you walk, E?"

I can barely breathe. I move my head back and forth weakly.

"Okay. Just hang on. Gotta lift ya." He leans in and unclips my seatbelt, slips his arms under my knees and back, grunting with the effort. I wonder if moving me will dislodge a blood clot, but I can't protest. He's right; we need to flee, find someplace safe. *Safe... A flash of memory, a small boat, beautiful water, sand, bronze skin in the sun... Another lifetime.* I black out, then I'm sitting in the passenger seat of the SUV. We're driving again. I close my eyes, wondering if they'll ever open again.

Not to Heaven without a hand to send me...

GIPPY JACKED ANOTHER RIDE, a dull gray Buick coal-emulsion burner parked under a dead street light in a dodgy neighborhood, and drove it back to where he'd stashed the SUV. He was afraid to open the passenger door but found Empa breathing weakly, though deathly pale.

Time to get invisible again.

A roll of paper towels and a bottle of water cleaned up most of the blood on his face and staunched the flow from the shallow cut above his ear. There was way too much blood in the passenger seat to clean up, but he wiped the worst off Empa's face and neck and lifted her into the Buick's cavernous back seat, laying her on her side. He shifted their gear and got some clean clothes and a towel from the bag. He also filled his pockets with magazines for his Glock.

One of the blades from the duster sliced the back of Empa's vinyl jacket, and he caught his breath. Clotted blood covered her back. The hole barely oozed now, bubbling with her gurgling breaths. Wiping it clean and slapping on five long strips of duct tape was the best he could do for a bandage, and the tape didn't want to stick very well. He draped the heavy coat over her, changed into clean clothes, got in, and drove. As a final precaution before they left the city, he traded plates with another big gray car. Still, he stayed off the main thoroughfares.

Cameras...fucking cameras everywhere.

He drove out of Memphis on a back road, knowing the naffies would be watching the freeway. They'd have their pictures from the Waffle House, might have them all over the net by now. Checking his phone to make sure they were headed in the right direction, he kept driving until the land got swampy and dark, flat country full of drowned farmland. On the edge of a dingy little town, he pulled over to a ramshackle roadside motel and parked behind it. Waking the manager at three in the morning might draw attention, so he decided to wait. He checked Empa, found her breathing but cold. He piled all their clothes on her, got in the front seat, and let the car idle with the heater on. He went to sleep with his Glock in his lap.

The thunderous roar of a tractor-trailer braking into town snapped Gippy awake to sunlight. The little town looked even dodgier in the daylight, which was fine with him. He checked the time: 8:30. The car still ran with half a tank of fuel. Empa lay in the back seat, pale, breathing, and warm to the touch. She didn't wake, which worried him, but breathing and warm was better than not breathing and cold.

He took his suit jacket, made sure there was no blood on his face or hands, and walked to the office.

A surly old woman answered the bell, squinting at him through thick, dirty Armorglass. "What you want?"

He nodded to her, keeping the injured side of his head away from her. "Need a room."

"Check-in ain't till noon."

"I'll pay for last night, too." He pulled the roll of cash from his pocket. "And tomorrow night. The room on the end there."

She frowned and squinted down the empty parking lot. "Where's your car?"

"Out back. Got in last night and didn't want to wake nobody, but the street traffic was keepin' me awake."

"Just you?"

"Me an' my girl. She's sleepin'."

She frowned again, looking at him, his clothes, and the money in his hand. "Two thousand."

Gippy would have argued at the ridiculous price, but he didn't care about the money. He peeled off two crisp T-notes and slid them through the slot. She ran them through a machine, frowned—he doubted her face could make any other expression—and passed him the key card.

"No funny bid-ness."

"No, ma'am." He went back to the car and drove it around the front, parking beside the room. A quick check made sure the key worked and the room was unoccupied and reasonably clean. It smelled musty, like a chain-smoker had lived there for a month, but it had a bathroom and a bed. Right now, that was all that mattered. He draped the duster on the bed and returned to the car.

Getting Empa out of the back seat proved a lot harder than getting her in. Her eyes fluttered, and she moaned a little as he sat her up, but she didn't really wake. If the surly woman in the office saw him carry her in, she might call the naffies, but she didn't look the type to want that kind of trouble. He'd paid her four times what the room was worth; that should satisfy her curiosity. Waiting until there were no cars passing, he hoisted Empa up in his arms and made it through the door in six steps. He lay her down on the bed on top of the coat—*probably not very comfortable, with all the stuff in the pockets*—until he could get her cleaned up. That would take a long time, so he brought in all their stuff and moved the car back out of sight.

Gippy was right; cleaning her up and getting her into bed took a long time, innumerable trips back and forth from the bathroom with damp towels, soaking them clean in the tub and wringing them out. He decided to leave his makeshift bandage in place. One bout of coughing when he rolled her onto her right side worried him, but it subsided when he finally got her propped up on the pillows. It also concerned him that she didn't wake up. He'd seen her recover from injuries in a few hours before. Why not this time?

He threw her ruined clothes into the tub and ran water on them, adding soap from their stash. They were trashed but throwing bloody clothes away might draw attention. It took another hour to clean up the place, then his own clothes, and wash out the gash in his scalp. Lastly, he got some water and carefully poured tiny dribbles into Empa's mouth. She swallowed reflexively, coughed a little, and swallowed some more.

Exhausted, Gippy tucked the blankets up around her and sat down beside the bed. Not knowing what else to do, he took her hand in his and, for the first time in his life, he prayed. *Please, God, don't let her die...*

IN AN UGLY NEIGHBORHOOD OF MEMPHIS, four NAFAS cruisers closed in on a beat-up white Mercedes parked at the curb. Troopers swarmed out of the vehicles, weapons poised, but found nobody in the car.

Commander Westerfield got out of her car, glowering at the Mercedes. The plate matched the number Duvara had given her.

One of the troopers approached her, saluting. "Nobody here, ma'am, but there's blood. A lot of it."

"Swab for DNA and search it."

As they complied, she walked a slow circuit of the car, followed the blood trail to where it ended only a few feet away. *Another car. Probably a third by now. They're skilled, whoever they are.* She didn't know for sure who she was chasing yet, but Duvara's information about the origin of the Mercedes gave her a good idea. She'd know soon enough. They had Empa's DNA from the Securotel. A match would confirm it.

"Commander!" She turned to find a trooper presenting a most curious object, a sheathed sword. "This was hidden under the back seat. Nothing else but garbage and blood."

Westerfield drew on rubber gloves and took the sword, examining it closely. She drew it a few inches and looked at the maker's mark on the blade. A cruel smile spread her lips. *Yes...this is the one...* "Check this for prints, sergeant, and run the DNA, but I believe we just found the trail of our wanted terrorist."

"Yes, ma'am!"

"Run the VIN on that car, too. I want to confirm the owner." Duvara could be mistaken on that score, or this could be a deception, a red herring, but the daughter of Ariquiel didn't think so. She knew the sword. Three of her cousins had been killed by this blade, at least temporarily. The question was, what had Empa been doing in Albuquerque, and why was she headed back in the direction she'd come from? There could be only one answer: *You're looking for something, aren't you? But what? Or who?*

LOST MEMORIES

I wake—a victory in and of itself—to warm blankets, crinkly sheets that smell of bleach, and Gippy's hand in mine. He's dreaming again, but different this time. *Flying over a sea of lights, joy, hope, love, so many souls to save...* Good boy.

I try to free my hand. I'm dreadfully weak and can barely lift it.

He stirs, wakes, blinks at me, still half asleep. "Good ta see ya breathin'."

"Good to...breathe." Talking makes me want to cough. My mouth is bone dry and tastes like blood. "Water?"

Gippy scrambles up and grabs a bottle from our gear. I can't hold it, so he helps me. I swallow twice and shake my head. Too much might make me sick.

"Where...are we?"

"Bullshit little town east of Memphis. I just drove."

I nod and try to shift under the blankets. My back hurts, but it's a dull ache, not the stabbing pain I remember. I can barely move. "How long?"

"'Bout a day." He frowns. "You gonna be okay?"

"Eventually." I shift again, and the blanket slips.

"Don't." Gippy looks uncomfortable and pulls it back up. "I...um... took yer clothes."

I can't suppress a smile. "It's okay. I imagine they were a mess."

"Never seen so much blood. Dunno how yer alive."

173

"Neither do I." I drink more water and begin to feel stronger, clearer-headed. "Have we any food?"

"Sure." He feeds me a gooey trail bar, washing it down with sips of water. While I eat, he fills me in on what I missed.

At the mention of switching cars, I ask, "What did you do with the Mercedes?"

"Left it." He shrugs. "If Chaki put 'em on us, they'll know where it came from anyways."

"Probably. I worry about Father Farrell. We should warn him."

"I messaged him. Dad's smart. They show up, he'll tell 'em someone jacked it."

"I hope they believe him. If they find my DNA in it, they'll be persistent."

"Nothin' we can do 'bout it. Not now." He tells the rest, his makeshift first aid and switching cars and plates again. Gippy's got a good grasp of being a fugitive. "You need food 'n sleep."

Truer words were never spoken, but I need him to do one more thing. "The bandage." I flex my shoulder and feel it pull. "Can you take it off? I need to know what the wound looks like."

"Um..." He looks uncomfortable again. *Embarrassment, worry...*

"Don't worry, Gippy. I trust you."

"Ain't that. I just..." He shrugs again. "Seem like I should'a *asked* before I cut your clothes off and cleaned you up, is all."

"I was a little unconscious, and now I'm giving you permission." I hold out a hand. "Help me sit up."

"Sure." He's gentle, but the tape stings when it comes off. "All closed up. A scar, but that's all. Fuckin' miracle."

"Yes, it is." The pneumothorax and bleeding have stabilized, at least. I don't tell him the bandage could easily have killed me by putting the pneumothorax under tension. I should teach Gippy some trauma medicine. "All I need now is time."

He sponges off a little dried blood and helps me into clean underwear —I'm too weak to do it alone—then tucks me back in bed. He'd make a good nurse. Another trail bar and a bottle of water make me sleepy. He turns off the light, and I let myself drift away.

When I wake next, it's dark and I have to pee. Gippy's sleeping soundly on top of the covers beside me. I feel better; my breathing is quiet, only stiffness in my chest. I'm stronger but still weak.

Strong enough to pee without help? I pull the blankets aside and work myself into a sitting position. My legs work, but I don't know if they'll hold me until I try. I rock forward, hands on knees, and push myself up. Shaky, but I don't fall on my face. *Good enough.* I use the wall for support and make it to the bathroom. The cold tile floor makes me shiver. I close the door and turn on the light.

The woman in the mirror looks like some I saw in Krakow, hollow eyes, bruised, beaten. *But alive, Empa. You're still alive. Never give up, never quit...* I remember Sergeant Gattish's grim sneer as he lay there bleeding out in a trench. *Now get up and fight.* His last words... they ring in my mind. *Fight...or die.*

I pee—the color of dark tea, full of blood—and consider a shower, but the tub is full of bloody water and my shredded clothes. I don't have the energy to clean it up and settle for washing my face and hands in hot water. I look at my face in the mirror and take out the lip rings and nose stud. I'll have to change my look.

"E? You okay?"

"Yes. Just cleaning up. Sorry I woke you." I peek out, and the light is on. Gippy glances at me and turns his back. "Thanks." I step out into the room.

"How you feel?"

"Better. Still weak." The bed looks inviting. "What time is it?"

"Mornin'. About five-thirty. Went out and got more food and some drinks. Filled up the car. We should go if yer strong enough."

So much for bed. "I'm strong enough, but I should probably change my hair color before we go. So should you." I root through our things and shrug into a sports bra and a thermal top. My old pants feel coarse on my legs. My Glock lays there, clean and holstered beside my phone. I pick them up along with a handful of trail mix bars and a bottle of Power-Aide. I sit on the bed, shaking from the effort. "I'd like to shower, too."

"No problem. There's an all-night drugstore in town." He gets up. "I'll go. What color you want?"

"Surprise me." I tear into a bar as he starts for the door. "Hey, Gippy?"

"Yeah?" He looks back.

"Thank you. For not giving up, I mean." I wash the crunchy bite down with a mouthful of the sickly-sweet drink.

He grins. "No thing, E."

"Why wash out my ruined clothes?"

"Didn't want no bloody stuff in the trash. Naffies might start snoopin'."

"Smart." I look over our gear and find one item missing. "The sword?"

Gippy's eyes widen. "Shit!"

I know without him saying that it's gone, left behind. A piece of my soul is torn away. My years with Musashi, the tenderness, the love, all his lessons, all mine, everything we shared feels like it will slip away, autumn leaves in a torrent, like all of my past inevitably does.

I stare into the emptiness opening up inside me, see a million dead faces, loves lost, my memories of them naught but footprints in sand. *Why...how can I forget them?* I see their faces, but their memories have faded: lovers, friends, enemies, children. Musashi was so special to me, so perfect a human being, so serene of spirit, the one man I loved without reservation, at peace with his own mortality and my immortality, so much more than I. I walk with him beside a pond, the grass strewn with cherry blossoms. He draws a katana from under his robes and presents it to me. His last gift to me. Without it...I'll lose him. Just like I lose everyone I love...

The emptiness within me is complete. I am nothing. I am a shell.

"I'm sorry, E."

Sorry... The gulf within me constricts, a cry welling up in me. "You don't *know* sorrow." A flush of anger, Gippy's, not mine. I'm empty. There's nothing left of me...

"I fucked up, okay? I forgot your precious sword because I was draggin' your bloody ass outa there. It's a fuckin' piece of *metal*, E, not a person! Don't tell me you got a corner on the market when it comes to grief!"

He's out the door before I can answer, gone. I wonder if he'll come back. Perhaps it would be better if he didn't. *I'm better alone. Nobody to hurt, nobody to love, nobody to forget...* I lay on the bed, curl into a ball, and weep.

GIPPY PULLED up in front of the motel and grabbed the bag of supplies, his thoughts a tornado of self-admonition. *Shouldn't've yelled. She been through enough. You fucked up. Own it and move on. She needs yer help, not bitchin'.* He got out and went to the room door, swiped the key, and opened it.

Empa lay on the bed curled up, unmoving, exactly where he'd left her. *That ain't like her.* He would have expected her to be up and pointing a gun at him. He closed the door, dropped the bag in the chair.

"Sorry I blew up. You didn't need that."

Silence.

"Yer pissed at me. I deserve it, but we gotta move."

"You should go."

The words felt like a kick in the gut. His mother had said something like that once, though she'd screamed it along with a hail of obscenities. That had hurt, but this hurt worse. He wasn't even angry with her, just shocked. It wasn't fair. He didn't know how to answer, but he wasn't about to walk out that door without her. He stood and waited, silent, patient, recovering from the blow. *Deep breaths... Steady spirit...*

He waited for quite a while.

Finally, she spoke. "Go, Gifford. Please."

"No."

"Please."

"My ma told me to get out once. Didn't mind her neither. You need to get up."

"No."

"So much for all that love bullshit, then, huh?"

"Love is *why* I want you to go."

"Bullshit, Empa. You want me to go because I forgot your sword. You think without it you won't remember this guy you loved. That ain't how it works."

"You're wrong."

"Am I?" Tired of talking to her back, he walked around the bed and squatted down. Her eyes were open, but her face was blank, eyes red from crying. "You lied to me earlier then? About loving people, remembering them, all of them?"

She closed her eyes. "This is...different."

"Is it?" He leaned back against the wall. "This Mushiato guy. You remember him."

"Musashi."

"Musashi, then. You remember him. His face." He wasn't asking but telling.

She clenched her eyes closed, tears leaking out of the corners. "Yes."

"Remember what he *felt* like. You loved him. You were *with* him. Taught him how to love, you said. You remember that?"

Tears coursed from her closed eyes. "*Yes.*" Her voice cracked.

"Every day, when you wake up, remember him. Feel him." *Like I remember Ma, Lennie, Macie and Jami...*

"It...*hurts.*"

"It *supposed* ta hurt." Now for the hard part. "You keep that sword too long, you won't remember *him*, just the sword he gave you."

Her eyes opened, blinking tears. "I don't want...to do this...anymore."

"*Want?*" Gippy's brow furrowed. "What's *want* gotta do with it?"

"Everything."

"Wrong! *Want* don't mean shit." He stood up, looking down at her. "My ma didn't *want* to watch her baby girl die; her other baby girl go off with some ganger pimp. She blamed me cause she didn't wanna admit her own fuckin' habit caused it all. I didn't *want* ta watch her die. I didn't *want* to shoot Lennie. Want ain't nothin'."

"I can't." She closed her eyes again.

"*Can't?*" That rainy night when he'd shot up three syringes of Trix trying to make the pain go away came back to him. He felt like he couldn't go on. Empa saved him, cleansed his soul from that horrific guilt. He couldn't do the same for her. She had to help herself. He could think of only one way he might be able to get her moving.

"Okay." Gippy pulled his Glock and pointed it at Empa's head. "Say the word. I'll send you home to yer daddy."

Her eyes opened, widened, a glimmer of life there. "You'd *kill* me, Gifford?"

"You can't fight anymore. *Finally*, maybe got a chance to beat these fuckers, an' you ready to let the whole fuckin' world burn 'cause you *can't* go on. You *done*. I *ain't* done. You get up an' fight, or you fuckin' die. Them's the only two choices."

"Fight or die." She closed her eyes. "No mercy in the world."

"This *is* mercy!" His hand started to shake. "Said so yerself. Killed people you loved to keep worse from happenin' to 'em. Who the *fuck* you think gonna walk through that door next if I go? What they gonna do to you?"

She didn't answer.

Gippy didn't know if he could pull the trigger. If she was too full of pain to even love anymore, too crushed to fight, sending her to Heaven would be the kinder fate than leaving her for the naffies to find. Could he do it?

"I love you, Empa." He moved his finger from safe to the trigger, felt the tiny ridge of the trigger lock depress under his fingertip.

"Wait." Her eyes opened, and she held out a hand. "Help me up."

He holstered the Glock and took her hand.

THE DROWNED EMPIRE

D riving is strangely therapeutic. The landscape and the mechanical feeling of the wheel, gas, and brake occupy me. Gippy worries I'm not strong enough to stay alert, but food, water, and a long hot bath have rejuvenated me, physically at least. I've never taken two days to heal before.

The drowned farms of the south stream past us, a few still trying to grow stunted crops to stave off the famine that's gripped the world. They work the land with their hands now. Without money for fuel, teams of oxen or mules do the work of tractors, fighting the climate, the blights that have devastated their genetically altered strains of corn, soybeans, and wheat. They're busy, bracing for the coming winter. Struggling to survive.

Survival...

My mind wanders. I think again of Musashi. The pain is exquisite, salt in a bleeding wound. I remember him, the lessons, his grace of mind and body. The *feel* of him. The serenity in him when we made love. The honor I felt when he gave me his sword, swearing to him I would carry it always, cherish it, and remember him.

Gone... I'm so sorry...

His voice visits me. *It is but a tool, Emiko. You should not have a favorite weapon. Relying on one weapon too much is the same as not knowing how to use the weapon well enough. May it serve you on your journey to bodhisattva.* His calloused palm on my cheek, a warrior's hand, a lover's.

It's a fuckin' piece of metal, E, not a person!

I see Musashi at his villa, only his bokken at his waist, how he favored the wooden practice sword to steel, even sometimes for dueling. *A piece of metal, not a person.*

It seems I've forgotten some of Musashi's lessons. Gippy's reminded me of one in particular. *It's supposed to hurt.*

It does.

I wonder again if Gippy would have killed me. If he loves me, and I believe he does, I think he would have. And he was right; a bullet would have been merciful. I'm in no condition to fight the Nephilim and their hounds, and I have little doubt that capture would mean long torment at their hands.

I look at my savior, bent over his phone, earbuds in, concentrating on his lessons, his lips moving. I know I can never ask him if he would have sent me to Heaven. He barely looks like the frightened young man who tried to rob me only a week ago, especially now with his hair bleached white and shaved on the sides, ears and nose pierced, eyebrows plucked and bleached.

We arrive in Nashville by midday, keeping to the back roads until we're in the city. I'm ravenous, and Gippy finds a diner, a seedy-looking place named Papa Cole's. It's busy, which is good; more camouflage. I check my look in the rearview mirror. *Another stranger...*

Gippy's choice of colors worries me, but he assures me that it's not over the top. I've seen more outlandish, but the street punk look, spiky blue hair shaved on both sides, scares me. I don't know myself anymore, outside or inside. The makeup, blue around the eyes, and dark red blush along the cheekbones, gives me an angry look, or maybe it's just my mood. Black lipstick, more piercings...enough hardware in my ears to make a clock. I would fit in nicely in a Berlin punk rock club of ninety years ago.

I get out—moving slowly because my chest still aches and I'm weak—and tug the short skirt down to mid-thigh. With the high-heel boots, another crop top, and my suit jacket over, I'm freezing, but I look very unlike anyone I've ever been before. Hardly invisible, but certainly not Empa.

"More you stand out, the less the naffies'll look at you," Gippy assured me. "They're lookin' for someone hidin'. They look at you and think 'Bitch couldn't hide in a housefire in that getup.'"

Again, I must trust his intuition—I'm too dead inside to trust my own.

We draw looks as we enter the diner, but surprisingly few. Jazz piano plays over a system, a beautiful tenor voice accompanying. *Papa Cole's... Nat King Cole... Of course.* Nashville is still a music city and draws all kinds. Cora loved this place. I wonder if she might be hiding here, posing as a musician, playing in bars and clubs.

Music... We take a booth, and a notion occurs to me. "Find a music store nearby. One that sells instruments."

"Why?" He starts tapping on his phone. I make him do our searches just for the literacy practice.

"Because we look like musicians, and guitar cases will carry our gear without drawing attention."

"'Kay." He nods and taps away. He's still worried about me; I can feel it. So am I.

A waiter brings us coffee and menus. I sip and gasp in surprise. Real coffee, roasted and brewed. *God truly loves me.* The music changes—*Unforgettable*—and I reconsider. *Musashi... oh God, I'm sorry...* I drop my menu and drain my scalding coffee. The searing heat blisters the roof of my mouth and throat, a slap in the face wake-up call.

"You okay?"

I meet Gippy's furtive gaze and shake my head. "No."

"You *will* be." He holds out his hand, and I take it. His worry for me, his love, and a core of determination I've never felt in him before humble me.

"I don't know." I try to inhale my unshed tears. I don't want to smear my ridiculous makeup. "Gippy, I need you to—"

"More coffee?" The waiter is busy and holds a steaming pot in one hand.

"Please." I nudge my cup over. "It's very good."

"Pop knows a dude with a solar-power greenhouse." The man grins with beautiful white teeth. "Man makin' *shit*loads of money."

"There's hope for mankind." I sip, relishing the pain on my burned tongue.

"Know what you want?" he asks.

"Couple'a barbeque san'wiches an' fries." Gippy noticed my disinterest in the menu.

The waiter nods and hurries off.

"So, you was sayin'?" Gippy releases my hand and stirs sugar into his coffee, a sin.

"I need you to promise me something."

His lips press into a thin line. "If I can, but I ain't leavin' you."

"I know you won't." Even if I beg him to, he won't. "I need to tell you that you were right. About me...about Musashi. He...told me..." I shake my head, forcing down tears. *No low spirit, no high spirit, steady spirit.* I breathe and reach for the calm center of my soul. It's there, but I don't know if I can grasp it. "I'm...not myself, Gippy. I don't know if I'll ever be."

"Bullshit. You'll come back. I know you will."

I shake my head. "Maybe...but if I don't..." I sip my coffee for a distraction. "You were right about what would happen if they ever caught me. I need you to promise me you'll...send me to my father if we're in a no-win position."

His face stiffens. "Mercy."

"Yes." I fix his eyes with mine, pleading. "I've seen it before. A cousin of mine, Gaia, Daughter of Sandalphon, Angel of Life, was captured by Nephilim during the Spanish Inquisition. They...tormented her for a quarter-*century* before I found her and ended her agony." The memory of that dark place, the chains, the blood, bare bone driven through with iron, the atrocities... "We all heal like I do, so you can imagine what they did to her."

Gippy looks ill, then nods. "We in shit too deep to breathe, I'll end it for you, E."

I look into his eyes and feel his determination. I think he can, and I think he *will*. "Thank you."

"Can we focus on *not* gettin' in that kinda shitshow?" he asks.

"I'll try." I sip my wonderful coffee—makes everything brighter—and struggle to get back to the business of survival. "Your disguise is good, I think, but I worry the car might have been photographed when you refueled."

"Yep. Me too." He glances around and lowers his voice. "Figured I'd jack a new one, or a new tag for this one, soon."

"A plate would be safer." Steal a car, and it gets reported. A tag might go unnoticed for months.

"Yep." He finishes with his phone and shows me the screen. "This okay."

A second-hand music store only a few miles away. "Perfect."

After eating and relishing another coffee, I feel marginally human, stronger and steadier. We buy two used guitar cases at the shop, cruise back alley neighborhoods until Gippy spots a likely car, and he trades plates in a flash. We're on I-40 East minutes later.

Fuel and another quick meal in Knoxville and the strip mines of Appalachia break my broken heart. Exhaustion forces us to stop in Roanoke. Not a huge city, but big enough for us to blend in. Yet another meal, and we find a nondescript motel where we can park out of sight of the main street. Thankfully, sleep comes quickly.

In the morning, I wake before dawn, feeling physically recovered. Emotionally, not so much. I dreamt of Musashi, and I swear I can feel him, his warrior's hands, his patient spirit, his love. Gippy's still sleeping, so I take a lesson from my new mentor and sit tailor fashion by the bed, hands on knees, and clear my mind. The old lessons come back.

Steady spirit... peace... breathe... focus... I remember Musashi and embrace the pain.

IT WAS a good thing Empa took over driving when they stopped for fuel in Allentown. Gippy couldn't keep his eyes off the city. It seemed they hadn't left it for the last hour. They crossed into New York State and turned east on the I-287, the traffic light, buildings blocking out the horizon, smog thick from coal-fired power stations.

"Can't believe they so many *people* in the world," he muttered, staring at the endless sea of buildings.

"Not nearly as many as there used to be. A hundred million were displaced along the eastern seaboard. Famine and disease killed half of them."

"This all New York City?"

"No." She gave him a wry smile. "This wasn't a city at all, or not a big one, before the flood. When they finally gave up trying to save New York, this whole area became a refugee camp, tents as far as the eye could see, but people started building, and just kept building."

"Save it how?" She'd already told him the sea swallowed up much of the cities along the coast. Gippy still couldn't conceive such a cataclysm and so, couldn't imagine the effort to save it.

"You'll see."

They turned from 287 onto another freeway that Gippy couldn't read the name of. Palace-something Interstate and a word he didn't know, Pkwy. He tried to sound it out and couldn't. The traffic here was even thinner. A big bridge loomed ahead, towering spires with cables supporting the roadway like the ones they'd seen across the Mississippi. Gippy could see the old freeway where it dipped down into the water and realized the bridge was new. As they rose, Gippy beheld New York City through the curtains of rain.

"Holy *fuck.*"

A mountain-range of buildings soared up, impossibly tall, too many, and far to his right, an immense black wall stretched from north to south, gapped and broken like a ganger's rotten teeth. And the *sea*…

Empa's voice brimmed with sorrow as she told him what he was looking at. "The New Hope Seawall, they called it. The second biggest construction project Man has ever undertaken." Her hand swept from north to south. "They intended it to stretch from the Bronx to Wilmington, protecting New York, Newark, and Philadelphia. When that failed, they tried to cross to the west south of Staten Island, but in the end, that failed, too."

The names of these drowned cities meant little to Gippy, and it wasn't the wall, or even the buildings, that struck his mind with impossibility. It was the sea. Massive rolling swells churned through the breeches in the mountainous barrier, spray flying hundreds of feet as they struck the embattled shore. He remembered Empa telling him how the sea had swallowed cities, a whole country, and now he understood.

As they descended and neared another new suspension bridge, he said, "Never imagined so much water, the waves."

Empa looked at him sidelong. "Mother nature's a bitch, ain't she?"

"No shit. Look like we pissed her off."

"That we did." Again, the sorrow in her voice broke his heart.

She'd been dangerously quiet, and he still worried about her mental state, but she seemed to be physically herself again, at least improving, moving toward their goal. He didn't know how she would handle a crisis, another firefight for instance. For his part, he didn't really remember much of the gunfight at the Waffle House. Just a lot of noise and broken glass. He remembered shooting up through the table, then it was all a blur. *Just as well*, he figured.

Empa slowed down as they climbed the next bridge, pointing. "That line of buildings is the New Jersey side, the Palisades. You can't really see Manhattan yet. When the city started to drown, they built the Palisades up, and most of the financial and business institutions moved there."

Buildings soared up like battlements, like the mesas they'd seen in the southwest. "Reminds me of that mountain range near Albuquerque."

"The Sandia Ridge? Yes, it does at that. There's a pull-out up ahead. I'll stop so you can see it all."

"Uh-huh." Gippy only listened with half his mind, the other half numb. Something she'd said long ago came back to him. *Armageddon... the end of the world.* It wasn't hard for him to believe that cults like the Church of the Coming Dark thought this was the end, the hand of God wiping mankind from the planet.

They descended, and buildings blocked his view, these no taller than others he'd seen, and his brain started working again. She took an exit, turning back onto another road that went back the way they came from, then ducked under the freeway. She then turned right onto a tiny road with a brown sign that read State Line Lookout.

He realized she wasn't using the phone to navigate. "You know your way around here?"

"Yes. I've been to Manhattan many times. Not recently, not since it died, but I've been to the Palisades just to look at it." Again, she sounded strange, as if talking about a dead family member. They drove for maybe a mile, then turned into a parking lot. There were a few cars here, people bundled up against the blustery wind and flagging rain. Empa pointed to an elevated concrete and rock platform to their right. "You can see it all from there." She pulled into a parking spot and stopped. "Come on."

He got out and flipped up the collar of Empa's duster against the chill drizzle. She walked fast, huddling in her inadequate coat, her short stride birdlike. They climbed the ramp, then a set of steps up to the viewpoint, then she stopped at a low stone wall.

Gippy stepped up beside her and gaped. "Mutha *fuck.*"

Ocean swells roared up the Hudson River, peaking against the outflow, crashing against crumbling megaliths. The eastern shore buildings lay in ruins, pummeled to rubble by the indomitable force of the sea. The taller buildings still stood, though water coursed around their bases. The scale of it all baffled him. It was too big, too much, and utterly destroyed, or at least looked to be from this distance.

"And people still *live* there?"

"Some, yes. The Church of the Coming Dark moved into much of the downtown area to the south there." She pointed to the tallest structures miles to the south. "There's quite a lot still above water."

"What's that?" Gippy pointed to a rusty and drooping span of steel across the water.

"The George Washington Bridge, or what's left of it. It was condemned in fifty-four. There were tunnels under the river, too, but those were flooded, of course."

"How we gonna get there?" Gippy peered at the raging river.

"You can get there from the north, but that would have meant a lot more driving. There's not a span across the Hudson for some way upriver." She pointed downriver toward the rusted bridge. "We'll cross by boat."

"Cross *that*?" He stared at her as if she'd told him he was going to be castrated. "No fuckin' way."

"Way." She smiled without humor. "There's supposed to be a break in the weather in a couple of days, and it's not so rough when the tide's rising."

He didn't know what tide was and didn't want to sound even more ignorant. "Where we gonna stay 'til then?"

She smiled genuinely then, the first one he'd seen since she was shot. "In the lap of luxury, my friend."

Empa drove them back to the freeway and south into the Palisades like she knew exactly where they were going. She exited onto an interchange to a major cross street, Palisade Avenue, and turned into the canyon-like streets between buildings. There were few other cars, but quite a lot of foot, bicycle, and little three-wheeled electric taxi traffic, people in decent clothes, even suits. Money. All of it perched on the brink of utter destruction.

"What keeps this place alive?" he asked.

"After the North American financial crash, most of the big firms just dissolved," she explained. "That left a lot of empty office space, high-tech telecom equipment, computers, and real-estate sitting unused. Nature abhors a vacuum, so other businesses moved in. There's not much industry left, but some of the big pharmaceutical corporations survived, telecom, construction conglomerates, and, of course, weapons manufacturers. And people have to eat, so food distribution corporations, energy conglomerates, and the like, took up the space. Fewer than a half-million people actually *live* here now, but they've got money."

"We gonna stick out," he said, eyeing the conservative clothes.

"Not so much once the sun goes down, I think. This is still a city that never sleeps, and people *will* have their distractions." She pulled up in front of a towering glass and steel structure with the stylized blue S of Securotel emblazoned above the gleaming steel doors.

Gippy recalled the symbol from the hotel in Cincinnati. "You wanna stay *here*? You *shittin'* me?"

"I shit you not." She didn't smile this time.

Gippy wondered if she had a death wish. "But if they was hacked like you said…"

She poked him in the shoulder. "That's why *you're* going to be our frontman."

"But I don't even have an ident!"

"You don't need one, Gip. All you need is money." Empa parked the car and gave him the details.

She'd been following the news, and Securotel had filed multiple lawsuits and even criminal charges against NAFAS officers for the assault on their Cincinnati branch. NAFAS didn't recognize the lawsuits but the corporation had done a complete purge of all of its records and customer profiles, scrapped their computer security firewalls, and contracted an entirely new cyber-security firm to put up a new one. They then launched a promotional campaign stating that no personal identifiers would ever be retained from a customer, and no internal cameras would keep recorded images for more than twenty-four hours. They positively guaranteed security and anonymity to everyone who stepped through their doors, regardless of identity.

Gippy didn't like it, but he had no choice.

Everything they had was packed into two battered guitar cases and a small worn shoulder bag Gippy had picked up. They carried it all up to a sheltered vestibule beside the huge steel doors. As Gippy wiped the rain from his eyes, a numeric pad folded out of the wall. He nervously tapped the star key four times.

"Please enter a valid account number," a computer voice said.

"New account." He tried to talk like Empa, all fancy and sophisticated.

"Initializing new account. Number of guests and length of stay?"

"Two people. Four nights." They didn't know how long it would take, but Empa had assured him money wasn't a problem.

"Amenities?"

He looked to Empa helplessly; he had no idea what that meant.

"I want somethin' nice, honey. A view, and a bathtub," she said. "Somethin' with a view of the river, and a bathtub."

"One bed or two?"

"One." He would have preferred two, but she'd told him one.

"Twelve point two kay North American Dollars. Will that be credit, debit, or PFT?"

He gaped for a second at the cost, then said, "Cash."

"This terminal is not equipped to accept currency of any denomination. Please enter and see the manager for assistance. Thank you, and have a pleasant day."

One of the massive steel doors popped open, and they lifted their cases and went in. The inside was much like he'd glimpsed when he rescued Empa what now seemed so long ago: a lot of white stone, security people with rifles and body armor, an attendant beside a scanner, and a vast wall of lockers. Of course, a truck hadn't driven through the front of this one, so it was cleaner. They handed over their instrument cases and put their pistols, phones, and other metal objects into a bin. Empa kept the shoulder bag since it only contained clothes and toiletries. The attendant put the two guitar cases and the bin into one cavernous locker. The scanner *bleeped* as he walked through, and Gippy handed over the money belt, submitting to another scan before being given it back. Empa handed their key ring over before passing through the scanner, looking bored.

They approached the wide stone counter.

"Welcome, sir?" An expensively dressed woman behind the counter smiled at them. "A new account and cash transaction?"

"Yeah." Gippy handed over two of the metal bars. "Put the rest on my account."

"One moment, please." She slipped the bars into a scanner, then nodded. "Very good. Anything else? Food, entertainment, libation?" She handed a paper card to him with nothing but a ten-digit number printed on it.

Gippy pocketed the card. "We'll call down room service."

"Very good." She pressed a tiny metal stud on her collar, and a man hurried up.

"May I take your bag?" As Empa handed it over, he gestured toward a bank of elevators. "This way, sir, ma'am."

Gippy felt a little strange with anyone calling him sir, but they followed and rode up to the eighteenth floor. Their escort showed them to one of many unmarked doors, swiped a tiny plastic card, and handed it to Gippy. The door *bleeped* and popped open.

"Anything else, sir?"

"No. Thanks." They went in, and he closed the door.

"Well done." Empa pulled the two sheathed carbon knives from under her jacket and handed him one. "Keep that handy."

"Sure." Gippy looked around the palatial room in awe. A huge closet, desk area with a big monitor, a bed big enough for a family of six, and a wall of curtains. The carpet felt springy beneath his feet. "Some place."

"Not bad. Drapes open, lights medium, draw a bath, hot." She flung her jacket on the bed and sat to unbuckle her boots. "Hungry?"

"Yeah." He stared at the view as the drapes drew open. It was starting to get dark, and lights were flickering in some of the drowned buildings of Manhattan. The river was a black ribbon cross-hatched with the white of breaking waves. The sea... He still couldn't grasp the enormity of it. "Don't look real."

"All too real." She kicked off her second boot and headed for the bathroom, unzipping her skirt as she walked. "Order whatever you want for dinner."

"How?"

She turned and blinked at him, then shook her head. "Sorry. Phone, voice only. Room service."

A bell chimed from somewhere, and a male voice answered, "Yes?"

Empa gestured for him to order and closed the door.

"Um, dinner fer two. What's good?"

"The chef's specialty tonight is fillet of cod in an almond glaze."

Gippy had no idea what that was. "Fine. Two of those."

"Very good. Anything else?"

On a whim, he said, "Yeah. Chocolate cake and a bottle of wine."

"Preference for the wine?"

Gippy had no idea about wine but knew how to fake it. "Whatever. Something that'll go good with the food."

"Very well. Thirty minutes?"

"Great. Thanks." Gippy took off his coat and stared out the window at the looming night.

He'd never imagined anything like this existed. More lights winked on in the towers of the drowned city, some flickering oddly, yellow instead of white, fires maybe. He could see bridges between some of the buildings. Huge rolling waves marched up the river, breaking against the outflow as rain slashed down. Such beauty, ugliness, majesty, and decay all in one incredible vista. A whole world he didn't know. He wondered how much more there was to see. He put a hand against the glass and felt the wind buffeting against the other side like a heartbeat.

A whole living world... A world worth saving.

22

THE COMING DARK

espite the war against science, humanity still maintains weather and communications satellites, and even though the weather has become nothing but a series of sequential storms around the globe, forecasting is reasonably accurate. A few planes still fly, after all, and some cargo traverses the oceans in the milder seasons. The forecast tells me that about forty hours after our arrival, the weather will break. This is good because Gippy's getting antsy.

At first, I think it's cabin fever and take him out on the town to ask around about the Church of the Coming Dark. You can learn things in bars and nightclubs that you'll never find on the net. I'm right that we blend in. That only makes him more nervous, however.

The affluent nightlife is something he's never experienced. Too many people, too many questions, and way too many women and men coming on to both of us.

"Relax," I tell him at the third club we visit. He's stiff as a board, clutching his drink so hard it ripples. "Enjoy yourself. Have a drink. Get laid if you want."

He furrows his eyebrows at me. "For real?"

"Sure." I sip my tumbler of whisky and let it sit on my tongue, savoring the flavor and the wash of memories it brings: music, laughter, and blood. "What's the use in living if you don't have fun occasionally?"

"Na." He looks around at the teaming crowd, the dancers, the men and women in their finery and flash hooking up, some casting us furtive glances. "Strangers. Not my thing."

"Suit yourself." I down my Scotch and wave the bartender for another. A man I don't know pays for it and smiles at me. I smile back and thank him, introducing us and shaking his hand. He's handsome, but there's only one thing on his mind.

The conversation goes nowhere, and we don't learn anything I didn't already know. Gippy's not having fun, so we go back to the hotel.

As a distraction, I teach him more lessons: meditation, focus, attentiveness, and some exercises. I also tell him everything I've learned about Pederson, the cult, and the city. We examine satellite images of drowned Manhattan, the island of Midtown where the cult has made its stronghold. He's not easy with our plan, but I have no alternative. When the weather breaks, we go.

There's zero security boarding the ferry, for which I'm duly grateful. We carry our guitar cases, pay our fares, and find a secluded spot. There aren't many passengers, but quite a lot of cargo. The big coal-fired engines belch filth into the air, and we leave the dock into the turbulent Hudson. The sky reminds me of 1960, pre-environmental protection, a dirty yellow-gray.

We've changed into more practical clothes for the trip since the chance of any NAFAS authorities in Manhattan is nil. I let Gippy keep my duster, much of our arsenal filling its inner lining. I see the weight in his stride. The guitar cases are awkward but carry our heavy artillery. I hope we don't need it.

Memory flashes: carrying ninety pounds of gear through the desert on legs hardened by years of training. *Hump your shit or stay home, soldier!* Gattish's voice will never leave me, it seems.

"So, these Coming Dark fuckers..." Gippy fidgets, pre-mission jitters.

I wonder why I'm not more nervous and don't like the answer I find inside myself. If I die, I go to Heaven. Not a bad reward for five millennia of war. *Never give up...you give up, you die!* That doesn't sound so bad anymore.

Gippy raps his knuckles against a pitted iron railing, staring out the filthy window at the looming decay of Manhattan. "They *all* crazy, you think?"

"Crazy?" I haven't intended to give him that impression. "No, just resigned to the only future they can see. Their dogma is that this is all

God's plan, that mankind isn't worthy of the gifts they were given. They see the end coming and think it's deserved. They embrace it."

He stares silently for a while. "Fuckin' crazy."

"Is it?" I shrug. "You've lived on the street, Gip. You know what desperation can do. These people have just turned desperation into resignation."

"'Cause it's easier to lay down an' die than it is to fight." He shakes his head. "Fuck that."

I have to ask him. "Where is this coming from, Gippy?" He looks at me askance. "You tried to end your life to stop the pain, once. I understand you wanting to help me fight, but why are you so determined? Our chances are about one in a thousand. What makes you so...indomitable?"

"What's that?"

"Um...you refuse to back down, even though we don't stand a chance. Why?"

He looks at me like I slapped him in the face. "*You.*"

I swallow hard. "How?"

He shrugs. "You gave me somethin' I can fight."

"But I *told* you, Gippy, the war's *lost.*"

"Ain't." He shakes his head. "Didn't even know there *was* a war 'till you come along. Thought the world was just fucked up 'cause *people* are fucked up. You say these Nephilim are doin' it, fuckin' us over, makin' people evil." He shakes his head again and looks out the window. "That pisses me off. Ain't right. Ain't nobody *born* evil. If people wanna be fucked up, that's fine, but the whole human race has been getting fucked for thousands of years, and we never even knew it. Now I got someone I can blame, someone I can point a finger at and say, 'fuck you!' even if it kills me."

I gave him something to fight, a real enemy. It makes sense. "I understand."

"Hope so." He looks back at me, dead serious. "I was worried you'd quit on me, E. Like maybe you come here to join these crazy fuckers, or just plain die."

I smile without humor. *Dear Gippy, you're a good soul...* I find myself listening to centuries-old lessons in the voice of the one man I loved more than any other. *Readiness is a constant state, Emiko. No high spirit, no low spirit, steady spirit. See close when far, far when close...* Miyamoto Musashi is still with me, and my spirit is steady.

"I have a feeling you won't let that happen, Gippy."

"Fuckin' *right*, I won't." He lifts his case as we come into the Washington Heights pier.

Protected from the ocean swells by the crumbling rubble of a hundred fallen buildings heaped into a breakwater, the pier is the sole access for deep-water vessels for the little remaining dry land in the uptown area. From here, we'll have to get a water taxi. We heft our gear ashore and look around.

"Ride, lady?" A skinny young man waves us to his bike-taxi.

"How much to the water taxi stand?"

"C-note."

The money means nothing, but I don't want to look like an easy mark. "Half-C"

He frowns. "Senty-fie."

"Okay."

"I hep." He reaches for our cases.

Gippy blocks him with a stern look. "We got this. Cash when we get there."

"Shu shu." He gestures toward his bike. "No needa be assho."

I nod and wink to Gippy as we load our gear and climb aboard. He's being careful. Good boy.

Our ride takes us down Pinehurst to 181st, then east. I try not to stare, but memories of the city haunt me. It's been a long time since I've been here. Things have changed so much, but then, most cities do over the centuries. *Paris, Rome, Hong Kong, Tokyo...* This one, however, has entirely changed in only fifty years. The biblical apocalypse is happening in slow motion; mankind simply hasn't realized it yet. Gippy's right about one thing, however: mankind isn't at fault; the Nephilim are.

Something to fight... I've fought in so many wars I can't remember them all, but always against the Nephilim. Even when I won, I lost. Now, I have a chance, a weapon... maybe. *All we need is to find it.*

We pull up at the water taxi dock, get our gear, and pay the fare. Our cabbie pedals off without a word. With the break in the weather, the water taxis are busy carrying cargo and passengers under their yellow awnings to and from hundreds of outlying high-spots still supporting life. Finding one to take only us and our baggage is impossible.

"Where to?" A surly woman looks us up and down, her wizened face a mass of wrinkled scrutiny, undoubtedly gauging our affluence and our ability to defend it.

"The Cathedral." I gesture to Gippy and our bags. "Just us."

She frowns. "I carry cargo, too. Five-C."

"Four."

"Five! No less. I gotta eat. My motor gotta eat." She waves to the six rail-thin youths loading cargo crates into the taxi, her motor. "Five, or fuck off!"

"Five, then. I'll pay you when we arrive. And we'll want a return trip later. Same price."

"Shu shu. Good weatha, I run two trip a day." She pulls a phone from a pocket. "You text when you wanna pick up." She gives me the number, waves us aboard, and takes the wheel. When the loading's finished, she snaps orders in Mandarin to her motor, and they take seats aft, slipping their feet into pedals geared to the propeller. They backpedal us out of the narrow trash-strewn slip into the open.

We're on the Harlem River for a short while, then our pilot guides us deftly into the canyons of Manhattan. I can't tell what avenue we're on at first, then glimpse the open area of Central Park, a rectangular inland sea. Most of the buildings are still standing, though some have fallen due to rust and decay. Gippy's in awe, and I can't blame him. I am, too. I remember what this city once was.

The Big Apple... Music runs through my head. *If I can make it there, I'll make it anywhere...* I wonder if we'll make it or not. *Not to Heaven will I go...*

We cruise into Midtown, turning east off Park Ave, then south on Lexington, skirting the shore. I spot the megalithic structures of once-iconic hotels soaring ahead of us, the distinctive peaks of the Waldorf Astoria, and remember staying there for one fabulous week a century ago. My eyes search the horizon reflexively for the twin towers, and I remember the day they fell, the Nephilim who flew the planes.

The water shallows, the tops of drowned busses and trucks visible, rusted hulks. Our pilot knows the waters well and guides us without mishap. We cross over again to Third Ave. The water ends at Fifty-Seventh Street. A quay wall has been fashioned out of debris from a fallen building. People stand upon it beside a mound of coiled cable. I can't tell if they're carrying spears or some kind of long tools. They're dressed in mismatched rags. As we near, I see the stylized inverted cross tattoos on their foreheads that mark them as cult members.

This is our stop.

We bump into the dock, and frayed ropes are secured. Nobody speaks to us or offers to help us with our cases. I nod to Gippy. He pays the driver, and we climb up with our gear. A quick count, seven of them, four men, three women, all rail-thin. The poles they carry have both a point and a hook, like boat hooks, but sharp. We get glances, but that's all.

"Wa-chu got?" our driver asks a man on the dock.

A man steps forward. "Sixty kilo, good wire. Coppa."

"Good, good! We trade plenty."

They start to barter, and I nudge Gippy on. There are no vehicles, no taxis, only the refuse-littered streets, and the towering buildings. Time to hump it. I wish for a good pack and web gear to haul our equipment. I have to shift my guitar case from hand to hand. The shattered glass of a million windows crunches underfoot as we walk.

"They trade wire for food?" Gippy asks when we're out of earshot.

"Probably anything they can salvage. Wire, metals, engine parts, any electronics that still work."

"If they don't use money, we could be fucked."

"That would be bad."

He looks up at the soaring buildings. "How many live here?"

"Now? I've no idea. Thousands, at least. The census bureau doesn't keep tabs."

He snorts a laugh at my attempted humor. "Don't look like they got guns, anyways."

I spot a few faces in the shattered windows, grimy, hungry, all tattooed. "Don't bet on it."

We reach Madison Avenue, and I point left. Several blocks later, I see that the spires of St. Patrick's Cathedral are still standing.

"That the Cathedral?" Gippy asks.

"It used to be a Catholic church, but it isn't anymore. The Church of the Coming Dark took over Rockefeller Center as their headquarters. They ran out every other religious group in the city." I point to the lofty edifice of Saint Pat's as we near. Skeletal remains hang on inverted crosses from the cornices. The word "Blasphemy," is painted in red across the edifice. "They weren't gentle."

Gippy looks up at the long-dead priests and nuns of the church and mutters, "And you sayin' these fuckers ain't crazy?"

"No crazier than the Romans, the British, the Nazis, ISIL, or a dozen other armies tricked by fear and lies into believing they're righteous and everyone else is evil." I glance at him, hoping he can understand. "*Everyone* believes they're on the side of right, Gip. That doesn't make them crazy."

"Think maybe the head of this cult's a Nephilim?"

"I've considered it. I hope not." I've also considered what to do if my hopes are dashed. "If I give you the word, don't hesitate. We open up, cut, and run."

He glances up at the corpses again as we pass. "Ain't gotta tell me twice." He reaches into the duster, and I hear Velcro part.

"Good boy." We turn up 50th Street, and I can see Rockefeller Center, The Cathedral of the Coming Dark. On to Fifth Avenue, and the promenade opens up before us. The tower and the adjoining buildings have been painted black. Red inverted crosses five stories high hang by cables over the promenade. Figures peer over the parapets where there used to be gardens. Armed guards stand in a rank where I once ice skated.

"The place isn't what it used to be."

THEY WALKED UP to the Cathedral steps with the eyes of six guards on them. Their uniforms, black tunics that hung to mid-thigh, emblazoned with the same red inverted crosses that hung overhead, didn't look like body armor. They wore helmets, low over the ears but without face shields. Their rifles were mismatched but looked like they would work well enough. Gippy doubted he and Empa could take all six of them down without getting shot, and he knew there were more atop the buildings.

"Shit hit the fan now, we dead," he whispered to Empa as they topped the steps.

"Just keep steady." She stopped as two of the guards broke ranks, one raising a gloved hand.

"Infidels are not allowed in the Cathedral," the hand raiser said. Their guns weren't pointed at them, but they were ready for trouble.

"We don't need to go inside." Empa held her hands out to her sides, empty. "We're just here to talk to someone. Do you know the name of Martin Pederson?"

"No."

"Can we speak to someone in authority, please?"

"No. You're not allowed. Your NAFAS means nothing here. You have no jurisdiction."

Gippy snorted a laugh and endured a glare from Empa. "Come on, E. It's funny. Dude think we *naffies!*"

The guard looked skeptically surprised. "You're not?"

"Nothing of the kind, I assure you." Empa took a half-step toward him, hands still up, empty. Gippy had no doubt she was putting some kind of angel-daddy whammy on him. He'd felt that, the sudden calm, peace, when she got close, like the warmth of a space heater. "We only want to talk to Martin Pederson, and we're willing to donate *considerably* to your church if we're allowed to do so. Please, tell your superiors we'd like to speak to someone in authority."

The man considered for a moment, looking from one to the other. "Stay here." He waved two guards over to cover them, then turned on his heel and walked into the Cathedral.

They were still alive; at this point, every minute was a win. Gippy looked up into the scattered clouds, patches of blue-gray showing through the smog, and felt a curious desire to laugh. "Could be pissin' down rain, I guess."

Empa gave him a sidelong look. "Yes, it *could* be worse."

He smiled at her, almost giddy. *Nerves...or her angel-daddy shit rubbin' off on me.*

They waited.

Gippy shifted from foot to foot to keep his legs from going numb. He blew on his hands and stuck them in his pockets. The cold metal there didn't warm them, but it was comforting, nonetheless. Finally, the guard reappeared with four more guards and a thin-faced Afro-Asian woman in a black robe with a cowl thrown back, the inverted cross emblazoned across the front. Curiously, she had no tattoo on her forehead. She stopped about ten feet away, examining them both as her guards fanned out in a semicircle.

"Why do you wish to speak to the prophet?"

Prophet? Gippy glanced at Empa, but she showed no surprise.

"We only want information about a patient he treated before he came to you. Nothing that involves your church." Empa made the same open gesture. "We're willing to pay for this information. Enough to feed your people for a long time."

The woman frowned. Gippy decided she would have been beautiful if she wasn't glaring. "We have food."

"But your people obviously struggle. We offer them help and only wish to talk."

"Infidels are not allowed in the Cathedral," she said, pursing her lips. Then she added, "But the prophet doesn't reside within. What are you willing to give?"

"G, show her."

Gippy unclipped the money belt and stepped up to lay it flat on the concrete. He opened it, flipping back the flaps to show the rows of precious metal bars. He stood and took a half-step back, thrusting his hands back in his pockets.

"Fifty thousand worth on the open market." Empa rested her hands on her hips. "And all we want is to talk to him."

The woman snapped her fingers and pointed to the belt. A guard pulled one of the bars from it and handed it to her. She looked at it closely, then at them. "You're fools to show this. What makes you think I can't take this and send you away with nothing?"

"G, show her."

Gippy pulled his hands from his pockets, brought them together, and grabbed the pins of the two grenades he held. He showed them to the woman. "See, you fuck wit' us, we fuck back."

Rifles rose, centering on him. The woman's eyes widened, then narrowed. "You would die."

"And so would you and all these nice men," Empa said, spreading her hands wide again. "The dark comes for everyone, eventually, yes? Is it so much to ask to take fair payment for something that costs you nothing and let everyone walk away alive?"

The woman's frown deepened. "What do you want to ask him?"

"Only information about a man he treated before he joined your church. It has nothing to do with you or your people. You have my word." She gestured to the money belt. "You take half now, half after we've spoken with your prophet."

The woman said nothing, glaring first at Empa, then Gippy, as if considering whether he could pull the pins before they killed him.

His hands started to sweat. "Don't be thinkin', bitch. I got nothin' ta lose."

She looked him in the eye but spoke to Empa. "You won't be allowed any weapons when you speak to the Prophet. We'll keep your friend as hostage. If any harm befalls the Prophet, you'll both die."

"And if any harm comes to my friend, I'll bring the wrath of God down upon you all." Something in Empa's voice sent a chill down Gippy's spine.

"I'll see to his safety *personally*." The woman smiled thinly. "You have *my* word."

"Then we have a deal." Empa pointed to the money belt. "Take half the bars from the belt."

The woman gestured, and a guard knelt to take half the bars, stuffing them clinking into his pockets.

"G, take the belt," Empa said.

He put the grenades back in his pockets and picked up the belt, folding it and wrapping it around his waist well above his holstered Glock.

The woman turned to another of her guards. "Bring the vehicle."

"Yes, Your Grace." He trotted off, tunic flapping.

"You have a car?" Empa asked.

She scowled at Empa. "We're *not* barbarians."

"I never thought for a moment that you were, Your Grace." Empa nodded respectfully.

No, just fuckin' nuts. Gippy lifted his guitar case.

They all turned toward the throaty roar of an engine. A huge vehicle, black with inverted red crosses painted on the hood and doors, rounded the corner and drove right up the promenade, turning at the bottom of the broad steps. It reminded Gippy of the one that drove through the front of Empa's hotel. The driver got out and opened the back doors. It was big enough to seat half a dozen.

"Come with me." The woman descended the steps without looking back.

They followed with their cases, escorted by four guards, and got in.

"May I ask what you carry in your cases?" the woman asked as they pulled away and raced down the street.

"Our instruments," Empa said with a perfectly straight face. "We're musicians."

"Perhaps your friend, G, will play something for me while you speak with the prophet." She arched an eyebrow at Gippy.

"Don't think you'd like my music." Gippy tried to ignore her. It wasn't easy; she wasn't glaring anymore.

23

THE FORTRESS OF DESPAIR

W e tear down 49th Street and squeal onto Sixth Avenue. I don't bother to tell the driver he's going the wrong way on a one-way and blowing the hell out of the speed limit. We're not likely to get a ticket. I study this woman, this high priestess or archbishop, if that's her title, and gauge her veracity. She's powerful, that's easy to feel, and comfortable in her position. The threat of death shook her confidence, and I worry she may seek to take that out on Gippy. I don't like the way she's looking at him.

We scream past Bryant Park, a field of weeds now, all the trees cut for fuel, no doubt. We race on, but we can't go too much farther. When the driver turns onto 34th Street, I realize where we're going. The sea crosses the road only a block further as we pull up in front of the Empire State Building.

I look to the high priestess. "You're kidding me."

"The prophet sees all. It seems apt that he have the finest view available." She gets out, and we follow, two of her guards flanking us.

The façade is even uglier than the original, painted black with the inverted cross of the cult emblazoned upon it, but inside it's as grandiose as I remember from a hundred years ago. Electric lights are functioning, the wood paneling hasn't been stripped away for fuel, and the gleaming metal hasn't been salvaged. This place has been cared for, revered, deemed holy. *Prophet.* I wonder at that designation.

"Pray that the elevators are working," I say to Gippy. "It's a long way up,"

"One is functional," our guide assures us.

More guards are posted here, heavily armed, though they look bored. Our arrival perks them up, and one presses a button beside the elevator doors. To my surprise, it opens immediately. We get in with our guide and two guards. *Steady spirit...center thoughts...see far when close.* It's the express. She presses 84, and the doors close.

Gippy staggers as we take off, muttering something under his breath. It's a long ride up. My ears pop repeatedly. We slow, and Gippy grabs the handrail. He looks ill. I put my hand on his, and he calms.

The doors open.

This part of the building isn't as I remember at all. Two more guards, both women, clad in black riot gear and armed with assault rifles. They're stationed by a pair of elaborate doors that should open to stairs leading up. The rest of this floor is lavishly appointed, warm, well lit, and comfortable, with what looks like natural wood and leather furniture, and plush carpeting. It reminds me of an upscale waiting room. The central area is large, pillared, and opens up at the corners to observation rooms, all similarly furnished. There's a strange smell I can't place. Our guards take station at the elevator doors, while the others don't even look at us, eyes front, immobile.

"Stay here," our guide instructs us, approaching the stone-like guards without looking back to see if we comply. "The prophet has a visitor. I must ask him if he'll see her." They nod, and one presses her palm to a print scanner, which opens the door. I glimpse stairs before the door closes.

I turn to Gippy and lower my voice. "Be careful with her. She wants something."

"Noticed. Damn near had to blow her up to keep her from takin' it."

"Not just the money. Something else."

He gives me a look. "She ain't one a them...suck-you-whacha call 'ems is she?"

"Succubus?" I suppress a smile. *Out of the mouths of babes...* "No, but she may try to recruit you. I don't know how long it'll take me to—" The doors open, and I turn.

That was quick.

The priestess gives us a surprised look as she approaches. "He's expecting you."

I doubt that, but I've met enough false prophets to know the drill. "Of course." I unclip my holstered Glock and hand it to Gippy, then the two carbon knives from the lining of my jacket and the four spare magazines from my pockets. "I'm ready."

"I must search you." She steps up, her eyes hard. "This is *not* optional."

"I expected nothing less."

She is embarrassingly thorough, right down to my hair, the hems of my clothes, inside my mouth, and every intimate nook and cranny. I don't blush easily. She insists I remove my boots and leave them. I've had more thorough examinations, but that was the first day of boot camp. At least there is no body cavity search. Gippy handles it well, but I feel him grinding his teeth.

"Be patient, G," I tell him as I approach the stairs. "I don't know how long I'll be. Please don't shoot anyone while I'm gone."

"No promises." He sounds pissed, or maybe just wary. I hope the latter. *Steady spirit...*

I climb the stairs and find myself in yet another world I don't recognize.

"YOU MAY AS WELL BE COMFORTABLE." The priestess gestured toward one of the corner viewing rooms and strode ahead without looking back. "Your mistress is going to be some time."

"Ain't my mistress." Gippy would have rather stayed right where he was, despite the eyes of the four guards on him, but he couldn't piss this woman off too much. Even if Empa got what she wanted from this guy, they had to get out of here. He picked up the guitar cases and followed her.

"What *is* she then?" she asked as she walked ahead of him into the lavishly furnished room. "Your mentor? Commander? Lover?" She smiled over her shoulder. "Dominatrix?"

He was sick and tired of people using words he didn't know. Never was a thing on the street, but it seemed now like everybody knew more than he did. He considered pulling his phone and looking it up but refused to give her the satisfaction.

"Might call her my guardin' angel." He took in the room and thought it was designed to be intimidating: wood paneling, or it looked like wood, comfortable couches and tables, sideboards laden with bottles and glasses of all shapes and sizes, light fixtures of cut crystal giving off a warm glow. *Money, power, comfort...* It paled when compared to the view.

Gippy tried not to gape, he'd seen it from their room on the Jersey side, but from here, the air reasonably clear with the break in the weather, he could take in the whole of the city, the ravaged wall, and the sea beyond, the two rivers converging at the apex of a mountain range of dead and dying buildings. A dying world he had never known and never would. Magnificence gone to decay and ruin.

Fuckin' shame, was all he could think.

"Quite a view, isn't it?" She turned to face him with an amused look.

He couldn't deny it. "Yep." He walked past her to the very corner of the room, put down the cases, and took it in, a little queasy with the expanse. "Make ya feel small."

"We *are* small." Glass clinked, and liquid splashed. "We are but a passing infestation of this world, one that God has decided to finally eradicate."

Gippy didn't know what infestation and eradicate meant, but he had no trouble picking out her meaning. She was wrong, but telling her so would probably be a mistake. Even *he* knew that telling religious fanatics their beliefs were bullshit didn't go well. He decided to take in the view and keep his mouth shut.

She walked up beside him, her feet silent on the plush carpet. "You don't believe in God, do you?"

He snorted a laugh and shook his head without looking at her. "Yer oh fer three."

"What?" She sounded put out, disappointed. He could see her frown reflected in the glass.

"Yer wrong." He looked at her now. She held two glasses with ice and some brown liquid, the scent of something spicy. She held one out to him, and he took it. There was no point in being rude, but he'd ride to Hell on a succubus' ass before he agreed with her bullshit. "We ain't small. God didn't fuck up this world; we did. And I *do* believe." He tried the liquid. It was sweet, and bit his tongue pleasantly, but the cold hurt his teeth.

Her eyes narrowed. Empa had been right, she was going to try to recruit him, seduce him into their cult, and she was upset that it wasn't working. She would take a different attack next.

She waved a hand at the view. "You think this world is redeemable?"

He frowned, sucking his aching teeth. The single sip of cold was giving him a brain-freeze headache. "What's redeemable mean?"

She laughed, low and soft. "You really *are* nothing but an ignorant boy, aren't you?"

"Maybe." He put his glass down on a nearby table. "But ignorant don't mean stupid, and I know some shit. Seen shit you wouldn't believe."

"No doubt." She smiled thinly and sipped her drink, eying him. "I apologize. Let me rephrase my question: Do you think this world can be saved?"

"The *world?*" He shrugged, thought about it seriously. Empa had said the war was all but lost, but now they had a sliver of hope, maybe a weapon, and there was something he could fight. But even if they destroyed every last Nephilim, there would still be evil in the world, people who hated out of spite, fear, greed, or simply because they'd been taught to. But there was good, too. Beauty. Love. Compassion. He'd seen it. He looked out the window at the drowned empire of mankind, remembered the hungry faces with inverted crosses etched on their foreheads, the hopelessness in their eyes, and shook his head. "Not *your* world, maybe, but some of it."

"The world is ending. The darkness is coming. You cannot deny it."

"Shit's fucked up, ain't no doubt, but the difference between you and me is, you figger it's easier to step in front of a bus than it is to git off yo ass and *fix* shit."

"There is no fixing what God seeks to destroy."

"There you go again, thinkin' God did it."

"Who if not God?" She gestured to the expansive view of ruin. "Whose hand but God's wields the might to drown a world."

Gippy raised his hand and smiled at her through his pounding headache.

"You have an inflated opinion of yourself." She sipped, looking amused.

"Nah, just not ready to step in front of the bus yet." He knew he'd never change her mind, but he wasn't about to back down. "Did that once already." He pointed up. "She saved me. Showed me we could fight."

"Fight the will of *God?*"

Bitch don't fuckin' listen. It was time for a little truth.

"No, fight the will of *Hell.*" He took a step closer to her. "Ain't *God* killin' the world, Yer *Grace*, it's his pissed-off little boy who got threw out the house for gettin' all uppity. Devil been tryin' to fuck us up the ass for five *thousand* years just to git back at daddy, but we still puckered up tight.

Some of us anyways." He looked her up and down. "Some figger it's easer just to roll over and take it than fight."

The glass shook in her hand. *"Blasphemer!"*

"Wrong again." He pointed up. "I'm on *God's* side, and I'm fightin' to fuckin' *win!*"

She slapped him hard, spilling her drink.

Gippy's head pounded, his vision blurring, darkening. *Bitch has a right.* He smiled at her. "Feels good to fight, don't it?" But the sting of her slap felt wrong. Her face swam in a blur. *What the fuck?* She hadn't hit him *that* hard.

She glared, shaking with rage. "I could have you killed with a *word.*" This was the same threat she'd made before, the same mistake of overconfidence.

"Say it." Gippy had his Glock out in a flash. "We can dance if you like, but I didn't come here to fight you. You ain't my enemy."

"You seem very determined to make me one."

"Nope."

"Then *listen.*" She looked down at the pistol, then up to his eyes. "Hell is a myth. Heaven is a myth. There is only God and his powers. Some of his powers walk among us, speak to us, help us understand. Others remain aloof, uncaring. There is no struggle between Heaven and Hell; there is only God. We are his experiment, his *failed* experiment."

"Who told you *that* shit?"

"The prophet."

Gippy didn't like the sound of that. This prophet was fucking crazy, and Empa was up there talking to him alone, unarmed. He didn't like this one bit.

"I see the realization in your eyes." She smiled, knocking back the rest of her drink and putting the glass down. "You know you're doomed, that mankind is doomed. You cannot save the world with guns and bombs?"

"You right there." He slowly holstered his pistol. "Don't mean it ain't worth savin'."

She laughed at him. *"How?"*

She didn't understand what he did. What Empa had shown him. "Love."

"Love?" She blinked, taken aback.

"Yeah, *love!* All that." He waved a hand at the view of decay and ruin. "That ain't *people.* It just *stuff.* The world maybe had a bitch of a car crash, but we still alive. Hell's real. Heaven's real. There *is* a fuckin' war, an' *that's* the battlefield!" He stabbed a finger at the view. "Hell wants us to hate each other. Kill each other. Give up and die. We do that, the muthafuckas win, and we *all* burn."

"And you think *love* will conquer all?" She curled a lip in derision. "How naïve."

"Nope, not all. There's always gonna be fuckers who hate. Bigots, Nazis, gangers, pimps who think women is nothin' but property, fuckers sellin' junk to kids to get rich. Sorry fuckers who *believe* the shit Hell pukes up." Gippy patted his holstered Glock. "*Them's* what the guns and bombs are for."

"How very noble of you." Still, she looked at him with derision. "And you think you can actually win, against *that?*" She waved at the view again.

"Didn't say that, either. You don't get it. You don't get *me*. You prob'ly never will, and it ain't my job to convince you."

"Convince me of what?"

"That it don't *matter* if we losin'. Don't matter that the dark *you* worship is comin'. I ain't done. I'm gonna fight it. Gonna light *up* the dark. There still *love* in the world. I seen it, *felt* it. As long as there is, the boss muthafucka in Hell ain't won."

"You'll *perish* fighting it."

"No doubt." He grinned at her. "But if just *one* more person loves one other person 'cause of what I do, I win."

"You're wrong." She stepped back from him. "You will lose. Mankind is doomed. Let me show you why."

Reaching for the collar of her robe, she turned around. He saw her reflection in the glass as she pulled down the long zipper and shrugged out of the garment. But it wasn't her satin skin, her shapely shoulders, breasts, and hips that drew his eyes; it was the jet-black tattoo that covered her back.

A long serpentine tail traced between her shoulder blades, feathered but reptilian, clawed feet on the legs of a man, also feathered, wings black as night, but burning red and orange, falling, the body and wings a perfect inverted cross. The head was that of a crow, its mouth agape, a red forked tongue writhing from its beak down to the cleft of her ass. A round red eye glared at him from that head, and he felt a chill, his head pounding.

Then the eye blinked.

24

THE THOUSAND EYES

The reek of decay, filth, old rotting paper, and a pervading chill greet me as I climb the stairs. The space is dark, curtains drawn to block out the view, lights turned low. My vision adjusts, and movement catches my eye. Four figures cloaked in black stand at the corners of the space, hoods shrouding their features, the cult's red inverted cross emblazoned on their raiment. There are pillars to support the upper floors and a metal staircase. Something rustles, more movement among the heaps of old papers, books, and general refuse. *Rats.* I recognize the acrid stench.

At the center of the central space, a human figure lies atop something that looks like an altar, though I can't tell. I feel cold, uncomfortable, uneasy. Something's very wrong. Something's here that shouldn't be.

"Welcome." The voice comes from the figure lying atop the altar. "Please, come in."

I walk closer, my stocking feet rustling the litter of old newspapers, pages torn out of books, faded photographs. The darkness becomes twilight as my eyes dilate. The altar is not stone, but wood, a desk, something a powerful businessman might have once sat behind.

"Forgive the clutter." The figure sits up slowly, legs swinging over the side of the desk toward me. "The cleaning lady doesn't get in much anymore."

I catch a whiff of urine, infirmity, decay. I can't see precisely, but his clothing looks like rags wrapped around and around, dark and stained, like he's been mummified. Still, something feels wrong here, but I can't discern where it's coming from.

"You're Father Martin Pederson?"

"I once was." He stands, seeming weak, frail, more so than his years should warrant, and hobbles around the desk to sit in a chair I hadn't noticed. "Not anymore."

I long to ask him what happened to him, why he left the Church, his calling, why he gave up, but that's not why I'm here.

"I'd like to ask you about a patient you performed an exorcism on twenty-two years ago. His name was—"

"Laurence Caldwell." He sighs and opens a drawer in the desk. Something rustles as he reaches in. "My greatest failure." He pulls out a bottle and puts it on the desk. Tiny shapes fall from it and skitter away.

Cockroaches. I shudder, but it seems ironically appropriate that the prophet of a doomsday cult would live amidst vermin, the creatures that will inherit the Earth if we are swept away. But I'm not done fighting yet.

"It wasn't a failure."

"He taught me the futility of my efforts. I destroyed his soul."

"No, you didn't."

"Would you like a drink?" He pulls two glasses from the drawer. More shapes skitter aside as he puts them down. "I can't offer many amenities, but single malt whiskey is rare these days."

I've lived in squalor for centuries, eaten vermin-infested garbage to survive while others died of starvation and dysentery around me. Pestilence has no grip on me, but something about cockroaches makes my skin crawl.

"No, thank you."

Four voices hiss from the cloaked figures. "Rude... Disrespectful... Heresy... Blasphemy..." I can't tell which voice comes from which, but they make my skin crawl worse than the vermin.

"Do not fail or refuse to offer hospitality to strangers," Pederson quotes, pouring into the two glasses.

Roaches thrash in the alcohol, trapped, dying in agony. The peaty pungent aroma reaches me, and my mouth waters despite my revulsion. My host pushes a glass across the desk toward me and raises his own.

"Drink with me, and I'll tell you about Laurence Caldwell." A cockroach gains the rim of his glass and crawls up his arm. He seems not to notice.

I focus on him, trying to feel his emotions, but I only get a roil of confusion I can't pick apart. Not unlike Emil, but instead of data, a hundred voices speaking at once. He's psychotic, delusional, perhaps unstable. The other four are blank, cold and lifeless inside, but they're obviously not happy with my refusal. If I refuse the drink, I may set them off or alienate Pederson. I need what's in his head. I pick up the glass.

"Good." Pederson smiles, and I see his face closely. He's emaciated, cheeks hollow, eyes sunken. He's only sixty, but he looks a century. "Bottoms up." He tosses back the liquor, roaches and all.

With three fingers, I scoop out my unwelcome insectoid garnish and flick them aside, then toss it back. Smoky peat explodes in my mouth, sinuses, throat, dredging up a thousand memories of the highlands from centuries past. I draw in a breath through my teeth... *Ah, Robert...such a wonderful fool.*

"You don't like my pets, I see." Pederson puts his glass down.

"I prefer my whiskey neat, thank you." An old joke comes to mind, but I don't think he would appreciate it. I place my glass carefully on the desk. "Now, about your patient."

"They're survivors, you know." He lowers a hand into the open drawer, ignoring my impetus. He raises it crawling with vermin, lifting it to examine them as they scurry about, falling to skitter away. "They'll outlive us all. God's chosen. Our worthy successors."

"They serve a place, as do all God's creatures." I don't want to get into a religious discussion about evolution. Been there, done that, burned the tee shirt. A dull headache swells up behind my eyes. "Your exorcism didn't destroy Caldwell's soul, Martin. You banished the Nephilim that had already *displaced* his soul. What I need to know is how you managed it."

"Nephilim?" Confusion, a flash of lucidity.

"Heresy... Lies... Sacrilege... Blasphemy..."

I'm getting sick of these assholes, and they're making my headache worse. "Can we speak in private, please?"

"They are my watchers. They help me see, help me atone." He pours more whiskey for us and picks up his glass. "Come with me."

I pick up my glass and follow. What else can I do? Unfortunately, the four watchers also follow. I feel their eyes on me like the skittering cockroaches.

Pederson ascends the metal staircase stiffly as if in pain. I consider touching him, taking his infirmity, but that would leave me at least momentarily incapacitated. Without any weapons, I can't risk it.

At the top, he presses a button, and the heavy metal door whines open to sunlight. He steps through, shielding his eyes, his wispy gray hair fluttering. There's nothing above him but sky; the upper floors have been removed. The former observation level is now an open platform. I see his clothing more clearly and cringe. They're rags, or perhaps bandages, for the stains are not just urine and feces, but blood as well.

Uneasy, I follow him onto the roof. I can't retreat. The four watchers block the stairs behind me. A cold breeze ruffles my hair, flinging back the hoods of the watchers' cloaks as they emerge into the light. I see their faces for the first time, two men, two women, their heads shaved, young, beautiful, eyes intense but expressions strangely blank. They have no facial tattoos. *Watchers.* I wonder what they are. My head is pounding now, and I know something's wrong. Something's assaulting my mind, trying to pry itself inside like a knife opening an oyster.

"Darkness is coming... Embrace the night... Our destiny... God's judgment..."

I *really* wish they'd shut up.

I squint against the light and take in the stupendous view. There are no railings, nothing but a man-sized inverted cross on a geared framework. It's painted red, but there are rust-brown stains beneath it. Blood.

"You want to know how Laurence Caldwell was exorcised." Pederson approaches the cross and turns back to face me. "I'll tell you, for a price."

There are straps on the cross. The watchers step around me. My head aches. "If you think for one second I'm going to—"

But the watchers walked past me to surround their prophet. Three begin to unwrap him while one cranks a mechanism that rotates the cross. Beneath the wrappings, scars, welts, wounds, and sores. His flesh is a tapestry of agony. I don't feel it from him. Why? I can't feel anything through the pounding in my temples.

I don't get headaches!

I look down at the whiskey rippling in my glass. *A drug?* I close my eyes and delve into myself, feeling the tenuous fingers of alcohol. *No, that's not it.* Deeper, subtle, a fog-like haze settling in. *Yes...there you are.* An elusive little poison, altering the tiny messengers that filter information. It's already assaulting my neurological pathways, changing them. I surround and destroy it. My headache vanishes.

Prophet... I have little doubt that they've been drugging him, feeding him chemicals to make him have visions. It's one of the oldest ploys of cults. I wonder what in God's name the drug is making Martin see for them. In his state of guilt and despair, I can only imagine.

But that's not why I'm here.

"Damn waste of good whiskey." I open my eyes and put down my glass to find that the robed watchers have finished preparing their charge. Pederson is strapped to the cross, nude, his flayed chest, arms, legs, raw and weeping, emaciated and shriveled by the cold. Upon his chest, however, is a most curious tattoo. It looks rough, like a prison marking, a raven falling from the sky, burning wings outstretched like an inverted cross.

"Penance." Pederson draws in a sharp breath as one of the watchers pours his glass of whiskey onto his flayed chest. It reaches me finally, a knife of pain through the fog, images, hallucinations, despair... His skin flushes, pulse racing at his throat. "God's punishment for destroying a human soul. Laurence Caldwell's soul. His grace transforms the pain to let me see the darkness. Embrace oblivion."

No, the drug they've been giving him perverts pain into hallucinations, some twist of biochemistry, I'm sure, but it doesn't really matter now. I pity him, certainly, but he's my key, my weapon to truly fight the Nephilim for the first time in my life. The key to saving mankind. Somehow, I have to get through it to find out how he exorcised Caldwell. As the watchers back away from him, one produces a ridged plastic lash made to inflict painful but not lethal wounds. He holds it out to me.

"For the information you seek, you must give me that which I deserve. God's judgment." One of the watchers cranks the mechanism that inverts the cross once again.

Rock and a hard place... If I take the drug from him, the unadulterated pain will likely throw him into cardiac arrest. If I take his injuries, I'll be incapacitated, and the watchers will probably kill me. I have to get past the hallucinations, the madness, to find out how this poor man banished a Nephilim to Hell, and there's no way I can do that except to do as he asks.

As I take the instrument of pain in my hand, I wonder what group delusion these watchers suffer from. I've seen brainwashing before, conditioning with drugs, starvation, pleasure, pain, sex, but nothing quite like this. They stare at us in rapt fascination.

"Embrace the darkness... Penance... Witness God's judgment... Watch and glory..."

Still, I feel nothing coherent from them, and it chills me. Something's not right. They're either whacked to their brainstems on drugs or hopelessly mad. If I don't do as they wish, I doubt I'll get off this roof alive. I kneel before Martin Pederson and weep for what I must do.

"God, forgive me." I grip the lash firmly and slash it hard across his scarred abdomen.

He cries out but not in pain. A flash of vision reaches me through his madness, the world in flames, the end of times. Armageddon. Can I work with this?

"Martin! *Confession* is penance! Tell me about Laurence Caldwell."

"Penance! Yes!" His cry wrings my heart. "I felt his soul die! I failed him!"

"No, you didn't. He was possessed at birth, his soul already gone. You banished a Nephilim!"

"Sacrilege… Blasphemy… Profanity… Lies…" the watchers chant.

"Give me penance!" Martin pleads.

I grit my teeth and slash across his abdomen again. More visions assail me, the end of mankind, a storm of fire wiping Earth clean. "Tell me how you did it!"

He cries out, shuddering, visions of a burning world exploding in his mind. "Penance! Yes. Again!"

"Witness… Witness… Witness… Witness…"

"Would you four shut the fu—" As I turn to glare, I see that the four watchers have divested and turned away from us. Upon their scarred backs, however, are etched the likenesses of one I have never faced but know well. Burning feathered wings, reptilian tail, and avian head in a perfect inverted cross.

Livid forked tongues writhe from the beaked mouths. The red round orbs blink, drinking in the spectacle, feeding on the torment. I wonder for an instant if I'm still under the influence of the poison, if I'm hallucinating, but no. This is real. The tattoos are alive, or rather *possessed*.

Everything crystalizes into sudden clarity, the tower, the island, a fortress, a bastion of deceit, the drug perverting pain into visions, an elegant lie. The coming darkness, ebony feathers, reveling in torment.

I suspected Hell was at work here. I should have trusted my intuition. Malphas, the raven of a thousand eyes, prince of demons, feeder on carrion and pain, is watching me through these poor deluded fools. An army of demon-worshipping cultists surrounds me, believing they're serving God, embracing their destiny.

I am well and truly screwed.

But Malphas doesn't know what I am…yet.

"NICE *INK*." For a moment, Gippy thought he was hallucinating, then the eye blinked again, the pupil rotating toward him. A chill grabbed him by the bowels.

"Do you like it?" The priestess looked over her shoulder at him. "Touch it."

"Um, no thanks." He would rather have touched a rabid rat.

"You fear God's mark, his eye." She turned partway round, the red orb tracking him.

Gippy found himself watching it, unable to look away. He'd seen some freaky ink but never anything that moved. "That some *shit*, woman, but I don't think that's *God's* mark."

"It is! He sees all, your soul, your sins, your desires. He lets me see the coming darkness." She turned full toward him now, the crimson eye eclipsed but still staring at him from the reflection in the window. "He can help *you* embrace it."

"Don't really want to." Gippy took a step back, repulsed. Her chest, abdomen, and legs were crisscrossed with thin scars from a blade or whip.

"But *I* want you to." She stepped toward him, raising a hand toward his face.

He grabbed her wrist. "Don't give a fuck *what* you want. We ain't playin' that game."

"It's no game." She struggled to reach him, but he twisted her arm away, his grip hard on her wrist. She gasped, eyes fluttering. "Yes... I see the darkness!" She reached with her other hand, and he tried to grab that wrist, but she met his hand with hers, intertwining her fingers with his. She was as strong as he, and her long nails bit into the back of his hand. "Feel it! Embrace it!"

And he did.

The pain ran up his arm like an electric shock, then up to his skull. The room around him exploded into fire, the world outside burning, fiery spears falling from the sky.

Gippy caught his breath. "What the *fuck*?" He'd been on some freaky trips once or twice, but this was something new.

"Yes! You see it! You *believe* it!" She dug her nails into the back of his hand. "See God's destiny!"

Gippy gritted his teeth and closed his eyes to the inferno surrounding him. *Not real, not real, not fucking real!* He opened his eyes and glared defiance into her eyes. "Don't know what the fuck's goin' on, but this ain't from God!" He shoved her away, his knees shaking. He could feel the fire crackling around him, the heat, the pain, his skin blistering.

She staggered against the table, sending the glasses clattering, her eyes still fixed on him. "Let me *show* you God's gift." Snatching up one of the glasses, she smashed it against the tabletop. Gripping the base, she drew the jagged end across her stomach.

"What the..." The cut wasn't deep, but her reaction to the wound redoubled his shock.

She gasped, eyes wide, alight with her own hallucination. "Feel it with me! See the world burn with me!" Leaning back against the low table, she ran her hand through the blood, then down between her legs.

"You're out of your fuckin' *mind*, woman!" Gippy caught movement in the window, her reflection, the gleaming red eye watching, the forked tongue writhing. *Oh, don't you even... Not real!*

"No. I feel God's gift in me." She lifted a leg wide, the red forked tongue of the tattoo on her back squirming up from her thatch of pubic hair to lick the blood trickling down her stomach.

Gippy took another step back, both revolted and trying to figure out if he was hallucinating or not. "Don't think God that kinky." *The drink?* He'd had plenty of drug-induced visions before, but nothing quite like this. The pain from the scratches on his hand was fading, but he couldn't suppress the images. He could, however, not believe them. *Not real!* "And I ain't into—"

A muffled cry and she jerked up as if she'd been shocked. She turned, staggering on unsteady legs to face the windows.

A naked man plummeted past, arms flailing, screaming, the same demon-crow tattoo on his back, its red eye wide with panic. Empa's conversation with their prophet evidently wasn't going well.

The high priestess screamed, whirled, and threw the broken glass at Gippy's face. He dodged, but a jagged edge cut a line across his cheek. As he reached for his Glock, pain shot through him, and the flames filling the room roared higher, consuming his flesh. He staggered to his knees, his skin crackling and burning, but managed to raise the pistol. His mind might be reeling, but his hands knew the drill.

"Don't!" Gippy fixed the sights on her as she reached back for the end table, his finger depressing the trigger lock.

She lifted the burning table up over her head, screaming, "Kill them!"

Well fuck! Things were liable to go straight to Hell if he killed their high priestess, but he'd be damned if he'd let her brain him with an end table. He lowered his aim and fired into her knee. Her leg folded, and the table crashed down between them.

Gunfire ripped through the room from behind him, shattering the windows left to right. Something slammed into his back, pitching him forward onto the broken table. He caught a glimpse of the priestess's face, rapt with visions from her injuries, an instant before bullets caught her full in the chest. She was flung back, her eyes wide with surprise as she fell through the shattered window.

Wonder if her fancy tat will fly away, Gippy wondered as pain-induced visions of Armageddon filled his sight. He knew he'd been shot, but not how bad. Even with Empa's duster he still felt like he'd been kicked in the shoulder. He also knew the visions weren't real. *Just a bad trip... Empa needs me!* He reached into his coat pocket for a grenade, fighting through the tornado of fire, pain, annihilation, the world exploding around him. More gunfire, bullets ripping through the fancy furniture.

Come on, Gip, you're not on fire! If you were, the grenade would already have exploded, and you'd be dead! He pulled the pin and pitched the grenade toward the chattering gunfire.

25

TO REIGN IN HELL

artin!" I reach out to cup his hollow cheek in my hand. I have no other choice now; with a demon watching, perhaps influencing his mind, I'll not get any details without delving his soul. His pain-induced hallucinations fill me, the entire world dying around me, flames, floods, earthquakes, billions dying...all God's will, a monumental lie. "Look at me!"

"No!" His eyes are tightly closed.

"Punish him... Penance... God's will... No mercy..." The chant goes on. I half expect them to break into Abba's greatest hits.

Talk about torture...

"Martin!" I lean close, whispering, pouring myself into him. "God *loves* you! Look at me."

"What?" His eyes open, startlingly blue, and I *delve*.

It's like diving into a hurricane of molten metal. I cry out, I think, but I can't tell. My mind reels as a thousand flaming swords pierce me. Through, deeper, swimming past piranhas feasting on my flesh, a sea of flames burning me, fighting to think through it. Amid the chaos, I find Martin Pederson, the brilliant young priest wishing only to help people. The guilt when he felt the empty shell of Laurence Caldwell, his crisis of faith. I see the tattoo being carved into his chest in prison, his first visions of Armageddon, the lie that has coiled around his soul. I surround the guilt, take it away; I can at least absolve him of that.

Back farther, deeper, memories, every nerve on fire, hard to breathe through the shuddering waves of pain. *No wonder they used him as their prophet.* In five thousand years, I've felt nothing like it. I'm burning, my flesh blistering. *Focus! Remember! See the exorcism! Details!*

The restrained figure of a man in a hospital bed, shoulders and forehead strapped down, a bite block in place, IV's hanging. Laurence Caldwell. He's not intubated, breathing rapidly, eyes moving behind his lids as the Nephilim struggles against the narcotic and physical restraints.

Another wave of flames score through my flesh, lightning bolts of agony. I can't see. I want to collapse, writhe, scream. *No! Think! See it!*

No, not narcotics. I see a syringe, a needle piercing a bottle with a yellow label. *Ketamine. Of course.* Not intubated, they'd use something that didn't suppress respiration. *Is that the key?* I delve Martin's memories for the dosage: 150 milligrams push for induction, maintenance drip from a one milligram per mL IV infusion. *Yes!* The dissociative anesthetic doesn't simply put the patient to sleep at that dosage but disconnects the conscious mind. It might make the Nephilim's grip on its host...slippery.

I get the whole procedure of the exorcism in one dump and fight my way back through the visions of Armageddon to the surface. I dare not take his pain or the drug. Instead, I give him something more: God's love.

Before I am fully back into myself, still writhing with the agony of my burning flesh, a hand grips my shoulder, dragging me backward. The floor hits me hard, jarring me back to lucidity.

"Blasphemer!" One of the watchers reaches down for my throat.

Millenia of survival reflexes and combat training brings my arms up to block his grip. I drive a kick into his side and roll away. My legs don't want to hold me up, but the memory of burning alive is fading. I don't know how Martin survives it.

Speaking of survival... The four cultists close in, faces contorted with rage, muttering their maniacal chant. They're between me and the door, and there's nothing behind me but a thousand-foot drop. A deep breath, and I banish the last of the false pain, but not the fatigue. I'd kill for a double espresso or a weapon, but I'm not going to get either one.

Weapon... They're unarmed, and the stupid little lash lies on the concrete before Martin. It might serve as a dagger if I can snap it off, but they'll be on me before I reach it. Even if they're not trained, four on one is a hard sell. Old lessons: *When in doubt, talk your way out of it, then run like hell. Don't let them get a grip on you. Don't get tangled up. Hit and run. Groin, knee, solar plexus, throat...*

"There's no need for this! I didn't hurt him!" I move sideways, hoping to get around them, but they corral me toward the edge.

"You're a blasphemer!" The man who tried to choke me takes center stage. He's big, thick, probably outweighing me by half, but he moves clumsily.

"I'm really not," I argue, moving away again.

"Liar! Whore!" Spits one of the women, closing in from the side, her hands held like claws.

"Says the naked, drug-addled, demon-possessed cultist." So much for negotiation. Baiting works, too.

She complies, lunging at me with hands outstretched. The others try to close with her, but she's in the lead. I drive a kick into her just below her ribs, and she folds. The beefy guy grabs for me, two hundred pounds of meat moving forward. *Perfect.* I grip his wrist, pull, and roll back, planting a foot in his gut as he pitches over me. A blood-curdling cry as I roll up, perilously close to the edge. My assailant is gone, plummeting to the street.

Grim gallows humor rises in me, an attempt to provoke the others into similar stupidity. "All those feathers, and *still* he can't fly."

The taunt doesn't score, and the other two close as the woman I kicked struggles to her feet.

"You'll die screaming, bitch!"

"Or *laughing.*" If I can just provoke them, I have a chance. "Why don't you—"

Gunfire from below, muffled at first, then a prolonged rip of full-auto and shattering glass. *Gippy! Damn it, Gip, don't get killed! Please!* I pray he's on the sending rather than the receiving end of the gunfire. Then a concussive CRUMP shakes the floor under my feet. *Grenade. Good boy.*

My assailants are at least momentarily distracted by the blast. *Now or never.* I spin low and put everything I've got into a kick to the guy's knee. It folds with a snap. I dive past as he starts to go down, but the woman to his left lunges, arms wide, and tangles up my legs. Concrete slaps me hard, but I'm already kicking, lashing out blindly to break free. My heel connects with something, and her grip starts to fail. I scrabble to my hands and knees.

Something heavy slams into my back, driving me back down. The floor cracks my chin, and I'm dazed for an instant. An instant too long. I flail out with elbows and feet, but all three of them are on top of me. Blows land, driving me down, numbing shock. A hand in my hair slams me down. Stars explode in my head. *Is that gunfire or the echo of my skull cracking?* The world spins for a moment, and I'm being dragged.

Better than waking up falling...

More gunfire, tremors from an explosion. *Gippy...I need you, buddy.* I blink away blood and twist to break the grip on my jacket. A hard blow, a kick, strikes me in the lower back. Numbing pain, and I almost black out again.

Voices and crushing weight. I can't understand what they're saying. I blink and see Martin lying in a pitiful heap, one of the cultists draping a cloak over him. He's breathing, at least. I try to rise, but there's a knee in my back, and my arm is folded back until the shoulder feels like it will pop out of the socket.

"Now who's laughing, cunt!"

I'd make a quip, but I'm having trouble thinking straight. I'm lifted, arm still painfully behind my back. A bloody face, the woman I kicked, her nose smashed, her teeth a bloody rictus. The man holds my other arm, but my feet are free. My vision clears, and the quip comes to me.

"My cunt's not laughing. Is yours?" I snap a kick into her crotch.

Getting the shit kicked out of me makes me stupid sometimes. My arm is wrenched hard, and I feel a pop. Now it's *definitely* dislocated. I scream, but it's cut off by a hard blow to the stomach.

I fold over the blow and retch, the world turning gray.

A scream—mine—as my shoulder's pulled straight, popping back into joint, and something tightens around my wrists, arms, thighs, ankles. A flash of memory: *Go not to Jerusalem. A hammer driving spikes through my poor uncle's hands and feet.* To this day, I don't know how he didn't cry out.

"Wake up, blasphemer!" A hand grabs my chin, and my eyes flutter open.

My head clears a little. The cultist's face is contorted with rage, an inch from mine. The two women stand behind him. One holds a short knife.

Not good.

I don't hear any more gunfire, so Gippy's probably dead. I was a fool to bring him here, a fool to hope. But we had to try. *See you in Heaven, my son.*

"Now, you'll pay for your heresy!" The woman brandishes the knife.

Sergeant Gattish's voice echoes through the pain. *Fight of die! You think there's mercy in this world?*

I don't have a lot left, and I'm tied to a cross. My only hope now is to die quickly before they discover what I truly am. I open my mouth to provoke them, taunt the woman into killing me. Better than years of torment. What comes out of my mouth surprises even me.

"Malphas, Raven of a Thousand Eyes, Eater of Carrion, Slave of the Serpent, Prince of Hell, be *gone* from these poor mortals!"

They look confused. Understandable, considering the language was ancient Hurrian. I don't know if my attempt has done anything, but it's given them pause. They're not possessed; I would have felt that. But they carry the mark of Malphas, and so are his. If I can drive the demon away...

I feel the wood behind me and realize I have one more weapon. "By the cross of Jesus Christ, Son of God, get thee back to Hell!"

Something fills me, then fades. Still, I don't know what's happened, if anything. My assailants look perplexed, confused, blinking at each other. Maybe it did work.

"I'm tired of listening to her blabber!" The man says. "Cut out her tongue."

Or maybe not.

I clench my jaw tight as the knife-wielder raises her blade. She tries to pry my mouth open, curses, and applies the blade to the muscle of my jaw.

I scream.

POP-POP-POP

Something spatters my face like warm rain.

EARS RINGING FROM THE BLAST, Gippy grabbed his guitar case and scrabbled out of the line of fire, emptying the clip of his Glock blindly. Something grated in his shoulder with the weight of the case, pain and visions lancing through him in jolts. Someone fired back randomly from the central room, panic fire that did nothing but tell him his grenade hadn't taken them all out. He slammed into the wall, and the pain exploded like a supernova, folding his knees. The visions flared up, his head swimming as he fumbled the Glock back into the holster and clicked open the latches of the guitar case.

Don't pass out, don't pass out, don't pass out. Blinking to clear the visions of flame and destruction, he looked down into the case. The hours of practice Empa had put him through clicked into place.

He slipped on the headset first and cinched down the strap. Flipping down the eyepieces activated the telemetry to the rifle. The ghostly overlay jumped and blurred for a moment as he lifted the weapon out and chambered a round. It was heavier than he remembered. One more switch powered up the sighting lasers and gave him crosshairs. Her lecture came back to him.

"The trouble with the LAWS system is that it's complicated, delicate, and doesn't handle field conditions well. The wifi can be jammed by EM interference, and rough handling knocks the lasers out of alignment, so don't expect to slam it around hard and have it work. It will, however, let you hit a target at a quarter-mile without much practice."

He'd put five hundred rounds downrange with this same rifle and had fallen in love with it. It was like the best videogame ever. However, the other trick it performed, that he needed now, was to shoot around corners.

Gippy slid sideways with his back against the wall, trying to calm his breathing. His heart pounded in his ears, and every move sent jolts through his left shoulder. Worse, the room around him refused to stop burning, and every shot of pain sent the flames higher. That, at least, he could do something about.

He hadn't taken any Vickies for almost a week, hadn't felt the need, but now he had more need than ever. He fumbled the plastic baggie out of his pocket and shook two of the little white gems into his palm. He swallowed them dry and stuffed the bag away. They wouldn't kick in for a few minutes, and he didn't know how they would react with whatever shit had been in that drink, but if he survived the next ten minutes, he'd need the help to get them out of Manhattan. *Them...* If Empa was still alive.

"Just stay alive, E. I'm comin'."

Nosing the rifle around the corner gave him a view of the room through the eyepieces. One figure lay sprawled and unmoving. He glimpsed a helmet over the rim of an upended table, and the two guards stationed at the stairs had taken cover in the far wing, standing with rifles poised around the corners of the opening. One of them must have spotted him and fired a burst. Chips of molding and drywall flew, but her aim was high. Gippy gritted his teeth, centered the crosshairs on her chest, and squeezed the trigger.

Holding the rifle unbraced made the recoil worse, but two of the three rounds hit home, one in the chest, one in her throat. The image in the lenses was crisp enough to show the surprise on her face as she fell.

A hail of fire forced him to pull back. He considered another grenade but doubted he could throw it far enough with his shoulder in flames. *Fine, then. Time to light up the dark.*

Working the pump action to chamber a grenade in the under-barrel launcher hurt his shoulder. He leaned out, centered the crosshairs on the far room, and pulled the launcher trigger. Shrapnel took out every window in the room, and hopefully, the shooter. Scanning the smoke and dust, he glimpsed the other guard going for the elevator. Just as he slapped the button, Gippy's burst dropped him.

Silence...nothing but the high-pitched whine of his ringing ears. He scanned the room—still nothing—and stood on shaky legs. The hallucinations seemed to be easing a little. *Only had one sip of the shit; maybe it's a short ride.* He could hope.

He heard a distant cry.

Move, Gip. She needs you.

He dumped the half-empty mag, picked another from the case, and slapped it in. That reminded him that his shoulder hurt. *Fuck it! I'm not dead! Move!* He stuffed two more mags from the case into his pockets, jacked another grenade in the launcher, and took up a proper firing stance at the corner. He leaned around and scanned, the red sighting lasers visible in the smoke. Nothing. He stepped out, sweeping, moving.

The guy by the elevator had caught a round at the base of his neck and was either dead or dying. He knew the woman he'd shot was dead. The other he couldn't spot. He pushed the call button beside the elevator and moved to the opposite observation room. It was shredded by shrapnel, a cold breeze wafting the smoke in eddies through the shattered windows, but he couldn't spot a body.

Then she stood up from behind an upset table, using her rifle to push herself up. Gippy swept his rifle and centered the crosshairs on her chest, the lasers jumping and blurring in the smoke. She saw the beams, then him, looked at him, her face bloody, shocked. She started to lift her rifle.

"Don't!" he shouted, gritting his teeth.

She hesitated. "Embrace the darkness." The rifle rose.

Gippy killed her, a centered three-round burst to the chest. That same surprised look and she fell back through the open window.

"Fuck!"

The elevator bell dinged.

He whirled, but it was empty. *Finally, a fucking break.* He hurried over before the doors could close and dragged the dead guard half in. That, at least, would keep anyone downstairs from paying them a surprise visit.

Next, the doors to the stairs. That posed a problem. They were locked, and the print scanner might be fragged. Limping over—Had he hurt his leg, or was he still just shaky from the hallucinations?—he poked the button above the pad. It lit up green.

"Fuckin' A!" But the pad wasn't keyed to his prints, and one of the guards was nothing but a sidewalk stain eighty-four floors down. He looked to the other guard. Her dead eyes stared blankly up at the ceiling.

"Come on, lady, time to open the doors to Heaven." He slung his rifle and dragged her over to the doors, then propped her up and pressed her hand to the pad. It *bleeped*, and the doors popped open. "Thank you, God."

He shouldered his weapon and peered up the stairs. *Dark up there.* He flipped the IR imaging switch on the rifle's scope, and the top of the stairs snapped into clear gray and white in his lenses.

"Sweet."

He went up, sweeping the weapon around to pierce the gloom. Filth, vermin, refuse, but nothing he hadn't seen during years on the street. One huge rustling rodent just about bought a ticket to rat Heaven, but he managed not to fire. Nobody home; only an old desk with a liquor bottle sitting there. His ears were still ringing, but he thought he heard voices from the stairs. Sunlight streamed down at a steep angle. He started up carefully, flipping off the IR as he neared the top.

Daylight, windy, and definitely voices.

Then a scream.

Empa!

Gippy took the last few steps at a run, rifle ready, and beheld a scene straight out of Hell.

Three figures—two women and a man—stood around a red cross. They were naked, and all three had tattoos like the priestess, but these were melting away like watercolor paintings in rain, the red eyes running like blood. That registered in a flash before Gippy realized Empa was lashed to the cross, and one of the women was cutting into her face with a knife. Her scream raked on his every nerve.

Sweet Jesus!

Crosshairs leapt to the woman's head, and Gippy squeezed the trigger. The three-round burst blasted her brains into a fine mist. The other two whirled to face him.

"Mutha fuckas!" Gippy put two bursts into the man. The woman started to raise her hands, eyes wide, but he didn't care. He killed her without a flicker of remorse. Then he was running. "Empa!"

Her face was bloody, a streaming headwound above her eye and a deep gash at her cheek. He slung the rifle and drew one of the carbon blades. He had her free in seconds, but catching her weight sent lightning stabbing through his shoulder and re-intensified the hallucinations. *Snakes, this time? Really? Not real!* They went down in a pile, but he cushioned her fall.

"Empa!" He pressed fingers to her throat, but she coughed blood into his face, and her eyes fluttered open. *Thank God!*

She looked at him quizzically for an instant. "'Bout *time* you got here."

He barked a giddy laugh. *Not just alive, but attitude!* "Hit traffic." He shook out a kerchief and pressed it to the head wound. "You okay?"

"Gimmie a second." She winced and coughed again. "I got my ass kicked here."

"Yer makin' a habit of that." He fumbled for his packet of Vickies and shook one out, then fished a bottle of water from another pocket. "Here, swallow that. Take the edge off."

"What..." She swallowed hard and nodded. "Better living through chemistry."

"Hold that to your head. Gotta do somethin' 'bout your jaw. Bleedin' bad." It was bright red. He cut a swath off his shirt and pressed it to the wound hard. "What the fuck happened? Three weak-ass punks. Figured you'd clean 'em up like scrapin' shit from yer shoe."

"There were four." She winced as he pressed the kerchief harder to stop the bleeding. "And I was...a little preoccupied with Martin."

"Ha! Tell me about preoccupied! That priestess bitch slipped me a roofie that has the whole world burnin' around me. Like I felt *myself* burning! Some freaky dope!"

"Yeah, I got that from Martin, too." Empa flexed her shoulder and winced, then struggled to sit up. She nodded to the other figure there, an old man lying under a cloak. "I had to wade through six shades of Hell to get what we needed from him."

"But you got it?" Gippy felt a surge of relief. "You know how he pitched that Nephilim fucker back to Hell?"

"I think so, yes." She pulled the kerchief away from her head and dabbed it. The bleeding had slowed to an ooze, so she pressed it to her jaw. "Help me up."

"Sure." He tried, but his knees folded when she grabbed his injured shoulder. He didn't quite scream. "Sorry. Don't grab there. Other side." He put his right arm under hers and lifted.

"You're hit?" She wobbled on her legs and helped him up in turn. "Where?"

"My back, but I'm okay, I think. Just every time I bump it, my fuckin' head explodes." He blinked and squinted away the illusions.

"I can fix that, at least." She put a hand to his cheek, and the illusions vanished.

"Thanks!" Gippy pointed to the smeared tattoos on the cultist's backs as they started to hobble past. "So, what happened to them. Look like the ink melted."

"They were being used by a demon. The tattoos were…like cameras for it to watch through. It was probably manipulating them at some level, too." She looked back at the bloody cross. "I sent it packing, with a little help."

"Talkin' help, here you go." He unclipped her holstered pistol and held it out. "We should move if you can. Shit's gonna get ugly 'round the 'hood."

"If it hasn't already." She looked down at the old man and started to go to him.

"Empa." Gippy grabbed her arm. "We gotta go. Can't be luggin' him 'round with us. Sorry, but we can't."

She nodded and sniffed. "Misguided servant of God, I'm sorry."

He tugged her arm, and she followed.

26

FLIGHT OF ANGELS

By the time we get in the elevator, I'm feeling a little better. At least my ears aren't ringing, and I'm not seeing double anymore. We look like death warmed over, but we're alive, armed to the teeth, and moderately mobile. I feel the fuzz of narcotics as the pill Gippy gave me takes hold. It won't last, but for a while, it'll take the edge off. A welcome numbness, for my shoulder is still killing me. I suspect Gippy's taken some as well. There'll be Hell to pay later, I'm sure. As we descend, locked, loaded, armored, and weighted down with the gear from the guitar cases, I have time to think.

Our survival now hinges on one thing. "We *must* take the vehicle."

"Won't be easy." Gippy seems steadier, though I can feel his pain still. I long to heal his shoulder, but I'm not in any better shape.

"*Walking* to the ferry pickup isn't an option." The numbers on the floor indicator descend to the teens, then single digits. We slow. "Get ready."

Gippy pulls a grenade and jerks the pin free. "Fire in the hole."

The bell dings a merry note, the doors start to open, and he pitches the grenade out. We hunker as gunfire and screams erupt. Bullets riddle the backside of the elevator, then the grenade explodes. Shrapnel clatters through the door, further marring the elevator's interior. We're through the doors, picking our targets before the debris settles.

While Gippy needs the help of the LAWS system, I prefer a simpler, more rugged weapon. Call me old-fashioned, but I humped an HK through more desert than Christ on a donkey—not a metaphor, I actually worked out the mileage once. Also, with everyone's auntie wearing body armor these days, I want more knockdown than a puny 5.56mm round. While he sweeps right, I go left. Two people are down in my field, and I make sure they stay that way with two rounds each. A shadow staggers in the distance through the dust, and I knock it down with three shots. There are no friendlies here. Gippy's firing bursts at my back, three, four...silence.

"Clear!"

"Clear!" he replies.

"Take the far wall. Lay down smoke behind us."

"Smoke out." The clink-clatter of a smoke grenade, and I spare a glance to make sure he's taking his position.

We advance on the doors, moving from cover to cover in leapfrogs, each covering the other. Through the entry, the big black vehicle is still parked by the curb. Luckily, no plummeting cultists pancaked the thing. I glimpse movement over the hood.

"Cover!" I flatten myself behind a column as full-auto rips through the entryway, sending glass and lead flying past us. The fire continues, a full magazine, a useless waste of ammo.

We're lucky they're amateurs. I lean out the instant the firing stops and put a single round in the shooter's face while he looks down for more ammo. I glimpse movement through the tinted glass and pop two more slugs home. No joy. Armorglass. I duck back.

"At least one more behind or inside the vehicle."

"Got it!"

More auto fire and chips of marble and concrete fly from my pillar. I yawn to clear my ears from the grenade blast, blink away the dust, and flex my aching shoulder. The rifle's recoil is killing me. Gippy holds his weapon around the edge of his own column, gazing off into space. He loves his new videogame. He squeezes off a burst and the firing stops.

"Get him?"

"Her. Yep." He slaps in a new magazine then takes another look. "Don't see... Wait. One more. Kneeling near the front wheel. No shot."

Kneeling...

I slide down the pillar, lay flat on my back, shoulder my HK and roll out. A round in the man's knee sends him screaming to the ground. Gippy's moving before I can get up, through the door, up against the vehicle, scanning the street by sweeping his weapon slowly around. I pop the screaming man's head with another round and follow, hunkering behind the rear wheel well.

"Well, that wasn't so—" Slugs ping against the vehicle a half heartbeat before the report. I spoke too soon. Luckily, they're lousy shots. I innately fix on the direction. "Up and left!"

"Right!"

"No, *left!*" I point.

He looks at me and makes a face. "Sorry! I meant I got it."

I lean out, but rounds crack against the pavement inches from my foot. Okay, maybe they're not such lousy shots.

Gippy props his rifle over the top of the vehicle, staring into the tinted window. More fire from above. He doesn't flinch, sweeps, freezes. The muscles of his jaw clench, and he squeezes off a burst. Silence.

"Get him?"

"Dunno. Shut him up, at least."

"In the car." I slap the side of the vehicle. "You drive. I've got to call our ride."

"Got it." He slings his rifle, pulls his Glock, and cracks the door, clearing the interior before he lunges inside. The kid's got promise. I pile into the back as the huge engine roars to life, and Gippy smokes the tires in a highly illegal U-turn.

"Can you find the dock?" I pull my phone and punch the water taxi woman's number.

"Think so."

I text: *Pickup at Cathedral dock ASAP. Coming Dark pissed. Hot LZ. Will pay for your trouble.* As I pocket my phone, something cracks against the side of the car.

Gippy swerves. "Looks like someone called ahead!"

I look around. We're screaming down Sixth past Bryant park. "Take a right on Forty-fifth. I don't want to get too close to their Cathedral."

"Fuckin' *right*, we don't!" He slows a little to take the corner.

No more gunfire, but quite a few curious faces from windows. My phone buzzes as we roar past Fifth Ave. "Next left." I pull up the return text. "Shit!"

"What?"

"Ferry trouble." The text reads, *FO. No way. You piss off my customers!*

I text, *10K NAD, cash!*

Gippy slows to take a left on Madison and shouts, "Shit!" Tires howl, and I slap the back of the seat as we screech to a stop. The street in front of The Roosevelt is blocked by a mob of about fifty cultists and piles of salvaged wire, copper pipe, and assorted junk. They're workers, not warriors, but the only way through is a circuitous route around the piles crowded with people. And they're all looking at us.

"Back!"

"Ya think?" Gippy smokes tires in reverse, screeches to a stop, and tears down Forty-fifth. He still doesn't quite have the finesse of evasive driving down pat yet. "So, we gonna *drive* back uptown?"

"I'm working on it! Drive!" We swerve around salvaged wrecks down the canyon of towering buildings under the Park Avenue overpasses. A few furtive faces hunker there, obviously living in the backs of old trucks and containers. I try to remember what cross street the dock was on.

My phone buzzes. The message reads, *20K Cash!*

I tap, *Done! Hurry!* and send it. We don't have time to haggle. "They're picking us up! Next left on Lexington."

"Good." He slows to make the turn; there are too many wrecked vehicles to take it fast.

We weave our way past clogged intersections at Fiftieth and Fifty-first, soaring towers of shattered glass and concrete glaring down. I glance west toward St. Bartholomew's and glimpse a crowd of cultists moving north. *Not good.* Word's out, and they know where we're going.

Water laps over the road ahead.

"Take it slow." The filthy water isn't deep, but it could hide hazards. I see a swirl and point. "Manhole. Don't drive over it."

"Gotcha." We plow through, throwing a wake like an eighteenth-century frigate beating windward.

The big vehicle handles it well, but we bump over unseen debris more than once. At the intersection of Fifty-third, we roll up and over a mountain of broken glass from a hundred thousand shattered windows, then back down the other side into shallow water, and finally dry asphalt at Fifty-fifth.

"Two more blocks, then right on Fifty-seventh."

"Got it." He speeds up, swerving to avoid mounds of broken concrete and red brick that used to be upscale apartments and hotels. Fifty-seventh is clearer and we take the corner fast.

Sporadic gunfire and I check behind us. A mob with a few black-uniformed guards carrying rifles fills the street two blocks back. A round strikes the rear window a foot from my face. *Note to self, send another thank you note to the manufacturer of Armorglass.* It's not the first time the stuff has saved my life.

We howl around the corner onto Third Avenue. The dock is empty; no cultists, but no boat either.

"Shit!" Gippy stops the vehicle. "Thought you said—"

"She said she was coming." I glance back, evaluating our position. We're exposed, but the cultists are coming down Fifty-seventh. We could make a stand at the corner, but that puts us half a block from the dock. We don't have many options. "Pull back close to the building. We've got to hold them off until the boat gets here."

"Great."

As Gippy maneuvers—parallel parking isn't his strong suit, but he puts us three feet from the building—I text, *ETA? We need evac ASAP!*

"Out. Keep under cover between the truck and the building."

"Fuck *yes*, cover!" He leaves the engine running and hauls his rifle out the driver's side.

Between the armored vehicle and the building, we have protection at least from small arms fire. I edge to the corner, take a left-hand grip on my rifle, and peer around at the mass of cultists. The black uniforms of the armed guards make them perfect targets. My crosshairs line up nicely with the inverted crosses, and I send some careful fire downrange. Three go down before they scatter and return fire.

The distinctive clatter of a Kalashnikov forces me to take cover. *And I thought I was old-school.* Bullets spall off the cornice, ricochet off our ride, and clang against the steel facing of a bank building across the avenue. I take another careful look. The crowd has split to the sides of the street, advancing behind wrecked vehicles. Behind me, the built-up pier blocks the alley, so they can't flank us without swimming, but they might come at us through the building.

My phone vibrates. "Switch! Got a call."

"Hope it's good news." Gippy takes my place, easing his weapon around the corner and scanning with his wifi scope. He fires a burst as I read the text.

Ten min. Hear gunfire. That you?

I tap, *FUCK YES! HURRY!* And hit send. "Ten minutes, Gip."

"Ten *minutes*?" He looks at me incredulously. "We got maybe *three* before they're up our asses, E."

"We need to hold them off." I pump a grenade into my launcher.

"Trade places and watch our backs. Anything comes out the building or the alley, kill it."

"Got it." He slips past and crouches with his back to the front wheel as I peer around the corner.

Cultists are crossing the intersection at Lexington. The rangefinder gives me an overlay in my scope, and I send a grenade into the wrecked vehicles on the north side of the street, pump in another, and fire into the cover on the far side before the first one detonates. I reload the launcher as the twin explosions echo along the man-made canyons. *Memories... building to building firefights in Syria, Berlin, Beirut, Bagdad, St. Louis...* I'd give my left tit for air support, armor, or even artillery.

I risk a quick look—they've gained a third of a block—and jerk back as more rounds send chips of brick flying. Whoever's firing the AK knows his business. I hold my rifle around the corner and fire two more grenades blindly, then lean out after they explode. I drop two more black-clad cultists, but not the marksman, and duck back before return fire can find me. They know where I am and are advancing under cover from their sniper. I reload grenades—I don't have an endless supply of those— check my magazine, and switch from semi to full auto. *Time to play some whack-a-mole.* But I'm the mole, and I need to take out the hammer before it gets me.

I stand, hold my rifle high around the corner, and fire two blind bursts, one up the street, one across. I jerk back as the marksman returns fire, dropping prone and flipping back to semi-auto. I scrabble forward and spot the muzzle flash in the dark recess of a building several floors up. Two rounds right on the flash shuts him up, hopefully for good. More incoming fire, this time wild, pings against the side of our vehicle as I crawl back.

A burst from behind me, and I glance back to see a figure with a pistol slumping on the steps of the building behind us. Young, a boy.

"Dumbass," Gippy mutters with genuine remorse. "Stepped out like this was an ol-time western shoot-out."

"Scout or a distraction." I dump my nearly empty mag and slap in another. "Keep sharp! If they get behind us, we're screwed!"

"Got it!" He opens the driver's door for cover and levels his rifle between the door and the windshield. Smart kid.

I lean out and find myself staring right at a cultist. He's running in the open, something in his hands, barely fifty feet away. I put two shots in his chest and duck back before his bomb goes off. Shrapnel and pieces of cultist clatter past. "Fucking suicide bombers! Watch close, G!"

"I'm on it!"

I peer out. More are coming. *Aim-fire-aim-fire-duck.* I hear two bursts from Gippy's rifle, but I'm too busy to look. *Cover my ass, Gip. Aim-fire...* I glimpse a figure leveling something over the hood of a wrecked car. I aim, but he fires first. A huge billow of smoke and an RPG screams past, missing our vehicle by a foot. I fire a burst into the smoke before it hits the bank building behind me. The explosion sends a rain of broken glass flying like an ice storm down on us.

"What the *fuck!*"

"RPG!" I shake bits of tempered glass from my hair.

He casts me an incredulous look. "You think this a *game*, E?"

My brain stumbles on that, then I realize. "Rocket-propelled grenade, not Role-playing game." I lean back around my corner and lay down some careful suppressive fire, watching for more bombers. They're holding back, maybe to find out if we're dead from the explosion. Gippy fires two bursts, swears, and an explosion behind me sends brick and debris flying past. I glance back just to make sure he's not dead. The building's entry is a wreck, but Gippy's still standing and looking for targets.

My magazine runs out on my next salvo, but I've taught them respect. I reload and check my phone; no messages. The dock: no boat. We have four minutes left. Time does weird things in a battle. I lean out and check for targets just in time to see another RPG fired.

"INCOMING!" I drop and roll under our vehicle.

The rocket hits the building we're hiding behind and all Hell breaks loose.

AT EMPA'S SCREAM, Gippy dove into the cab of the vehicle and covered his head with his arms. The explosion rattled his ears and sent chunks of the building crashing down all around and on top of their ride. A piece the size of a body hit the cab and crumpled it down a foot. Another smaller one shattered the windshield but didn't entirely knock it out. The rain of debris subsided.

Gippy looked up, but he couldn't see far through the dust. The engine was still running by the gauges, but he couldn't hear it. His ears rang.

"Empa! You alive?"

"Think so. You?" Her voice sounded like it was coming through a big pipe.

"Just *great!*" He slid out the driver's door and looked for her. "Where?"

A bloody hand thrust out from under the vehicle. He grabbed it and pulled her out. She had a new contusion on her face, but she still had her rifle.

She looked up at him through the dust. "How's the car?"

"Runnin', but insurance gonna be a *bitch.*"

"No sweat. Non-owner policy. Help me up. The damn muffler smacked me in the—" Her eyes widened, looking up past him. "Gip!"

He shot a glance over his shoulder up at the building. The stone facing was shot with cracks, the crumbling fissures widening. The entire front of the building began to lean outward.

"Get in!" Gippy jerked Empa to her feet and lunged back into the driver's seat.

Empa didn't bother with the door since it was bent with the crumpled roof, but threw her rifle through the shattered window and followed it, screaming, "Go! Go! Go!"

Gippy slammed the shifter into drive and stomped the pedal to the floor. They lurched forward over debris, the big tires spitting rock and dust behind them. He couldn't see a thing through the shattered windshield, but the ridiculously intact side view mirror showed him the avalanche of stone, rebar, and glass behind them. When the front of the vehicle rode up on the inclined quay, he hit the brakes.

"Empa?"

"Still here." Her spiky blue hair, dusted white with powdered concrete, rose from behind the seat. She blinked and looked around. "Nice driving."

"Thanks." He chuckled. "Graduate of the Drive or Fuckin' Die Driving School."

She coughed a laugh and shook her head. "Smartass."

"Gotta laugh or lose your shit, right?" He nodded back to the massive pile of debris. "Think that'll slow 'em down?"

"For maybe a minute or two." She leaned out the window and squinted. "Pull up to the end of the quay and turn this beast sideways. We'll use it for cover while we board the boat."

Gippy glanced out his shattered window and saw the yellow-awning of the water taxi coming around a corner a block away. "Fuckin' A!" He pulled up and jockeyed the vehicle around. The steering wasn't working too well, but he managed. He turned off the motor and patted the splintered plastic dashboard. "Good girl."

A bullet spanged against his door, and he ducked reflexively. "Thought you said a minute or two!"

"They're persistent!" Her rifle barked three times in quick succession.

"They're fuckin' *insane!*" Gippy crawled out the passenger window, dragging his rifle behind. When he leveled it over the dented hood of the vehicle, however, his lenses glared with a red ERROR message. "Fuck!" He ripped off the headset and fired blindly to cover Empa as she squirmed out of the back-seat window.

"What's wrong?"

He hunkered down. "Fuckin' scope's fucked!"

"Here." She reached over, flipped a catch lever, and jerked the high-tech laser sighting system off his rifle. It clattered to the ground. "Welcome to old-school, baby." She hefted her own weapon, its scope also gone, and grinned.

"Bitch, I'm too *young* for this old-school shit!"

"Just keep 'em pinned down." She leveled her rifle through the passenger window and fired another three rounds. "And pray they don't have another RPG."

"I ain't stopped prayin' since we landed on this rock!" He rested his rifle on the mangled hood and took aim through the open sights, sending careful single rounds downrange at anything that moved.

"Good!"

They kept up a steady fire, but Gippy doubted he hit anything. Every time a cultist broke into the open, Empa dropped him. He glanced over his shoulder when his magazine ran empty. The boat was only yards away. The old woman at the wheel looked angry and scared.

"Ride's here!"

Empa glanced back and nodded. "Lay down all the smoke you've got and get aboard."

As Gippy threw three smoke cannisters, one after another, she lay down suppressive fire. He looked back as the boat bumped into the dock bow first.

"Come on, come on, you asshos!" the driver screeched.

"Time to go, E!" He stepped aboard and lay flat on the bow.

Empa emptied a magazine into the smoke as she backed up to the edge, then turned and stepped aboard. "Go!" She dumped the empty magazine and slapped in another, dropping to kneel beside him. "You okay, G?"

"Any better, and I'd be twins!" Something moved in the smoke as they backed up, and Gippy fired at it. An explosion rocked the pier, blasted debris splashing all around them. "Fuckers don't give up."

They backed, picking up speed, both of them continuing to fire steadily.

"You asshos fuckin' *crazy!*" their driver screamed, swinging the boat around when they were half a block away from the pier.

"Just a friendly argument about religious doctrine." Empa jacked a grenade into her launcher and fired. Their vehicle exploded. Standing, she shuffled past the wide-eyed driver to cover the stern. The six peddlers were hunkered low over their stations, pale and pumping madly.

"You ruin my bidness!" the driver screeched. "Where my fuckin' money?"

"Twenty K. Pay the nice lady, Gip." Empa fired into the smoke from the stern, standing like a statue.

Gippy stood, unclipped the money belt, and dropped it in the woman's lap. "Keep the change."

She peeked inside the belt and went silent, guiding them around a corner into safety. Gippy sat down and cleared his rifle. He felt suddenly numb, even the pain of his shoulder only a faint background irritation, like the ringing of his ears.

Empa sat down beside him, filthy, bloody, bruised, and beautiful. "Good work."

"You too." He reached into a coat pocket and pulled out a bottle of water. It was empty, holed by a bullet or some shrapnel. It had been *inside* his coat. The bullet could have just as easily killed him. He stared at it for a full minute before dropping it into the boat. "Fuckin' *fuck.*"

"You okay?" she asked.

He shook his head. "Damned if I know."

"You will be." She clapped him on the knee. "We got what we came for, Gip. Dinner's on me."

Gippy tried to laugh but coughed and choked on it. He put his head in his hands and felt her hand on the back of his head. He closed his eyes and saw the faces, surprised, angry, screaming as he squeezed the trigger of his rifle, and didn't feel anything. He was alive; they weren't, done deal.

The trip back to the hotel was a blur. People boarding the ferry gave them strange looks. They stowed their long guns in the trunk of their car and got cleaned up as best they could, dampening a towel with a bottle of water and wiping the dried blood off each other's faces. Empa drove. Gippy drank half a bottle of water to ease his throat and passed it to Empa, who drank and passed it back without a word. When the bottle was empty, he stared at it. *Inside pocket...could have killed me...* They stopped in front of the hotel.

Gippy leaned out the passenger door and threw up.

Security at the hotel looked worried, but Empa said something witty. Rough gig, bad crowd, never play this town again... Did they need medical attention? No, just bumps and bruises.

Gippy couldn't remember the details, tried to join the conversation but felt like if he spoke, he would scream. They handed over their weapons, submitted to the scans, and took the elevator up to their room. He couldn't find the key, couldn't remember where he'd put it. Empa fished it from the inside pocket of his jacket and pulled him through the door.

He stared at the room, ridiculously clean and tidy. It didn't look real. Empa helped him out of his coat, and he felt lighter, like he'd float away. Wincing as his shirt came off, sitting, boots, socks, pants, gentle coaxing to stand, stumbling, then stepping into the warm spray of a shower. Hands, arms, smooth olive skin against him. He held her close.

He realized she was naked, holding him in the shower. Was he dreaming? No, dreams didn't feel like this. *Numb... blank... empty.*

"Empa...I...can't *feel* anything!"

"It's okay." She held him closer. "It'll come back. Just breathe and let it come back. You're alive. I've got you. You're safe."

Safe? It seemed an alien concept, but her arms felt good; the warm spray felt good. The pain was slowly returning, the fog of numbness lifting. The faces of those he'd killed came back again, startled, screaming, dying. He held her, prayed to God for forgiveness, and sobbed into her shoulder.

27

FULL DISCLOSURE

Gippy's pretty quiet in the morning. So am I. Some things are better left unsaid.

I took his injuries and tried to soothe the mental trauma, but it's hard to do when I'm still recovering from my own. A night's rest and food have healed the physical damage. Breakfast, another shower, clean clothes, and we check out looking like human beings. I worry about Gippy, but I think he'll be okay. I've done all I can for him; the rest is up to him. I wish it got easier but it never does. Killing is harder for us, we who love people instead of hate. I don't tell him that. I also don't tell him that holding him, healing him, feeling him come to grips with what we did, helped me as much as it helped him. I think I'll be okay, too.

I always am, eventually.

In the car, he asks, "Think it was worth it?"

"Yes." My answer comes without hesitation. "If it works, yes. It's the weapon I've been seeking for five-thousand years."

"What is it?" He looks back at the city as we roll over the parkway spans. "How did Pederson exorcise the Nephilim?"

"Ketamine."

"What?" he gives me a look. "Like, *Special K*, ketamine?"

"Yes. It's an interesting drug. At the right dose, it dissociates the consciousness from the body."

"Don't gotta tell me. Rode that train a few times."

"Well, then you know. I think that loosened the Nephilim's grip enough to allow the exorcism to work."

"No shit, so like all we gotta do is score some K and find a Nephilim to shoot up?"

"That's the theory."

"Well, I can score you some K easy as takin' a piss, but where we gonna find a Nephilim, and how we gonna convince the fucker to hold still long enough to test this *theory* of yours?"

"That's where we're going." It's time to tell him everything about Emil. Now that I know how it was done, I have to return. I have to convince Gippy of that, but I need to make sure he's ready to hear it. "So, you remember when you and Jeri found out…about me."

"Yeah."

"Remember when I said the blonde woman in the picture with Father Farrell was my cousin? The daughter of an angel, like me?"

"Yeah."

"Well, she and Father Farrell had a relationship. That was before he joined the priesthood."

"Lucky Father Farrell."

"Yes, but she left him, and it pretty much crushed him."

"That sucks."

"Yes, it does, but it was necessary for two reasons. The first is that she was carrying his child."

"What? I thought you said—"

"I did, and it's true. My kind can't procreate." I look at him. "At least not with *humans*."

"Wait. *What?*" Gippy's quick, he's figured out where I'm going with this, and his disbelief hits me before his verbal denial. "No fucking way. Father is *not* one of those fuckin' things."

"No, he's not."

My agreement catches him off guard. Confusion. "But you said—"

"Listen, Gippy. Remember how I said Ketamine makes the Nephilim's grip on their host slippery?"

Silence, then, "Yeah."

"Now, you *know* Father Farrell. You know he's autistic, that his mind works differently than most people's, right?"

"But that don't make him a—"

"You're *right*, Gip; it doesn't make him a Nephilim. In fact, it saved his soul when one tried to possess him at birth. *Because* his mind is different, always flooded with information, decisions, alternatives, colors, smells, names, so much stuff it makes it hard for him to even *think*, the Nephilim couldn't get a grip on him."

"So, where is it?"

"It's *in* him, Gippy. It can't escape and can't take control. He doesn't even know it's there."

"And you want to exorcise it. Destroy it."

"Send it to Hell permanently, where it belongs. Yes."

"But why even bother? If he's not in danger, why risk going back to Cincinnati?"

"Two reasons: First, the Nephilim tracked us down because of the Mercedes' plates, right? Chaki, the succubus, must have figured something out about you, sensed me through you or something, and contacted them."

"Okay, you already said that, and we sent Father a warning, and he said no problem. He'll tell them it was stolen."

"Yes, but if a *Nephilim* goes to Saint Luther's, which is a real danger if they've matched my DNA from the Mercedes, it might...feel one of its own inside Emil. If it does, it'll kill him, instantly, to free its cousin."

"Shit." Silence again, and I glance at him as we merge onto 287 West. He looks worried. "What's the second reason?"

"You're not going to like this, but Emil's a...*safe* subject to try this procedure on. Capturing a real Nephilim alive will be dangerous. If it works on Emil, we know it'll work on a real Nephilim, and taking that risk will be worth it."

His bleached eyebrows brows knit. "That's *cold*, E."

"I know, but it's all I've got." We drive in silence for a while, and I can feel his worry mounting. "You understand?"

"Yeah, I understand, but let me ask you somethin'."

"Please do."

"You don't know if this'll work or not, right?"

"No, I'm not positive."

"So, if this was a *regular* Nephilim, there wouldn't be a human soul left, right?"

"Correct."

"But if this *doesn't* work, if ketamine makes Father Farrell's grip as slippery as the Nephilim's, could it...hurt him, kill him, destroy him and take over?"

"I don't *think* so, but I can't be sure. An exorcism won't send a human soul to Hell, but if something goes wrong...I don't know what might happen."

Silence again, then, "Could the Nephilim grab hold of Father's soul and drag him down with it?"

I honestly hadn't thought of that. "I don't think so, Gippy, but I can't be *absolutely* sure."

We ride in silence for a long while.

"You gonna tell him before you try this, right?"

"Yes. I'm going to tell him."

"Okay then. He says we do it, we do it. He says no, we don't."

"Gippy, if Father Farrell dies—"

"The Nephilim respawns, I know. But if Father dies, *his* soul goes to Heaven. It's *his* soul, Empa. It's *his* choice, not yours, not mine."

I glance at him and feel his resolution in this. He won't back down, even for me. I've been fighting these things so long and losing that I would try anything to tip the balance the other direction, even risk a good human's soul. I think of the destiny of a priest's soul banished to Hell and shiver. Ironic that a drug-addicted street kid is my voice of conscience.

"You're right, Gippy. It's Emil's choice, not ours."

"Fine, then. We get to Cincin, I'll score you some K, and we'll pop the question."

"Good. Text him again. I'd like to know if he's had any visits from the authorities."

"Sure."

I drive on in silence as Gippy sends the message, thinking ahead, wondering if there would be another way to test this procedure before using it on Emil. Short of capturing a Nephilim, I can't think of one. I'll just have to tell him the truth and pray to God he makes the right decision.

We'll be there in ten hours.

IT WAS SNOWING in Columbus when they stopped to get money and fuel. Gippy felt strange about walking into the bank alone, all spiffy and clean in his best outfit, but they were nearly broke. *Shouldn't have given the water taxi driver that tip...*

He felt stranger about Empa putting him on her account. She made him memorize the nonsense phrase that put his voiceprint into her system—the keys to the kingdom, or at least one of her kingdoms. She told him she was doing it because she was undoubtedly still being hunted in Ohio, and while they hoped her disguise was still good enough to fool facial recognition software, she couldn't be sure. Banks had more cameras than a maximum-security prison, and if she went in and activated some alarm, she'd never get out.

Gippy thought there might be another reason, one she wasn't telling him. If Empa died, he could still access her money and carry on the fight. *No pressure.*

He stopped just inside the atrium door, stepped onto the white foot-shapes painted on the floor, and held still. *Just relax. Just a scan. Ain't got nothin' for them to see.* The scan was silent. He didn't feel a thing. Then a green light blinked on the inner door, and it popped open into a short Armorglass-walled hallway. There were two guards, one to either side, holding carbines, and narrow slits in the Armorglass just wide enough for the muzzles of their weapons. They watched him as he walked the gauntlet.

Nervous fuckers, bankers.

A middle-aged woman in a suit expensive enough to have made him salivate a month ago greeted him with a blank look. "May I help you?"

"Courier picking up a transfer." Empa had made him practice his performance.

"Account number?" she held up a phone for him to tap in the sequence.

Gippy didn't touch it. "Encrypted. Voiceprint only. I've got a voucher." He pulled his phone and showed her the screen, the voucher's encrypted code block filling the screen.

She raised an eyebrow and smiled thinly. "Follow me, please."

He did, trying to ignore the eyes and dozens of cameras on him. *Nothin' to see, folks...* In a small cubicle, she directed him to a seat before a tiny terminal and sat on the other side of a desk.

"Just place your phone on the scanner and recite your key into the terminal."

Gippy put his phone face down on the green-lit pad and recited, "Voice print: Epsilon minus three whiskey alpha tango plus twelve. Picking up transfer."

"Processing," the artificial voice responded.

He waited while the woman stared at him.

"Approved. Funds released."

"Very good." The woman consulted her phone, her eyes widened, and she got up. "Please wait here, sir. I'll be back with your funds in a moment."

"Thank you." Gippy pocketed his phone and watched her leave the cubicle, worry niggling his gut. If something had been hacked, or his voiceprint set off an alarm, he'd never get out of here. However, he could do nothing but wait, and tried not to fidget.

About ten minutes later, she returned with a small metal box. "Sorry for the wait. We're a small branch and don't usually handle large withdrawals in bullion." She smiled again, warmer this time.

"No problem." Gippy stood and untucked his shirt as she opened the box with an old-fashioned metal key. He unclipped the money belt and lay it on the desk, folding it open. Platinum ingots gleamed inside the box. Less than he'd carried before, but still a fortune he never could have imagined only weeks ago. The money made him feel perversely guilty. The teller unloaded the box, thirty thin wafers stamped with the Swiss-bank emblem and serial numbers. He slipped them into the belt one at a time.

"Anything else?" She smiled again.

"No. Thanks." Gippy folded the belt closed and secured it around his waist, then tucked his shirt in.

"Very well. This way, please." She gestured, and he followed her to the exit. She paused at the Armorglass door. "Thank you for your business. Have a nice day." She pressed her palm to the print lock and pulled the door open for him.

"Thanks." He tried to smile at her, but his face didn't want to take that shape. *Too much shit in my head to fuckin' smile.* Gippy walked the gauntlet again, waited in the entry vestibule for the outer door to click open, and stepped out into the bitter cold. Empa waited in the car, the engine running. A long walk across the parking lot. A water bottle in the gutter caught his eye, a flash of memory—*Empty... bullet hole... inside my coat... could have fuckin' killed me.*

He got in the car.

"Everything okay?" Empa gave him one of her looks, the ones that told him she was gauging him, eavesdropping on his feelings. He would have felt violated if it hadn't been her.

"Fine." It wasn't really a lie. He was as okay as he was going to get. "Just makes me nervous, ya know."

"I know." She drove. "Too many cameras."

"Think the naffies watch *all* the bank feeds?"

"Most. All in the name of national security." Empa sighed and eased onto the onramp. "Privacy takes a back seat to fear when people fly planes into buildings. The Nephilim orchestrated the war on drugs, the war on terror, the war on gender, the war on the media, all in the name of keeping people safe. They're very good at it."

"To make people hate each other." Gippy retrieved his pistol from the glovebox and clipped the holster to his hip. Empa wore her old duster. He remembered how flash and new it seemed to him when he first saw her. Firefights and road miles had frayed it, but he still felt more secure wearing it. The coat had saved his life, both of their lives. Maybe he'd ask her to buy him one.

"Any message from Emil?"

Gippy checked his phone. He'd messaged Father Farrell that morning but still had no reply. "Nada."

"I don't like that. Might mean trouble."

"Dad's smart. Naffies show up, he'll send 'em packin'."

"I hope so."

They drove in silence for a time. Gippy checked his phone twice more. Still no answer. The tires groaned on the snowy road. God, he hated winter. He squinted at a road sign, thirty miles to Cincinnati.

"Mind if I sleep?"

"No. I'll wake you when we get close."

"Thanks." Gippy slouched down in the seat and closed his eyes. He didn't expect to sleep, nerves and fatigue, memories and fears, love and worry, all vying for bandwidth in his brain. He didn't know why, with all that he'd been through recently, but of all the faces that plagued his dreams, Jeri's came into his mind. He saw her smile, always teasing about sex, nudging him, clicking her teeth against her studs and the rings in her lip. *Love and worry...* He dreamed...

"Look at me, Gip," Jeri said, with her lopsided smile. "I'm invisible."

She faded away to nothing.

THIRTY MILES AWAY, Jeri stood with the other homeless in the shelter common room of Saint Luther's, trying not to look scared. Four NAFAS goons watched them through the tinted visors of their riot helmets, their faces stony, emotionless, hard. She kept her hands in the pockets of her hoodie, her eyes down. *Never look 'em in the eye. Just be invisible. Blend in. They got nothin'.*

But it wasn't the goons who worried her; it was their boss. The hard-looking bitch, Commander Westerfield, wore a long black trench coat with gold stars on her collar. She called the shots and hadn't let up since they walked in. Father met her questions calmly: the car had been stolen; no, he didn't report it; no, he'd never seen the woman they sought. Sister Janice just met their questions with silence and her patented stone-cold glare. Jeri could tell by the look in the woman's eyes she wasn't buying it.

Westerfield showed them the photo again. Empa's unmistakable features, beautiful, calm, mouth half-open in the middle of a word. That mouth sent a pang of longing through Jeri. "This person is a known terrorist, has murdered several NAFAS officers, and is a threat to national security. We *know* she was in Cincinnati two weeks ago and that she had Father Farrell's car in Memphis a few days ago. Anyone with information about her is required by *law* to cooperate with our investigation. Withholding information is a federal crime."

The homeless looked at one another. Most of them were regulars at Saint Luther's, and some might remember Empa's brief appearance, but none of them were stupid enough to speak up. Street people didn't cooperate with naffies as a general rule. Or at least that was what Jeri thought.

Then Drake stepped forward, his face hard, lean, sweaty, hungry for a fix, his hands twitching at his sides. "Yeah, I seen her, right here in this room."

The NAFAS commander's eyes fixed on him like a magnet onto steel. "And do you know where she might be?"

Drake shrugged. "What's it worth to ya?"

"A great deal." Westerfield stepped up to him. "Where is she?"

"Dunno," Drake said, but then pointed a shaky hand to Father, then to Jeri, "but they do."

FIGHT OR FLIGHT

Yet one more skill Gippy has that I don't: he can find a drug dealer in a city of half a million people as easily as I can locate my ass with both hands. He gets back in the car, holding a plastic bag in his hand, five syringes preloaded with ketamine inside.

"Told ya. Easy as takin' a piss."

"Way too easy." I pull away from the curb and head north out of downtown. "Still no answer from Emil?"

He checks his phone. "Nothin'."

"That *really* worries me. He might be too busy to answer right away, but all day?"

"Think they tracked the car to him?"

"Probably, but they should have already come and gone." Unless they found something more. Matching my DNA would take a day or so, and they'd probably watch the church for another day before going in. I doubt NAFAS has Cora's face in their system, but a Nephilim might recognize her in Emil's photo, as I did. If that happened, they'd arrest and interrogate him. That would certainly explain him not answering our texts.

"Can those Nephilim feel each other like you can feel them, from a distance, I mean?"

"I don't know. I don't think they can detect Ageless that way. I've gotten the drop on them before by spotting them before they spot me."

"So, if one shows up at Saint Luther's, they might not feel the one in Father, right?"

"Possibly. At least not until one of them touches him. Then they'd probably know."

"And then he's dead." A storm of worry, anger, eagerness emanates from Gippy.

I can offer him no solace, for my mind is just as troubled.

Finally, we see Saint Luther's through the rain-soaked night. I do a drive-by, looking for something amiss. It's 9 p.m., and there are lights on in the rectory. I'm circling the block when Gippy spots them.

"Black SUV's, two of 'em, parked up the side street."

"Shit." I was looking at the church, and the vehicles are parked half a block away. "They've staked it out." I drive on.

"Really *crappy* stakeout." Gippy gives me a look, cocking one eyebrow. "Two flash cars, exactly the same, sittin' right together? They'd use unmarked cars and park all 'round if they was just watchin' the place."

He's got a point. The other alternative is even more terrifying: "They're inside."

"Gotta be." He looks at me, his face like stone. "This ain't good, E. Goin' in's gonna get bloody, and we got friends in there. Night like this, the shelter's packed."

"I know." I turn a corner, trying to think of a way to get everyone I love out of this alive. "They don't have anything solid on Emil, and Jeri's a nobody. If they search the rectory, they might find the pictures of him with Cora, but that was decades ago. We could just drive away, but—"

"Nope. Ain't happenin'." His adamance in this rises up like a brick wall.

"All right. That means going in, but we've got to do this *right*. Did you see anyone in the cars?"

"Nope. Tinted."

"We've got to find out. We can't go in with them out here to call for backup." I turn again to circle around behind the two parked SUV's.

Gippy squirms out of his jacket and pulls on his old threadbare hoodie. "Lemme check the SUV's. Nobody gonna pay attention to a street punk."

"That'll be dangerous, Gippy." I turn again and kill the headlights, trying to think of an alternative. I pull the car to a stop. "You think you can do it without being spotted?"

"I'm *invisible*, remember?" He shifts his Glock to the front pocket of his hoodie and pulls up the hood.

"Be *careful*."

"Got *that* right." Frigid air slaps me in the face as he gets out. Gippy's gone by the time my eyes adjust from the dome light, vanished into the darkness. I crack my window to listen and pull my pistol.

The wait is physically painful but blissfully short.

Even with my eyes adjusted, Gippy's hard to spot. I turn off the dome light before he opens the door. Another cold blast and he's beside me.

"One at the wheel of each. Engines runnin'. The dash lights lit 'em up enough to see through the tinted glass. Nobody in the passenger side up front, but I couldn't really see in the back. They're lookin' at the church and neither one's wearin' his helmet."

"Damn." I doubt they're Nephilim, but we must neutralize them somehow. The windows are doubtless Armorglass. "Taking them both will be hard. Doing it quietly before they can use the radio will be damned near impossible."

"Especially if the doors are locked."

I think for a minute. "Think you can open one of their doors?"

Gippy frowns. "Dunno. High-end cars have them fancy electronic locks, harder to jimmy."

"Could you do it without the driver noticing?"

"No way."

I think for another minute, but Gippy interrupts my fruitless effort.

"Look, these naffies ain't street cops, not if they here trackin' *you* down. They like special, right?"

"Federal officers, probably, why?"

"Then they think they're badasses. Ain't gonna call for backup to handle one skinny street punk."

I don't like the sound of this. "What are you thinking?"

"Thinkin' it's time to be bad."

GIPPY SMASHED the rearmost SUV's driver-side mirror with a brick as he strutted past. *How dare these fuckin' naffies park their fancy cars on* my *street!* A muffled shout from inside the car reached him, but he just kept strutting. The brick smashed the other car's mirror before the door to the first one opened.

"Hey, you little fucker!"

Gippy dropped the brick, turned, and flipped them a double bird. The instant before the front car's headlights came up, he saw the naffie from the back car draw his gun, then a shape moved in the dark behind him. Blinded by the headlights, Gippy concentrated on listening. The front car's door opened.

"Freeze, you little shit!"

Empa's plea came back to him: *Just don't get shot, Gip.* He raised his hands and froze, every nerve in his body screaming to move, hide, take cover, draw his gun, but even though he couldn't see the naffie, he knew the man had a gun on him. *Run and get shot...*

"Damn right I'm freezin'!" Gippy tried to look cold. It wasn't hard. "Arrest my ass and put it in a nice warm cell! Jail better than this shit!"

"On your knees, motherfucker!" Movement beyond the headlights as the naffie stepped out from behind his door. No sound from the other one.

"Don't shoot me, man! I give up! I just *cold*!" Gippy knelt slowly, hands still up.

The naffie stepped into the light. "Nelson! Cover me while I cuff this little fuck!"

No answer.

"Nelson!"

Still no answer and a flicker of movement behind the man with his gun trained on Gippy's chest. He kept his eyes on the gun, on the finger resting *near* the trigger, but not on it.

"Man, I think Nelson *dead*," Gippy said.

The gun wavered. "Nelson?"

Nothing.

The naffie started to turn. Gippy reached for his weapon, but Empa burst into the light, her long fighting dagger in one hand. Even watching, it happened almost too fast to follow.

As the naffie's pistol swept around, Empa crashed into him, slapping her right arm down to trap the man's weapon. Her momentum bore him backward, but she tangled his legs with hers, and he fell. His shout turned into a gurgle. As they landed, Gippy saw the knife in his throat. She jerked savagely, blood sprayed across her face, a mist in the headlights. As the man convulsed, she stabbed again, burying the blade to the hilt in his eye, and twisted.

Gippy grabbed the pistol from the dying man's twitching grasp. He hadn't even gotten off a shot. Blood still fountained from the man's throat. Gippy felt like he would puke.

Empa rolled off, her face painted crimson. "Get the lights!"

"Um...right." Gippy hurried to the open door and fumbled for the light switch. *Every damn car got it in a different place.* He found it, and the world plunged into darkness. After the headlights in his eyes, he couldn't see anything. He heard something being dragged.

"Help me get him in the back."

"I can't see shit, E! You okay?"

"Fine. Just a mess. I don't suppose there's a towel in there."

Gippy blinked away the afterimages of the headlights but still couldn't see much, even under the dome light. "Don't think so. I still can't see a thing."

"Unlock the doors and help me get this heavy asshole into the back seat."

"Sure." He found the door lock and stepped out. The naffie lay there staring up at the sky with one eye; the other was nothing but a bloody hole, his throat a gaping wound. His chest jerked as he lay there, bloody bubbles frothing up from the wound. "He still movin', E."

"Just reflexes. He'll twitch for a few minutes; they always do. Grab an arm."

Gippy didn't know if her casual tone bothered him more than the fact that she knew so much about how people died. Shooting someone was one thing, but this... He helped muscle the beefy man into the back seat, then the other. That one lay face down on the icy pavement, a wide red stain under his head.

"You fuckin' scary, E," he said as he helped her lift.

"What?"

His eyes had adjusted enough to see the surprise through the blood on her face. "You scary. You kill people way too good." He pointed to the gaping wound in the man's throat. "Like that, up close, personal like."

"Killing *is* personal, Gip." She wiped her mouth with her sleeve, smearing the congealing blood. "Knife, sword, gun, bomb... it's *all* personal. And you're right, I'm far *too* good at it. It makes me sick. These two men probably thought they were on the right side, the good guys. I just pray their souls go to Heaven and they learn the truth."

Gippy closed the door on the man's boots, the old dread rising in him again. "Think God'll send me to Hell fer this? Fer killin' good people just 'cause they was in our way?"

"No. Soldiers on both sides of war kill people without ever knowing if they're good or evil. Nobody's innocent, but that doesn't condemn them to Hell."

"How do you know?" He felt stupid asking *her* that. "Yer daddy tell you?"

"No," she admitted. "I just... *know*. I couldn't go on if I thought otherwise. Now help me get cleaned up and get their uniforms off before rigor sets in."

"You think they'll buy it?" he asked as they trudged back to their car.

"All we have to do is get through the door."

"And take out the bad guys before they kill everyone."

"Yes. That."

JERI WATCHED the NAFAS commander stroll around Emil's den while one of her guards held her and Father Farrell at gunpoint. The other three guards were holding the homeless and Sister Janice downstairs. The woman prowled around, inspecting everything, her posture a confident swagger. Drake stood aside, twitching for a fix, waiting for his reward for ratting them out.

"You pose a problem, Father Farrell. I know you're not telling me everything, but arresting you will get my investigation nowhere. You languish in prison, and a terrorist goes free." She stopped before the mantle and peered at a picture, the one Empa had said was her cousin. "Why did you lie to me, Father?"

"Because I know what you are." Jeri didn't like the burr in Father's voice. Defiance would only get them killed, or worse.

The captain looked at him, her eyebrows knitted. "I'm a commander in the NAFAS Federal Security Force, Father. What did you *think* I was?"

"That's *who* you are. I know *what* you are." Father glared at her, more sheer malevolence in his voice than Jeri had ever heard.

The captain turned away from the mantle. "And what *am* I, Father Farrell?"

Father rattled off a phrase in a language Jeri didn't know, Latin, maybe, but its effect on the woman was astonishing. Her face paled, and the muscles of her jaw clenched hard.

"Then you know what I'm capable of, Father." Westerhouse reached into her coat and pulled out a handgun, small and sleek. She pointed it at

Jeri and clicked back the hammer. "Tell me all you know about the daughter of Raphael, or I send your little whore to Hell."

"What the *fuck*, lady?" Drake took a step back, his eyes wide.

Father Farrell stepped in front of Jeri into the line of fire. "No. We have nothing to tell you. She came and went. We don't know where."

That was true enough, but it only seemed to anger the captain. "We will *see* what you have to tell me, slave of an ungrateful master." The sleek little pistol moved and barked, blasting Drake's brains into a fine pink mist against the wall.

29

HALLOWED GROUND

I follow Gippy down the stairs to the sanctuary door and stand aside as he pushes the call button. This is the weak link; if the NAFAS have a strictly radio-only communications order, they won't open the door. I hope the story we've concocted holds up.

We wait.

The view slot clacks open. "What the hell are you doing here?"

"Caught a little bastard prowlin' around the church. Didn't fit any descriptions on file, so we wanna stow him with the rest." Gippy's been practicing his speech, but I can still hear a little street slang beneath the surface. Thankfully, the tinted visor of his helmet hides his features, and the security light shines down from overhead, casting his face in shadow.

"Why didn't you call it in?"

"Bother the commander with *this*? You kidding me? Open the door. We gotta get back in position."

"Fine. Don't flip out." The view slot clacks closed, and I draw my fighting daggers.

Musashi's lessons come back to me. *Two short blades for close conflict, Emiko. The short is better. Faster. You cannot be fast while close with the longsword. Close, you must be fast. See far when close, see close when far. Practice what I teach you day and night.* I hide the blades behind my forearms and step into the light. The door opens; the man's weapon is slung. *Close, quick, deadly, silent.*

"Where's the—"

My right-hand blade stabs beneath his helmet's visor, taking him under the chin, silencing him. He reacts quickly enough to raise a hand, and my left blade goes into the gap in his body armor in the armpit. He tries to draw a breath, but my knife is in his larynx. With twin twists, the brachial artery and both carotids are severed. All blood flow to his brain ceases, and his eyes roll up, knees fold, his weight bearing me down.

Gippy grabs the falling man's vest before he hits the floor, bless him, and lowers the body down. While I clean and sheathe my blades, he takes the man's weapon and closes the door.

We're in.

I take the man's radio and turn it off, then check the short carbine. The magazine is loaded with flechette ammunition, basically an armor-piercing 7.62mm shotgun. The round is made to penetrate light armor and then fragment, sending metal shards into the flesh beyond. They have less range and knockdown since steel weighs less than lead or uranium, but produce horrible wounds. I wonder briefly if I have fragments like this in my chest. Probably not. If I'd been shot with one of these in Memphis, I'd have died before Gippy even reached me. Someday, I should have an X-ray. Or maybe not.

"You first." I give him a quick once-over on the carbine. He's got to take it; if he shows up without it, the other naffies won't believe for a moment he's the man we killed. "Go for the farthest one. The carbine should pierce their body armor from close up. Give me a number when you tell them what happened. Get close, point-blank, and try to muffle the shot against his armor."

Gippy nods and takes a deep breath. "Farthest one is mine, draw attention, give a number, and shoot him point-blank." He slings the carbine, hand on the grip, finger off the trigger. "You got my ass on this one, right?"

"You know it, buddy." I pull my Glock.

He nods and tries to smile, struggling to get in the zone. "Party time."

I feel his determination solidify. *Please, God, give him strength.* "I'm with you."

Gippy walks boldly down the hallway, and I follow two steps behind, matching his stride so our footsteps sound like a single person. He goes through the door without pause, opening it only halfway to shield me from view. I flatten myself against the wall and listen.

"What was that about?"

"Some skinny kid wantin' food. I sent him packin'. You two get lonely or somethin'?"

Only two? Can't be all of them. I start to move, but a muffled gunshot, far away, brings me up short.

"What the fuck? Call in."

A burst of fire from a carbine, and I'm through the door. Gippy is right up against one of the two troopers, the muzzle of his weapon wedged against the man's stomach. The other is aborting his reach for his radio and lifting his carbine one-handed. I don't have time to get close, and there are people behind him. Two rounds in the body at least ruins his aim, and his burst frags the ceiling—Thank God, no innocents are hit— then I'm on him. The muzzle of my Glock at his neck. The bullet blows right through the inside of his helmet, painting a fine mist on the ceiling.

A woman is screaming, holding a child close. I scan the faces, but Emil and Jeri aren't here. Sister Janice is.

"Quiet!" the nun barks with astonishing authority. "Who in the name of God—"

"'Sokay, sis." Gippy takes off his helmet. "It's me. Gippy. We're here to help."

She glares at him. "By murdering policemen?"

"By doing whatever's necessary to save your lives, Sister." I lift my face shield. "The NAFAS are here looking for me, and they'll not leave until they've interrogated every person here. Now, we heard a shot. Where—"

Gippy's radio squawks, "Heard shots! Report!"

"Answer," I tell him, though he looks hesitant. "Tell them we heard a shot, and one of the prisoners pulled a gun. Threat neutralized. Every- thing under control."

He nods and presses the button on his shoulder mic. "We were about to call you. Heard a shot, and one of the prisoners pulled a gun. Threat neutralized. One dead punk. Everything's under control. You okay?"

"Situation nominal. Clear." The radio goes silent.

"What's nominal?" Gippy asks.

"It means nothing to worry about." I turn to Sister Janice. "Where's Father Farrell?"

"Their...leader took him, Jeri, and Drake upstairs with one of their troopers."

"Shit! E, you don't think..."

I can't read Gippy's mind without touching him, but it's not hard to figure out what he's thinking. One shot. If the squad commander is a

Nephilim and discovered Emil is harboring a Nephilim soul, they might have killed him. "Did they say where they were taking them, Sister?"

"No, just...someplace comfortable to talk."

"The rectory." I nod to Gippy. "How many troopers with them?"

"Just one."

"Why'd they take *Drake*?" Gippy asks. "He don't know shit."

"He..." She frowns, but one of the other homeless interrupts.

"He wanted a reward. Ratted out Father and Jeri for a fix."

"Mutha..." Gippy grits his teeth. "We gotta get up there, E!"

"Yes, we do." I pull one of the fallen trooper's pistols and hold it out to Sister Janice. "Do you know how to use this?"

She glares at it. "No. I won't touch it."

"I do." The same man—the older man who served me dinner here once—steps forward. "I served. I'll keep watch."

"Good." I hand him the weapon. "If we're not back in a few minutes, do whatever you think is right."

"Gotta go, E!" Gippy's at the door, champing at the bit.

I flip down my face shield and follow him up the stairs.

THE NEPHILIM in Father Farrell's den looked down at her smoking pistol in disappointment. "Firearms are so very unsatisfying." She holstered the weapon and reached into the other side of her long coat to withdraw the scabbarded length of Empa's sword. At the sight of the weapon, Emil's eyes widened. "I see you recognize this, Father. It's how I knew what the woman we seek is."

"How did you get that?"

"I found it in *your* car after they abandoned it." She drew the sword smoothly and dropped the scabbard, examining the blade. "Truly a masterpiece, isn't it? So beautiful and so deadly." Her eyes slid from the polished steel to Father Farrell. "Step aside."

"No. We don't know anything about Empa. Kill us, and you get nothing."

"Kill *you*?" She smiled and took a two-handed grip on the sword, raising it level with Emil's chest. "Oh, I wouldn't *dream* of killing *you*, Father." She jerked her head toward the guard. "Move him."

The trooper advanced, but Father didn't move. Instead, he reached for the man's gun, but the trooper was well trained, and the butt of the weapon struck him hard in the chest, driving him aside. The trooper's eyes were on Father Farrell, not Jeri, so when she fired Gippy's little snub-nosed revolver through the pocket of her hoodie, it caught everyone by surprise. The bullet smashed into the trooper's body armor, driving him back hard enough to allow her a second shot. That one hit the Nephilim in the abdomen, doubling her over.

"Little bitch!" The trooper smashed his carbine across Jeri's face, knocking her down.

She didn't quite lose consciousness and tried to pull the pistol out to fire again, but he kicked her hard in the stomach and jerked the weapon away. Another blow sent Father Farrell sprawling to the floor.

When Jeri could breathe, she blinked in surprise at the Nephilim, standing with the sword in hand as if she hadn't been shot. Blood stained her uniform, but she seemed not to notice or care.

"Stand her up against the wall."

The trooper lifted Jeri bodily and pinned her against the wall. The Nephilim grabbed her by the throat with her left hand and leveled Empa's sword low with the edge up.

"Let me show you a trick we used in Bataan during the war." She plunged the sword in hard just above Jeri's belt and slightly off center.

Jeri's scream shivered the air.

The blade, so sharp it would shave like a razor, slipped through her viscera with almost no resistance, then pierced the wall behind her. The Nephilim hammered her palm against the pommel of the sword, driving it through the plaster until the round guard was inches from Jeri's belly. She released the sword and stepped back. Jeri gripped the hilt, gasping for breath, blood trickling down her leg.

"Now, Father, you'll tell me *everything* about the Seraphim-spawn you've known, both the woman who was here and the woman in that picture on your mantle." The Nephilim gestured to Jeri. "Do it quickly, or your little whore will be slowly cut in half as her strength to remain standing fails."

⸻

WHEN GIPPY HEARD THE SHOTS, he stopped to look back at Empa. Then a scream tore his heart out, and he was running. *Jeri!* Empa hissed something in a stage whisper behind him, but he wasn't listening.

The door to the rectory had a stout lock, but it didn't hold up against a burst from the carbine. The hall, maybe sixty feet to the doorway of Father's den, seemed like a hundred yards. A naffie trooper leaned out of the opening with a raised weapon, but Gippy was already firing as he charged, adjusting his aim by the trail of disintegrating plaster and wood. A muzzle flash from the trooper's weapon lit the hallway, but two of Gippy's rounds hit the man, and he vanished into the room. Gippy dropped the empty rifle and drew his Glock, dodging into the room as fast as he could make the corner.

Jeri... blood... the trooper... muzzle flashes... a woman in a long coat reaching to grab Father... a gun in her hand. Something hit him, but the hours of training with the Glock paid off. He walked rounds up the trooper from thigh to face.

The floor hit his knees, and he knew he'd been shot. The tall woman grabbed Father, her gun pointing at him. She screamed something at him, but he couldn't raise his arm to shoot her. She redirected her pistol to Gippy's face, and he saw her finger move to the trigger.

Something hit him hard, and the world exploded.

30

HEAVEN SENT

Gippy's out of control.

I've been taught by a dozen different warriors of as many ages of warfare that out of control in combat is bad. Even John Rackham was a cold and disciplined fighter, even drunk off his ass. Robert the Bruce was the single exception. *No good man surrenders but with his life.* It worked for him, but this is likely to get us killed.

Another of Musashi's lessons: *Versatility in strategy, weapons, tactics, environments, conditions, and opponents is key to victory. Nothing ever goes as planned in battle.* I can't stop Gippy, but I can use his reckless charge to our advantage.

As I follow him through the shattered rectory door, a round from the trooper's carbine spalls off Gippy's flak jacket, and the shrapnel clatters against my face shield. A splinter of steel sticks through the high-impact plastic an inch from my nose. Gippy empties a mag, spraying drywall, wood, and steel fragments down the hall. Dust puffs from the trooper's jacket, and he retreats back into the room.

Gippy drops the empty rifle and pulls his Glock.

No, no, no... But he wouldn't hear me if I was screaming, and dives into the room full tilt.

I'm three steps away when simultaneous fire breaks out from a carbine and Gippy's Glock. Two steps, a woman's voice screaming commands. One step and the room begins to open up in my view.

Look at nothing, see everything.

The trooper is down, torn from crotch to crown. *Good shooting, Gip.* The hilt of a sword—*My sword!*— stands out from the wall...no, from a body, for two pale bloody hands grip the hilt. *Jeri's hands... Oh, God, please no.* I'm through the opening, and Gippy's on his knees, his shoulder a mass of torn meat.

Hate blasts through me like heat from a kiln. *A Nephilim.*

She holds Emil but is bringing her pistol to bear on Gippy. I bowl him over, and the round slams into my body armor. I'm firing as I roll, but not accurately. She's holding Emil, and I dare not hit him. A chair between us, and bullets send cotton batting flying like snow. One hits me, but her pistol doesn't have the punch to penetrate my body armor. I level my Glock over the back of the chair, but she's got Emil in a chokehold, her weapon arm over his shoulder. I can barely see her and have no shot that will stop her dead.

We stare at each other for a heartbeat, her hate beating against me in waves. Her gun is shaking, and I see blood on her leg. She's been shot.

Then something on her face changes, the rictus of battle rage evolving to curiosity, surprise, wonder. She looks at Emil.

She knows.

The pistol in her hand moves, the muzzle sweeping around toward Emil. She's going to kill him.

I still have no shot. I drop my weapon—Sergeant Gattish would kick my ass for that—and use the chair as a springboard to launch myself at them. Her surprise turns to horror, and she starts to bring the gun back toward me.

I slam into them both. My hands lock onto her wrist. We go down in a heap, twisting and rolling. The gun fires, but I can't tell if I'm hit. She's got both hands on the weapon now and is fucking *strong*. Damn me if she's not on top, her legs wrapped around mine. Another shot, and the bullet slams into my helmet, shattering my face shield. I close my eyes reflexively against the shower of splinters.

A scream like nothing I've ever heard in my five thousand years, and the woman's grip suddenly goes utterly limp. Warm wetness sprays my face as I thrust the pistol up and away. I taste blood. Something heavy lands on me, thrashing, and I shove it away, rolling on top. I blink away blood to find the Nephilim lying beneath me, screaming obscenities in dead languages, her arms both severed at the elbow.

Jeri lays in a bleeding heap, gripping my sword. She must have pulled it out of the wall and her abdomen to save me.

"Emil, see to Gippy!" I don't have time to give a shit about the Nephilim right now. I crawl away from her thrashing body to Jeri. Her eyes are open, but her viscera lie in a bloody pool beside her. "Oh, Jeri..."

"Knew...you'd...come back." She smiles and coughs blood. "Missed me. Admit it."

"Shhhh, of course I did, you beautiful fool!" I cup her spilled intestines and roll her onto her back. She screams again, weaker. There's no arterial spray, so the aorta isn't violated. "Now just breathe."

"Did you see...the sword? I could be...a fucking...samurai. Ninja Jeri..." She's going into shock, trembling all over. She grins through the blood. "Fuckin' badass bitch with a blade. That's me."

"Shut up and breathe, Jer. I've got to..." I turn to see how Gippy is, and Emil looks grave.

"He's shot. His shoulder and abdomen. Bleeding but not horribly."

"I'm not fuckin' dead!" Gippy snaps, clearly lucid. "Fix Jeri first."

The Nephilim's still screaming and thrashing, kicking at me. *First things first.* I place my hands on Jeri's abdomen, easing the viscera back into her. A piteous wail rises up from her throat with another gout of blood. She's a mess, but if I can just put her back together, I can close the wound and deal with peritonitis later. The last of the slithery intestines slides back into her, and I take as much of the surface wound as I can without spilling my own guts. My body armor should keep me intact. Pain, yes, but nothing like what she's feeling. Deeper and I close the exit wound, less critical, and mend a few severed arteries and veins. Her eyes flutter closed, but she's still breathing.

I try to stand, but my legs are suddenly weak. Of course, they are; I'm now bleeding internally. I crawl to Gippy. His eyes meet mine, the obvious question in them.

"She's alive. Now it's your turn."

"Sorry I got shot." He grimaces as I cut the straps of his body armor for a closer look. "Kinda lost my shit. I couldn't think...or stop."

"Yeah, we'll talk about that later." I look up at Emil. "Can you please shut that thing up for me?"

He blinks at me, shocked. "I can't *murder* her, Empa."

"It's not human, Emil! It's a Nephilim."

"E! Wait." Gippy grabs my arm. "Don't kill her. We can...send her to Hell! K in my pocket!"

Now I'm the one who's not thinking straight. "Yes!" I fish the bag full of syringes out of his pocket and hand it to Emil. "One full syringe IM and tourniquets for her arms. It should stop struggling. We'll deal with it later."

"What is this?" Emil takes the syringes.

"Ketamine. Please, Emil. I have to see to Gippy, then make sure Jeri's okay."

"Very well." He doesn't sound happy, but right now, I can't care. I place a hand on Gippy's abdomen and feel the horrific wound deep within. His body armor stopped the outer casing of the round, but seven thin shards of steel went tumbling through him. I control the bleeding, feeling another wave of weakness, and heal the worst of it. His shoulder's shattered, but the main arteries and nerves are intact. I align the bones and knit them just enough to hold them together. The pain entering me makes my head swim.

"That's enough, E! I'm okay for now." Gippy's hand closes on my wrist, pushing me away. "I'm not gonna die. Go see if Jeri's okay."

"You've still got a lot of metal in you," I warn. "It should come out."

"Not *now*." He nods to Jeri. "She's worse."

"Let me judge that, would you?"

"Please, E. Go fix Jeri. She...shouldn't be hurt. It's *our* fault she's hurt. It was stupid to take Father's car. I should'a *known* better."

He's right. "*We* should have known better." I nod and go back to Jeri, though even crawling now is a challenge. I place a hand on her brow and assess her condition. She's lost blood, and the shock has taken its toll, but she's resting for now. There's still much to mend, but if I take much more, I'll pass out. With a church full of dead NAFAS troopers and a dismembered Nephilim, that wouldn't be good. I take what will become a raging infection and seal up her viscera to prevent more. Her eyes flutter but don't open. For that, I'm thankful. I don't need the distraction of her thoughts.

I look to Emil. The Nephilim is quiescent now, its severed arms tied with white shoelaces. "How is she?"

He looks at me and shrugs. "The bleeding's controlled, but I don't know how she's still alive. Jeri shot her before, and all this blood..."

Now for the hard part. "Emil, I can't stand yet. I've stabilized them both, but I can't do more right now. We have to—"

"I'll get Sister Janice to help." He stands. "What happened downstairs?"

"We killed three more troopers and two outside. Their vehicles are parked on the side street and should be gotten rid of along with the bodies."

He nods, a deep sadness piercing the deluge of his chaotic thoughts. "I'll pull them in the garage, and we'll get things cleaned up. I don't know about the other residents, though."

"I'll explain to them, Father," Gippy says. He sits up, holding his arm gingerly. "Nobody'll say a fuckin' *word* after I tell 'em what that bitch did to Drake and Jeri."

"I pray you're right, Gippy." Emil frowns and sighs. "Such a waste of human life."

"It's *war*, Emil." I have to remind myself that he hasn't seen the things Gippy and I have. I can't offer much solace, except, "What's done is done. Let God sort them out."

EMPA HAD TAKEN as much of their injuries as she could without killing herself, but they still needed mending. Gippy's arm was in a sling, and his guts still felt like someone had kicked him, but Jeri had been worse off. After he hobbled down to help explain what the NAFAS had done to coerce Father into giving up Empa—Father had taken Sister Janice aside, thankfully, and Hank had already volunteered to help protect the church if more naffies showed up—he'd returned to find Jeri asleep in the tiny bed in the rectory guest room and Empa all but passed out in Father's bed. Sitting beside the bed and taking Jeri's hand, he'd intended to just watch her for a while. He hadn't meant to fall asleep, but woke when Jeri stirred, her hand flexing in his.

She blinked at him. "Hey."

"Hey." He reclaimed his hand, embarrassed. "How you feelin'?"

"Like a bitch stuck a sword through me, but..." Her other hand moved under the covers, and she winced as she rolled. "All healed up. Empa do that?"

"Yeah." He struggled to stand up, caught his breath, and barely made it to the chair. "Sorry. Didn't mean to fall asleep. E took most of our hurts but couldn't take it all. She'll fix us both up later."

"You...shouldn't be up." She scooched back and pulled the covers back. "C'mere."

He looked at her, wearing only a pair of tiny black panties, and swallowed hard. "Jeri, I gotta tell you...somethin'."

"So crawl into bed and tell me." She smiled that teasing smile. "Don't worry, Gip. I'm way too sore to fuck."

He had to admit, the bed looked good, and Jeri looked even better. He hadn't realized how much he missed her, how close they'd gotten in the few days after Lennie was killed. "Okay." He stood and shuffled over to sit on the bed. His right arm was bandaged under a cast-off shirt Father had given him, but he managed to unlace his boots and kick them off.

He started to lay down when Jeri reached around and grabbed his belt buckle. "Off with the pants, mister. There's blood on 'em."

She was right; they were bloody. He sighed and shucked out of his pants. Lying down on his back—he couldn't lay on his injured shoulder—Jeri pulled the blankets over them and snuggled close, warm and pleasant. She snaked an arm over his chest, her chin on his shoulder.

"So, what do you want to tell me?"

"Long story." He didn't know where to start.

"I ain't goin' anywhere, Gip."

He thought for a moment, then just dove in headfirst. "I...was... broken, Jer. I been broken more than once, and I don't mean just shot up. Broken in my head. What I went through with my mom, my sisters, Len, then with Empa...I never thought I could keep goin', but she...fixed me."

"How?" There was worry in Jeri's eyes.

"Not how you think, Jer. She just...fixed me." He went on to tell her what had happened in Albuquerque, Memphis, then about Manhattan, and after, how Empa had just held him in the shower until he stopped crying, then held him some more. Just held him. Learning what it really meant to be at war, what it meant to sight down a rifle and take a human life, had shattered him. "It was like she scooped up all my pieces and held them together until I healed. I...understand now. We're at war with people who'll run into gunfire with a bomb strapped to 'em to try to kill you, even if it means blowing themselves up. It scares the shit out of me, but I'm gonna keep at it, help her fight, as long as I can. It's my life now."

"Okay." A tear slid down her nose and dripped onto the pillow. "So... why tell me?"

"'Cause I'm..." He sighed again, not knowing how to say it. "Look, I know you got a thing for Empa."

"Fuck *yeah*, I got a thing for her. She walks into the *room*, I get a boner."

"I know, right? She's like that, but me and her...we more like family, ya know?"

"Yeah, I know. So?"

"So, when we was comin' up the stairs, and I heard you scream…" He took a breath, held it, then said it. "I fuckin' *lost* it, Jer. I been in some freaky shit fights and never once lost my head until after, but when I heard you scream, I lost my shit. Felt like someone had my guts in a knot. That's why I barged right in and got my ass shot."

She stared at him for a long moment. "What are you sayin', Gip."

"I'm sayin' I didn't know how much…how much I cared for you 'till that happened. When those cult fuckers had Empa tied to a cross and were cuttin' on her, I didn't lose my shit. I love her like I loved my mama, Jer, but…you… I don't know; it's like you're a piece of me that I'm missin'. Like…"

"Like we should be together." Another tear dripped off her nose, but she smiled.

"Yeah, like that, but it ain't simple. I know you got a thing for Empa. Gettin' into some weird love triangle thing ain't a good idea. Especially doin' what we do."

She stared at him again a long while; he could see her going through the thought process he had while he watched her sleeping. Then she said, "Why does shit always have to be so complicated?"

"Dunno, but it is. Life's fucked up. The world's fucked up. I'm tryin' to fix what I can and helpin' Empa's the right way. I *know* it is. I wanna be with you more than damn near anythin', but you comin' along with us… would be too complicated."

She frowned. "It wouldn't *have* to be."

"How you figure?"

"Well, I could fuck you on Mondays, Wednesdays, and Fridays, and her on Tuesdays, Thursdays, and Saturdays." She grinned her mischievous grin and ran her hand down his chest to his crotch. "I'd probably have to rest on Sundays."

" Jeri…" He took her hand in his before she could slip her fingers into his underwear. "Don't joke."

"Not really jokin'." She gripped his hand hard. "Love ain't somethin' you run out of, Gip. I got enough for both of you, but I see what you mean. I'm not a fighter. Shit scares me; I freeze up. I'd suck at your job."

"That'd come with practice. What makes it complicated is that I'd do stupid shit if you was with us. Stayin' here with Father would probably be dangerous, too. We gotta talk to Empa about this. Ask her what she thinks we should do."

"Why ask her?"

"'Cause she's…" His brain stumbled; what *was* she, really? His mentor? His friend? His guarding angel? The answer was simpler than that. "'Cause we both love her, but different."

"And you both love me, but different."

He hadn't thought of it that way but couldn't keep from smiling. "Yep, I think so."

"And I love you both." She nodded. "Complicated."

"Right."

She frowned. "Gotta admit, Gip, I lied to you about one thing."

"What's that?"

"I'm not too sore to fuck." She slipped her hand out of his and down under the hem of his boxers. "And neither are you."

3 1

STRAIGHT TO HELL

I stumble into the kitchen, following the scent of coffee. Emil looks up at me and offers a weak smile. He looks like I feel, which isn't particularly good.

"Sorry. I didn't mean to wake you." He pulls another cup down.

"I should be up. There's too much to do." The clock on the microwave reads 4:23, and the light from the den tells me that's p.m., not a.m. I still feel weak, but Gippy and Jeri should be well enough to travel by sunset. Finding them asleep together this morning surprised me, the scent of their lovemaking even more so. Maybe it shouldn't have. I managed to take almost all of their injuries without waking them and went back to bed. "How is everything?"

He shrugs and pours boiling water onto instant coffee and passes me the cup. "Well enough."

"The NAFAS cars? The bodies?" I inhale the intoxicating aroma.

"At the bottom of the Ohio River. Hank is quite resourceful, and Janice didn't put up too much of a fuss after I explained what their commander did. Gippy and Jeri are downstairs talking to the other residents. I don't know if they believe all of it, but they're not about to go running to the authorities. I'm afraid there was no way to explain it other than to tell them the whole truth about you."

"I thought not." I'll have to leave Cincinnati as soon as I can.

Emil sips his coffee and stares at me, his eyes questioning. "Are you okay?"

"I will be." I sip and burn my tongue. "And the Nephilim?"

"Alive, though I don't know how. I've kept her under with ketamine, though I had to have Hank go out and get more."

"They're tougher than humans, Emil. Anything short of a lethal injury won't stop them." I blow on my coffee and risk another sip. "Emil, we learned how to exorcise them, send their souls to Hell permanently. I want to try it on this one."

"You're sure it *is* one? A Nephilim, I mean?"

"I'm sure. I can feel them." I look around the kitchen. "Mind if I make some toast? I'm starving." I've lost blood, and healing both Gippy and Jeri has wrung me dry.

"Oh! Of course. I'm sorry." He opens a bread box, pulls out two different loaves, then pulls butter, peanut butter, jelly, jam, and Nutella down from the cupboard.

"I need to tell you more, Emil." I push down two slices of wheat bread and face him. "And it won't be easy for you to hear."

He frowns. "Is it about Teri?"

"Partly, but most is about you. I didn't find any clue where she went, but she...discovered something about you, Emil. Something different. It resulted in the reason she had to leave."

He looks mildly surprised. "What about *me* made her leave?"

He's misunderstanding where I'm going with this, and there's only one way to straighten him out. "She was pregnant, Emil, with *your* child."

"My...*what?*" He staggers back, confusion, shock, heartbreak hammering through the deluge of data clouding his mind.

"Your *child*, Emil. Now, let me explain. I told you what I *thought* was the truth when I said that my kind can't have children. I *thought* it was true. As it turns out, I think it may be only true if we couple with humans or other Ageless."

"Wait! So, you're saying I'm not *human?*"

"For the most part, you are, Emil, but you carry something else inside you." I must press on; he must know the absolute truth. "A Nephilim soul tried to possess you at birth, but your autism protected you. It couldn't grasp your soul well enough to destroy it. It's trapped, impotent, in you." My toast pops up.

Emil collapses into a chair at the kitchen table, clearly stunned speechless.

I smear peanut butter on my toast and take a bite, giving him some time to accept it.

"How do you know this?"

"A letter on Teri's computer. I'll show you if you don't believe me. I wasn't sure until I shook your hand when we left. I felt it in you, Emil."

"So, when I die…"

"It'll respawn into another human, destroy their soul, and continue fighting to corrupt mankind. Also, it'll know all that you've experienced in your life. Teri, me, Gippy, Jeri, your child…everything."

"Good God." His coffee ripples in his cup. He downs a gulp and stares into space for a moment.

I eat my toast and let him think it through, process the data. I must let him make the connection, then the right decision. I know he will; I've felt his soul.

Finally, when my toast is gone and I've made more coffee for both of us, his eyes refocus on me. "Can you exorcise it? Send it to Hell forever?"

"I think so, I pray so, but it's not without risks." I sit at the table with him, impressed with his calm. "I need to test the process on the Nephilim we captured first, then I'll know if it works."

"Then you do the same to me, but I've got to be anesthetized with ketamine first?"

"That's the theory." *All the truth…* "But Gippy brought up another danger. If the ketamine dissociates *your* mind as it would a Nephilim, there's a chance it could get a grip on your soul or even drag you down with it."

"Drag me down…" His eyes widen. "To *Hell?*"

"Yes."

"Sweet Jesus, Mary, and Joseph…" He shakes his head, staring down at the table. "But you don't know if it'll work at all yet. You have to test it on the…the other Nephilim first."

"Yes, but *you* have to make the decision about yourself, Emil. We can't force you to risk your soul."

He snorts a laugh. "Not much of a choice there; risk my soul, or release a devil's spawn back into the world to destroy another innocent human soul and wage war on everyone I love when I die?" He smiles and looks up at me. "Of course, I'll do it. How could I not?"

"Thank you, Emil." I lay my hand flat on the table before him. He takes it, and once again, I'm immersed in a tidal wave of unfiltered information, his shining soul a beacon at the center, and behind it the impotent malev-

269

olence of the Nephilim lurking like a cowering shadow. "May God bless you and keep you."

He smiles sardonically. "That's my line."

GIPPY FELT A LITTLE WEIRD, and it wasn't because he'd never been with a woman before. Jeri wasn't like most women, and he had to admit, even sore as hell, she was a pretty amazing lover, gentle, attentive, and relentless. What made him feel strange was waking up virtually healed beside her. He'd realized immediately that Empa must have come in while they were asleep, healed them both, and left without waking them. Again, if it had been anyone else, he would have felt violated, but not Empa.

Of course, that took a bit more explaining to Jeri before she settled down. Then, being Jeri, she attacked him again for another much more vigorous round of lovemaking. He was still walking stiffly but not from any lingering injury.

Talking to the other homeless had been easier than he thought, and Hank had astonished him by greeting him with a hard embrace. Gippy saw understanding in the older man's eyes; he knew what it meant to be a soldier. Gippy told them all as much as he could without giving too many personal details away. There was no way to know if they believed him, but Father had told them all that he'd been shot and Jeri stabbed, and none of them could doubt that their injuries were gone.

Then Sister Janice interrupted them with a summons to the rectory. Empa was awake and had asked for him. It was time to deal with the Nephilim.

The rectory was still a mess despite a hasty clean-up; bullets and blood had left their marks. Father's den had been scrubbed, the rugs removed, and the shredded furniture taken down to the garage. The Nephilim strapped to a folding table in the middle of the room didn't do much for the décor.

"Hey, you two." Empa smiled as Gippy and Jeri came in, her eyes twinkling with love for them both. "How do you feel?"

"Great! I—" Gippy stopped because saying anything more would have been useless with Jeri grabbing Empa in a crushing embrace and passionate kiss.

"Jeri..." Father smiled and shook his head. "You could have said hello first."

Jeri broke off the clinch, completely unembarrassed. "Said hello last night. This is thank you." Her eyes never left Empa, and damn if a blush didn't rise to Empa's cheeks.

"You're welcome, Jeraldine. And thank *you*."

Once again, if it had been anyone but Empa, Gippy would have been jealous. Instead, he stepped past Jeri and took Empa in his arms.

"Sorry I lost my head, E. Don't know what happened to me."

"I do." She smiled and winked at him as they separated. "We'll talk about it later."

"So, Gip told me you can oust one of these fu...um...Nephilim jerks back to Hell permanently." Jeri stepped over to the table and glared down at the sleeping form. The woman's breathing was fast, and her head moved back and forth as if not entirely under. "That right?"

"We hope to, yes." Empa caught Gippy's eye and nodded. "With Emil's help."

"You told him?" Gippy asked.

"Yes, and he's willing to try as long as this first trial works."

"Try what?" Jeri looked from face to face.

"Another exorcism," Father said with his usual steady smile. If Empa had told him the truth, he was taking it remarkably well. "On me."

Jeri took a step back from him. "On... *What?*"

Father Farrell explained the Nephilim soul trapped in him, unable to destroy his soul because of his autism, the possibility of sending it to Hell, and the danger that Father's soul might be banished with it. Gippy watched Jeri try to wrap her head around it. He couldn't tell if she managed it or not.

"But we must deal with *this* one first," Empa interjected. "I wanted you here, Gippy. You should know how to do this, just in case."

He didn't like the sound of that—*Just in case she dies, and I have to go on alone*—but he nodded. "Sure, but I ain't no priest."

"Technically, you don't have to be." Father put a hand on Gippy's shoulder. "It *is* Church law, as is permission from a bishop, but what the Church doesn't often tell its parishioners is that anyone can perform the ritual. This..." he gestured to the Nephilim, "isn't a case of possession, strictly speaking, but an entity of Hell destroying a human's soul to utterly occupy the body. The Church would never sign off because there's no soul to save, only one to condemn. But in the end, all you need is faith."

"Well, I got *that!*" He nodded to Empa. "Hangin' with an angel's little girl'll do that to ya."

"I know." Father said it like he meant it. "So, in my opinion, we're answering to a higher order here. Don't tell my bishop I said that. I'd be excommunicated."

Empa smiled ruefully. "One reason I don't associate with organized religions regularly is their propensity to make rules to consolidate their power, rather than to perform God's work."

"A sad truth," Father agreed, stepping to the side of the table. "I've tried to bring the level of anesthetic down to the point where the Nephilim can hear us. That's key. Without an IV, unfortunately, I can't be precise, and we're not equipped for that here."

"Plus, she's got no arms to stick a needle in." Gippy nudged Jeri. "Badass bitch with a blade."

She gaped at him. "You *heard* that?"

He just grinned at her and pulled her close as Father and Empa started the ritual.

As far as Gippy was concerned, it was a lot of repetitive praying, crosses painted on the Nephilim with holy water and sanctified wine, a host placed in her mouth. They spoke in Latin, English, and Empa in several other languages. The Nephilim began to struggle, thrashing her head back and forth, straining against the straps, but only mumbled. The ketamine wouldn't allow anything more.

Jeri held him tight, watching closely, and whispered, "How do we know if it works?"

"Empa'll know. She can feel the fucker in there." Gippy could see the strain on Empa's face as she continued the ritual, pressing a hand down on the struggling woman's forehead.

A sweat broke out on her face as Empa chanted the words over and over. "Be *gone* from this vessel, get of Ariquiel. In the name of Christ, be *gone* from this world. Go to your father's master and *atone!*"

It went on for hours. Gippy and Jeri sat down to watch, but Empa and Father Farrell continued relentlessly, never pausing to rest.

Then, suddenly, the Nephilim's mouth gaped wide, she strained against her bonds, shuddering all over, and finally went still. The chest rose and fell shallowly, a pulse beating at her neck.

Empa pressed a hand to the woman's forehead, her brow furrowed. She opened the eyes and stared down into them, then broke away, taking a step back. "It's *done!*" She sounded stunned. "It's gone, and the body lives." She looked to Emil. "We've done it."

Father Farrell sat down hard in a chair, crossed himself, and sighed deeply. "Thank God."

"Indeed." Empa stared at the empty human shell in disbelief.

Gippy got up and went to her. "You okay, E?"

"Yes, I…" She looked at him, and there were tears pooled in her eyes. "It *worked*, Gippy. I hardly ever hoped…" The tears spilled.

"We got our weapon." He gripped her shoulders and smiled. "Cheer up!"

"Five *thousand* years…and *finally*." She smiled through the tears. "Only one-hundred ninety-eight to go."

"And I'm next," Father Farrell said flatly, staring at the still-breathing human shell.

"I have to rest first, Emil, and eat something." Empa wiped the tears away and took a deep breath.

"What about that?" Jeri asked, stepping to the side of the table. "I thought she'd…die."

"The body will die eventually, Jeri. Probably sooner rather than later, considering the trauma it's endured. The Nephilim was keeping it alive by sheer force of will. Without that…"

"So, it's really empty then? Like, nobody inside at all?" Jeri didn't sound like she believed it. Like she was still afraid the woman would wake up and stab her again.

"Really." Empa went to her and put an arm around Jeri's slim shoulders. "Come on. Let's eat."

32

SLIPPERY SOULS

At Gippy's suggestion, we eat with the homeless in the basement common room.

"They need ta *see* you, E. Need ta know you're real."

It's the least I can do. Hank is behind the counter again, slinging hash and grinning. I get some strange looks—fear, shame, discomfort—from the others. Nothing I can do about that. Hopefully, by tomorrow I'll be nothing but a rumor for them.

We get our food—literally hash, and I don't ask what kind of meat is in it—and sit. I'm ravenous and dig in, replacing the calories I burned healing their injuries. Emil picks at his dinner. Gippy nudges me under the table; he's noticed it too.

"I'm sorry for all this, Emil. I imagine you're wishing I never walked through your door."

"Not so." He smiles that calm smile and takes a bite, eating mechanically. "If you hadn't, I wouldn't know I had a child somewhere. Maybe, when you're finished here, you could try to find Teri?"

"I'll do my best. I promise." I have no idea where to start looking, and finding her could be dangerous for both of us, but I need to know about the child, though for different reasons than Emil.

He takes another bite, chews, and swallows. "What...do you think my chances are, with the exorcism, I mean?"

So, that's what's bothering him. I can't blame him for being nervous;

he's risking more than his life here. "Good. Exorcisms, in general, don't risk the human soul." I'm not lying to make him feel better.

"So, the risk," Jeri asks, looking from face to face between the three of us. "I got a question about that."

"Ask."

"So, the ketamine makes the Nephilim's grip on its host *slippery*, so you can exorcise it, right?"

"Yes, that's the theory."

"Why don't other drugs work?"

"I don't know, but I've seen others tried. Opium, Propofol, fentanyl, all used for restraint in light enough doses to allow the patient to hear the practitioner. Nothing ever worked."

Jeri frowns, pushing her food around on her plate, unusual behavior for someone who never knows where her next meal is coming from. "And the reason the Nephilim in Father didn't take over when he was born is kinda the same, right? His mind makes him...slippery."

"Yes, that's right." I exchange a look with Emil and realize I've been stupid. "Holy...um...forgive me, Emil, but I'd completely forgotten! Cora, your Teri, thought an exorcism might work on you *without* any drugs. That's how she got her theory to look for other cases of successful exorcism in the first place!"

He looks startled, hopeful. "And *not* using it would lessen the risk." He thinks for a time, seeming remarkably calm about the revelation. his emotions as impenetrable as always. "Seems logical, but...what if it fails?"

I shrug. "Then it fails, and nothing happens. We're free to try again under anesthesia. It's certainly the safer route."

"Then we'll try without first." He takes a bite and chases it down with the vile soykaf they serve down here, his eyes still on me, his mind still churning. "There's one other thing to consider before we do this, but it's...personal."

"Personal?" I have no idea what he means and can't get his feelings through the deluge, but I have to respect his privacy. "We can talk it over in the rectory, then."

"I'd prefer to speak to you privately if I may." Emil smiles at Gippy and Jeri. "No offense, but—"

"Holy shit!" Jeri's eyes widen suddenly. "You're gonna ask her if she wants you to—"

"Jeri!" Emil's tone cuts her off, but Jeri's blushing furiously, and so is

Emil. Embarrassment and a surge of jealousy from Jeri, which makes no sense...unless.

The connection finally clicks into my mind. "Ah, *that*." It's my turn to blush. "I've thought about it, Emil, and while the prospect of motherhood intrigues me, I don't think so. I need to find out what happened to Teri first, exactly *what* her child is, if you know what I mean. Also, I've finally got the weapon I need to fight the Nephilim, and I can't imagine employing it while pregnant or caring for a young child." I put a hand on Emil's and squeeze. "But I appreciate the offer."

"Well, I..." His blush deepens. "I thought I should. You'll likely never get another opportunity to bear a child."

"Perhaps." Other options have occurred to me, none of them tasteful. "Time will tell."

We eat in silence, Emil with a better appetite, until our plates are empty. I take the dishes up and thank Hank for his help.

"Wanted to thank you," he stammers, sticking out a hand.

"For what?" I take his hand and get a flood of peak memories in a painful info dump, all the familiar horrors of war. He's carrying a lot of baggage.

"Cause knowin' there's a *reason*, a fight that might *mean* somethin', gives me hope."

"Where did you serve?" I ask.

"Third Battalion, seventy-fifth Rangers."

I squeeze his hand hard. "We chewed some of the same desert, then. Combat medic, Fast Response Force, Kurdish CTG."

His jaw drops, but his grip remains firm. "*Lexoman Parastin*," he says, and my jaw drops, too.

I think through the thousands of US soldiers I saw in the Middle East, but I don't recall him. We both know there's nothing left to say; you had to be there.

Gippy, Jeri, and I follow Emil up to the rectory. The body the Nephilim occupied has expired, which doesn't surprise me. After so much trauma and blood loss, the only thing keeping it alive was the will of a truly evil soul. We wrap it in a sheet and carry it down to the garage without much conversation. I wonder who this woman would have been had she not been devoured by evil. I mourn death often, but the loss of a soul shakes me to my core.

Only one hundred ninety-eight more.

Emil makes us coffee, and I remember the wonderful coffee in the restaurant in Nashville where Gippy and I ate. Maybe I'll find some and send it to Emil.

"I don't mind telling you I'm nervous about this. It's necessary, I know, but this...thing's been a part of me for so long. I don't know who I'll be when it's gone."

"I don't think it's really a *part* of you, Emil. If it was, if it could influence you at all, it would have twisted you into a completely different person."

"I pray you're right."

"So, you think we need to...I dunno...tie him down or somethin'?" Gippy asks.

"Probably not. If the Nephilim doesn't have any control over him now, it won't while we're exorcising it." But that brings something to mind that I read in Cora's notes. "But you *are* on medications, aren't you, Emil?

"Yes. An antidepressant and an anxiolytic to control OCD. Why?"

"Because Teri mentioned in her notes that when you're off your medications, you're very different, even dangerous."

Emil frowns. "To myself only, as far as I know, but I'd hate to hurt any of you. Perhaps some restraints would be wise."

Fortunately, one of Emil's comfortable armchairs survived the battle. We use a couple of robe ties and belts to secure his arms and legs and call it good. Lastly, I enlist Gippy's help and run through the basics.

"Just keep it up. Concentrate on your faith. Say what comes to mind while you touch him." I rest a hand on his shoulder, trying to ease his anxiety. "Don't worry. You can't do this wrong if your heart's in it and your mind's on your faith."

"It can't...jump to possess the exorcist, can it?"

I grin at him. "No. That's Hollywood. You're safe."

"Okay. Good to know." He takes a deep breath as if we're about to walk into a firefight. In a way, we are. "Let's do this."

We begin.

This is very different than the previous exorcism. The ketamine anesthetic created a fog around the other Nephilim's soul, like thick cotton batting that I had to delve through. It clung tenaciously to its host, even with the anesthetic loosening its grip. This one has no grip and nothing insulating it from me; I feel its hate like a wall of thorns. It's fully conscious and knows what we're doing. Azkeel's spawn is not only enraged but afraid. It would slaughter us all if it could.

I pause my chanting long enough to say, "Emil, tell me immediately if

277

you feel anything unusual." I don't know what might happen as the Nephilim's soul is expunged.

"You'll be the first to know." He's remarkably calm, concentrating on his faith, reciting The Lord's Prayer in his head like a mantra.

Holy water and sacramental wine have no effect. The Nephilim is insulated from Emil's physical body. Our faith, our love, however, torments it. Its mind is open to me, and it knows who I am. As the spawn of Hell always do, it spits a thousand curses and threats, promising torture to everyone I love, living and dead, telling me of the atrocities Hell serves out to all those I loved who died in centuries past. Lies, of course. I've loved thousands over the millennia, and I feel confident that they all reside in Heaven.

I can't resist a twist of the knife. *It is you who will receive torment in Hell for all eternity, Azkeel's get. Your father's master will not be pleased with your failure.*

I will be a prince among the damned, daughter of Raphael! I will tell my Lord of you! All your weakling friends will be hunted and tortured to death! You will be vivisected a thousand times before we allow you to die screaming!

Those, unfortunately, are credible threats. The Serpent can communicate to the Nephilim through its earthly minions. They'll learn we have a weapon with which to fight them. I'll be hunted, but I've always been hunted. Jeri, Gippy, Emil, Sister Janice, and others will be found and murdered. Doubt of this path enters my mind for the first time, but what alternative is there? What options do I have? If I don't banish the Nephilim to Hell, it'll respawn and still tell everything it knows to its cousins. But that will be years hence.

It's already happened, I realize. The other Nephilim we exorcised is already in Hell. Word is likely already spreading. The war will come to Saint Luther's, could be coming as we perform this ritual. We have no time to spare.

"By the love of Christ, by the grace of God, by my faith in mankind, be gone from this vessel, spawn of Hell. Go to your father and tell him you failed. Go to the Serpent and tell him he's lost the war. I am the sword of God. I cut you free from your ties to this Earth. Begone!"

Gippy's chants are more colorful. "Out the house, bitch! You ain't welcome! We *love* each other! Ain't no room for your hate shit here! Go burn with yo devil-bitch daddy!"

"I feel...something. Afraid!" Emil's voice comes out harsh, strained.

"That's its fear, Emil! Concentrate! Focus on your faith! Feel God's love filling you!"

Emil begins to recite his prayers aloud, now, and I feel the Nephilim fading, crying out in a last gasping effort to hold on to its tenuous grasp. The ritual is working.

The cries of hate and spite fade and finally cease.

It's gone.

"Stop!" I take a step back. "It's done."

Gippy stops and blinks in surprise at me. "So quick?"

"Yes. It didn't have a firm grasp on Emil's soul." I start to untie the bonds on Emil's wrists. "How do you feel?"

"I don't know. Not really different." His relief is palpable, his fear ebbing. "I felt its fear, though. I wonder if it made me feel...other things."

"It could have, but it's over, Emil." Gippy and Jeri help me release him. "But there's something I have to tell you all. Something I should have thought of before. We're all in grave danger. We've got to leave."

"Leave?" Emil looks stunned. "But..."

"Emil, please let me explain." I give him the bad news and watch his horror rise up. "Everyone here, the staff, the homeless, has to flee, or the Nephilim will take them."

"Shit, E! We gotta get our shit together and scoot!" Gippy alone realized instantly what Empa feared. "If they got more friends in NAFAS, we're *all* fucked!"

"But, how?" Emil rises, his mind awhirl as always with a thousand details. "Where will we go?"

"I don't know where, but the how is simple: Money." Empa grabbed Gippy by the arm. "Go tell Sister Janice to come up here. Then tell Hank to get the homeless together. We've got enough cash to get them all out of the city, maybe out of the country. The Nephilim won't hunt most of them, but the rest of us will be in the crosshairs. Go!"

Gippy grabbed Jeri's hand and pulled her away. She looked scared, and Empa's fading pleas for Emil to pack up as much as they could didn't calm her.

"Where will everyone *go*, Gip?"

"Anywhere but here. With enough cash in their pockets, they'll get by."

"And what about..." She faltered and tugged his hand to stop him, lowering her voice to a whisper. "What about *us*? What about Father and Sister Janice? What about you and me?"

"Jeri." He gripped her hand hard. "We'll get by. Empa's got more money than she knows what to *do* with. Enough to get all the homeless south for winter. Enough to set you up in style wherever you want! Father's smart, and Sister Janice, she's like a damn pit bull. She'll survive. We'll be okay, but we gotta scoot!"

Jeri didn't look convinced, probably couldn't conceive anyone with that much money, but she went with him. Sister didn't even ask them what was wrong, just made a face and went upstairs. Hank pulled the residents together in the common room quickly, and Gippy laid it out.

"Naffies gonna come down on this place like a ton of flamin' shit. We got enough cash to get you all outta town and set up for a while, but you can't *ever* come back to Saint Luther's. This place gonna be crawlin' with naffies, and they'll take you and squeeze you for everthin' you know."

"But we don't *know* anything," one woman insisted, looking scared. They all looked scared.

"Don't matter. They'd still squeeze you. These fuckers don't play nice." He hooked a thumb to Jeri. "Bitch stuck Jeri through the gut with a fucking *sword* to make Father talk."

He assured them that money wasn't a problem. There were twenty-four residents, a full house with the weather turning cold, but after their stop at the bank in Columbus, they were flush. Sister came down with a double armful of cast-off clothing and dumped it on the floor.

"Take it all, and there's more. Jeri, help me." She sounded like a drill sergeant.

"I'll help, too," Hank said, obviously picking up on the urgency.

Things moved with astonishing speed. The homeless didn't have much to pack but took whatever Janice offered, wearing layer upon layer of clothing and stuffing more into bags and packs with what food they could fit in. Empa came down and spoke to them, each individually, asking them to forgive her for throwing their lives into turmoil and handing out money. Some stared at the thin platinum bars in wonder, never having seen money in non-script form before. Jeri explained how much they were worth, which dropped jaws, and where best to exchange them. Many were already planning bus trips south, new lives in Atlanta, Charlotte, or Birmingham. Gippy drove some to the bus station in small groups, dropping them off a block away to avoid the NAFAS who were undoubtedly watching.

When he came back the last time, he found a curious group waiting for him in the garage.

Father Farrell, Jeri, Empa, Sister Janice, and Hank stood around a small pile of suitcases, boxes, and bags. A beat-up old Nissan sat on the other side of the garage, the trunk open. He got out of the Buick and scanned their faces.

"Whassup?"

"We're ready to go," Father Farrell said, nodding to the Nissan. "Sister Janice's car. We'll travel together until we find someplace to settle down. We just wanted to say goodbye." He offered his hand to Gippy, and they shook warmly.

To Gippy's astonishment, Sister Janice gave him a fierce hug, her eyes gleaming with unshed tears. "You be good, Gippy. Stay clean. You look *so* much better than when I first met you."

"I *am* better," he assured her, nodding to Empa. "It's the company I keep."

"We'll keep in touch, but it's probably best if neither of us knows where the other is." Father picked up a bag and put it into the trunk of the Nissan. "Just to be safe, you understand."

"You best ditch that car or get other tags quick," Gippy said. "Naffies'll be lookin' for it when they find this place empty."

"That *would* be wise," Empa agreed. "And don't access your bank accounts or show your faces where there are cameras."

"That'll be difficult." Father looked worried.

Welcome to the war, Gippy thought.

"Just be careful." Empa smiled and embraced Sister Janice, who looked a little uncomfortable with her. "Stay strong, Sister. God loves you."

"I will, and I know." A brief uneasy smile flashed across Janice's face, and she turned to continue packing.

"And you, Hank? You goin' with 'em?" Gippy asked.

The grizzled old man grinned at him. "Nope. Asked Empa if she could use someone along who wouldn't shoot his own dick off by accident, and she said yes."

Jeri chucked Hank on the shoulder. "Hey, I happen to know from personal experience that Gippy did *not* shoot his dick off!"

"Jeri!" Gippy, Father Farrell, and Sister Janice all snapped at once.

"Be good to have another guy along." Gippy shook Hank's hand. "All these women be drivin' me nuts."

"Just good to be fightin' the good fight for a change." He looked at Empa strangely. "*Lexoman Parastin*, you know."

"What?" The words meant nothing to Gippy.

"It means every man saves his country by sacrificing his life," Empa said with a sad smile as if remembering too many bad things. "Well, we better go. Emil, be safe." She embraced him long and hard.

"I will be, and thank you for everything, daughter of Raphael." They parted.

Jeri and Hank loaded the last of the luggage into the cavernous trunk of the Buick. Empa got in back with Jeri, and Hank rode shotgun. Gippy got behind the wheel and waved once more to Father and Sister, thinking a short prayer that they'd be okay.

Outside, the rain had turned to sleet. He turned south toward the freeway. "Where too, E?"

"South. I hate the cold. Too many years north of the Arctic Circle."

"The what?"

"Nevermind. Just head south."

"How far south?"

"Atlanta, I think. I know the city well enough, and we can set up a safe house easily."

"Atlanta, it is." Gippy took the onramp south on I-74 and glanced in the rearview mirror. Jeri had her head pillowed on a bundle of clothes and stared out the window. Hank was already dead asleep. "You okay, Jer?"

"Yeah." Her eyes met his in the rearview. "Yeah, I'm good. Just never thought I'd leave this city, is all."

"You'll like Atlanta." Empa gripped her shoulder warmly. "Cheer up. There's a whole world out there for you to see."

"Yeah, that kinda scares me, too." Jeri smiled and shrugged. "I'll get used to it."

"I'm sorry for everything that's happened, Jeri," Empa said with regret.

"I'm not." Jeri flashed a broader smile, her old lopsided mischievous one. "Got more now than I've ever had in my life. Hot boyfriend, hot girl-friend, and a warm place to sleep."

Empa laughed, and Gippy smiled. Of course, they couldn't stay long in Atlanta, just until the search for them cooled off. Maybe until spring. He hoped to have that long before he had to go back to war.

"One hundred ninety-seven to go, E." He sighed and stretched his neck.

"One hundred ninety-seven Nephilim, and one cousin to find, if she's still alive."

"You think she is?"

"I pray so." Empa sighed deeply and leaned back. "I pray it with all my heart."

EPILOGUE

WAR IS HELL

Word spread through the minions of Hell like wildfire. Two Nephilim had been banished to Hell by one of the last get of the Seraphim. They'd found a way, a weapon. Images of their faces raced through their network, and the hounds began to hunt.

One unlikely recipient of the bulletin sat behind a desk in an autobody shop in Albuquerque. The succubus, Duvara, examined the faces, considering them carefully as she filed her nails. There were four: the Ageless get of Raphael, whom the succubus fantasized about strapped down to suffer all of her darkest whims; a priest named Farrell, who had evidently harbored a Nephilim in his autistic brain for his whole life; and two street punks who were helping them.

Two street scum and a retard priest... Leave it to an Ageless to scrape the bottom of the barrel, Duvara thought.

The latter had no official identities, and so no photos, voice prints, or DNA on file. They did have sketches, however, and those circulated with the others to every NAFAS headquarters in North America, and even abroad. International terrorists, the story went. The noose would tighten, and they'd be found.

Duvara wasn't usually a part of dragnets like this, but one of the faces struck a chord of familiarity. She put down her nail file and examined the face closely.

"Well *fuck* me!" The hair was wrong, and she didn't remember earrings, but finally she recalled where she'd seen that face: right here in this office. Her failed attempt to seduce the mulatto boy still grated on her pride. There had been something different about him, angel touched, and now she knew the source. "Hangin' with a Seraphim's daughter. So *that's* how he could resist me."

She took pride that not many men or women *could* resist her. Seduction was what succubae *did*, after all. Chaki was riding a dozen men and a few women right to Hell even now, corrupting their souls a bit more every time she fucked them. She'd sent hundreds to burn and would send hundreds more. She assuaged her pride with the fact that the boy had been in the thrall of a Seraphim's spawn. She'd been hunting out of her league.

Duvara pulled her phone and tapped a message to her Nephilim contact, outlining where and when she'd seen the boy, and that she'd sent her the license plate of his old Mercedes earlier. She got an error message moments after she sent it: Recipient's account deleted.

"Fucking Hell!" There were only two reasons the woman's account would be deleted. She was either dead, or worse, one of the ones who'd been banished. Duvara forwarded her message to another contact, an incubus she knew in LA who worked in the porn industry and human trafficking, telling him to send it on to his superior.

She got a reply immediately. "Not your bitch. Do it yourself."

Duvara typed, "My contact's dead or banished. Do it, or I go over your head and have your dick cut off."

The reply came back. "Done. Don't be a cunt."

She laughed at that and sent. "You are what you eat…"

His reply was predictable. "Then why aren't you a cock?"

She sent him an obscene emoji, put her phone away, and went back to filing her nails. The boy wasn't her problem, but still, he'd been interesting. Maybe she'd do some searching, contact some of her thralls, put out some feelers. Who knew, she could get lucky. Bagging one of the few remaining Ageless would be another jewel in her crown once she returned to Hell, and Daddy would certainly reward her.

That thought brought a smile to her lips. Once the war was won, and the horsemen scoured this dying planet clean, she would be free to torment all the souls she sent to Hell. Maybe, with a little luck, the boy who had escaped her would be among them. That would be a delicious eternity indeed.

To Be Continued

ACKNOWLEDGEMENTS

Thanks to all who have helped me with this story, especially my wife, Anne, for her invaluable input and wealth of ideas that made Empa who she is, and my friend Steve, who let me peer into the mind of a soldier. A special thanks to my author friend, Howard Andrew Jones, for his input and referrals for more help. Thanks finally to John for believing in me enough to have a look.

ABOUT THE AUTHOR

Born and raised in Oregon, Chris met his wife and soulmate, Anne, while attending graduate school in Texas. Since then they have been gaming together since 1985, sailing together since 1988, married since 1989, and writing together off and on throughout their relationship. Most astonishingly, they have not killed each other during the creation or editing of any of their stories…although it was close a few times. Visit Jaxbooks.com for more.

ALSO BY CHRIS A. JACKSON

FRIENDS OF FALSTAFF

www.ingramcontent.com/pod-product-compliance
Lightning Source LLC
Chambersburg PA
CBHW020358110726
47899CB00006B/1757